HERO'S ROMANCE

T. Edward Redd

Copyright

About the Author

T. Edward Redd is currently a college freshman in Indiana. He is pursuing a degree in English.

His passions are fitness, travel, meeting people and writing. He is constantly meeting new people and exploring the wonders of the world. He loves to blog, make people laugh and share the pleasures of life with others.

You can find T. Edward Redd at:
www.fictionfanaticandromance.wordpress.com
www.facebook.com/TeamAwesme
www.twitter.com/tedwardredd

Acknowledgements

This is my very first book and a step into the realm of my dreams. This is a meaningful experience and I'd like to thank everyone who helped.

First and foremost I thank family and friends, who've helped me every step of the way. I love you all dearly.

I would also like to thank those of you who have followed me and supported me on my sites as well. I hope you all enjoy this.

Lastly I would like to thank those of you who took the time to read this. I hope you enjoy it as much as I enjoyed writing it.

Dedication

I would like to dedicate this book to a person who is very precious to me. This is more than just a book. It's the first step for me as I pursue my dreams.

I dedicate the actions I take to grasp those dreams, to you. I don't think I'd be this far if it wasn't for her. So thank you.

A dream…

CHAPTER ONE

I hear your cries. I feel your pain, sadness and despair. Your heart was broken at such an early age. You grew up feeling as if you didn't belong. You wanted to be accepted and acknowledged but you were rejected and ignored. You still feel as though you don't belong. I feel it and I see the built up tears behind your smile. You go to sleep wondering each night "where are you?". Where am I you ask? Waiting for you. Waiting for you to finally find me.

End log

A girl sleeps soundlessly in a soft bed coated with white sheets and a blue blanket. Her room is painted light pink with fresh white carpeting. Papers, pencil, pens and a pink diary clutter a table near her bed. As the morning sun begins shining light through the window shades, an alarm clock goes off. Slowly, she opens her eyes.

As she rubs sleep out of her eyes, a soft yawn escapes her mouth. She sits up and leans to a nightstand beside her bed to turn off the clock. A cell phone lies on her desk. After grabbing it, she examines the screen. It reads: **March 4th, 2011, 7:00 a.m.**

With another yawn, she thinks, *"It's morning already? I hardly got any rest. The big day has finally come. Yet, it doesn't feel special quite yet."*

Her feet plant on the soft carpet as she gets out of bed to tidy up her sheets and blanket. She goes into her bathroom and begins washing her face. The water is cold as it touches her delicate skin. A relieving sigh frees from her lips as she looks into the mirror. She stares at herself as she thinks.

"They say if you start the day with a smile, you'll end it with a smile. I do my best to find something to smile about each day. But, I also look in the mirror each day and wonder if life has something more to offer."

After brushing her teeth, she paces out of the bathroom and begins getting dressed for the day. Her outfit of choice is blue jeans and a pink t-shirt. She walks to her dresser and grabs a brush. While brushing her long brown hair, she observes herself in a mirror above her dresser.

"I'm no one special at all. Walk beside me for a day and all you will see is a plain girl with a simple life. My neighborhood isn't exactly the best place to live. My parents divorced when I was young and I don't have the best relationship with the parent I live with.

"My high school life is ok I guess. This is my last year. My grades are seemingly perfect. I'm the head cheerleader of the cheer team, and school president. Oh, and I date the captain of the football team. I'm pretty much everything a teenage girl could want in high school. Yet I'm not happy."

She checks her cell phone for messages. Disappointment spreads across her face because she sees no one has messaged her. She grabs a backpack and exits her room.

As she walks downstairs, she looks around to see no one is present. She grabs car keys from a table as she leaves the house.

She gets into a car and begins to drive down a rural road. The travel lasts for a few miles, while she occasionally passes cars and school buses along the way. The drive ends with her arriving at a high school. She parks her car and begins to walk towards the school. Unimpressed while she strolls inside, she lets out a somewhat mellow sigh.

"Each day I go to a place where I'm surrounded by people I don't prefer. I have maybe one or two actual friends. The rest just hang out with me because I'm popular. My boyfriend probably doesn't even realize that today is my birthday. But I don't complain. It could be worse."

She watches a few jocks picking on a student. They knock his books out of his hands and laugh. The boys laugh and smile as she approaches. A smile forms across her face while she watches a tall boy, with dark curly hair and freckles. He laughs with the other jocks.

He says, "Yeah guys the party was crazy. The girls were all on me." He shows an arrogant smirk as his friends flatter his ego.

His friend Jaxon says, "That's crazy Regan. You're the man."

The girl watches Regan socialize with his friends. She politely interrupts saying his name soft yet firmly. Regan and his friends look back at her. His happy expression fades into a look of annoyance.

"Good morning baby," she says. "I missed you last night. I called a few times but you didn't answer. I know how busy you can get with football and work."

Regan's friends snicker softly as he replies, "Well you know. I'm *always getting busy*, with work that is. How are you Aliyah?" His friends snicker when he looks back at them.

"I'm doing pretty great babe. I'm really excited about today," she says.

Regan watches as she looks at him smiling. There's a moment of awkward silence while Aliyah waits for his response. He asks in a crept out tone, "Why do you keep smiling at me like that? You're being weird again."

"I'm not being weird," she laughs. "Aren't you excited about today too? It's a pretty special one don't you think?"

Regan becomes confused. He looks back at his friends who are just as oblivious. Regan becomes surprised and quickly looks back at her.

He smiles and says, "Oh! Ha of course I'm excited about that! Isn't everyone? It's going to be one of the biggest nights of the year. We're going to throw a huge party."

Aliyah becomes excited and screams. She hugs him as the feeling of joy runs through her. Regan holds her as he smiles.

She shouts, "I can't believe you're throwing a party!"

He says, "Aliyah calm down. I haven't won yet. Don't jinx me. You know I hate that."

She becomes confused and looks at him, "What are you talking about? Win what?"

Regan looks at her like she's an idiot. He says, "The championship game. What else? It's only the biggest day of the year. How could you forget? You're going right? You have to be there. You're the head cheerleader and my girlfriend."

Aliyah shouts in frustration, "You were talking about the stupid game?"

Regan rolls his eyes, "Oh yeah I forgot. You're thinking about going to school to be a nurse. Look Aliyah today is *my* big day. If I do well the scouts will be impressed. I wish you would be a little more considerate and cheer me on with this. You know college football is my dream."

Aliyah becomes depressed, as she says, "No, no you're right. I'm sorry. The game isn't stupid. It's really important. I just thought that-" she begins to feel selfish and stops herself.

Regan says, "You thought what?"

Aliyah shines a fake smiles and says, "I thought you were confident enough not to be afraid of the jinx thing. You know you're going to win for us babe."

Regan says, "Ha that's my girl. Isn't she great guys?"

He smacks her butt as his friends root him on. Aliyah becomes offended but doesn't let it show. She walks away as Regan waves her goodbye. She crosses her arms as discomfort shadows her. She walks sadly down the hall as if alone and cold.

"Story of my life, same old same old. This is typical. But I still smile. I can't really complain can I?"

"Even though he forgot, he has his good moments. I have everything a high school girl can dream of but yet...I feel so empty. Is it wrong to feel like that? Is it selfish? Am I wrong for wondering if life has more to offer than what I've been given?"

She walks into a chemistry classroom and sits towards the front of the class. Class begins and time begins to speed along. Aliyah watches Regan, who's sitting with his friends in the middle row. He throws a paper ball at a student towards the front of the class. Boys laugh as the paper ball hits the student in the back of his head.

The student turns around and says, "Knock it off. Let's grow up a little. We're seniors, not kindergartners."

Guys woo as Regan laughs. He says, "Oh Tim. You sound so angry today. Loosen up man."

Aliyah watches as the student rolls his eyes and turns around. She looks sympathetic for him but gets distracted as her two friends Robyn and Snow get her attention.

Robyn whispers, "Aliyah, you're going to the game today right? You can't bail again. It's the championship game."

Aliyah says, "I don't really want to go. I'm not sure."

In a convincing tone, Snow says, "But your boyfriend is playing and you're the head cheerleader. You have to go. Come on it's the last game."

Aliyah ignores her and asks, "Do you two know what today is?"

Snow replies, "Yes. It's Thursday, the 4th of March, 2011."

She says, "Well yes, all of that is right. But something special happened today 17 years ago."

Robyn guesses, "Hailey's Comet?"

Aliyah becomes annoyed and says, "Hailey's Comet was in 1986."

Snow and Robyn watch in confusion. Aliyah covers her face in a stressed out fashion. Snow says, "What's on your mind? You seem moody."

"What happens today?" Robyn adds.

Aliyah sits up and brushes off their thoughtlessness, "Nothing. Today isn't special. Not at all. I was just messing around because I'm so bored with class."

Snow says, "Hey you're going to Regan's party tonight right? They plan to throw a victory party. Robyn and I wanted to know if you could get us invited. You can do that for a couple of friends right?"

Robyn adds, "Plus, if I get Tim to come, I'm pretty sure I can get him back with me. He's been so different this year. But I know he still loves parties. What do you say?"

Aliyah shines a smile, "Of course I can. That's what friends are for."

Robyn says, "That's why you're our best friend. Thanks Aliyah you're amazing. We love you lots."

Aliyah smiles at them. Her smile fades into displeasure as she turns away from them. She looks down to her desk and thinks, *"Love me enough to forget my birthday. You're awesome best friends."*

Her thoughts are interrupted as she hears something hit a chair. She looks to see Regan kicking Tim's chair.

Tim hits his knee on the desk. In annoyance, Aliyah watches, as the jocks laugh with Regan. She watches in suspense as Tim gets out of his chair.

Regan mockingly says, "Uh-oh. I think Timmy is mad."

Tim stares at Regan as if looking at his soul through Regan's eyes.

Regan laughs and says, "Do you need a pencil or something Timmy?"

Tim stares as if he feels sorry for Regan. He turns to his desk and grabs his things as he says, "Grow up Regan."

Regan laughs and mocks Tim as he switches seats. Tim ignores rude and taunting comments Regan throws at him as he sits down. The teacher firmly says, "Regan, knock it off or go to the office. I won't ask again."

Aliyah sighs in annoyance. She glances at Tim who is writing in diligent silence. In her mind she makes a comparison of Regan who continues to goof around, to Tim who, focuses on his work in a mature manner.

Tim stops as he realizes she is watching him. They make eye contact for a couple of seconds that seems to last for ages. Tim breaks contact as a paper ball hits him in the head. He looks back to see a jock waving. Regan laughs and says, "Stop staring at my girlfriend Timmy. She doesn't like creepy guys."

Tim looks back at Aliyah and becomes somewhat bitter towards her simply because she's associated with Regan who constantly torments him regularly.

He looks away as the teacher kicks Regan and his friends out of her class. Aliyah sits at her desk bored and frustrated not with class, but her daily life. She sighs in defeat.

Time passes and the class bell eventually rings. Aliyah gets up and quickly paces out of the class. She walks to a long row of lockers lined along a wall in her school hallway. She opens her neat and organized locker. A picture of her and Regan during junior prom hangs inside. A sigh of disgust makes its way from her as she grabs a bag and shuts her locker as if wanting to get away from the picture.

She turns away and becomes startled to see a student standing in front of her. She flinches and nearly drops her books.

After gaining her senses, in an annoyed tone she says, "You scared the life out of me! What do you want? How long have you been standing there just watching me?"

The student says, "Like two seconds."

Aliyah stares at him as she tries to calm down, not wanting to release her stress on a stranger. She notices him holding a birthday card. In utter surprise she asks, "Is…is that for me?"

The student jokingly says, "No it's for the locker. Of course it's for you. Happy Birthday from Tiger Southeast High School."

Aliyah takes the card overwhelmed with shock and joy.

She says, "Oh my gosh! Thank you so much. No one even realizes it's my birthday. Not even my own boyfriend. I feel awful. I didn't mean to yell at you. I'm having a bad day. Thanks, um?"

The boy says, "Tim Derr. You know, the guy you had class with less than five minutes ago with?"

Aliyah becomes embarrassed, "Oh! Yes, I remember you. I'm sorry. Like I said, it's a stressful day."

"It's fine. We all have them so I can relate."

Aliyah says, "Yeah. Hey, I'm really sorry about Regan. Him and his friends can be really juvenile sometimes."

Tim interrupts as he says, "You don't have to do that. It's ok."

She replies, "No it's not. I'm sorry. He's a sweet guy. He just likes showing off for his friends."

Tim says, "Loud and obnoxious. That's the best. Well, bye."

He waves as he turns away. Aliyah grabs his arm and says, "Wait!"

Tim looks back, "What?"

Aliyah looks at the card then to him and asks, "Why did you give me this? I know it's for my birthday but we don't even know each other. Do you give random people cards every day?"

Tim smirks and says, "Yup."

She raises her eyebrow with confusion. Tim smiles and says, "I work in the school office. I'm part of the special events team. It's my job to keep track of birthdays and hand out those letters from the office.

Aliyah opens the card. It reads: *A special card for a special girl. Happy Birthday!* She smiles as she sees a smiley face near the bottom of the card.

She smiles and says, "Thank you. This just put me in a better mood. Do you make these?"

Tim says, "Yes. The office forces me and a few others to make handmade cards so the birthday people feel special."

Aliyah replies, "Well it worked. You're the only person who remembered my birthday today. Not even Regan knows."

Tim smiles and says sarcastically, "Wow he's really sweet like you just told me. He's a keeper."

Aliyah becomes annoyed as she says, "Thanks, I know you're mocking me."

Tim reassuringly asks, "Aren't you the most popular girl in school or something like that? I'm sure I'm not the only person who remembered."

Aliyah begins to unknowingly vent, "Everyone likes me for the wrong reasons. My friends like me because I'm with Regan or because I'm a cheerleader captain. No one really takes the time to get to know me. I've been missing cheer lately. I'm starting not to like it that much. I'm thinking about quitting. I'd rather stay home and read, you know?"

Tim smiles politely as he looks around as if in a hurry, "Aliyah, that's really sad. I'm sorry about all of that but I really need to go."

"Oh, it's fine." She shines her signature fake yet convincing smile as she says, "Thanks for the card." She reads the signature: "Timothy Derr."

He becomes annoyed at hearing her call him by his full name. As he turns away Aliyah asks, "Hey are you going to today's game?"

Tim says, "I didn't go to the last 12 games. There's no point in going to this one. No."

"Come on. Where is your school spirit?"

Tim smiles and says, "I hate it here. See you around Aliyah. Happy birthday."

She smiles and thanks him as he walks away. Time continues to pass leading to the school day's end. Aliyah eventually makes her way to the championship game. She stands on the sidelines with her teammates in a royal blue and white cheer outfit. The game bores her stiff as she watches and occasionally leads a cheer with the other cheerleaders.

She eventually makes her way to a bleacher as the last three minutes of the game come. Excitement finds its way to her mind as she begins reading a book. She smiles at the story as she is momentarily taken away from the stress in her life.

A buzzer from a time clock sounds and snatches her out of her fantasies. The crowds let out a loud cheer as the winning touchdown is scored. Aliyah watches as Regan cheers with the other players. She looks somewhat alone as she watches cheerleaders and football players surround him as he shows off. She sheds a single tear as she thinks of the fact that it's *her* birthday.

She leaves to her car and drives away in tears. Listening to love songs she can relate to somewhat calms her down as she drives for a few miles. After a few minutes she arrives at a medium sized white house with a black rooftop. She pulls into the driveway.

She steps out of the car and walks into the house. As the familiar aroma of beer attacks her nose she becomes disturbed, stepping across the threshold. She steps into a dining room and quickly makes her way into a living room.

She watches her bald and hefty middle-aged father slouch on a couch. To no surprise, she sees him drinking alcohol with his feet on a table as he watches sports. She watches him drink and becomes upset.

She smiles anyway and says, "Hey dad! I'm home."

Without looking at her he asks, "Did you bring home dinner? You're late and your brother and I are starving."

Aliyah says, "The championship game was tonight. No I didn't bring dinner."

He puts down his beer in annoyance as he changes the channel. He looks at her and asks, "Why?"

She replies, "I didn't think I had to tonight."

Her father becomes more annoyed, "Your brother and I have to eat. What made you think you didn't have to get us food?"

Aliyah smiles gleefully and says, "Because it's my birthday. I figured you had something planned. Can't we go out to eat tonight for my birthday?"

Alvin rolls his eyes and stands up. As he takes out his wallet he says, "That stuff is for little kids Aliyah. Here's twenty dollars. Order something for us to eat."

Hurt begins to overwhelm her as she pleads, "Can we please go out for my birthday? Please? Did *you* even remember?"

The sound of her voice irritates him. He raises his tone, "Aliyah, order the damn food you're getting on my nerves. Do it before I get mad."

Aliyah takes the money and walks away saddened. She gets onto the phone and begins ordering pizza. After a couple of minutes on the phone she hangs up and walks to the dining room table to sit. Her father walks in towards the kitchen.

He watches as she takes out her birthday card. His hand instantly binds with another beer from a refrigerator in the kitchen. He looks at Aliyah and asks, "Is that from Regan?"

Aliyah sighs, "No, he forgot it was my birthday today."

He replies, "Well football players get busy a lot. Don't take it personal. When he's rich and famous he'll make up for it and get you a big house. Maybe he'll get me one too." He laughs greedily.

Aliyah laughs and doubtfully says, "Yeah right."

Her father walks to her and looks at the card as she reads it with a smile, "So who's that card from?"

Aliyah says, "This boy who works in the school office."

Her father gets a look of repugnance as he says in a strict tone, "Are you cheating?"

Aliyah becomes offended as she says, "What? No, this is just an innocent card. The office makes him give out cards for special events."

He takes the card away and examines it saying, "This looks handmade."

Aliyah confirms his statement saying, "It is."

He reads the card, "A special card for a special girl. His name is Timothy? Sounds familiar."

Aliyah says timidly, "He's the only one who remembered it was my birthday today."

Her father looks at her in shame and disgust as he says, "So you're going to cheat on a football player who is going to make millions with a boy who passes out cheap cards? Stupid!"

Aliyah looks with dismay and shock as he rips the card in two. She shouts, "What are you doing?" She reaches for the card, only to be knocked down by her father. She flinches as he throws the ripped pieces of the card at her shouting, "I didn't raise you to be a loose cheater!"

Aliyah cries, "I'm not cheating! I love Regan!"

He glares at her and says, "You're a damn slut! Just like your mother!"

She gets up and runs up a staircase as teardrops fall from her eyes. Frantically, she rushes into her room, shuts the door behind her and locks it. Nothing but hurt and the feeling of weakness overpowers her. She turns and leans her back against the door. The tears refuse to stay in her eyes even though she wants to be strong.

As she gasps for air she begins to breakdown in tears as she slowly sits against the door defeated. She cries silently as she covers her face.

Looking for a way to release her stress, she looks beside her to a dresser.

She grabs a diary and reads her last entry.

I hear your cries. I feel your pain, sadness and despair. Your heart was broken at such an early age. You grew up feeling as if you didn't belong. You wanted to be accepted and acknowledged but you were rejected and ignored. You still feel as though you don't belong. I feel it and I see the built up tears behind your smile. You go to sleep wondering each night "where are you?". Where am I you ask? Waiting for you. Waiting for you to finally find me.

End log

Aliyah begins writing in the journal as she cries.

CHAPTER TWO

You know what the worse feeling is? Having everything that anyone could ask for and still feel desperately alone...money, clothing, shoes, I have it all. Yet, I hurt all the time. I believe that a certain person exists. They can take this pain away. Relieve me of isolation and this pain of having no one by my side. When I cry and when I hurt, I do it all alone. I wonder...sometimes I wonder if she can hear my cries...where are you...

End Log

Timothy Derr works in a school office close to sundown. While finishing up paperwork, his principal, Kurt Frawgs walks to him with a worried look saying, "Tim, it's getting late."

"I don't mind. It's not like I have anything better to do," he replies.

Kurt pats him on his shoulder and says, "Come on Tim. It's time to go. Take a break and go home."

Tim nods as he begins to pack his backpack. He thinks.

"Most kids can't wait to leave school. I on the other hand hate going home. There's nothing to go to. Father works long hours so I hardly ever see him. He comes home and goes to sleep. My mom left us when I was 16.

"Hell, things weren't that great when she was here. We didn't have the best relationship. I'm sure it's messed me up to some degree."

He finishes packing his things and puts his bag over his shoulder.

"Since mom left, the house has been so quiet. Peaceful I guess. But is it wrong that I somewhat miss the drama? Although I hated her, at least I didn't feel this alone."

He walks out of the office towards the exit. Aliyah's friend, Robyn waits for him at the exits. They begin walking together while leaving the school. Robyn talks while Tim looks somewhat uninterested. His deep thinking drowns Robyn's voice out.

"Since mom left, well before she left, I always had this empty feeling. Over time, I've found that being with a girl that I'm attracted to and like eases that feeling. It makes me feel, not so alone."

He smiles and holds Robyn's hand, as she kisses him on the cheek. They walk through the school park and share a few moments with each other. After a hug, Tim watches Robyn wave him goodbye as she walks to a car alongside the park. The wind blows leaves past Tim as he stands alone. He begins his walk home.

"There it is again. That empty feeling. I've had this feeling since I was in middle school. I've had friends but never a lot. I've always had one best friend. I usually lose them after a year. They switch schools and I lose contact with them. I'm also shy. I guess that's why I hardly talk to people."

A girl walks towards him and smiles as Tim's good looks charm her. He says nothing out of sheer shyness. She becomes annoyed, taking his silence as rejection. She speed walks past him.

He walks for a couple of miles and arrives home. Nothing but the silence and warm air of the house, greet him as he enters. He lets out a greeting but his father has already gone to bed. Upon walking into to the kitchen he sees that dinner has been made. He begins making a plate.

"The quiet bugs me. I hate it. Though nothing is said, the truth can be heard so clearly. I am alone. There is no one here."

After barely eating half, he throws out his meal. He walks into a living room and sinks into a hospitable and pleasant couch. He grabs a remote and turns on the television. A happy couple on TV hug each other. For a moment their joy brings peace to his heart, seeing something so pleasant.

But as he snaps back to reality, he realizes, *that* isn't *his* life. There isn't anyone present. There is no one to hug, no one to speak to. He is alone. Anxiety overtakes him as the feeling of loneliness and solitude cloud his mind.

He has trouble looking up but he forces himself to stare at the emptiness around him. Eventually his will to fight his pain dies out. He drops his head in defeat as a single tear falls onto the remote.

"I never really had problems with depression until my mom left. I remember cutting myself one time in front of my mom. I got in trouble at school that day. She embarrassed me at school in front of my classmates. I was scared of what she was going to do to me.

"While she drove me home I remember thinking about how much I knew she would yell and spank me when I got home. I was scared. When we got home she yelled at me outside. I grabbed branches from a tree and started cutting my arm. That's when she hit me. I was expecting tears and a hug, but she hit me across the face."

He turns the TV off as his unwanted seclusion overwhelms him. Tears bleed from his face but he refuses to make a sound. He rushes up a staircase, trying to flee from the quietness, the loneliness. A sigh finds its way out of his body as he closes his bedroom door behind him.

He's escaped to his room once again. Though he is still alone, this feels like a haven. His feet drag him limply to his bed. He lies down as he removes his shoes with his feet. The warm and soft bedding calms his heart. Hugging his pillow as if holding someone, his sea of sorrow settles down. The storm has passed for now.

"I think when she was around all I really wanted was a hug from my mom. She favored my sister a lot more than she favored me, if she favored me at all. I tell myself that I don't need her and that I hate her. But as I get older I start to think that the relationship I have with her has had a really bad effect on me.

"Since she left, I've become a lot more withdrawn, depressed and quiet. The only thing that makes me smile genuinely is a girl's affection. When my mom left I felt abandoned and on top of that I had already gotten little to zero affection from her.

"I think I try to fill the void my mom failed to fill by subconsciously seeking a girl's affection. Having someone by my side just makes me feel, here. I feel seen and not abandoned. The girls I talk to probably aren't good for me at all."

He grabs a black journal and a green journal. He begins writing in the black journal.

"Writing usually keeps me sane. It's what I like to do and I'm good at it from what people say. I usually write stories."

He continues to write. He stops and thinks. He closes the black journal and opens the green journal. He reads it as he thinks.

"I also have this journal I write in from time to time. I started writing in this back in 2007. I was in counseling at some point in my life and it was suggested that I write in a journal daily in order to get my emotions released. Writing actually does help calm me down.

"It's funny. I think in a weird way I should thank my mom. If I weren't so depressed all the time I would have never started writing. Now I've written 4 stories, the longest has more than 260 chapters. I'm sure I'll make a career out of writing novels since, I'm good at it.

"When I first started writing in this thing, my mom was living with us. She was the main subject of my journal entries. It was usually entries about the things she did to cause trouble in the house. You can see the pain in my pen strokes. I think that's one of the reasons I started fiction writing.

"It was and still is an escape. I create characters with breathtaking lives, friends and a lot more. My characters have the life I wish I had, mainly the part about not being alone. The funny thing is, you can see some of me in my characters. You can see my personality and my actual life in some characters. Some characters are heroes.

"I always try to be the hero in most situations. I like helping people out. Some characters in my stories want to be the hero, but the main character keeps outshining them. This causes them to spiral into depression and eventually causes them to become the story's main villain.

"In a way, I feel like that sometimes. Sometimes I feel like a monster and times I feel like a saint. The way I used to argue with my mom and scream at her makes me feel like a monster. I've said some really cruel things to her in the past. She has too but that's not an excuse.

"The way I help out other people for no reason makes me feel like a hero. I give out money without thinking about it. I feel obligated to help people out if I'm able, so I do. But I'm still so alone. It makes me question God's existence. Why would he put me here, knowing my own mother would leave me and basically mess me up for life? On top of that, I'm still alone. I only ask for one person who will take this feeling of isolation away.

"Yet, I sit in bed alone every night hurting, slowly dying on the inside. I'm supposed to place my beliefs, my hopes and faith into this higher being that I have never seen with my own eyes. Yet this being doesn't seem to hear my cries for mercy, freedom from this isolation. I've concluded that there is a God, but maybe it just doesn't care as much about us like we think he or it does. If it cared, it wouldn't have let my mom leave me.

"But I don't blame God for anything that's happened to me. Some things that have happened I take the blame for. Other things that have happened like my mom leaving, that's just life I guess. But this God I was raised to put my hopes and faith into is said to have infinite power and greatness.

"So if it's responsible for creating me, in some sort of sense, can it not feel my pain? Can it not see how much I've suffered? And if it can see and feel my pain, why, why hasn't it sent or made me this person who's going to take the pain away?

"I answer these questions with a simple 'because he doesn't care as much as you'd like him to'. I've concluded that God has everything set in stone from the very start. Before you were even born he mapped out your entire life; beginning, middle and end.

"So to ask God, this almighty being, to change a plan he has already made for you is a bit pointless. Its mind was made up before you breathed your first breath. I'm hypocritical; sometimes I love God, and sometimes I get mad at it. I'm sure everyone has at some point. If they say they haven't, they're breaking one of the precious Ten Commandments, bearing false witness or lying.

"And that's fine. I get it, it made everything and it call the shots. All I am is a simple creation. Its plan for me has already been decided. But exactly what is its plan? That's my only question.

"What genius plan requires me to go through all of this pain and suffering? Never getting a mother's affection, watching your father mistreated for years by her then watch her leave. To top things off, she made me carry her bags to her truck the day she left.

"I will remember that painful day forever. What plan requires all of this? What child needs to go through all of that? I'm not mad. I just need to know. What do you want from me? What's your plan?"

He hears a door shut and looks out the window. He sees his father leaving for work.

"My father works hard to give my sister and I a good life. He's been really great before and after my mom left. I believe if it wasn't for my father, I wouldn't be so sophisticated and civil. My mother would have messed me up completely. I definitely wouldn't have a future like I do now. This is where my hypocritical view on God comes in.

"Sometimes I'm really grateful to God for allowing me to have a father in my life and a good one at that. So in a sense, God isn't so bad after all. It's a love and anger type relationship I have with God. Sometimes I love God more than anything. Sometimes I'm just angry and hurt. So I blame God for not making it easier. I'm only human. At least I don't pretend to be the perfect Christian."

He closes his eyes, trying to fall into a sleep.

CHAPTER THREE

Another typical day in the life of Aliyah Conrad. No one told me happy birthday. Well one boy Timothy Derr did. I don't know if it counts since the office makes him do it. It still felt nice regardless. I love how everyone tells me I'm their best friend yet only a boy I have never seen till today told me happy birthday. Not even Regan remembered. My dad called me a slut and hit me again...it hurts a lot. Going to sleep every night crying...wondering when it all will end. I can hear his cries but I'm still waiting for him to find me...my warrior, the one who will take me away from this pain...

End log

Aliyah stands in front of her dresser during early nighttime. She stares at the bruise she received to her side from falling down, after being knocked down by her father.

She sadly says out loud, "Happy birthday, Aliyah."

Weakly, she smiles as a tear falls from her eye. She picks up a picture on her dresser. Comfort makes its way into her heart as she stares at a middle-aged woman. The lady bears a striking resemblance to Aliyah. She has long straight brown hair, soft pale and milky skin and grey eyes. The only difference between her and the woman are the freckles on the woman's face. It is her deceased mother.

"My mother died a few years ago. I was fourteen at the time. My mom and dad had been divorced for three years before she died.

T.Edward Redd   **32**

"The affair was with her friend from college. When my father found out, he kicked her out without even thinking about it. She pleaded and begged for his forgiveness, but he just shut her out completely.

"Cheating is wrong and I still don't agree with what my mother did. But I do understand how defenseless and weak she felt against his abuse. My father has always had a drinking problem. When he drinks, he loses control of his anger. No one wants to be abused. My mother sought help. A cry for help turned into an affair I guess. My mom wasn't a bad woman. She had no one to go to. He pushed her into the affair.

"Since mother died, dad's drinking has gotten worse. I can tell he's taking his pain from mom out on me. He always calls me a slut and says I'm just like her. I know what she did was wrong. But I miss her so, so much. I'd do anything to have her with me right now. She would free me from this nightmare they call living."

Sitting on her bed by the dresser, she holds the picture to her chest as she shuts her eyes. The peaceful yet painful moment lasts for what seems like minutes. Tears fall from her eyelids as she gasps for air. She becomes desperate to escape the pain, the sorrow.

Quickly she grabs her phone and begins messaging Regan in an attempt to find comfort in his responses. Though he treats her badly, he is one of her few reasons to stay hopeful. She is hopeful that one day, he will turn into the hero who will wipe her pain away.

To her disappointment he doesn't reply. She tries calling, but the call gets sent to voicemail within two rings. This is typical but in her mind, waiting for him to change seems logical. Losing hope in him means having no hope at all. She sits her phone down as she covers her face in frustration.

"Is it wrong to want an escape? To want more than what I already have? Yes I date the captain of the football team. I'm head cheerleader, and I'm school president. But none of that even matters to me. I hate it. I hate all of it. I hate having fake friends and a boyfriend who barely knows I exist. It's like I'm in limbo. I have everyone and everything and yet...I have no one and nothing. It hurts. If feeling this way is a crime, then I'm serving forever."

She grabs her diary and smiles as she flips through past entries.

"This diary has been my place to vent since I was a little girl. I don't write regularly. Whenever I'm stressed, in love or just bored, this is what I go to. When I was younger, I always wrote about my prince charming. I doubt Regan is my Prince Charming, but he's as good as it gets. There's good in him. If he would just get over trying to impress his friends, I'd be happier with him. I know he'll change. He just needs time to grow up."

Aliyah shuts her journal and wipes her face with the palms of her hands. As she stands, she takes in a deep breath. Upon releasing her breath, strength forms in her demeanor and eyes. She gets up and leaves her room and begins walking downstairs.

She sees her father asleep on the couch. Several bottles of beer are lying around the couch and one in his hand. Quietly she collects the bottles and places them in a trash bag. Before taking the bottle from her father's hand she takes a moment to stare at him.

"My father isn't a bad man either. Hurt has its way of changing you. It can make you pitiful, angry, evil and nasty. We do what makes the most sense to battle that hurt. He finds help in drinking. All it does is damage his health and attitude though."

She gently takes the beer bottle from him and kisses him on the forehead. As she stands up, she sees a redheaded toddler. He stands in the dining room in blue pajamas as he sucks his thumb. Aliyah finds joy in his presence.

"I have a little brother, Liel. He makes all my pain and stress vanish just by seeing his precious smile. He's five. When I look at him I see so much of my mother."

The little boy asks, "What's wrong with daddy?"

Aliyah shushes him gently, whispering, "He's sleeping Liel."

"But I'm hungry. I didn't get to eat any of the pizza. Daddy ate it all."

Aliyah walks to him and kneels to him whispering, "Go get dressed and I'll take you to get something to eat. Then we'll go to the park. How does that sound?"

Liel smiles with excitement and runs upstairs. Aliyah smiles at his innocence. Suddenly, she hears the fridge door close. She looks back to see a half dressed woman walking, out of the kitchen. The woman waves at Aliyah as she holds a beer in her hand.

Aliyah becomes alarmed and loudly whispers, "Hey! There's a little boy that lives here. Please cover up!"

The woman smiles seductively as she squeezes her own breasts saying, "Don't be jealous. You'll fill out soon."

Aliyah argues, "That is *not* the point! My brother is way too young to be exposed to…"

"Aliyah, shut-up."

Aliyah halts as she looks back to see her dad glaring at her with spite. Her strength weakens as she sees the anger and hate in his eyes being directed right at her soul.

She softly says, "But father she…"

He interrupts again by saying, "Your brother is going to see a woman like this sooner or later, and it's not a big deal."

She shouts, "He's too young to be exposed to things like this now. You'll screw him up!"

Her father gets angry and with an intimidating tone says, "Watch your damn mouth! Leave us before I get upset."

Aliyah watches in defeat as the woman sits on her father's lap and kisses him. She feels a tug on her shirt and looks back to see Liel. He breaks the negative energy flow as he smiles blissfully.

She smiles as he says, "I'm ready sissy."

Liel notices his father kissing the barely clothed woman. His eyes light up with joy. He slowly walks to them. Aliyah tries to grab him but he unknowingly pulls away. Not wanting to upset her dad, Aliyah hesitates to stop Liel.

He stares at the woman as he says, "Mommy?"

Aliyah becomes alarmed and quickly walks to him. She grabs his hand saying, "Don't look Liel. Let's go."

Liel looks back at the woman in confusion thinking it's his mother. Aliyah leads him out of the house.

Liel asks, "Who was that with Daddy? It was mommy wasn't it? Can we go back Li, Li?"

Aliyah ignores him in pain as she gets him into the car and buckles his seatbelt.

T.Edward Redd

He pleads, "Li, Li can we go see mommy please?"

Aliyah fights her tears as she tries to pay no attention to him with patients. Liel begins to cry, "I want mommy!" repeatedly as she struggles to adjust his seatbelt.

"THAT'S NOT HER," she shouts.

Liel argues, "But daddy was kissing her. I saw it! You're lying! Why would he kiss someone who's not mommy? Take me to see my mommy!"

Aliyah slams the door shut. Realizing her anger is slowly getting the best of her, she stops herself to take a deep breath and calms down. She gets into the driver's side of the car and starts the engine. Her brother cries loudly as she tries to focus on driving.

In hurt she ignores him, waiting as he slowly gives up on yelling. He leans against the window sadly as he cries quietly. Aliyah sheds a tear as she looks away.

"Liel is only five. He was two when our mom died. He was born a year before the affair. Mother wasn't allowed to see us too much after the divorce and Liel was barely two. My dad started dating multiple women no sooner after he kicked her out.

"She had no money and the guy who had the affair with her bailed when mother asked for help with winning custody. She couldn't afford an attorney and had no chance at winning guardianship.

"Liel saw all of the women Dad was with and eventually just saw Mom as just another woman. He was so young. After mom died there wasn't a way for me to remind him who mom was without pictures. Now he grows up seeing a different woman every other day with my dad. I'm the closest thing he has to a mom.

"I've basically raised him since she died. I try to keep him away from my dad and his lifestyle. I don't want Liel growing up confused about love and sex. My father brings over so many women and never thinks about how it could affect Liel. I doubt Liel remembers what mom actually looks like now.

"He's so young and innocent. Liel thinks that only moms and dads kiss. That's what I taught him. So when he sees my father kiss on other women, he assumes it's our mom. It makes me mad that my father doesn't see what he's doing to Liel. I don't want Liel growing up thinking it's ok to kiss and sleep with different women daily. It's bad enough that he thinks these random whores are his mothers. It's hard. He's all I have."

She looks at Liel as he stares out the window crying. After stopping to get food, they arrive at a playground. After parking the car, Aliyah gets out and walks to Liel's side. She opens the door for him. He holds a bag of food tightly as he looks away from her.

"You're not going to eat," she asks.

He frowns as he ignores her. She kneels to him and says, "A lot of kids can't eat from restaurants or even at all. Eat your food Liel, please."

T.Edward Redd   **38**

He snatches the bag, digs into it and begins to eat. Aliyah sighs as she holds her arms as if cold from the night temperature. Liel struggles to open his drink.

Aliyah watches and says," Here, let me help you."

Liel snatches the juice away and shouts, "No!"

Aliyah tries to gently grab the juice and insists on helping. Liel pulls away shouting, "No! I don't want your help. I hate you! You wouldn't let me see mommy! I want my mommy!"

Aliyah shouts as her tears fall, "SO DO I! But that wasn't *our* mom!" She sits down and leans against the car as she cries. Liel watches as his sister covers her face, crying silently. Concerned for her, he gets out of the car and walks to her.

He holds the drink to her and says, "Sissy..."

She peers up and looks at her brother who holds a guilty look. Wiping her tears she says, "Here. Let me open that for you bud."

She opens the drink for him and gives it to him.

He thanks her as he begins drinking. She pats him on the head and hugs him saying, "I'm sorry I yelled Liel. I love you so much."

Liel hugs her back saying, "I'm sorry I said I hated you Li, Li. I love you."

Aliyah smiles at him. In a mother like fashion she grabs his bag of food and digs into it. After handing him his food, she watches Liel as he eats his burger and fries. Teasingly, she steals one of his French fries. She laughs as he becomes upset and pouts. He smiles and lets her take more as she pats him on the head. They sit alongside the car as the moon shines over them. Liel leans against Aliyah as he finishes his food.

She looks to him and asks, "Liel. Do you remember what mommy looked like?"

39

Liel shakes his head yes as he says, "She has black hair."

Aliyah says, "No Liel. That wasn't mom." She takes a picture out of her purse and hands it to him and smiles saying, "That's our mommy."

Liel takes the picture and examines it. He sees a woman in her late-thirties with long a beautiful brown hair. She's almost identical to Aliyah only she looks more like and adult and has freckles on her motherly face.

Aliyah asks, "Do you remember now?"

Liel becomes confused asking, "But what about the mommy dad kissed?"

Aliyah sorrowfully answers, "It wasn't her. And I hope she *wasn't* a mommy."

He questions, "Why would daddy kiss her then?"

Aliyah hugs him and says, "Come here. Don't ever grow up to be like daddy. He hurt mommy and made her go away."

Liel looks in shock, "He hurt mommy? But why?"

She holds him saying, "Look at me Liel. Our mommy is gone."

He says, "But where is she? Will she ever come back?"

"Mom is in this beautiful and magical place called Heaven. There is no pain, she is never sick and she never cries. One day, we will be there right with her. She's looking down on us with a smile each day."

Liel looks to the sky. He becomes curious as he looks back at Aliyah. He says, "That's really cool. When will mommy come see us? Can we go see her in Heaven?"

Aliyah struggles to answer his question as she looks away, "We, we can't see her. Mother isn't coming back Liel. Heaven is a special place for special people. One day we will go, but no time soon."

She watches as Liel puts his head down in sorrow. Aliyah holds his hand smiling and says, "But I talked to her before she left. She gave me a secret message for you."

Liel becomes excited saying, "Really? What?" Aliyah smiles as she sees his face brighten once more. Liel eagerly says, "Tell me!"

She says, "She wants you to be good. Always be respectful towards girls and never hurt them. Find someone special and protect her, never hurt her, ever. But most of all she said that she loves you very much and that she misses you."

Liel asks, "Can you tell mommy something for me? Tell her that I promise I won't ever hurt my big sister and that I love her too! I hope she has fun in the magical place and I miss her a lot." Aliyah smiles and says, "I will Liel."

Liel asks, "Hey. Is mommy safe?"

Aliyah gets excited saying, "Of course! In Heaven, no one can hurt her. She never cries, and she's always happy. You don't have to worry about that." Liel smiles and looks at the picture Aliyah gave him.

He says, "Mommy be safe mommy. I love you. Li, Li can I have this picture please?"

"Yes, put it somewhere safe and never forget who your mommy is. She isn't any of the women you've seen with dad and no woman you'll ever see."

She points at the picture. "That's our mommy. Promise you'll never forget."

Liel smiles and says, "I promise."

Aliyah replies, "Good. Let's go play on the swings bud."

She holds his hand as they walk to the swings. They begin to laugh as they swing under the night sky.

CHAPTER FOUR

Buddha said human suffering is caused by not accepting change and having attachments to things that eventually break or die. I have no one and nothing to attach myself to. So why do I suffer from isolation. It's not something that can break yet it can die by me finding this person...where are you, I need you...make my sadness die...be my attachment...

End Log

Tim works in his room, on a school report, on his laptop towards the coming night. He creates a lunch menu for the next month, April. He receives a text message from Robyn as he finishes the menu.

Tim says, "I wonder what she wants. It'll have to wait though."

He works on the school paper.

"I tend to bury myself in school and office work. If I spend all my time on work, it'll distract me from things. Things like my parents' divorce, my mom being with another man and my father crying. Working is better than cutting or overdosing on nighttime medicine."

He finishes an article for the school paper. Having nothing left to do he closes his laptop unwillingly, knowing silence waits. Checking his watch to see it's 8pm, he looks around his room as if looking for someone, only to realize he is the only one there. He sighs as he checks a message on his phone.

He smiles as he says, "Robyn wants to hang out?" He begins to get dressed.

"A typical day for me consists of me waking up, getting dressed, going to school, coming home, and going to sleep and then it starts over the next day. On the weekends I usually do work or sleep the day away."

He leaves his room and exits the house. After walking for a few blocks he meets Robyn. He smiles at her.

"I don't really have a lot of friends to hang out with. I don't really try to make friends. One person is all I need."

Robyn smiles saying, "Hey!"

He replies, "Hey there miss."

Tim breathes in air as she hugs him gently. It's as if her presence brings him to life. He becomes happy as he hugs her back warmly.

"It's weird how my moods go from depressed, to at peace and happy. All it takes is a smile and a hug from someone special to me. Right now, that's Robyn."

Robyn smiles at him as he smiles at her. They walk through a park as the moon shines bright like a diamond. Robyn looks at him and sees his muscle tone. His perfect fitting black V-neck hugs his broad chest and stomach. She looks at his well-defined arms as she gets close, infatuated by his features. She holds his hand asking, "Have you been working out?"

he says, "Oh, well yeah I've had a lot of free time. So I work out at the house a lot."

Robyn blushes and smiles saying, "It's sexy." Tim smiles at her as she continues, "You should get back on the football team."

Tim ignores her annoying and commonly used conversation starter, hating the words "Get back on the football team".

She says, "Come on! You were great Tim. Besides if you joined the team I'm pretty sure you and Regan would become best friends aga…"

He interrupts her saying, "Stop."

She continues to pester, "But Tim you were really good babe. Why don't you join?"

He says, "I don't like football the way I used to Robyn. It caused too much competition and fights."

Robyn says, "You're talking about Regan aren't you?"

He ignores her. She tries to continue her persuasion simply to be stopped by Tim.

"I'm not part of the team anymore Robyn. I never will be again. It's not who I am anymore."

Robyn says, "That's the type of attitude that makes the jocks target and pick at you."

Tim looks at her irritated as she continues, "You put on this front like you're better than them, or that you're too good for them. You and Regan were best friends. But then you stopped football. You quit the team and walked out on the championship to publish novels that don't even sell."

Tim let's go of her hand and pulls away saying, "Why would I want friends who only like me for their personal interest? But when it comes to my dreams, they're stupid."

She says, "You were good at football and you were our team star player. You walked out on us and let us down for a damn publication meeting. Why would you choose writing books over a chance to play college football? You had everything: popularity, friends, everything. You threw it all away for book writing. It's selfish."

Tim stands up and turns away from her. She says, "What? Now you're walking away from *me*?"

Tim walks away saying, "Have a good evening Robyn."

She becomes frustrated and walks away, "Thanks for wasting my time! I thought I'd give us another chance, but you'll never change. Have fun writing your books."

She storms off in a fury. Tim stops walking to think, "One moment, the person you care about the most is all over you. She treats you like you're her world. Than the next moment it's all gone."

He begins walking on a sidewalk.

"I just want one person to help me get through my days. I want somebody who would be supportive of my dreams. That's part of the reason why I purposely quit the team on championship day. I knew they would lose it without me. They're so fraud and I hate it. I would always talk about my novels."

"They thought it was dumb. They were never supportive, but when it came to football I was their best friend. I felt betrayed, used and somewhat ignored. I didn't even have a publication that day. I was just tired of being used.

"So now almost the whole school hates me for making them lose the championship game. But I never imagined Robyn of all people would disapprove too. I was sort of expecting her to motivate me. But she's obsessed with me returning to football."

On arrival to his home he sees his father's car parked in the drive through. He quickly walks into the house excited. The scent of fresh food being cooked tickles his nose. It's satisfying, but not anywhere near as fulfilling as the presence of another person in the house. Loneliness doesn't exist at the moment.

His father Robert sees him as he walks into the kitchen. He smiles and says, "Hey Tim. How was your day?"

"It was pretty awesome dad. I just had an amazing date with Robyn from school."

Robert becomes happy saying, "Oh that's nice. What did you guys do?"

Tim smiles, "We just took a walk in the park. Nothing too crazy." He thinks.

"I've never told my dad about how I always feel depressed or alone. I always lie and tell him I've had the best day. If he knew I felt so alone, I think he'd quit his job just to spend more time with me. That's the kind of man my father is."

Robert speaks as he cooks, "This Robyn, is she a respectable lady Tim? I don't want you dating anyone who will get you off track. Dating is great, but don't get distracted."

Tim interrupts, "No dad. Robyn is great. She's really supportive and reads every book."

Robert says, "Just make sure, whomever you choose to be with loves you for you. Make sure you treat her with respect too son."

Tim adds, "And always show her that I care. I know dad."

He smiles at his father. His father proudly says, "I raised you well. I made dinner. It's on the stove. Well I'm going to take a shower and go to bed. I have a long workday tomorrow. I won't be in until late so I'll leave money for groceries or take out, you pick. You can have company. You know the rules. Girls need to be out by twelve."

Annoyed Tim says, "I know, I know."

Robert says, "Alright son. I love you."

Tim says. "I love you too. Goodnight."

His father walks up the stairs. Tim makes himself a plate of food as his mind wanders.

"It was all a lie. Robyn hates reading. But how could I tell father that I'm depressed and that I feel alone every day? How could I tell him Robyn hates the fact that I write? It would break his heart. He thinks his son is happy and has the time of his life. He could never begin to imagine what I go through.

T.Edward Redd   **48**

It would bring him to tears and I won't do that to him. I will figure this out, alone. No one's coming over this weekend. I don't have any friends. Robyn was the only person I talked to until today. But he doesn't need to know that. No parent wants to hear their child is depressed."

He sits at the dinner table alone eating, occasionally looking around as if waiting for someone. Slowly he loses his appetite as the silence begins to bother him. He stops eating and throws out the plate covered with food.

Trying to run away from his troubles as always, he walks up to his room and lies on his bed. He hugs his pillow and shuts the lights of his room off. His peace is brought to a short end as his phone rings.

He let's out a frustrated and heavy breath as he sits up in annoyance. His hostile feelings shift to confusion as he sees that it is Robyn who is calling. He answers, "Hello?"

Robyn cheeringly says, "Hey! What are you up to?"

Tim replies, "I'm going to bed."

She replies, "But it's only 9pm on a Friday. Baby get out of bed and come meet me at Regan's party!"

"Baby?"

Robyn says, "Yeah babe! Regan is having a party tonight because they won the championship yesterday. They couldn't have the party last night because Regan got in trouble so his father was too pissed at him. But his father left town so he's throwing it tonight! That's only the first part. He's letting you come!"

Tim asks, "Why do you want me to come?"

Robyn answers, "Because I like you. I hate fighting with you and I want to see you tonight ok? The party is at Regan's. Hurry up!"

Tim asks, "Regan said, he's fine with it?"

Robyn replies, "Yes baby! Aliyah did me this huge favor by getting us invited. Just come on. Don't keep me waiting! Hurry!"

Tim says, "Ok, ok. I'm coming."

Robyn giggles and says, "Ok. See you later then babe."

CHAPTER FIVE

Didn't do a lot of anything today. I took Liel to the park today. He saw dad kissing another woman and thought it was mom. It made me upset. I don't hate my father. But sometimes I just can't stand him. I'm doing everything I can to raise Liel to be a respectful and loving person. I don't want Liel to be like our dad. Well tonight I'm going to Regan's party. Hopefully I have a good time. I can hear my hero's cry. But I've yet to see his face or feel his presence. I hope he finds me soon...

End Log

Aliyah stands in front of a mirror with a gorgeous black and silky dress on. She brushes her long and brown hair gracefully. Liel walks in with a cheerful expression on his face.

He looks at Aliyah and says, "Li, Li you look like a princess."

Aliyah smiles and replies, "Thank you Liel."

She turns off her curling iron and grabs her purse. She checks her phone for messages as she walks to her door. Liel stands as if not wanting to leave.

Aliyah says, "Ok, out of my room buddy."

As she leads him out, Liel asks, "Are you leaving?"

"Yes, but not for long ok? "

Liel's innocent face quickly forms into a face of sorrow and anxiousness as he holds her legs saying, "No! Please don't go."

Aliyah smiles and pats him on the head, "Awe Liel. Don't worry, I'll only be gone for a couple of hours."

Their father walks in from the kitchen with a beer. He looks at Aliyah and notices she's dressed nicer than usual. It revamps memories of his wife, triggering hurt buried with disgust in his tone as he says, "Why are you dressed all fancy?"

Aliyah doesn't hear him, only noticing the hundredth beer in his hand. She begins to worry and becomes annoyed with the daily alcohol abuse habit asking, "Do you have to drink one of those every hour of the day? It's bad for you. Plus you shouldn't be drinking with Liel around."

Her father gets irritated asking, "Aliyah how old are you?"

"Seventeen. You know that yesterday was my…"

Interrupting, he counters, "Yeah seventeen. So that means you're still a child right?" She becomes annoyed knowing a lecture is coming.

He says, "Have you ever paid any bills around here? No. I pay for everything in this house, I feed you, I pay for your car, phone bill, your clothes, everything. If I want to drink a damn beer then I'll drink a damn beer. Don't lecture me about shit. You're not grown. You act just like your mom."

Liel becomes excited as he says, "Mommy went away to Heaven."

They look back at Liel. Alvin starkly says, "What are you talking about? Your mom died years ago. She hasn't went anywhere but six feet under."

Aliyah shouts, "DAD! Don't say things like that around him!"
Liel says, "No, Li, Li said that she's in this magical place where she's always happy."

Their father mockingly says, "What the hell are you teaching him this God crap for?"

Aliyah angrily disagrees, "It is not crap!"

Liel says in a sensitive tone, "Mommy went away because you were mean to her."

Aliyah looks at Liel in shock not expecting him to repeat her words. She becomes fearful as her father looks to Liel asking him to repeat what he had said. Aliyah tries to distract her brother, only to be told "shut-up" by her father as Liel continues

He cries, "You hurt my mommy…"

Aliyah becomes more and more fearful as Liel continues to viciously attack their dad screaming, "Why did you hurt my mommy? You made my mommy leave me!"

Tears form in their father's eyes as Liel weeps, "I want my mommy. I can't see her, because you hurt her. Why would you hurt my mommy? Daddies aren't supposed to hurt mommies! Why daddy? Why did you hurt her? Why daddy? Why??"

Aliyah becomes scared as her father sheds tears as he violently shouts, "SHUT-UP!" He flips over the dining room table in a tearful rage. Aliyah runs to Liel and grabs him as glass shatters against the floor.

Aliyah brings herself together, protecting Liel from possible dangers as she tells him, "Go to my room Liel. Play on my laptop." Liel initially refuses. Aliyah firmly whispers, "No Liel. Go to my room and lock the door. Now."

Liel runs to her room as their dad gains his senses. Aliyah bravely stands tall, ready to face a familiar conclusion. She becomes empathetic as she watches him wipe tears from his face, slowly turning to her.

He glares at her with a brutal rage as he fumingly speaks, "You're teaching my boy that I hurt his mom? That I killed her? You're trying to turn the only thing I have left against me?"

Aliyah stands tall as he approaches her. He slaps her across the face and she falls to the ground. She holds her face as he shouts, "You're mom was a slut! Just like you and she cheated on me! Don't go feeding him these lies that I killed her!"

Aliyah sheds a few tears as she stares at the ground. She's hurt but not from the slap but from the emotional trauma of his words. Her dad continues, "I don't care if you hate me like your mom did. But you're not taking Liel from me. He's all I've got left."

Aliyah stands, as she cries in empathy, "No dad I don't hate you! Liel misunderstood me. Dad I love you. I don't like fighting with you. You're my dad."

She walks to him in an attempt to receive a long awaited hug from her father. He discards her, pushing her away shouting, "Get the hell out Aliyah! You disgust me right now. Just go!"

Aliyah grabs her keys and leaves the house. She starts her car and drives away in tears.

"Even my father breaks down sometimes. Life is hard like that. Everyone has to put up with pain."

She drives a few miles. She tries to drown out her despair with loud love songs. At Regan's spacious house, she parks her car near its gate. Her face throbs as she pulls out make up and looks into a mirror. A bruise shows on her face. Desperately, she tries to cover it with makeup only to see it partially hidden. The bruise refuses to hide behind the expensive face paste as she gives up. She puts her makeup away and steps out of her car.

Before making her way to the mansion, she watches another car pull up. A familiar face drives the 2005 silver Saturn as she stares into the tinted windows. He turns the car off and steps out. He's dressed in dark wash blue jeans with a white V-neck and a black leather jacket. She watches as he begins to walk her way, somewhat bothered.

"It's that boy from school..."

She watches as Timothy Derr walks. As usual he notices nothing around him, including her as he thinks deeply.

He notices her watching him at the last second. He looks as she waves kindly to him as she greets him with a simple, "Hi."

Tim raises his eyebrows as if surprised she's speaking to him. He politely waves back.

"Uh hey. Leeyah," he says.

Aliyah smiles and corrects him saying, "**Aliyah**. How could you forget it? Ha I remember your name, Timothy."

Tim looks irritated, nonchalantly saying, "I never said I was good at remembering things."

Aliyah joins him in walking as she says, "Are you alright?"

Tim sighs saying, "Yeah, I just don't want to be here." He sees her bruise and asks, "What happened to your face? Did you get into a fight or something?"

Aliyah becomes embarrassed not expecting anyone to notice, as they never notice anything wrong. She laughs in embarrassment.

"Oh this? Haha, no I didn't get into a fight. I actually fell in the shower."

He interrogates, adding, "Onto your face?

Aliyah smiles weakly as she counters, "It's a pretty big shower and I'm pretty clumsy." She looks away somewhat depressed remembering what actually happened.

Tim let's out a concerning sigh as he casually says, "You're lying."

Aliyah becomes nervous as she defensively says, "I'm not! I fell in the…"

Tim breaks her sentence saying, "It was something more serious. I can tell. Aliyah looks down in overwhelm and shame. Tim comfortingly eases her.

"It's not my business so I won't dig the truth out of you. Just hang in there ok? If you ever want to talk about whatever happened, I'm always in the office during school."

Lost for words she stutters a "Thank you." She becomes suspicious and asks, "But what are you expecting in return?"

Tim looks at her in confusion as he replies, "Excuse me?"

She becomes annoyed as she continues, "Sex? A date? Boys always want something in return."

Tim becomes more aggravated as he states, "I don't *want* anything from you. I was being nice to you. Don't judge me based on the guys you choose to let into your life Aliyah. Excuse me." He begins to walk ahead of her towards the mansion.

Aliyah stares and becomes guilty as she runs after him, saying, "Hey, I'm really sorry. That was horribly rude. Can we start over Timothy? I'm having a bad night. Can you please forgive me?"

Tim relaxingly says, "Don't make a big deal of it. It's ok."

They walk towards the mansion. There's an awkward silence as they walk. Aliyah glances at him every other second, not trying to get caught staring. She watches with interest at his peaceful yet depressing silence. She becomes longing for him to speak if just a word.

"You're really quiet aren't you," she asks.

He explains, "It depends on who I'm with."

Aliyah becomes slightly annoyed, "What? So you don't want to talk to *me*?"

He corrects her simply saying, "I never said that."

Silence soon interrupts the awkward connection. Aliyah looks at him repeatedly, not being able to read his hot and cold body language. Her inability to comprehend him slowly begins to annoy her as she looks away. She tries to connect again and looks to him asking, "So who invited you?"

He says, "Robyn."

Aliyah becomes surprised as she repeats the name along with her last name; *Green.*

Tim says, "Yes. We dated at one point not too long ago."

Aliyah becomes excited as she begins recognizing a pastime Tim. She eagerly speaks, "Wait, you're the kid from last year aren't you? You were the star running back and you were amazing! What happened to you at the championship?"

Tim responds in annoyance, "I left."

Aliyah asks, "Why". Not because the team needed him, but because he was so superb. She can't understand why he would leave something he was so good at.

Tim lies, "I had a publication meeting for my novels. I want to be a writer, not a football player."

Aliyah becomes intrigued, "Oh, I understand. That's really productive. I hope you do well."

Tim looks at her, happy but confused to hear such foreign yet the long awaited words he'd always wanted. Aliyah asks, "Wait, why don't you want to be here?"

He sighs, "Well your boyfriend and his friends hate me. I don't really like too many people. But I like Robyn, so I came for her I guess."

Aliyah blissfully yet naively says, "Regan hates you? Haha no Regan is sweet."

Tim glares as she clearly and painfully takes up for Regan, while knowingly blinding herself, "I mean he can be mean sometimes."

Tim refuses to hear her sad and pathetic attempts to make Regan look good saying, "Save it, ok?"

She becomes offended saying, "Excuse me?"

Tim attacks her, "Regan isn't exactly the nicest guy. If you think he is you're dumb and blind."

Aliyah attacks back, "He's my boyfriend! Don't talk trash about him."

Tim brushes her off without any hesitation and walks ahead of her. She glares at him walking away but becomes happy to see Regan walk out of the mansion. She smiles at him. She watches as Regan and Tim cross paths. He purposely bumps into Tim and shouts at him, "Watch it loser!"

T.Edward Redd

Tim ignores him as he continues his soundless walk into the house. Regan walks towards Aliyah. She smiles and hugs him but watches Tim in pity as he walks into the house alone. Without looking she says to Regan, "How's your day going Tim?"

She gasps as she stops herself. Regan looks at her with alarm. Aliyah becomes fearful as she corrects herself, "I meant Regan. Babe, I…"

Regan gets angered asking, "Were you talking to that loser?"

Aliyah begins to panic, "We were just having a normal conversation babe. I'm sorry!"

She becomes scared as Regan aggressively grabs her by the arm, pulling her to him. She pleads, "Ouch! You're hurting me."

He gets in her face demandingly asking, "Do you like that reject?"

Aliyah can't bring herself to speak as the sheer fear overwhelms her. She sheds a tear as he shakes her shouting, "DO YOU?"

"No! I love you Regan!"

Regan quickly calms himself as he notices people watching him as they walk by. He waits for them to pass. He glares back at Aliyah and points to her as if he's her father quietly but in a bullying fashion demands, "I don't want to see you even look at him. Understand? He's a loser."

Aliyah cries silently. She remains quiet not wanting to upset him any further. He looks at her face and mistakes her bruise for ruined makeup. Disgusted, he says, "Clean your face before you come into my house. You look horrible."

He walks away. She watches in pain as a group of girls greet him. He hugs one and walks inside with her. Feeling as if she's a failure to him she drops to her knees and cries.

"I always seem to mess up with Regan. I miss how things were when we first started dating. Now not only am I a disappointment to my father, but I feel I'm a disappointment to Regan too. It's like he doesn't even see me anymore. I need to do better."

She stands up and wipes her tears.

"And I will." She smiles and walks to the house.

CHAPTER SIX

Tim sulks around the luxurious mansion with a blank expression. As if expecting to eventually meet some point of interest, he walks around. He looks at the dozens of people that fill the house. He looks aimlessly for Robyn.

He mutters, "This is stupid. Why am I here?"

One of Regan's friends, Chance agrees, "Yeah. Why are you here reject?"

Tim looks back to so see Chance, Jaxson, Fred, Matthew and Ben, who are all friends of Regan. They laugh at him as Andrew points out that Tim was talking to himself.

They ask, "Who invited you?"

He answers, "Robyn Green."

Fred points behind Tim laughing, "Does she remember you're coming?"

Tim looks back in dread to see Robyn kissing another guy as he caresses her beautiful body. The jocks woo as Tim allows his bottled emotions to surface. He unleashes his rage onto a lamp, slamming it down.

Regan walks in and becomes shocked to see the glass and ruined light across the floor. He becomes raged to see that it is Tim who has caused the commotion.

The party suddenly stops as Robyn looks back to see an enraged Tim. She becomes shocked and quickly stands as he shouts, "What the hell are you doing?"

Before she can respond Regan's voice roars across the room at Tim. He calls, "REJECT!"

Tim looks at him slowly as Regan approaches. He angrily shouts, "You're destroying my house now? That's a one thousand dollar lamp! You're going to pay for it."

Unconvinced Tim objects, "One thousand? There's no way it cost that much!"

Regan takes his words as an insult as he shouts, "What loser?"

Not wanting to cause a fight Tim says, "Guys come on. We don't have to do this."

Robyn rushes to his aid. She holds his arm as she talks to Regan, "I'm sorry. I invited him. I'll pay for the lamp ok?"

Regan grins and gets the attention of the house. The music volume lowers as he makes Tim the center of attention.

He points, "Take a look."

Everyone begins to stare at Tim. He slowly begins to feel a rush of anxiety. The anxiety suddenly stops as he notices Aliyah in the crowd. She watches in sorrow, as if trying to apologize with her eyes.

Regan looks to the crowd, "Does he look familiar guys? Can anyone tell me who he is?"

Andrew goads Regan on by saying, "That's Timothy Derr. Last year's star running back!"

Regan smirks as he continues his harassment, "That's right. This was our team's star running back. On championship day this *reject* bailed on us. Costing us the game of the year."

Tim stands in defeat as most of the house boos him with Aliyah and Robyn being a part of the few exceptions. Tim bravely takes the verbal assault knowing if he walks away he will prove to be weak and afraid.

Regan continues, "Can anyone guess why he left? For a stupid book publishing."

The crowd boos even louder. Not being able to take any more, Tim storms towards the exit trying his best to keep his anger at bay. As he gets close he walks past Aliyah. For a brief moment their eyes connect for what seems like a time stopping marvel. Time returns to its normal pace as he walks out, slamming the door behind him. He stomps the ground as he shouts.

"Damn it! What do they want from me?"

He sees a brick and looks at Regan's expensive orange Charger. Tim takes the brick and throws it viciously at the car. The glass caves into the car's interior as the brick collides with it. Robyn shouts for Tim. He looks back at her.

"Tim are you crazy? What are you doing!?"

He snaps at her, "What do you want? Don't you miss your boyfriend?"

"Tim I don't have a boyfriend. Not even you. So don't get jealous when you see me with other guys."

Tim looks angered as hurt rings in his voice, "So why have we been talking all this time? What's the point of all of these dates? I thought you wanted to get back with me."

Robyn says, "I do, but you can't let go of this writer's career or whatever. I want my football player back Tim."

Tim becomes frustrated and shouts, "That isn't *me* anymore! Why can't you accept that? Is the only reason why we went out was because I was the star running back?"

She replies, "Tim I like you for you. Football was part of the reason. But now I don't even know who you are. You sit by yourself, you never come out to parties, and you're just different."

He calms down as he uncaringly says, "Maybe I was just trying to live up to everyone's expectations but my own. Honestly I just got tired of being with fake people. I never changed; you guys never knew the real me."

Robyn defensively says, "Did you just call me fake?"

Tim questions her, "Be honest. If I don't get back with the team will you get back with me?"

Robyn begs, "Tim why don't you want to get back with the team? You were really amazing!"

Tim turns away in annoyance, "I'm going home."

Robyn shouts for him but is ignored. She walks quickly, following behind him, calling for him. Tim gets into his car and tries to start the engine. To his dismay he is out of gas. He becomes more irritated as Robyn knocks on his car window. He opens the door and asks, "Can you give me a ride to get some gas?"

Robyn rolls her eyes, "Get out of the damn car. We need to talk."

He gets out and looks at her. He finds trouble keeping his heart hardened as her deadly beauty quickly overwhelms his eyes and spirit. Soft peach skin, curvy and petite figure with supple pink lips, Robyn is a knockout.

He fights his feelings saying, "About what Robyn? You're only concerned about me being your star player again."

His feelings soon overwhelm him as he stares at her light pink lips as she says, "I'm not obsessed ok? I just want the old you back." He gets close to her and gently grabs her soft and curvy hips. She looks at him as her soft pale cheeks begin to blush. She slowly smiles saying, "What?"

He shushes her softly as he kisses her mouth. The scent of her captivating perfume excites his hormones as she wraps her arms around his shoulders. Holding her face with one hand while caressing her back with the other, he kisses her.

With every kiss he takes, his dark sea of emotions slowly get gated away, deeper inside of him. His mind wanders as he holds her.

"It's like a disease. It's similar to a fly, flying to a street lamp. The heat will burn you alive and it's not good for you. But the warmth feels so good. You can't help but to go back no matter how many times the heat has hurt you. I know she's not good for me. But what other choice do I have? At least I'm not alone. This is as good as it gets."

Tim kisses her as he says, "I love you."

Robyn says, "Let's get into your car babe."

She holds his hand and leads him into his car. She pushes him onto the seat and gets on top of him.

He watches as she removes her shirt saying, "I missed you Timmy."

She rubs on his defined chest as she kisses his neck. Tim says, "Come on don't call me Timmy."

He smiles as she flirtatiously whimpers, "Please be my Timmy baby?"

Seductively and slightly, she licks his cheek as she nibbles and kisses it. As she runs her hands through his soft and black curly hair, he kisses her. She begins to stroke his inner thigh as she pushes her breasts against his chest sexually. Tim becomes slightly unfocused, as the romance has suddenly shifted into unattractive lust.

He tries to gently caress her sides as he attempts to cuddle her more. She begins to unbuckle his belt. Tim tells her that he loves her once more only to become unsatisfied as she unfastens his belt, ignoring his words.

He stops her and says, "Hey."

Robyn becomes frustrated as she lets out a big breath saying, "What?"

Tim repeats, "I love you."

Robyn barks, "Ok Tim I get it. You love me. How many times do you have to say it? It's freaking annoying. You just keep saying it over and over again."

Tim says, "I say it because I mean it and I want you to say it back and mean it too."

Robyn argues, "I do say it!"

Tim says, "Do you mean it when you say it Robyn?"

She rolls her eyes again saying, "You really know how to kill the mood don't you?"

He repeats, "Do you?"

She loses her patients, "YES! I wouldn't say it if I didn't mean it. Stop asking me over and over. It gets on my nerves."

Tim becomes hardened again saying, "I guess I say it so much because I wish you'd say it first for once. Sorry that I'm getting on your nerves. I just care a lot. Robyn just get out of my car. I'm going home."

Robyn becomes confused as she says, "What? But Tim-"

He stops her, "Robyn leave."

She pleads in frustration, "What did I even do? I said I loved you! I'll say it one thousand times! I love you, I love you, I love you. I freaking love you! Is that better?"

He looks at her smirking as he mocks her, "You're heart wasn't there. Try it again."

Robyn becomes frustrated, "What's your problem? This is what I'm talking about! You act so detached and emotional all of the sudden. One minute you're hot and the next you're ice cold!"

He opens the door and pushes her out. He throws her shirt at her saying, "I need to be left alone. You're not going to get it."

Robyn tries to say I love you, only to have the car door slammed in her face. She walks away in frustration as she puts her shirt on. Tim slams his fist in anger.

"My life is like an emotional rollercoaster. One moment I'm happy and the next I'm frustrated.

"I just want someone I guess. Someone who is truly here. Yes she said she loved me. But it wasn't genuine. If she loved me, she would support my dreams.

"It's been like this since my mom left. I don't know what the hell is wrong with me. I feel so weak. The fact that I want someone this badly, I hate it. But that's just the way things are for me."

CHAPTER SEVEN

Aliyah stares at Regan who angrily picks up glass from the floor in his living room. Soothingly she says, "Are you ok babe?"

He replies, "I can't believe that idiot wreaked my dad's lamp. He is going to be pissed."

Aliyah comforts him, "It's ok babe. I can pay for it if you need me to."

Regan rejects, "No that idiot Tim is going to pay for it."

"Did you really have to humiliate him like that," she asks.

Regan stops and shoots her an evil look, "Are you taking up for that loser?"

Aliyah says, "No I'm just saying. You never know what people go through." She thinks about her home life, "Sometimes people have it a lot worse than we think."

Regan becomes jealous as he says, "Do you like him or something? Why are you so obsessed with him all of the sudden? Go get him if you want him."

She says, "I'm not obsessed. You made the entire house boo him. Do you know what that can do to someone's self-esteem? Just be nicer to people Regan."

He laughs at her as he gets up, "Everyone isn't a pushover like you Aliyah. That idiot is going to pay for this."

Someone rushes inside yelling, "Regan someone smashed your windshield dude!" Aliyah watches as Regan runs outside.

"A pushover...maybe I am a pushover. I care a lot about people. Maybe it's a weakness. I just imagine everyone living my life. Being called a slut, losing your mom and being hit by the one you're supposed to call father."

She walks outside towards a crowd surrounding Regan's truck.

"I know how damaging words alone can break someone down. It's happened to me my whole life. I would never wish that upon anyone. Not even my worst enemy. So I try to be kind to everyone. I wish Regan would see it like that."

Regan screams, "What the hell! My truck! Damn it! I'll kill that loser!"

Aliyah runs to him saying, "Babe calm down!"

"Don't tell me to calm down! Look at my truck," he shouts.

Aliyah says, "Babe it can be replaced. Please, just calm down."

He says, "No! I'll kill him!"

Aliyah says, "Please don't talk like that Regan! You don't want to be like that." She tries to hug him but he sees Robyn and pulls away from Aliyah. She watches as he begins talking to Robyn.

"He reminds me so much of my dad. Deep down he's a good and loving man. But he's so angry and full of hate. He takes everything out on everyone around him. Even his loved ones. I wish I could get through to him and maybe save him."

Robyn motions towards Tim's direction. Regan walks towards Tim's direction as the crowd follows.

"But just like my father. Some people are just beyond saving."

She chases after Regan, watching as he approaches Tim's car. Tim doesn't notice as he sulks on the wheel drowning in his own sea of hurt feelings. Aliyah watches as Regan bangs on the car door. He yells for him to get out. She runs towards the front of the crowd trying to call Regan to stop.

Regan opens the car door shouting, "Get out here reject!"

Without looking he scoffs, "No Regan. Now is the worst time to mess with me. Walk away before you trigger something dying to be let out of me. I don't want to hurt you. But if you push me too far, I'm not sure if I could help myself right now."

Regan shouts, "You wreaked my truck asshole!"

Tim shoots him a sarcastic stare as he smiles, "Sorry. I guess I'm a sore *loser.*"

Regan pulls him out the car and throws him on the ground, "Do you think you're funny loser?" He kicks Tim in the stomach. Tim coughs in pain.

He holds back not wanting to be overtaken by his anger as Regan kicks him repeatedly. The crowd cheers Regan on as Aliyah races to him. She tries to stop him screaming, "Regan stop it! Leave him alone! You're out of control! Look at how you're behaving!"

Regan pushes her away as he exclaims, "Shut up and get back!" He repeatedly kicks Tim, who refuses to fight back. Regan grabs Tim by the shirt, teasing him, "Come on Tim, Tim."

He holds Tim by the collar as he mockingly slaps him across the face twice. Pain bleeds from his face as he in defeat says, "Just, leave me alone."

Regan lets out a cruel laugh as he mocks Tim's tears, "Haha he's crying! What's the matter Tim? Do you want your mommy?" The dark ocean of emotion floods the gates of Tim's heart and breaks through as he hears the word, *mommy* echo in his mind.

He unleashes a violent rage upon Regan, ferociously punching him in the nose in the blink of an eye. Regan stumbles back, in shock as he holds his broken and bleeding nose. Tim rushes and tackles him in a blind rage. He begins to punish Regan with violent blows to the face.

The crowd starts wooing as Tim repeatedly hits Regan who can do nothing but take each hit directly. Aliyah screams in terror for Tim to stop. He snaps out of his rage as he hears her screams. He looks at her. The two stare at one another.

He looks back at Regan in shock. Regan's face is patterned with bruises and blood dripping from his nose. Suddenly jocks blindside him and begin ganging up on him as they attack.

Regan gets up, holding his nose as he shouts, "Hold him! You're dead reject."

The jocks pull him up and hold him. Aliyah jumps in between Regan and the jocks holding Tim. She holds her hands up as she blocks Regan's path. Tim stares in confusion as she protects him.

She shouts, "No more. Stop this Regan! I won't let you continue this childish behavior. You need to grow up."

Regan shouts, "Aliyah MOVE!"

Aliyah shouts back, "NO!"

Regan says, "Why are you protecting him? *I'm* your boyfriend not *him*!"

Aliyah yells, "He's had enough! You already humiliated him and they just beat him up. Why is he such a big target for you? Leave him alone. You beat him baby. Just let it go."

Regan glares at Tim, and says, "No. He hasn't had enough." He pulls out a hunting knife. Tim watches in fear as Regan walks towards him. Aliyah becomes alarmed shouting, "Regan don't!"

Tim struggles to get free. He gives up as he watches Regan approach him. He awaits his fate, slowly accepting what's to come as if not caring to live. Regan holds up the blade and walks past Tim, towards his silver Saturn. He begins carving into the vehicle. Tim shouts for him to stop.

He writes in *loser* on Tim's car with the knife and slashes his back tire. Regan smirks, "Now it's over. Next time you won't get off so easy, loser."

He walks to Aliyah who looks at him with disappointment, "Come on Aliyah. Let's go."

She speaks with discontent, "Why did you do that? When are you going to grow up?"

Regan says, "Whatever. I'm going back to my party. Stay out here with the trash if you want." He walks towards his house. The jocks let Tim go as the crowd follows Regan back to the house. Tim rushes to his car and kneels to the writing.

Aliyah looks back at him as she thinks, "*Everyone has a story. No one ever thinks about how his or her actions may affect another person's life. I know from my own experience that it can be Hell.*" She takes a single step towards him. The wind blows as if welcoming a moment between the two.

T.Edward Redd

She hesitates to speak, "Are you…are you ok?"

Tim looks back at her in annoyance, "What do you think?"

She becomes silent as the guilt for her boyfriend's actions overtake her. Tim unknowingly vents, "Was the championship that important? So important that he has to break me down every chance he gets? What do they want me to do, kill myself?"

She quickly walks to him saying, "Hey don't talk like that! Your life is meaningful."

He becomes angered saying, "How would *you* know? You don't know anything about me."

She says, "Well you're right I don't know anything about you. But you were the only person who remembered my birthday. Not even my own dad celebrated my birthday. I begged him to take me out for dinner. But he says that stuff is for little kids. So delivery it was."

She laughs at her pain as she kneels to him. He looks at her with empathy saying, "I'm sorry to hear that."

Aliyah says, "I know the office makes you do it. But it really meant a lot to me. Thank you."

He becomes modest as he replies, "It wasn't that big of a deal."

Aliyah smiles, "It was to me Tim. It was special. I still have the card."

"I'm glad. I made it special for you. Well, I'll see you around." He begins walking towards the road. Aliyah gets up asking, "Hey where are you going?"

"Home."

She becomes dumbfounded as she says, "You're going to walk?"

Tim says, "Your amazing boyfriend slashed my back tire."

Aliyah walks to him and grabs his hand, "Don't walk home it's late. It's not safe to walk home at night. Hasn't your mom ever told you not to walk at night? I bet she cares a lot about you."

He ignores her but stops walking. The pain in his heart grows as he hears the word mom yet again. The hate subsides as Aliyah gently squeezes his hand saying, "Come on Tim."

She begins walking him to her car. He stares in confusion saying, "What?"

She smiles and says, "I'm driving you home. Don't say no either. Just come on."

Tim gets into the car. He watches her walk around the car to get into the driver's side. He stares at her, not knowing how to react to a kind gesture from his enemy's girlfriend. Was this some sort of sick joke? Or was she genuinely being kind?

He brushes his thoughts off, not wanting to deal with any more stress. Going along with whatever is in store for him, he buckles his seatbelt. He notices Aliyah watching. He asks, "What?"

Aliyah says, "Nothing you just remind me of my little brother. He always puts his seatbelt on. He makes me wear mine," she laughs.

He explains, "You should wear it. It could save your life."

She puts it on as she laughs. Starting the car, she drives away. Repeatedly, she glances at him as she drives.

Without looking at her he demands, "If you keep staring at me like that I'm going to get out and walk."

Embarrassed to be caught staring, she focuses on the road and apologizes. They drive for a few miles of cold and awkward silence.

The silence begins to make her itch. She looks at Tim who silently stares at the night sky as if wishing for something. She attempts conversation, "So Timothy-"

"Please stop calling me by my full first name," he interrupts, "I go by Tim."

Her patience shortens as she rolls her eyes, "Ok fine. *Tim.* Tell me about yourself."

Tim says, "What do you want to know?"

Aliyah smiles stating, "Anything. For starters why are you so freaking quiet?"

Tim looks out the window as he scoffs, "I don't know. I just am."

She smiles and asks, "Do I make you shy? I get that I'm pretty but don't be shy. I won't bite."

Tim ignores her. The silence births once again as they continue driving down the road. Tim becomes comfortable with the familiar muteness as Aliyah becomes more and more bothered. She becomes fed up and pulls the car over. Tim sits up and looks around. He looks at her as she puts the car in park.

"Aliyah what are you doing? Why are you parking the car?"

She crosses her arms, "This silence stops now. It's too weird. I'm being kind enough to drive you home. The least you can do is share a conversation with me."

"Ugh! What do you want me to say?"

She looks at him and says kindly, "Just talk."

Tim becomes frustrated and retreats back into his shell as he leans back, watching the moon. Aliyah takes out the keys and leans her seat back. "Fine. We'll be here all night I guess. It's a good thing I have cozy seats in here huh? Should I turn on some heat?"

Tim rolls his eyes as she begins to relax in her chair. Time passes as Tim continues watching the sky in silence. He becomes annoyed and unbuckles his seatbelt. He sits up and looks at her.

"What's your problem? Just take me home! I will seriously get out and walk if you don't start this car *right now*."

Aliyah smiles as she looks at him, "Hey you're talking! Now just tell me about yourself. But not in a mean tone. Try talking kindly with compassion in your voice."

Tim scoffs in frustration as he sits back again in silence. Aliyah smiles at him. He turns away from her in annoyance. Time continues to pass. Aliyah begins to lose the silent battle as she begins to become bored. She looks at Tim whose eyes are fixed on the sky.

"It's been an hour and he hasn't said anything at all. What's wrong with him? Maybe he just doesn't like people. It's so strange though. He's the same boy from last year right? He was so open and popular. I never paid much attention but I know him by reputation. He's so different now. Well, if he wants to get home he's going to have to talk sooner or later."

CHAPTER EIGHT

An hour of silence passes as Aliyah and Tim sit in the car. Tim looks at Aliyah through the window's reflection. She is slowly beginning to give up.

"Why does she want to know about me? It's not even a big deal. No one ever tells me to talk about myself. I'm usually always hearing people talk about themselves."

He looks back as Aliyah sits up. She fastens her seatbelt and puts her key into the ignition. Tim pauses before speaking. He wants to speak but something inside tells him to remain silent.

Before she can start the car Tim manages to say, "My full name is Timothy Edward Derr." She stops and looks at him. He stares out the window as he talks, "I was born on July the 8th, 1993."

Aliyah leans back to listen. He continues, "I live with my father. My mother left me when I was 16. I don't have a lot of friends anymore. So I like to spend my spare time working. For fun I like to draw and write stories."

"My favorite color is red. I like to listen to soft, hard, punk, and alternative rock music. After high school I want to go to college and become a professional writer and a cartoonist. That's all you get," he looks at her.

Aliyah smiles and says, "You sound really interesting Tim. Thanks for sharing. That was nice of you."

She starts the car engine. Tim stares at her as they drive away.

He says, "Wait, that's it?"

Aliyah says, "What do you mean Tim?"

"Well I mean tell me about *yourself*. You made me talk. Now it's your turn."

Aliyah smiles as she begins her short tale, "Ok. That's fair. My full name is Aliyah Starla Conrad. I was born March 4th 1994. I live with my father too. My mother died a few years ago in a car accident. I actually have a lot of friends. But I prefer to spend time by myself. I like to read, write music and sing for fun. My favorite color is green. I like the music you just mentioned along with country and pop music. After high school I want to go to school to become a nurse that helps deliver babies. That's about it."

Tim says, "That was pretty good. You're an interesting person too Aliyah."

Aliyah becomes thrilled, "Hey! You got my name right."

Tim fails to keep his smile hidden as her lovely smile softens him. Aliyah asks, "So what type of stuff do you write?"

He says, "I write a lot. I write songs, poetry and stories. Mainly just love stories though."

Aliyah becomes excited and says, "I love to read. What genre do you favor when you write?"

He speaks about his work vividly, "Most of them have been romance novels. I have one action based graphic novel. It has over 270 chapters."

Aliyah becomes impressed saying, "Whoa you're dedicated! Haha I don't think I could write that much without getting bored."

Tim slouches saying, "When you always have a lot of spare time, boredom becomes the norm."

Aliyah asks, "Are you saying you're always bored?"

"Well, kind of yeah. Like I said, I don't have a lot of friends. So I spend a lot of time at home."

Aliyah brainstorms, "You should do something with your dad then."

Her smile fades as Tim puts his head down. Her home situation makes her think his reaction to her words, is because he may have a bad relationship with his father as well.

She says, "What's wrong? Oh no I'm so sorry. Do you have a bad relationship with your dad?"

Tim defends, "Huh, no! Of course not. He's great. He just works a lot so I hardly ever see him. I'm usually home alone. Since my mom left the house has been really empty."

She feels as if she can relate as the feeling of her mom lingers in her heart. She sympathizes, "I'm sorry to hear that. You miss her don't you?"

Tim casually says, "No. I *hate* my mother. I can't stand her."

Aliyah becomes alarmed at his cruel words and shouts, "Don't say stuff like that!"

Tim argues, "You don't know her. I do. I'll say whatever I want."

Aliyah says, "I know she gave birth to you. I don't know the relationship you two have but I'm sure she loves you Tim."

He counters, "Then why did she leave? Giving birth to me was the only good she ever did for me. Don't lecture me. You don't know what it's like. You're just a spoiled rich girl."

She softly says, "Don't judge me Timothy. You don't know me either. I don't have the best relationship with my father. I don't know your mom, you're right. But I do know I wish my mother were still alive. Be thankful that you have both your mother and father."

Tim feels remorse as he hears the barely hidden pain in her voice, "As for my home life. You don't know anything Tim."

He stares at the bruise on her face and says, "So I was right. You didn't get that bruise from falling." She becomes teary eyed as he asks, "Did you?"

She tries to smile her pain off but tears fall from her face as she shakes her head no. Tim watches in grief. Wiping her tears, she pulls into Tim's driveway. "You're home."

Tim stares at her. She looks at him and says, "What's the matter? You're home. Go on home."

Tim asks, "Aliyah how did you get that bruise?"

She remains silent but watches him trying not to cry. She looks away as she gasps for air as she weeps, "Why do you care? You're home now, so go. It's not your problem. Why do you care?"

Not knowing how to express his feelings comfortably, he awkwardly says, "Well I don't know. It's just you're..."

He stops as she looks at him. She asks, "I'm what?"

"Special," he says.

She wipes her face as his words confuse her, "What are you talking about?"

Tim says, "The thought of someone hitting you, well it hurts me. You seem so nice and caring."

Aliyah smiles and laughs as she wipes her tears saying, "You don't mean any of that. You act like I'm annoying or something every time we talk."

Tim says, "I don't think that. You're nice. You're the only person who's been this nice to me. You might have saved me tonight, the way you stood up to Regan. And it was nice of you to drive me home."

Aliyah says, "Well I couldn't let you walk home with it being so late. And no one deserves to be beaten. I had to defend you. It was the right thing to do."

Her strong character unknowingly moves him. She doesn't look it but she is a tough individual and her kind heart adds to her womanly grace. Seeing the battle wound on her face causes sorrow in his heart. Not for himself, but for this kind and caring person who cries at the wheel of her car.

Tim stares at the bruise and asks, "Did your father do that to you?"

Aliyah stops breathing for a brief moment and chokes. She begins to cough. Tim watches as she gets herself together.

Looking at his house, she says, "Hey it's getting pretty late. You better get going."

She looks at Tim whose eyes look deep with concern. He says, "Did he Aliyah?"

She looks away as she sheds another tear. She laughs saying, "It doesn't matter."

Tim says, "Yes it does."

He gets out of the car and walks to her side. He offers his hand saying, "Come inside. Please?"

81

Aliyah questions, "Won't your dad be upset? It's so late."

Tim says, "He won't be back until late tomorrow. Come inside."

She takes his hand and he leads her to the front door. She watches as he unlocks the door. She thinks, *"No one's ever took me under their care for the sake of me. Even with Regan my venting usually ends with him talking me into sex."*

Tim opens the door for her and let's her walk in first. She stands at the door as she watches him walk into a kitchen. He begins pouring a glass of lemonade and asks, "Do you want something to drink Aliyah?"

She says, "No, but thanks for offering."

He walks to her with a glass and holds it to her smiling, saying, "Here. Don't say no. Just drink it."

She smiles and takes the glass. She takes a sip and says, "Don't steal my quotes Tim. I better not see that in one of your books."

They exchange smiles as he leads her into a living room and sits. He picks up a remote asking, "Do you like TV?"

He turns on the television. A sappy love movie that Tim was watching earlier plays. A man says to a woman, "For the longest, I've wanted to hold your soft and soothing hand. Here we stand with nothing to separate us."

The woman says, "You've longed for my touch just as I've longed for your warmth. Here we stand with nothing but restrained-"

Tim quickly changes the station out of embarrassment. Aliyah says urgently, "Hey turn it back! I love romance. Hurry, hurry!"

Tim changes back to the station. The two lovers embrace each other with a kiss and intense holding of one another. Aliyah's eyes soften as she watches.

"That's so beautiful. What ever happened to old school romance Tim? Why aren't things the way they are on TV?"

Tim watches as the woman looks into the man's eyes with passion. Tim too wonders why real life isn't that way as he says, "I'm not sure."

He looks at her. She looks at him. There's a moment of silence. This time the silence isn't awkward, but suspenseful. Tim looks at her bruise. He scoots close to her and gently rubs the bruise with his hand. She slightly flinches.

"So it happened today," he says.

Aliyah looks at him with surprise asking, "How do you know that?"

He explains, "Your face was fine the other day. Plus it hurts when I touch it right?" She nods as he gently rubs her face in a consolingly manner. "It's an artist thing," he says. "I pay attention to small details. So..."

Aliyah says, "Yes ok? He hits me."

He says, "Don't be so casual about it. You don't deserve to be hit, especially not by a man. I'm sorry this happened."

She stares at him in pain, "Why do you care so much? What are you planning on getting out of this?"

Tim patiently says, "Hey, would you stop asking me stuff like that? It's degrading. Just because a guy treats a girl kindly doesn't mean he wants something from her. Relax and breathe. Tell me what happened. I don't want to take advantage of you, I promise."

Aliyah says, "Ok, ok I apologize. My mom died a few years ago. I was 14. I have a little brother who was 2 or 3 at the time. He was too young to understand that she died. So after my mom died. My father started seeing other women frequently. Today a woman dressed in a bra and panties came out of my kitchen."

"My little brother Liel is so young. He saw her kiss my dad and thought it was my mother. It hurt me badly. My dad is messing him up. I've basically raised Liel."

"My mother had an affair with my dad after he hit her. So my father kicked her out. After she died my father started drinking a lot more. I told Liel that our dad hurt mom and made her leave us for good. He repeated it to my dad."

"But the way Liel said it. I think it got to my dad. I know it made him feel responsible for her death. He broke down and cried. He told me not to turn Liel against him, that Liel was all he had left and that I wouldn't take him away."

Tim comforts her as she cries, "He calls me slut and says I disgust him. My father hates me. It hurts so much. All I have is Liel. I can't let my dad raise Liel to be like him."

She cries. Tim awkwardly hugs then holds her comfortingly. His awkward feelings begin to dim as she cries on his shoulder.

"Stay strong Aliyah. Your brother needs your strength. I'm sure he loves you very much. Protect him ok?"

Aliyah says, "I know. It's just so hard. I have zero support."

Tim asks, "What about Regan?"

Aliyah becomes frustrated saying, "Regan didn't even remember my birthday. I've talked to him about my personal life. He barely cares. All he cares about is sex, parties and football. He doesn't even know I exist. My father is in love with him. He thinks Regan is so amazing because he's a quarterback. He wants me to marry him so if Regan goes pro I'll marry into wealth."

Tim rolls his eyes saying, "Life is so easy huh? Look at you, marrying for money. You've got the life."

Aliyah says, "No, I never said I wanted to marry for wealth. I said my father wants me to. I want to marry someone I love. I don't care about money."

Tim asks, "Do you love Regan?"

She wipes her tears as she calms down saying, "I used to think I did. But lately I've been questioning why I like him. Lately he makes me cry more than I do smile."

Tim says, "Well at least you have someone to care about. I don't have anyone period."

In a questioned tone Aliyah says, "Robyn?"

He doubtingly says, "She's in love with the old Tim. Not me. Robyn wants me to play football. I want to write. She can't respect that. She says it's annoying when I tell her I love her a lot. I only say it so much because I want her to say it first."

Aliyah says, "Well at least she says it. Regan has never said it back. I mean he jokes about it. But he says he doesn't want to get serious right now. He says he wants to have fun before he settles down. At least Robyn says it."

Tim says, "I'd rather not be told it at all, then to hear it and it be a lie. How can you love someone and not respect his or her dreams? I want someone who pushes me to go for my goals. Not someone who thinks they're dumb and a waste of time."

Aliyah says, "I bet you're a great writer."

Tim replies, "I guess. People say they like my work."

Aliyah smiles as she grabs his hands, "I want to read one of your novels!"

He looks at her in confusion questioning her words, "You want to do what?"

She smirks saying, "You heard me. Go grab one for me. Do you write romance?"

Tim says, "I do. But you wouldn't like any of my books. Trust me they're-"

Aliyah interrupts, "Shut up and go get one of your novels. I love romance. Where's your room?"

Tim says, "Up the stairs, why?"

Aliyah looks past Tim and stares in shock, "Oh my gosh!"

He looks back asking, "What? What is it?"

Aliyah grins and sneaks away as her clever diversion distracts Tim. He looks back as he hears footsteps going up the stairs. He says, "Oh come on." as he walks after her.

"I can't remember the last time I had a girl over. Robyn was the first and only girl I've ever had over here. She was my first everything. It was last summer. I never thought it would have ended. But time flies and people change."

He stands outside his bedroom and looks at Aliyah as she reads one of his books. She lies relaxingly on his bed as what she is reading intrigues her. Tim watches, changing his mind about yelling at her to get out.

T.Edward Redd   **86**

"It feels kind of good having company. She's pretty. But she's not my type. She likes guys like Regan. Football jocks who mistreat girls and use them for other things besides love. She's the kind of girl who would stay beside the worst guy on the planet and see the good in him.

"She believes if she waits long enough he'll change. That's not me. She wouldn't know what to do with someone like me. The lack of abuse and drama would scare her. She'd find it too good to be true. She would get paranoid or bail out of fear. It's not worth my time. She would just push me away."

Aliyah smiles at Tim as she closes the novel. Tim walks towards her, as he says, "Didn't like it huh?"

Aliyah pretends to frown, as she says, "Well no." She quickly smiles, "I love it!"

Tim becomes offended saying, "Stop kidding around. It's not funny." He takes the novel.

Aliyah says, "Hey! I wasn't finished."

Tim proudly looks at the novel saying, "Stop playing with me. It's not funny. This is the first novel that I have ever published. It doesn't sell as well as it did when it first hit stores. I'm proud of it though. So don't mock me by saying you love it when you hate it."

Aliyah takes the novel back, "For your information I wasn't mocking you. I actually do like the story. I like how Glen's character has inner conflicts with himself. He's in love with his girlfriend but she's being distant. Then his ex comes back into his life and confesses her love to him."

Tim stares in amazement saying, "That was incredible. You really read it?"

Aliyah smiles saying, "That's as far as I got in the story. Then you snatched it away. It's suspenseful and dramatic. I like it. I can relate to Glen's character. I hate it when I text Regan and he doesn't reply for hours or not at all. It hurts. It makes me feel so..."

Tim finishes, "Alone."

Aliyah agrees, "Yeah, alone."

Tim sits beside her. He looks at the novel saying, "I of all people know that feeling. Glen's character is based on me. A lot, if not all of my novels are based on things I went through or feel."

She says, "Can I borrow that?"

Tim says, "My novel?"

Aliyah shakes her head yes, "Yes, I won't steal it. I'll buy my own copy when I get the chance. It's in stores right?"

Tim says, "Yes. But don't worry keep that one. I can..."

Aliyah stops him with a shush, "I'll buy my own Mr. Derr." She smiles as she starts reading again. She lays back asking, "Where's your dad?"

"He went to work. He's a truck driver. He doesn't get home until late tomorrow."

Aliyah looks at him and smirks, "Oh, so do you always bring girls over here when he leaves?"

Tim corrects her, "You're the first girl to come over here in a year. Robyn was the first and only girl who's been over up until now."

She becomes caring saying, "You're not lying are you? So are you here all alone every day?"

Tim looks at her and confirms her question with a smile.

She becomes dumbfounded with grief saying, "Why? You should get out with some friends! Go have some fun. You're an amazing person. Don't waste time alone."

Tim looks at her saying, "Friends? Did you see what your boyfriend did tonight? The entire house booed me. I have no friends."

Aliyah says, "I'm sorry that happened tonight. You didn't deserve that. No one does."

Tim smiles saying, "It's no big deal."

Aliyah can't help but smile at his obvious tough guy front as he smiles. She playfully pushes him saying, "Stop it. You're lying. You shouldn't be alone like that all the time. It's not healthy."

Tim becomes defensive saying, "What would you know? You're friends with everyone. You have no idea what it's like."

Aliyah gets up saying, "I know a lot more than you think. Well, I should get going. It's pretty late."

Tim agrees with her. They walk to the front door. Aliyah looks at him, "Thanks for tonight. It was relieving. I hope I didn't bore you to death with my silly venting."

Tim smiles and says, "It wasn't silly. Thank you for opening up. I hope it helped you release some stress. Oh ha, and thanks for the ride home."

Aliyah smiles and says, "It wasn't a big deal Tim and yes, you helped relieve me of some of my stress. Thank you."

They stare into each other's eyes. There's a moment of connection between them as time stops for them once again. They stare deeply into one another's eyes as if they can see one another's soul. They stop after realizing they are staring at each other deeply. They both embarrassingly look away from one another.

Aliyah blushes saying, "Um, I uh."

Tim shies away saying, "Yeah I should uh."

Aliyah says, "Sorry! Ha. I'm so sleepy."

Tim says, "Yes me too! I kind of spaced out."

They both laugh and stare at each other once more.

She awkwardly says, "So, I should go."

Tim embarrassingly replies, "Have a nice drive."

Aliyah shows the novel to him smirking, "I'm reading this when I get home. I'll let you know what I think about it."

Tim smiles, "Alright."

Aliyah teases, "Are you smiling Mr. Derr?" You always walk around with that *the world bores me* expression. I didn't know you smiled."

Tim replies, "Everyone smiles. Sometimes they just need a reason to smile."

Aliyah encouragingly says, "Well you have a nice smile Mr. Derr. Use it more often."

Tim smiles peacefully saying, "Thank you, Ms. Conrad."

She smiles at him for mocking her formality. She slowly backs up as if not wanting to leave as she says, "I'm going home now. Sleep well Tim and thanks again."

She walks out the house. Tim watches as she walks to her car to make sure no one bothers her along the way. He thinks.

"When our eyes met there was this moment of familiarity. It felt like I belonged. It was only a few seconds but it felt like I knew her for years. I misjudged her to some degree. She's not like the other girls. She wasn't snobby or self-centered. She was caring and sincere. On top of that she enjoyed my novel."

He calls for her. She looks back saying, "Yes?"

Tim says, "Take care of yourself ok? Be safe at home. Don't let it bring you down. You sleep well too." She smiles as he continues, "If you ever want someone to talk to and someone who actually listens, I'm always in the front office or even here."

Aliyah smiles, "Goodnight Mr. Derr and thank you. This meant a lot."

Tim watches as she gets into her car. She starts it and drives away.

"But she isn't my type. We live in two completely different worlds. She's stuck in her world and I'm stuck in mine. That's just how it is."

He watches Aliyah drive away. She honks as she waves him goodbye. Tim smiles as he waves back.

"Oh well." He walks back into the house and closes the door behind him.

CHAPTER NINE

Last night was ok I guess. Just a typical day in the life of Aliyah Conrad. But I'm not going to complain. Yesterday was longer than usual. I did a lot. The party was boring. Regan and I barely spoke to each other. He got into a fight with Tim Derr. He's the boy that remembered my birthday. Regan's friends jumped him after he punched Regan in the nose, which I'm sure is broken. I managed to stop Regan from hurting Tim even more. I drove him home after Regan slashed his car's back tire. Regan can be so immature sometimes. It's very annoying. I wish he would grow up. I spent some of the night with Tim. He's an interesting guy. Caring too. He invited me inside after I told him my father hit me. It's weird how he saw the bruise but Regan didn't. It hurts a lot. Well I'm going to start my day now. I still wait for my warrior. The one who will take the pain away. Where are you? Can't you hear my cry or feel my pain? How long must I wait...

End Log

Aliyah lies on her bed reading Tim's novel "Hero's Wake".
She squints as the sunlight from the morning sun, beams through the window blinds. She thinks.

"This novel is amazing. He really wrote this?"

She flips the page as she continues reading as if caught in a spell.

"He said Glen was based on him. Does that mean he actually went through this? I wonder if all of his novels are this good."

She checks her text messages only to see no one has sent any memos.

"What a surprise," she scoffs.

T.Edward Redd   **92**

She begins reading again as someone knocks on her door. She looks back to see Liel slowly peeking his head in. In his childlike voice he says, "Li, Li can you make me some breakfast? I'm hungry."

She answers, "I'll be right out Liel."

She bookmarks her page and places the novel on her dresser. Staring in the mirror as she flips her hair behind her, she looks at her bruise. She says, "It looks horrible."

She walks out of her room and closes her door. Walking downstairs and towards the kitchen, she sees her dad sitting on the couch. Several beers are on the table, while one is in his hand. She speaks, "Good morning."

He doesn't respond. She becomes let down and walks into the kitchen. She grabs a carton of eggs, bacon and sausage out of the refrigerator and places them on a counter.

"My dad hasn't looked at me, let alone talk to me since last night."

She places a frying pan on the stove burner and turns it on.

"It feels weird. He's never ignored me before. Our relationship has never been good but at least he always talked back to me."

She begins frying bacon and sausage on the pan.

"But now there's nothing from him. I don't want my father to hate me. I don't know what to do. Is it bad that I miss him calling me names and the drama? At least he was recognizing my presence."

She places the cooked meats onto a plate and begins scrambling eggs. She looks at her dad as he drinks beer and watches TV.

"But now he doesn't even look at me. It's like I'm a ghost now. He really doesn't care about me. I disgust him."

She sheds a tear. The tear evaporates as it falls onto the skillet.

"I wish mom was here."

She finishes scrambling the eggs and scrapes them onto a plate with a fork. She turns off the stove eye and prepares two plates. As she calls for her brother to come eat, she walks into the dining room. Placing a plate on the table, she looks at her dad. She walks a plate of food to him.

She smiles, "Here dad. I made you breakfast."

He ignores her as he belches and changes the channel.

She continues, "I made eggs. I know that's your favorite."

He continues his silence as she tries to talk to him again, "I'll just leave it here on the table."

After placing it on the table, she watches in worry as he takes a giant gulp from his beer bottle.

She asks, "Do you want anything healthy to drink? Like apple or orange juice?"

He continues ignoring her as he searches for something interesting on TV. Aliyah slowly backs away in defeat. She tries once more, "I love you dad…"

He burps and turns the station. Hurt, she says kindly, "Ok well, enjoy your breakfast."

Sadly she walks away towards the dining room table. Her pain gets washed away as she sees her hope eating happily at the dining room table. She sits beside her brother and asks, "How does it taste?"

Liel cheeses as he swallows the delicious meal saying, "It's the yummiest breakfast ever Li, Li!"

She smiles. Her dad walks to the kitchen with the plate she made. Aliyah smiles with excitement, "Did you like the eggs? I scrambled them the way you like."

Her joy ceases as she sees the plate is filled with food. Her father had touched not one bit. He tosses the food into the trash and makes a bowl of cereal. Aliyah sheds a tear and calmly walks to her room.

Shutting the door behind her she lets out a sigh. She sits on her bed as she grabs a pillow. Her sulking begins as she holds the pillow. She squints in frustration.

"Why does he hate me so much? Why am I the one who has to suffer all the time? It isn't fair. I've never hurt anyone. My father hates me. My mother died. My boyfriend barely knows I'm alive. Why? I've never complained. I'm grateful for everything that I've been blessed with. But I still suffer."

She grabs her phone and sends Regan a text message. She waits, placing hope in the text she knows won't arrive. She becomes antsy as moments of silence pass. She grabs the phone and calls him.

To her surprise, he answers. She barely hears his voice as background noise drowns out his voice.

Aliyah cheeringly says, "Hey babe," she sits up happily.

Regan becomes surprised to hear *her* voice, "Aliyah? What do you want?"

"I need someone to talk to. You make me feel better so I called."

Regan tries to end the call saying, "Aliyah I don't have time right now."

Aliyah hears girls in the background and says, "Who is that?"

Regan replies, "No one I'm at the store. Aliyah I can't talk right now."

Aliyah cries, "Regan I need you! You never have time for me. I need you baby."

In an annoyed tone he says, "Aliyah I don't have time to listen to you whine. I'll call you back."

She begs in distress, "Babe I won't whine I promise! Can we talk for five minutes? I'm your girlfriend for crying out loud! Spare me five minutes. Please."

She hears music and laughter in the background and says, "Where are you? It's so noisy."

Regan says briefly, "I'm at football practice. Babe I have to go bye." He hangs up.

Aliyah pleads, "Regan!"

She slams her phone down and holds her head in frustration.

"You're not supposed to complain about what happens to you. Never focus on the bad. Only the good. But what if there isn't anything good? What if nothing but bad things happen to you? Is it wrong to cry? Is it wrong to want an escape? To want someone who understands you?"

She walks to her dresser and picks up *Hero's Wake*. She opens it and reads. For a quarter of an hour she is taken away from her sad world as the writing moves her word for word. The more she reads, the more she becomes curious about the mysterious author.

She closes the book and grabs her car keys. After walking out of the house and getting into her car, she takes a drive. She arrives at her high school after a few miles. After parking in front of the building, she gets out and walks towards the building.

Once inside, she looks at the absence of students that Saturdays tend to bring. Voices and phones ring from the office. She makes her way to the office as she looks at the novel. As she steps into the office the aroma of coffee welcomes her.

"It's like a regular school day minus the students," she mutters.

The secretary looks at her as she walks in. She searches the office and spots Tim sitting at a desk filled with papers as he types on a laptop. She smiles. The secretary gets her attention with an attitude filled tone asking, "Can I help you?"

Aliyah says, "Um could I," she points at Tim.

The secretary rolls her eyes in annoyance as she motions her to come in. Aliyah walks to Tim and sees the table filled with papers. She sees him playing games on his laptop and clears her throat. He quickly clicks out of his activity and grabs some papers saying, "Here I finished next week's newsletter. I hate the fonts you pick so I changed it up," he laughs, "I know you'll love it Kurt."

He looks back and becomes surprised to see it's Aliyah and not Principal Frawgs.

"Aliyah," he says in confusion.

She smiles saying, "Hi Mr. Derr"

Tim checks his watch and looks at her saying, "Hey. Why are you here on a Saturday?"

She sits beside him saying, "I was going to ask you that same question."

Tim says, "I work here on Saturdays."

Aliyah teases, "They pay you to play card games on your laptop?"

Unenthused he says, "I was bored. Why are you here?"

Aliyah says, "Why are you so forward? Can I not be here on Saturdays?"

Tim says, "Well yeah. But I've never seen you inside the building on Saturdays."

She says, "Well, since you're always alone I thought I'd visit." She opens her bookmarked page of *Hero's Wake*.

Tim asks, "You're still reading that?"

She replies as she reads, "Yeah. I'm halfway through it. I stayed up until 3 am reading it. It's a really good story. Do you mind if I sit here and read it?"

He reopens the card game as he says, "Not at all."

She giggles at him. He lightheartedly shushes her. They share peaceful silence as they on their task. They occasionally glance at the other while one isn't looking. Principal Frawgs walks in and looks at Tim.

He scoffs and says, "Tim you know the rules. Students aren't allowed to be here past 12 on Saturdays."

Tim smiles and says, "Come on Kurt. Besides it's not 12 in Missouri."

Frawgs replies, "This is Indiana Tim. Come on. Don't stay in this old office all day. How can you love this place more than the staff does? Get out and have some fun. Take your girlfriend out on a date."

Tim shouts defensively, "She is NOT my girlfriend."

Frawgs says, "Leave or go to the detention room."

Tim asks, "For how long?"

Aliyah interrupts, "Hey, Tim do they feed you here."

Frawgs pats him on the back and smiles at her saying, "We sure don't. I bet you're hungry huh Tim? Take your girlfriend out for lunch. Somewhere outside the building."

Tim repeats, "She isn't my girlfriend!"

Aliyah says, "That's a good idea. Come on Tim, let's go grab lunch."

Tim says, "You want to buy me lunch?"

Aliyah smiles saying, "Only if you promise to leave this depressing office."

Tim gives in as Frawgs begs for him to take her offer silently behind her. Tim rolls his eyes and packs his things.

"Fine. Let's go."

Frawgs goofily shouts, "Thank you! You got him out of the seat! You're a godsend Aliyah. Take him far away. He spends way too much time in here."

Tim sticks his tongue out at Frawgs. Frawgs counters with a goofy face. Aliyah grabs Tim's hand and leads him out the building. They get into Aliyah's car and drive away.

"I've never seen Principal Frawgs joke and laugh like that. He must really like you," she says,

Tim says, "Yeah they all do in there. I'm basically one of the staff members. Only except I have no authority, I'm a student and I don't get paid."

Aliyah laughs. Tim smiles but stops to look at her face asking, "Hey have you been crying?"

Aliyah ignores him asking, "Do you work at the school every Saturday?"

Tim says, "Yeah. It's volunteer work. I used to stay at school to avoid going home to mom when she lived with us. After she left it got really cold and lonely at my house. So now I'm at the school a lot to avoid the cold loneliness."

Aliyah holds his hand caringly saying, "That's no way to live Tim." She smiles at him as they arrive at a Mexican restaurant. "Do you like Mexican food? We can go somewhere else if you want," she says.

Tim says, "No we can eat here. Thank you."

She parks and turns the car off. She gets out and signals him to get out. Tim walks to her saying, "Look, I don't have any cash ok?"

She grabs his hand and smiles saying, "I'll pay for you. Come on. You need to have some fun for once."

They go inside and order food. They find a table and sit. Aliyah notices Tim didn't get a drink and says, "Hey do you want a drink?"

Tim says, "No it's ok."

She says, "Yes you do. Wait here. I'll go get you a drink."

She walks to the counter and gets him something to drink. She takes it to Tim who takes a sip immediately.

Aliyah laughs, "I thought you weren't thirsty."

Tim pants, "No. The burrito is just really spicy!"

T.Edward Redd

She laughs at his goofiness as he fans his tongue. They begin to eat. Aliyah watches as Tim eats his burrito. She smiles as she thinks.

"He reminds me so much of Liel, only except he's really shy and quiet. He hasn't always been like that. I can tell. Something happened that made him retreat into this shell. When he's comfortable he comes out of it. It's cute."

CHAPTER TEN

Tim eats his burrito as Aliyah watches him, not caring if he notices or not anymore. He looks at her and wonders.

"Why did she buy me lunch? Does she really just want to spend time with me? Did Regan put her up to this? No. She's way too nice to do something like that. It's just strange. Maybe it's strange because I'm not used to someone doing this for me. No drama or yelling. It's peaceful."

He looks at Aliyah, who is still staring. He says, "Look Aliyah. You're nice and everything, but you seriously need to stop staring at me."

She smiles and teases, "Why are you so defensive? I can look at you if I want."

"You're weird then."

Aliyah counters, "You're always shy and quiet. You're the weird one. You're the only eighteen-year-old boy I know who's this quiet."

He shrugs, "Well maybe we're both weird."

Aliyah says, "You should meet my little brother. I think you too would get along." She smiles, "You remind me a lot of him."

He asks, "How old is your brother?"

She answers, "Five. He'll be six in May."

Tim says, "That's nice."

Not wanting him to retreat back into his shell, she encourages him to speak more by asking, "Do you have any siblings Tim?"

He says, "I have a sister. She's off in college though. I hardly ever see her."

She hesitates to ask her next question but says, "Can I ask another question?"

Tim shakes his head yes as he takes one of the last bites of his burrito. She asks, "Why do you hate your mother?"

Tim stops chewing. Aliyah stares in suspense as the familiar silence returns. She quickly says, "I'm sorry. I didn't mean to offend you."

He finishes the burrito and says, "You didn't. It felt like I was going to sneeze but it went away." He nonchalantly wipes his mouth and drinks the last of his drink.

Aliyah asks, "Well, why do you hate your mom?"

Tim takes a deep breath and begins to explain, "For the longest time my mom and I haven't really had a good relationship. I never got that motherly affection from her. My mom is bipolar. I was too young at the time to understand.

"I grew up being yelled at, name called and disciplined for the smallest things by her. She was cruel. I grew up watching her mistreat my father. I've always had a great father and son bond with him. So when my mom mistreated him it fueled my anger and hate towards her. My mom always used to show favor towards my sister. Things I got spanked for she got away with easily and even hugged. I never got that."

He lifts his left shirt sleeve and reveals cuts and burn marks.

Aliyah says, "I saw those the other day. I figured you got cut or something. Did she do that?"

As he points to a specific scar he says, "No, I did it. I did this when I was in the seventh grade.

Aliyah morns, "That's so young. You were, what twelve or eleven?"

"Eleven," he says. "I got in trouble at school that day. I didn't turn in an assignment, so I had to pull a green card. The teacher told my mom. She came to the school and beat me in front of the class. My friends, well the whole class laughed. There might have been two or three kids who didn't laugh. My mom told me I was getting more when we got home."

Aliyah looks in sorrow yet somewhat relieved. The more he speaks of his pain, the more she feels that he can somewhat understand her. Finding someone who understood *pain* and *loneliness* was like finding ice-cold water in a weary desert. It's alleviating.

He continues, "On the way home I was scared. When we got home I grabbed tree branches and tried to cut my wrist. I thought my mom would of cried or something and hug me. I wanted her to say that she didn't want me to die and that she loved me."

A single tear he doesn't seem to notice escapes his right eye as he continues, "But she didn't. She slapped me across the face and told me to stop. It hurt. Not physically but emotionally. It felt like getting stabbed at the soul. Cutting was my way of transferring the emotional pain to physical pain. Physical pain goes away faster. But emotional pain lingers. It's worse than physical pain."

The more he speaks the more she innocently becomes drawn to him. Underneath this quiet and tough exterior lies a hurt and lonely boy who simply wants to be loved. The strength he upholds daily with these tormenting feelings inside of him displays his courage and strong will. She finds him to be brave.

She rubs her hand on his scar and says, "Don't ever cut yourself again ok?"

He looks at her as she wipes tears from her face. He asks, "Why are you crying?"

She wipes her face, "No one should have to go through that. You were just a boy. I'm sorry she didn't show you the love you wanted. The love you needed as a child."

Tim brushes it off saying, "It's not a big deal. It's just my life."

She stares at his scars and rubs them with her hand. She continues, "It shouldn't have to be. You're a pretty good kid Tim. I never would have imagined that you of all people lived like this."

Tim stares at her face. He touches the bruise on her face. She grabs his hand. He pulls away saying, "Sorry, I didn't mean to-"

"No. Like this," she guides his hand and places it on her bruise and comfortingly says, "There."

"Does it hurt?"

Aliyah says, "No not anymore. It looks a lot worse than it is."

Tim asks, "What did Regan say about it?"

Aliyah mocks herself with a smile, "He didn't notice it. He never notices anything about me."

Tim holds her hand saying, "I'm sorry."

She smiles and says, "I'm still standing Tim. I'll be fine."

Tim smiles at her bravery and strength as he wanders.

"She's a special girl. She's strong. I can tell just by looking at her that she's hopeful. I don't know what about. But she's fighting for something or someone. Maybe I misjudged her."

Aliyah jokingly mocks Tim saying, "If you keep staring at me like that I'm going to walk home or whatever you always say."

Tim smiles at her humor.

She says, "Another smile? That's like ten since we've been hanging out. I'm good for your health huh Tim? Hey do you want to get out of here?

Tim asks, "What do you mean?"

She grabs his hand and says, "Come on. It's boring here." She pulls him up and leads him towards the exit. She drags him unknowingly as she smiles.

He hastily says, "Aliyah where are we going? Aliyah!"

She replies, "Live a little and just come on." She continues to lead him down a street.

Tim impatiently says, "Why did we leave the car? Aliyah seriously!"

She becomes annoyed and says, "Just shut-up and follow me! Geez." She looks back and smiles at him kindly. Tim smirks at her and follows. They arrive at a playground. Tim looks nerve driven as he stares saying, "Seriously?"

Aliyah lets out a refreshing sigh as she says, "Finally. Here we are. I take Liel here all the time.

Tim says, "Your brother? But he's five."

She taps his shoulder, "Tag you're it!"

She runs away cheerfully. Tim stands and watches her run away.

"That empty feeling. Since I've been around her, I haven't felt it. Not at all. But she's not my type. I can't get drawn to her. We're two completely different people. She's used to being abused and mistreated. The sudden change would scare her. She's not the girl for me."

Aliyah stops running and looks behind her to see Tim standing in the same spot. She says, "Tag you're it!"

He stands in place, finding the idea of tag childish. He stares at her with a *no way* expression on his face.

Aliyah says, "Hey come on! Stop being so boring. Don't you know how to play tag? Or am I too fast for you?"

Tim smiles peacefully.

"But still, it's been a while since I've felt this good. So I'll enjoy it. At least now I have a friend."

He runs at her. Aliyah runs away excitingly. She looks back and teases, "Come on Tim. Weren't you a running back," she giggles. They run through the playground. Tim chases her up a grassy hill and slowly catches up. He playfully tackles her and she laughs.

He smiles and holds her saying, "Gotcha now."

Aliyah laughs joy filled as she tries to get free. Their heads bump and they fall onto the hill. Tim gets on his knees holding his head over dramatically.

"Ouch! What's that head of yours made of? Steel?"

Aliyah laughs, "Don't be a cry baby."

Tim smiles and says, "Oh I'm a cry baby?"

Aliyah pokes her tongue out as she says, "Are you going to prove me wrong?"

"How about this?"

He gently pinches her side. She screams in shock. She gasps and looks at him smiling as she says, "You did not just do that!"

He pokes his tongue out and gently pushes her saying, "You know I did."

She pinches him back smiling. He tries to pinch her again but she playfully grabs his hand. They begin to harmlessly wrestle in the grass. They tussle and roll as they laugh while they play fight. They slowly roll their way towards the edge of the grass hill. Aliyah begins to lose balance.

She panics saying, "Oh my gosh Tim!"

She reaches for his hand. He grabs her only to be pulled down the hill with her. They both roll down the hill, laughing freely and carelessly as they forget all about their worries as the moment takes them away from it all. They roll all the way to the bottom of the hill.

Tim rolls on top of her. Aliyah laughs so hysterically that she begins to cry. This time her tears are tears of joy. Tim laughs along with her. They stop laughing to stare into each other's eyes.

Tim asks, "Are you alright?"

She breathes hard trying to catch her breath as she says, "I am. Are you?"

"I'm alright."

Their smiles fade into looks of restrained passion and anxiousness. Tim looks at her beauty. Now that it's free from the dark clouds of her pain he can truly see her loveliness. Aliyah is now able to see the softer side he always hides, fearing the world wouldn't understand him otherwise. They both unintentionally begin to understand one another's heart. Tim stares at her.

Tim thinks, "She's beautiful. I can't even put what I'm feeling right now into words. But it feels, great."

He hesitates to lean towards her and Aliyah does the same. He leans in for a kiss as Aliyah closes her eyes. The playground sprinklers come on, cutting the moment to an end as they both get sprayed. They flinch and get off of each other. Aliyah screams in laughter, as she gets wet. Tim grabs her hand and leads her to the playground.

She looks at her wet clothes upset and says, "Oh my gosh. I'm soaking wet." Tim takes off his shirt and offers it to her. Aliyah stares at his breath taking body.

His chestnut brown skin glistens as the sun shines on it. She watches as water runs down his seemingly flawless and toned body. Biting her lip, she unknowingly and slowly becomes love-struck. She gains her senses as she sees him holding his shirt to her. He offers it for her to dry off with.

She blushes, "Oh no, you don't have to do that. You dry off with it. You look really soaked. Not that I was staring! I mean I was looking but not like that. I'm not saying I wouldn't look. I mean you have a pretty nice body. Not that I was staring or anything! I'm not creepy or anything. I just mean that's a really nice shirt. I don't want to ruin it."

He holds it to her willingly and says, "It's fine. Dry off so you don't catch a cold."

Aliyah gently takes the shirt. She smiles and says, "Thank you Mr. Derr."

He watches as she drains her long brown hair gracefully. She gently begins drying herself off as she pats her soft and beautiful snow like skin. Tim can't resist watching as her blushes of red on her face and body moves him. She continues to wipe herself down elegantly as if preparing for a special occasion.

"She really is amazing," he thinks. *"I never really paid attention to her. But just being around her makes me feel so happy. I don't feel alone or depressed. I feel the exact opposite. It feels amazing. If only I could feel like this forever."*

He smiles peacefully. She looks at him and says, "What? Oh the shirt."

Being distracted by her breathtaking presence he says, "What shirt? Oh! My shirt. Of course."

Aliyah smiles and hands it to him saying, "Thank you Mr. Derr. That was a kind gesture."

"It was my pleasure Ms. Conrad. Thank you. Not just for that but today. I can't remember the last time I had so much fun."

Aliyah says, "Well thanks for having so much fun with me. I honestly can't remember the last time I had this much fun either. Regan doesn't even take me on dates anymore. He's always busy with football and work."

The sun begins to set as they sit on the swings. They share peaceful silence, as it has now become part of their slowly forming bond. They take the moment in, enjoying the peace as the sun begins to set.

Aliyah smiles and looks at Tim saying, "Thank you for the drama free day Mr. Derr. I needed it."

She notices he's looking at her with a look of wonder. She says, "What is it?"

He looks away saying, "It's nothing. I just don't get it. What do you see in Regan? Do you honestly love him? I mean he's just not right for you. You deserve better than him."

Aliyah says, "What do you mean?"

"I see how you act when you talk about him. You want to believe in him. But things aren't the way you want them to be. He ignores you, bad mouths you and mistreats you. You don't honestly think that's what you deserve do you? I mean look at you. You're beautiful."

She blushes and smiles. She looks away laughing as she says, "Of course you being a boy would say that."

Tim corrects her, "I wasn't talking about beauty as in the physical aspect. I mean you as a person. You're so bubbly. You don't have the best home life and yet you never complain. You *always* smile. You make me beam. I haven't genuinely smiled in over a year. You glow. Your energy is just amazing. I really enjoy being around you. You make my day worthwhile. Most of the time I just want to sleep the day away. But you make me want to live. Thank you Aliyah."

Aliyah stares, lost for words as her mouth manages to voice, "That's the sweetest thing anyone has ever said to me…"

Tim looks at her from head to toe then makes eye contact, "I'll admit you're very affecting. But there's way more to you than looks. You're a special girl Aliyah."

Aliyah says, "Thank you, Tim." She looks away as she becomes sad, feeling as the moment of joy would soon be ended by the approaching night sky.

Tim notices and asks, "Hey, what's the matter Aliyah?"

She says, "I don't know. It's nothing."

He replies, "I can tell when you lie. Tell me what's on your mind."

Aliyah smiles at him as she says, "Nothing, Tim."

He stands unconvinced but doesn't push the truth out of her. He stands beside her as the sun begins to make its way behind the horizon. Aliyah smiles at the beauty of the horizon saying, "It's getting pretty late huh?"

Wishing he could understand what was troubling her, he looks to her saying, "Yeah, it is. Let's get back Aliyah."

They look at each other for a moment. They look into each other's eyes as if they can read each other's thoughts. Tim looks away as he fights his growing feelings.

He thinks, *"No. I can't fall for her."*

His thoughts are brought to a halt as Aliyah grabs his hand. He looks at her surprised to hear her say, "You're a good guy Tim. You're not like these other boys. You're actually about something. Please stay that way. Don't ever change. Not even for Robyn."

Tim says, "I wasn't planning on it."

Aliyah says, "Good."

They begin walking back to the car. Aliyah begins to drive Tim home. Although he's quiet she begins to be able to understand his muteness. She knows this silence is happy silence and not the silence of sadness. She smiles and shares it with him as she drives, losing memory of all of her despair for this brief moment.

Tim occasionally looks to see if her smile has faded. Each time he looks, he is pleased to see the smile still perfectly constructed on her gorgeous face. He tries not to smile as his hardened feelings unwillingly diminish the more he shares time with this scenic beauty. He's slowly developing feelings of care and romance for her. He looks away trying not to be caught smiling.

They arrive at Tim's house. Both are brought out of their separate yet connected worlds of happiness as they both stare at the house. He looks at Aliyah and she looks at him.

She says, "Well, here you are Mr. Derr. Sleep well, ok?"

Tim opens the car door looking at her saying, "Thank you. Have a safe drive Ms. Conrad."

They smile at each other as he slowly shuts the door. He watches as she slowly drives away. They share one last moment with a wave of goodbyes to each other. Tim smiles as she drives away.

For the first time in a long time I smiled. I was happy today. I laughed and I felt at peace. There was zero drama. Aliyah Conrad visited me at work today. We hung out all day. It was fun. I haven't felt this way in so long. Now that she's gone I miss the feeling. Could I be falling for her? The idea of being with her makes me happy. But at the same time I know how it would end. In the end I'd be alone and hurt even more. But she cries and she feels pain. When I look into her eyes I can see her pain. I can feel her pain. Aliyah, can you feel my pain and hear my cries?

End log

CHAPTER ELEVEN

Yesterday was one of the greatest days I've had in a really long time. I called Regan but he was busy as always. So I decided to go see Timothy Derr at the school. Haha it's funny. He calls it his work but all he does for the most part is play card games on his laptop. He's cute. I bought him lunch and we hung out at the playground where I take Liel. We played tag, which ended with us rolling down a hill. Timothy landed on top of me. There were a few moments of us looking into each other's eyes. I felt something for that short moment. It was that familiar breath taking feeling that I've wanted so long. I wanted to cry. I wish that Regan would treat me the way he does. Timothy notices every small detail about me. He told me I was beautiful not just physically but as a person. I could see myself falling in love with him. But I know he wouldn't return my feelings. He's too good for me.

End Log

Aliyah sits at her dresser early in the morning reading, Hero's Wake.

"Today my feelings are so mixed up. All I can think about is how much fun I had yesterday. How badly I wanted him to kiss me." She covers her face feeling guilt, *"But I'm supposed to be in love with Regan. He needs me. I can't give up on him. Since yesterday I'm questioning my feelings for Regan.*

"I used to think I loved him. I wanted to marry him and have kids with him. We would have had the perfect family. But since I spent time with Timothy, all of those dreams seem like fantasies and not reality."

She takes a deep breath as she flips a page.

"Regan isn't going to marry me. He wouldn't propose. Not this early anyway. He doesn't even say he loves me when I say it. How can I expect him to want kids with me, let alone marriage? Timothy was so sweet yesterday."

She smiles as she reads.

"He was kind and genuinely sincere. I could tell that he honestly cared about me and wanted nothing more than to see me well. Why does he have to be so different? He didn't try to have sex with me or even touch me inappropriately. He barely flirted with me. The closest thing was he saying I was a beautiful person. Guys like him don't just show up. He'll end up marrying a princess type of girl."

She flips another page.

"He'll end up with the kind of girl that would always make him smile. She'll be beautiful too. Her smile would bright up the whole room. She would always know how to make his day better. She would be caring and nurturing like a mother. Most of all, she will be family oriented and they will welcome him with opened arms."

She gets depressed unintentionally as she starts comparing herself to the girl she describes.

"She won't come from a broken home. She will know how to treat him as a man. She would know how to trust him as a man. She'd know how to make him feel like a man. She would be a really good wife and would help heal his emotional scars. That isn't me. I have my own emotional scars. Timothy doesn't need more drama in his life."

She bookmarks her page and lays the novel on her dresser. Getting up, she takes a look at herself in the mirror for a moment. Staring at herself, she tries to picture herself as a princess with the life she dreams of. She smiles briefly as her imagination sways her. The bruise on her face brings her back to her not so fairytale like world. The smile on her face fades into a plain look.

"I don't want to live like this every day. I want to truly be happy. Who wants to wear fake smiles for the rest of their life? Don't I deserve to be happy? Is it wrong to want to be happy? I love my father and I'm grateful for the things I've been blessed with. But is it so wrong to want liberation from the pain in my heart, or at least have it truly eased?"

Her phone rings. She looks at her cell phone and sees a message from Regan. The message reads: ***Call me.***

Aliyah becomes overjoyed as she calls him. He answers.

Aliyah smiles as she says, "Baby! Hey how are you? I missed you yesterday, but I still had a good day. Ok so I…"

Regan becomes annoyed, stopping her in mid-sentence, "Aliyah, be quiet for a minute. Gosh you're talking my ear off. I called for a reason."

Aliyah becomes somewhat affected, "Don't you want to hear about my day babe?"

He replies, "I want to go see a movie with you tonight."

Aliyah screams with happiness, "You want to do what?"

Regan replies, "I miss spending time with you."

Aliyah says, "Awe baby. I do too, let's go to the movies."

Regan continues, "Let me take you to a drive in? It should be nice. I'll pick you up around seven."

Aliyah holds her heart saying, "Awe baby! I'll get ready right now. You're the best. I love you so much Regan."

Regan uncomfortably replies, "Ok well I'll see you at seven."

Aliyah says, "Babe don't you love me?"

Her words are cut short as he hangs up on her quickly before he can hear her words again. Aliyah's facial expression goes from happy to disappointed. She smiles blissfully as she begins getting dressed.

"He'll say it one day. He doesn't want commitment right now. I can't expect him to suddenly change his mind. I need to be more understanding. I just need to be patient."

She brushes her hair and looks in the mirror.

"He just needs some time." She dresses up in a fancy dark blue dress.

Her hair flows gracefully down her back and her eyeliner and makeup can be barely noticed as she perfectly paints it onto her already striking face. She finishes and grabs a small black purse. Placing her phone into it, she leaves her room.

She makes her way downstairs and looks into the dining room not surprised to see her father lying with a new half-dressed woman. She looks to the living room to see Liel staring at the woman. Frustration shrouds her as she walks to Liel.

She says, "Liel do you want to play on my laptop again?"

He shakes his head no as he plays with an action figure. Aliyah looks at her father feeling the woman up as they share tongues. She becomes repulsed and ashamed of her father.

She slightly begs, "Come on Liel don't you like playing on the laptop?"

Liel plays with the toy as he says, "Yeah but I don't want to play on it right now Li, Li."

"Well how about you go to my room and watch a movie?"

Liel becomes annoyed, as he says, "No."

Aliyah pleads, "Please Liel?"

He shakes his head no. She looks to her father who continues to kiss the woman as if trying to suck out her soul. Aliyah becomes infuriated and summons the needed courage and confronts him. He ignores her initial attempts to get his attention. She grabs the lady's shoulder angrily.

The lady looks back and shouts, "Hey!"

Aliyah whispers, "Dad your five year old child is right across the room! You're making out with a woman who is barely dressed. Don't you think this is a little irresponsible?"

He replies, "You're the only one complaining."

Aliyah shouts, "HE THOUGHT THE LAST WOMAN YOU KISSED IN FRONT OF HIM WAS HIS MOTHER!"

Her father becomes angered saying, "Lower your voice! This is my house. You don't make the rules I do!"

Liel watches the confrontation as his father shouts at his sister. He slowly begins to hate this monster who continually torments his beloved sister. Liel watches as his sister shouts at the monster.

"It's not about the rules! Start watching your behavior around him! You'll mess him up and have him turn out like you did!"

He gets up and slaps her. She falls to the ground. Wanting to protect his sister as he promised, Liel runs screaming, "STOP IT!"

Liel runs to Aliyah and kneels to her. Aliyah says, "It's ok Liel. Just go to my room and lock the door. I'll be fine. Hurry."

Liel says, "No. I promised mommy I would always protect you remember?"

Aliyah stares, moved by her five-year-old brother's bravery. He stands in front of her as he stares his father down with resolve in his eyes. He is not angry. He's just protecting his big sister.

Their father yells, "Move Liel! Your sister is being bad."

Liel shouts back, "No daddy, you're being bad. Stop hurting my sister!" Their father stares in shock, not knowing how to react to being yelled at by his favored child.

Aliyah protests, "Liel stop."

Liel doesn't hold back any longer, "No daddy, you stop! Don't hurt my sister. You're going to make her leave me too. I hate you!"

Their father stares in shock as if stabbed through the heart with a thorny sword. His anger slowly dies as deep seeded shame and regret surfaces. Aliyah grabs Liel.

"No! Don't say that. You don't *hate* your dad. Don't ever, ever say that again."

He cries to her, "He hurt my mommy and made her go away forever. I don't want you to leave me forever too. Don't go away forever Li, Li please. I won't let daddy hurt you I promise! Please don't leave me."

He holds her tight. She holds him as a mother would hold her child after they fall and scrape their knee. Their father watches as Aliyah comforts Liel. As he watches Aliyah soothe his son, it's as if he's watching his dead wife comfort Liel. His heart softens as his eyes water, seeing his wife after so long.

The alcohol causes the similarity between Aliyah and her mother to cast an illusion upon him. He sees his wife looking at him, not with hate or sorrow in her eyes, but disappointment. She shushes Liel as she soothes him, stopping his tears.

Their father becomes overwhelmed as he flees into the kitchen.

Aliyah holds Liel saying, "I'll never leave you. I promise." Her cell phone rings. She sees it's Regan, who is calling. She looks at Liel and says, "Hey I have an idea. Do you want to come to the movies with me and Regan?"

Liel becomes alarmed saying, "No! I don't like Regan. He's mean to me."

Aliyah says, "He won't be mean I promise. Come on let's go."

She grabs his hand and leads him towards the door. Feeling his cold glare, she looks back to see her father. A guilty feeling causes her to turn away. She leaves and walks outside to see Regan in an expensive black truck. He becomes upset when he sees she's bringing her brother. She opens the door.

Regan says, "Hey, hey what's the brat doing here?"

Liel barks, "I'm not a brat!"

Aliyah becomes upset saying, "Regan don't call him that. You know he hates it. It hurts his feelings." She helps Liel get into the backseat.

Regan argues, "No! Take him back inside Aliyah."

Liel sticks his tongue out at Regan as Aliyah says, "I don't want him left alone with my dad. He has another woman over. She was barely dressed making out with my dad."

Regan says, "Ok, so?"

Aliyah says, "So I don't want my five-year-old brother exposed to sex so he isn't confused about love when he's older."

Regan nonchalantly says, "He'll be fine. Just let him stay in your room until we get back."

Aliyah says, "I'm not letting him stay without me here. That's the end of it. Let's go enjoy the movie babe."

He begins to drive as Aliyah puts her seatbelt on. She looks to Regan as she smiles, and asks, "How was your day babe?" He ignores her.

She repeats, "Hey, how was your day babe?"

He replies, "Fine I guess."

Aliyah smiles saying, "So tell me about it."

Regan scoffs in annoyance, "Ugh! Aliyah why are you talking so much? Listen to the radio."

Aliyah says, "I want to hear about my boyfriend's day. Sorry if it's a crime to be interested in my boyfriend's day."

Regan says, "You ask every day! It's fucking annoying."

Liel becomes hysterical saying, "Awe! You said a bad word!"

Aliyah becomes annoyed and says, "Regan don't curse in front of him! My gosh, you act like such a child sometimes."

Regan becomes irritated as he continues to drive. Aliyah looks out the side window and sighs. She thinks.

"It's always like this. When we spend time together, we either argue or have sex. We argue about everything. He pressures me into sex. I feel if I don't have sex with him, he'll cheat or even leave me. I love him. I don't want him to leave me."

They arrive at the drive in movie. Regan pulls up to the ticket booth and says, "Three tickets for *Bloodbath Nightmare*."

Aliyah firmly says, "No."

Regan looks back with shock, "What?"

She says, "I hate scary movies. Besides, Liel is too young to see all that killing and blood. He'll have nightmares."

The ticket lady adds, "He's too young anyway. You have to be 17 or older to see rated-R films unless accompanied by an adult legal guardian."

Regan looks to Aliyah as if she's a pest asking, "Are you going to be difficult all night?"

Aliyah argues, "You know I hate blood and gore! Can we see *Our Wedding Day*?"

Regan says, "NO! I'm not sitting through that romance crap."

Aliyah smiles and pleads, "Please babe?"

Regan gives in saying, "Ugh! Three tickets for *Our Wedding Day*."

The lady gives them three tickets and requests 25 dollars. Regan pulls out a ten dollar bill and looks at Aliyah, "Where's your money?"

Aliyah becomes confused, "I thought you were paying?"

Regan angrily pulls out 15 more dollars saying, "This was a bad idea."

He gives the ticket lady the money and drives to the movie screen. Time passes as they watch the movie. Aliyah watches as the movie touches her. Regan stares out of his window in boredom. Aliyah sees Liel sleeping in the backseat. She smiles and looks at Regan and says, "Thanks for bringing me out."

She kisses his cheek as he replies, "Whatever."

Aliyah says, "I love you."

He rolls his eyes in annoyance as he slouches.

Aliyah repeats, "I love you, Regan."

Regan shouts, "Ok I heard you, Aliyah! Watch the stupid movie you made me pay for."

She looks at him deeply asking, "Do you love me back?"

Regan says, "Ugh, you're being so irritating!"

She asks once more, "Regan do you love me back or not?"

He shouts, "I don't fucking know!"

She becomes hurt and alarmed to hear his obvious thoughts finally free from his heart. She becomes teary eyed saying, "What?"

"I said I don't know," he says.

She fights her tears as she begins to whimper, "I don't understand. How do you not know? What have we been doing this past year?"

Regan says, "I like you a lot. But I don't want to focus on love so soon. I want to have fun and live a while."

She starts to cry as she says, "We've been together for a year! How can you say you don't know? We do everything together. What am I to you?"

Regan becomes more annoyed as he says, "God, why are you crying Aliyah?"

She cries, "Regan I love you! I spend all day thinking about you. I want to be with you for the rest of my life. Don't you want to be with me for the rest of your life?"

Regan becomes disturbed as he says in a disgusted tone, "You mean marriage?"

"Eventually yes! That's what people who fall in love do. They get married, they have children and they settle down. Then they pass that joy and love onto their children. They live together long and happily."

Regan says, "That's exactly why I didn't want to see this stupid movie. You need to slow down. You're asking way too much right now. I'm not marrying *anyone* for at least ten years. I don't even want to be in love this early."

Aliyah says, "So you don't love me?"

Regan says, "You're going to dig the truth up, fine. No Aliyah. I don't love you, not right now."

Aliyah heartbreakingly cries, "Why Regan? You mean the world to me. You always treat me like a nuisance, and then you treat me like a princess. How can you not love me? Can't you see how much I care?"

Regan ignores her as she cries to herself. She looks away. Her tears stop in defeat as she sighs. Her mind wanders.

"I don't know why I bother. It's fear of being alone probably. I don't want to be by myself. Not now. Being alone and going home to be abused and mistreated would be worse than this."

After a few minutes of tears, she calms down. She opens her purse and pulls out *Hero's Wake*. She begins reading from where she left off, no longer interested in the movie. Time passes. Regan looks at her. He leans to her and kisses her cheek.

He says, "Hey babe."

He rubs her arm. Aliyah rolls her eyes in annoyance saying, "No Regan. Not tonight."

He insists, "Come on babe. Your brother is asleep." He rubs her butt. She becomes angry and slaps him across the face. She shouts, "I said no!"

Regan rubs his face and shouts, "Why are you being a bitch?"

She becomes angry and shouts back, "What did you just say?"

Regan says, "You have done nothing but bitch all night. You're so boring! You never want to do anything. Now you don't want sex either?"

Aliyah says in a fed up tone, "You just told me you didn't love me! I'm not a piece of meat. You can't expect sex whenever you want it. I'm not being a bitch. You're being a jerk. You've been one for a long time now."

She tries to calm down as she continues reading. Regan says, "Look maybe I'll love you sometime later." She ignores him.

Regan shouts, "Did you hear me?" He snatches the novel.

She shouts, "Stop! Give that back!"

Regan shouts back, "Don't ignore me like that!"

Aliyah pleads, "Regan give it back! That's not even my book!"

Regan looks at the book asking, "Whose is it?" He becomes alarmed to see the author name *Timothy Derr*. He becomes outraged shouting, "What the! Timothy?"

She says, "Yes! That's his original copy. He let me borrow it. Give it back!"

Regan tears it in half down the spine saying, "I told you to stay away from him!"

Aliyah screams, "No! What have you done!"

Regan shouts, "I told you not to talk to him! When did you see him?"

Aliyah shouts back, "It doesn't matter. Nothing happened. He let me borrow his novel, that's it! Why did you rip it up! This is his original copy. It's the first one ever printed!"

Regan shouts, "I don't care! I don't want you talking to him and don't even look at him!"

He tosses the novel out the window. Aliyah yells at him and gets out to get it. Regan gets out and grabs her by the arm. People begin to watch them fight.

Regan shouts, "I said NO!"

Aliyah pulls but doesn't get free as she says, "You're hurting my arm! Let me GO!" She claws him across the face as she tries to get free. He lets her go in pain. Out of rage he slaps her across the face. She falls to the ground.

He demands, "Don't *ever* talk to him again! He's a loser!"

Aliyah shouts, "At least he remembered my birthday!" She cries, "It was last Thursday. It was on the day of your special football game. How could you forget my birthday?" She looks at the novel and sheds a tear. The tear lands on the word Hero.

She says, "He was the only person who remembered. Not even my dad remembered. I needed you more than anything that day and you forgot about me! I'm not a bitch. You ignore me all the time and it hurts. Now you say you don't love me after we've been together for over a year...I don't deserve this and I can't take it anymore."

Regan watches as she holds the torn halves together. He says, "Do you like Tim?"

She says, "I told you that I loved you. I barely know Timothy."

Regan repeats, "Do you like him?" She remains quiet as he repeats, "Do you?"

She replies, "I...I don't know." She rubs her face, not from the pain, but from the lingering comfort of Tim's touch. She stares at the novel.

She thinks, *"I've never met anyone like Tim before. In a way he reminds me of my mother. The way he shows he cares and makes me feel loved. It's not a lustful love either. He shows genuine care and concern. When our eyes locked I could see inside of him. I could see the nature of his heart. He'd never hurt someone he loved, not even a friend."*

Regan becomes more frantic as Aliyah continues staring at the novel in deep thought. He grabs her again shouting, "Stop ignoring me!"

She screams, "No! I like how he treats me and how he is as a person! I love you! That's why it hurts so much. How can someone who barely knows me make me feel so good? But a guy I've been with for a year and fell in love with can't! Do you know how painful that is? It hurts Regan!"

Regan says, "What do you want from me? I'm with you aren't I? There are plenty of girls at school that want to date the quarterback. But I chose you Aliyah!"

Aliyah says, "I want you to grow up! You chose me over everything a year ago. I remember when you used to spend all of your time with me. We stayed up every night on the phone. But now you choose everything over me. I come last all the time. You choose football, parties, and your friends over me. How could you forget my birthday? It's one day out of the entire year. Am I that insignificant to you?"

Regan says, "I brought you out on a date tonight because I missed you. You brought your brother, you picked the movie and now you're complaining. I can't believe how selfish you're acting. I'm just going to take you home."

Aliyah says, "Fine. I'm done trying. Just take me home Regan."

She looks away. Regan starts the truck up and drives away. There's silence as Regan drives the truck on the street towards Aliyah's house. She takes note of the silence.

Although it's just silence, it's not the same as Tim's peaceful mysterious and alluring silence. This silence is cold.

Aliyah sees Liel through the rearview mirror as he sleeps.

Regan says, "You need to stay away from that loser Tim."

Aliyah asks, "Why do you always call him a loser?"

He repeats, "Stay away from him."

Aliyah says, "I'm allowed to have friends. You can't control who I talk to. You're not my..." She stares at him in shock as she finishes her sentence, "...my father."

Regan stops the car and glares at her as he shouts, "You're right, I'm not your father!" She stares in fear as she sees a similarity between her father and Regan as he continues, "I'm your boyfriend and if you want it to stay that way you'll leave Tim alone! If I catch you with him you'll regret it."

They continue to drive. They eventually arrive at Aliyah's house. Regan parks in the driveway. Aliyah gets out and wakes up Liel, "Come on buddy let's get you into bed." She picks him up.

Regan says, "I mean it, Aliyah. Stay away from him." He drives away. She carries Liel into the house and to his room. After tucking him in, she walks to her room.

She lies in her bed, letting the events of the day replay in her mind constantly. She holds *Hero's Wake* in one hand and her cheek with the other.

"The more time I spend with Regan, the more of my father I see in him. He's full of anger and hate. Deep down inside he's kind and caring. But on the surface he allows his anger and hate to engulf the good side. I know there's good in him. But will it ever come out?"

She stares at the ripped novel's cover. She rubs dirt off the cover and sees the title: *"Hero's Wake"* By Timothy Derr. She stares as she becomes depressed

"Where is *my* hero?"

CHAPTER TWELVE

Since yesterday I've been really confused about my feelings for Robyn. I used to think I loved her. She was the only person I ever thought about. I wanted her more than anything. But now all I can think about is Aliyah. How she came to see me at school, how she bought me lunch or even how badly I wanted to kiss her on the playground. But she's not right for me. I can't., I don't want to fall in love with her. It wouldn't work out. There's no point. I meet with Robyn tonight. Hopefully things go better than they've been..

End Log

Tim and Robyn hold hands as they walk through a park. Tim stares at the beauty of the trees and flowers dully. Robyn rambles senselessly but can't be heard as Tim's mind drifts. He can't bring himself to enjoy the moment. He thinks about him and Aliyah having the time of their lives on the playground the other day. He thinks about being on top of her as he prepared to kiss her. He tries to fight his feelings.

"What's wrong with me? Why is she the only thing I think about? I barely know her."

Robyn looks at Tim and smiles. He dimly smiles and looks away.

"Robyn and I are finally together again. I should be happier than ever. This is what I've wanted for the longest. She's here. But now ,it doesn't feel the way I thought it would. I still have this empty feeling. But why?"

Robyn gently pulls his hand.

He looks at her as she smiles saying, "Hey you. Why are you so quiet today? It's like you keep drifting off into another world."

Tim apologizes. She takes hold of both of his hands as she leans to him. She holds him saying, "It's ok Tim. I'm enjoying the time I'm spending with you."

Tim runs his fingers through her hair. He kisses her expecting his feelings for her to return but the kiss is no longer the same. To his surprise he hears her voice, "I love you so much Tim." He stares at her, not knowing how to react. He thinks.

"She said it first this time. Shouldn't I be happy? This is Robyn Green, the girl of my dreams. This entire year, all I wanted was for her to say she loved me and truly mean it. But now, all I want to do is be around, Aliyah. That's dim! She isn't right for me. She would push me away. I know she would. Stop thinking about her!"

He forces himself onto Robyn as he kisses her, "I love you too Robyn."

She smiles at him and grabs his hand. She says, "Come on. I made something special."

She leads him to a picnic table. Tim becomes surprised as he sees a meal prepared. His favorite dish of meatloaf casserole, macaroni, spinach and mashed potatoes is neatly prepared on the table. He looks at the final touch of the romantic scenery as she lights two candles lying on both ends of the table.

"Robyn this is incredible," he says.

She smiles and says, "I made your favorite, meatloaf."

She leads him to his plate. He sits down. She leans over him as she points to the different side dishes saying, "There's macaroni, spinach and mashed potatoes. I even brought us apple juice baby."

Tim looks at her in shock not being able to imagine her ever thinking to put such a passionate scene together.

He says in a surprised tone, "You put all of this together?"

She smiles saying, "Well duh Tim. I remember small stuff like that about you."

She sits beside him. He grabs her and kisses her. They hold one another as they lean on the picnic table bench. He kisses her neck as she holds him and shuts her eyes. She let's out a soft moan as he cuddles her breasts and kisses her neck.

She moans his name softly, "Oh Tim, baby." She holds his face and kisses him. She holds his hands as she barely resists him saying, "Baby, we're outside."

Tim says, "I'm sorry. But I want, no, I need you Robyn."

She blushes as she says, "I'm not going anywhere baby. We'll be together all evening. Don't worry. We'll have time for this later."

They sit up. She grabs a fork and cuts a piece of meatloaf for him. She feeds him, "Let's eat first and enjoy dinner with each other."

They begin to eat. Tim can't find himself to eat as his wondering mind takes his appetite with it. Robyn looks at his untouched plate asking, "What's wrong? Is the meatloaf bad? I used a different recipe. I'm sorry babe. I thought-"

He stops her and says, "No, it's perfect Robyn."

She smiles at him and continues to eat. Tim stares at his plate as the feeling of emptiness engulfs him. He thinks.

"Just perfect. Yet the feeling isn't the same. Everything is at the point I wanted it to get. But nothing feels the way I expected. I can't stop thinking about Aliyah. How she smiles, her laugh and how she plays with her long brown hair when she gets nervous. But most of all, I can't stop thinking about how I feel when she's around me. My feeling of emptiness and isolation is gone. I don't feel that with Robyn."

Robyn looks at him and says, "Hey if it tastes bad just say so. We can go out to eat babe."

Tim replies, "No it's fine. I'm just really full."

She says, "Well that's fine babe. Let's go for a walk."

They get up. Robyn gets close to Tim and holds his arm as they walk down a trail in the park.

She rubs her face on his warm arms as they stare into the graceful twilight. She says, "It's a nice day isn't it?"

Tim agrees, "Yeah, it is."

As they walk Robyn begins to speak, "You know Tim. This is how our first date went. Only except it was your idea at first. I just reinvented the memory. I miss being with you. I did all of this to remind you how things used to be. I want to be with you again."

Tim replies, "I'm not a football player anymore Robyn."

Robyn brushes off the comment saying, "We can talk about that later. I just want to be with you." Tim tries to convince her but she stops him with a hug saying, "I'm sorry. I'm really, really sorry."

Tim holds her and gives her a serious look, "Robyn, look at me. I will *never* be your football player again. That Tim is gone forever. I'm a writer now."

Robyn looks away with disappointment. She puts it aside with a smile as she says, "Ok Tim fine. I won't like it at first but I'll get past it."

Tim questions, "What do you mean?"

Robyn explains, "I just want to be with you. I don't care if you don't play football anymore."

"You don't?"

She holds him saying, "No baby. Just say you want to be with me. I need you too." Tim stares at her as she lays her head on his chest and wraps her arms around him.

His feelings begin to confuse him. His old feelings want to resurface but are eclipsed by the one's he's developed for Aliyah. He thinks.

"Aliyah isn't the girl for me. Even though I've developed feelings for her. They're just silly ones. Aliyah and I would never work out as a couple. We come from two different worlds. She's used to abuse but she's always had people in her life. But I've had no one besides my father. I've learned to appreciate the people I care for through isolation. Not having someone for a long time will do that to you."

He holds Robyn as he fights his feelings for Aliyah.

"But Aliyah has always had people in her life. Even though she's been mistreated she's made bonds with people. She doesn't know the feeling of isolation, to be completely alone. The lack of drama and abuse would be unfamiliar to her. She'd eventually leave me for someone who gives her that abuse. There's no point."

He kisses Robyn and holds her.

"So I need to erase these childish feelings."

He speaks, "I want to be with you Robyn. I love you."

Robyn says, "I love you too."

They walk for a while until they arrive at his house. Tim walks Robyn to her car. He says, "Well, here we are."

"Isn't your dad gone," she asks.

Tim checks the time on his cell phone. It's 12:30 a.m.

Robyn says, "Let me spend the night then."

Tim says, "What?"

Robyn continues. "You told me that you've never slept with anyone right?"

Tim says, "I've had sex before. But I've never spent the night with anyone."

She grabs his hand and pulls him towards the house requesting, "Sleep with me tonight. I want to take your sleepover virginity. Let me be the first and maybe even last girl you sleep with."

Tim smiles and kisses her saying, "Ok Robyn."

They go inside and Robyn leads Tim to his room. She relaxes on his bed, while he begins to work on a story in progress on his computer. An hour passes. Tim continues typing diligently as Robyn watches a movie. She looks around and notices the room is very neat and organized.

She says, "It's a lot cleaner in here. Last time I was in here it was so junky."

"I've just had a lot of time to myself. Cleaning takes up time so I do it daily," he says.

Robyn takes her top off revealing a stunning black tank top beneath it. She says, "Come here baby."

Tim says, "Come read my story first. It's really good. I've reformatted it finally. I want your opinion on it."

Robyn says, "Ugh, You know I hate reading."

Tim says, "Just read a few paragraphs."

Robyn becomes annoyed, not interested in his work, "Tim no. How about in the morning when I'm awake?"

She takes off her tank top and shows off her fancy blue bra. Tim gets aroused as he gets up and walks towards her smiling. He sits on the bed and holds her as they kiss.

Robyn slightly sucks on his bottom lip and gently pulls away teasingly saying, "You tried to have dessert before dinner earlier. Do you still want it?"

They begin kissing lustfully. Tim tries to transform their lust into love with romantic caressing and cuddling. Robyn rejects with naughty touching and seductive kisses. Tim kisses on her neck and she lets out a moan. The more they kiss the more Tim's desire for passion dies. All he can taste is her spit and feel her overly aggressive touches.

"Robyn is kissing me. But when I close my eyes, I see Aliyah. Why can't I stop thinking about her? It's like my feelings for Robyn have completely faded away. Now the only person I want to be with is Aliyah. My mind says Robyn but my heart cries Aliyah Starla Conrad. I want her to be the first girl that spends the night with me. But my mind says no. I already know how that would end."

He forces lost feelings as he begins matching her lustful and sexual drive as he gets on top of her kissing her neck.

She giggles as he rubs her butt. She rubs his chest saying, "Someone is naughty tonight."

Tim closes his eyes and allows his mind to run freely as he thinks about Aliyah. He hears Robyn's words but sees Aliyah say, "I love you Tim."

"I love you too, *Aliyah*," he says with pleasure.

He gasps and opens his eyes to see Robyn looking at him with confusion asking, "What did you say?"

Tim struggles to speak, "No! I meant..."

She says, "Aliyah as in Aliyah Conrad? You love her?"

Tim panics, "No! I wasn't thinking clearly."

Robyn says, "So you've been thinking about her? Why have you spent time with her?"

Tim confesses, "She came to the office and we had lunch. It was nothing serious. We were just passing time. She means nothing to me."

Robyn says, "Wait. So is that the reason why you've been acting so weird today? You've been thinking about Aliyah? You like her don't you?"

Tim remains quiet not knowing what to say.

She asks, "Do you even love me? Wait do you *love* Aliyah?"

Tim struggles to look her in the eye and looks down. Robyn hurtfully looks away saying, "Oh…" She begins placing her clothing back on as she says, "I should go."

He says, "Robyn wait, I care about you."

She gets off of his bed and stands up.

He says, "Robyn listen to me. I want to be with you."

She shouts, "You love Aliyah!"

He argues, "I never said that Robyn!"

Robyn shouts, "You literally just said it ten seconds ago!"

Tim says, "Robyn. I love you!"

Robyn says, "I can see it in your eyes. You want to be with her. You don't have to say it out loud. "

"It was an accident Robyn! How can I love someone I barely know? Aliyah doesn't mean anything to me!"

Robyn walks to the door infuriated. He gets up and gently grabs her hand. She snatches her hand away shouting, "Get OFF!"

Tim says, "Robyn let me talk!"

She looks to him and calmly but in defeat says, "I'll call you later ok? Get some sleep and clear your mind."

Tim watches as she backs away towards the door and sheds a tear.

Tim pleads, "Robyn don't go. I'm sorry. I need you in my life not Aliyah. I want to be with you." She walks out of the room wiping her face.

He lays back into his bed in defeat. His feelings for Aliyah refuse to leave hi heart. But his mind continues to orbit around Robyn. He closes his eyes as he let's out a deep breath.

"Even though I felt empty when she was here. Now that she's gone I feel even emptier. I can't be with Aliyah. She's not right for me."

CHAPTER THIRTEEN

*I hate Mondays. Well I don't really **hate** anything. I just don't like them very much. All Mondays are to me is the reset of everything that makes me cry. Being ignored at school by the person I love. Being yelled at and abused by my father. Pretending to be happy when I'm miserable. Last night was the worst night of my life. Regan was horrible. He was jealous that I was reading Tim's novel. He wants me to stop talking to Tim. He asked me if I liked him and I couldn't answer. Tim made me feel a feeling I haven't felt in a long time, maybe ever. I honestly could see myself falling in love with him. He's so warm hearted and caring and yet so reserved. He isn't arrogant or cocky but he talks with so much confidence. He's a man. But I'm not the girl for him. I wouldn't know what to do with someone so perfect. I'm not enough. I don't deserve him...*

End Log

Aliyah sits in her room early in the morning at her desk. She's dressed for school as she finishes taping *Hero's Wake* back together. She reads the book peacefully.

"I like how I can relate to the characters in his novel. Has he felt these characters' feelings? This isn't like anything I've read before or seen on TV. I don't think he steals inspiration. I think he gets it from experience. If he gets it from experience than I can relate to him and his pain. How his character Glen feels alone and ignored after Mai stops talking to him for long periods of time. He understands me."

She grabs a book bag and puts the novel inside it as she walks out of her room.

She walks down the stairs and into the dining room.

"Liel! It's time to go to school." She sees him with his backpack by the door and asks, "Are you ready buddy?"

He smiles excitingly saying, "Daddy is taking me to school today!"

"He is?"

Her father walks out of the kitchen eating a bagel saying, "Yes, I am."

Aliyah looks at him saying, "But I always take Liel to school."

He smiles saying, "Not anymore. I'll take him to school from now on. I'll pick him up too."

Aliyah becomes affected saying, "Why? I can do it dad. "

He firmly says, "You're not filling his head with anymore lies. I'm taking him and I'm not changing my mind." He looks at Liel, "Are you ready to go get breakfast buddy?"

Liel shouts happily, "Yeah!"

Aliyah stares, heartbroken as Liel holds his father's hand. She feels traded off as they walk out of the house, leaving her alone. She grabs her chest and sheds a tear after a moment of silence. She drives to her school brokenhearted and doesn't bother to turn on any music. Songs don't seem to help her smile this time. She walks hopelessly through the halls in silence as if the world has ended.

She voices, "Liel…"

She walks towards her locker. Like a lifeless corpse, she stands at her locker aimlessly. Her face holds no sadness or happiness, just bleakness.

"Liel is the only person I have. Regan doesn't love me the way I love him. My father hates me. Without Liel, I have nothing and no one."

She begins to put her books away.

"I've had my depressed days. But this feeling of lost is a whole new hell all together. I've never felt so...alone. My father will try to break our bond. I know he will. If he breaks the bond Liel and I have. I don't know what I'll do. I can't survive without my little brother."

She puts her head in her locker to hide her silent tears.

"He's all I have. Without Liel I'll be completely alone. Why can't anyone hear my cries? Why do I have to be the one that suffers so much? I wish mother were here. Since she left nothing has been ok. I don't want to be alone. Please, where are you? Can't anyone hear me? Please save me from this misery."

Tim's novel falls out of her locker. She looks at it and stares for a moment. She kneels down and picks it up. She looks at it for a while. She stares at the title: *Hero's Wake.*

"Hero?"

She looks towards the school office. As she looks down, she thinks. Her feet drag her towards the office as she nervously fiddles with the novel. Her heartbeat becomes loud as thunder as she gets closer. She stops at the entrance to the office. Time pauses as she slowly peaks in to see Tim at a computer unproductively playing card games again. The storm in her heart subsides as she breaks a smile and laughs to herself.

"What is it about him that makes everything feel better? I've only hung out with him twice and yet, I can't. I can't stop getting this feeling for him. The feeling that I belong."

She slowly walks in as butterflies flutter in her stomach. Her face becomes red as she becomes nervous. She fights as she takes a step back. As she struggles to make a choice, Tim looks back at her as if he knows she's been standing there.

His gaze freezes her in place as she becomes surprised. Tim raises his eyebrows curiously. Aliyah looks embarrassed. Their eyes lock again. The butterflies in her stomach begin to burst into fireworks as her anxiety shoots up.

Her mouth seals shut as she tries to speak. Tim smiles and waves. She lets outs a girly squeal. She covers her mouth in embarrassment and quickly races away out of the office.

"What the heck happened to me back there? I screamed like a little girl! That was so embarrassing. What if he thinks I'm a complete weirdo now? Ugh! Or worse, what if he thinks I'm stuck up for not waving? As if any of that matters. I'm not the girl for someone as great as Timothy."

She pays zero attention to where she's walking as she continues to worry. She bumps into someone.

They shout, "Hey!"

Aliyah says, "I'm so sorry! Oh my gosh are you," she becomes surprised to see Robyn as she finishes, "...ok..."

T.Edward Redd   **144**

Robyn becomes jealous and annoyed to see the girl her boyfriend has confessed love for to her, "It's fine, *Aliyah*," she says.

Aliyah laughs nervously, "Oh hey Robyn. How are you?"

Robyn says, "I didn't know you skipped class."

"Oh I'm not. I just came from the office."

Robyn becomes mad knowing the office is Tim's typical living space during school hours. "For what," she asks.

Aliyah fidgets with the novel as she becomes more nervous as she struggles to speak, "Oh um well. I mean I was just-"

Robyn becomes alarmed to see a familiar book in Aliyah's hands. She takes the novel and looks at it. "Um, could you give that back? It isn't mine," Aliyah says weakly.

Robyn says, "Tim wrote this didn't he? I didn't know you were a fan. Did you buy this?"

Aliyah says, "Oh no. He let me borrow it a few nights ago. But I plan to buy my own soon."

Robyn heightens her tone as she becomes envious saying, "You spent the *night* with him? When? You know that I like him!"

Aliyah panics, "No! No we just hung out. He let me borrow his novel, that's it."

Robyn flips through the novel as she says, "Did you know Tim and I got back together?"

Aliyah becomes stunned, "You're with Tim now?"

Robyn smirks evilly as she arrogantly says, "That's right. We got back together. He told me he needed and loved me. It was cute."

Aliyah looks away, hurt saying, "That's great," She puts on her fake smile finishing, "I'm happy for him," she catches herself, "I mean you! I'm happy for you."

Robyn walks a half circle around Aliyah saying, "It is great. Here."

She hands Aliyah the novel. Aliyah takes it and asks, "What did you think of this? It's pretty addicting isn't it? I stay up late every night reading it. I try to get four chapters in each day. I bet you love his books don't you? I bet it's amazing being with a writer."

Robyn says, "I've never read any of his books."

Aliyah becomes shocked, "Why not? Your boyfriend is an awesome writer. He's so eloquent and he knows how to feel." She looks at the novel with a sad expression as she continues, "He's pretty amazing."

Robyn says, "I personally don't find his writing career exciting. I'm trying to get him to play football again."

Aliyah becomes upset, defending Tim's passion, "Why? He likes to write. You should support his dream to be a great writer! He's really good. Timothy doesn't even like football. I think he might even hate it."

Robyn rolls her eyes and looks at her, "Look Aliyah, I can tell that you care about him. I can see it in your eyes."

Aliyah plays clueless saying, "What? No, don't be silly. I'm with Regan."

Robyn strikes, "Exactly, so stay away from Tim."

Aliyah becomes hurt saying, "What?"

Robyn snaps, "You heard me! I *just* got back with Tim. If I'm patient I can get him into football again. I don't need you encouraging this writing stuff and I especially don't need you confusing his heart into thinking he loves you."

Aliyah becomes stunned, saying, "Love? *Me?*"

Robyn says, "Stay away from him. I mean it. If I see you with him I'll tell Regan."

Aliyah argues, "I don't like him like that! We're friends. I'm-"

Robyn finishes for her, "Not good enough for Tim!" Aliyah stares with hurt in her eyes. As Robyn continues, "He's not some dumb jock who goes around cheating and messing with other girls' hearts."

Aliyah says, "What are you talking about? Regan would never cheat on me!"

Robyn says, "Stop playing dumb! Everyone knows but you. I'm sure you just play dumb because you know you can't do any better!"

Aliyah looks down sadly. She struggles to swallow her pain as tears flood her eye sockets. She whimpers, "Please go away."

Robyn continues, "You aren't good enough for Tim. He's the type of guy that girls want to marry. If you hadn't noticed, those kinds of guys are impossible to find. He doesn't need to be distracted by you. You aren't good for him. He's mine so just stay away."

She storms away off, leaving Aliyah to slowly succumb to her agonizing words. Aliyah walks towards a restroom at a fast pace, trying to outrace the coming tears. She struggles to keep calm as she tugs on her shirt and fidgets with the novel.

"She's right. I don't belong with someone like that."

Calmly, she walks into the restroom. Whimpering as the tears begin to fall, she begins to break down. She runs inside the very back stall. She locks herself in and kneels down crying as she pulls on her hair.

"I don't belong in that type of world. I belong in this hell of a life. I'll never get out. I'm stuck. I want to be happy for once. I hate living like this. Nothing ever changes. I wish mom were here. I need my mother. Why did she have to die so soon? None of this is fair!"

She calms down and sobs. Looking at the novel helps her gain control of her breathing. She begins reading the last chapter of *Hero's Wake* as the writing usually helps her find a happier place in her mind and heart.

She reads out loud, *"'He gently brushes her hair with his hands as she stared into his eyes with deep passion. She looked away and said, "Glen I can't, you love Mai. I can't pull you away from her."*

Glen looked into her eyes as he gently pulled her to himself. He said, "Mai doesn't see what you can see in me. Mai doesn't feel what you feel."

Aliyah begins shedding tears as she continues to read, *"'Marcella squeezed his hands as she hesitated to lean towards him and said, "Why do you like me this much? I'm not as amazing as you make me out to be Glen."*

She said, "I'm not as pretty as she is. I don't come from a good caring family like she does. I can never offer what she can Glen. Don't waste your time on me please."

She shed a tear and looked away. Then he said, "You're wrong Marcella."

T.Edward Redd

She looked at him as he said, "You're the most beautiful person I've ever laid eyes on. The way you bite your lip when you're nervous. Or the way you stare into the sky when we lay in the grass. You stare into the sky smiling as if there isn't a care in the world. The way you make me sing when you're on my mind. Most importantly, you have something she can never get. You have my heart.'"

Aliyah smiles and sheds a tear as she flips a page and continues reading, *"'Marcella stared at him with passion in her eyes, as if hearing words from the heavens. Glen said, "Mai doesn't have your love to offer. Only your love feels the void in my heart Marcella. I need it,' Glen kisses Marcella. Marcella let's go of his hands and holds his face as he holds her waist.'"*

Aliyah closes the novel and wipes her tears.

"I wish I could have that. The more I read this novel, the harder it becomes to finish it. I fall for him the more I read what he has written. Does Timothy write how he feels? Does he want someone like Marcella? A girl who makes him forget all of his pain? The type of girl that makes crying around her impossible unless they're tears of joy? I can kind of guess how the ending will be. He ends up with Marcella. A perfect girl for the perfect guy. I can't finish this."

In defeat she walks to the office. She walks inside towards Tim. She watches as he plays a frog game on the computer. He loses. He becomes annoyed and says, "Darn."

Aliyah can't help but laugh. He looks back at her as she says, "Do you seriously stay in here all day playing computer games? How much work do you actually do?"

Tim smiles saying, "You just keep catching me on breaks. I'm pretty productive in here. I saw you earlier. Are you too cool to wave at me?"

Aliyah blushes and says, "Oh no I'm sorry. I was late for class."

Tim examines her red face and left over tears slowly draining back in her eyes. He asks, "Is everything alright?"

Aliyah says, "Huh?"

Tim replies, "I can tell. You've been crying. Is everything all right? Your father hasn't hit you has he."

She laughs softly as she wipes her face. This time she isn't laughing at her pain. But she's laughing at the fact that he always notices when something is wrong. It's as if good keeps mocking her miserable life.

She says, "It's nothing, Tim."

Tim argues, "Stop saying it's nothing. You don't deserve to be hit!"

Aliyah shushes him saying, "Stop being so loud or someone will hear you! I didn't come here to vent." She holds the book to him.

"Oh. My book. So you finished it. How did you like it," he says.

Aliyah smiles, "It was great. I loved it."

He examines the tape holding the recently torn book together. He says, "You loved it enough to rip it in two? How ironic."

Aliyah lies, "Oh um, my dad did that. He thinks novels are dumb. I can buy you a new one."

Tim laughs, "I wrote the story. You might as well pay me upfront. But don't worry about it. This is an original. It can't be replaced anyway. At least it's not completely ruined. It being damaged like this makes it look a bit epic. It's like it's been around for years now."

Aliyah expresses regret, "I'm really sorry."

Tim genuinely smiles, "No it's fine. I'm glad you liked it. Don't be sorry. You can't control other people's actions. I'm more worried about you than some silly collection of paper and ink."

Aliyah shies away, "Oh, ok. Well I should go."

She slowly turns away. Tim watches as she hesitates. She can't bring herself to walk away. She turns around asking, "Where do you get your inspiration from? Other authors, TV, movies or what?"

Tim answers, "Experiences and dreams."

Aliyah becomes surprised and says, "You've experienced that stuff?"

She sits beside him as she flatteringly obsesses over his writing, "I can relate to Glen so much. Wanting to feel noticed and not wanting to leave someone who hurts you hoping they'll change. Wanting someone you know you don't deserve. So you..." Tim finishes, "...So you stay with someone who's bad for you, because that's as good as it gets."

Aliyah says, "Yeah, exactly."

Tim explains, "There was a girl I liked a while back. She had this habit of putting off my calls and it bugged me badly. I would always wish someone would enter my life so I could make her pay for hurting me with her cruel silence. Someone new would come along and she would become jealous. Her jealousy would eat her from the inside out. She would feel the pain and loneliness her silence placed upon me."

Aliyah listens intrigued as he continues, "A new girl never showed up. So I expressed my thoughts and feelings by writing it into a story. I initially stopped writing after I was over the heartache. But after looking over it I decided to tweak and finish it.

"The girl hates me for writing the book though. I kept her name the same but scrambled her last name so she couldn't do anything about it. Now she gets to watch other people read a successful love story written by the guy she hurt. I never took her back."

Aliyah becomes admiring, saying, "That's so freaking cool! That's beyond amazing. That's the best form of karma I've ever heard. I bet she regrets hurting you now that you're a successful writer huh?"

She smiles at him. Tim smiles back as he continues, "It wasn't about revenge. I just liked the story enough to make it my first publish. All of it is from me. Most of the depressing stuff is experience. Sometimes I exaggerate in order to emphasize emotion in my writing. But I try to stick close to experience."

Aliyah says, "Does that mean you feel like Glen?"

Tim says, "Exactly."

Aliyah says, "That's so deep. I mean it's weird how I can relate to you."

T. Edward Redd   **152**

Tim smiles saying, "It looks like I did a good job then. Someone can relate. That was the whole point of sharing my story. I'm glad you enjoyed it."

Aliyah says, "Wait. So if you write based on experience does that mean you've met someone like Marcella? Who is she?"

Tim stares at Aliyah with infatuation as he says, "Um. Well I wrote that about two years ago. So when I wrote it, no I didn't know anyone like Marcella. Not back then anyway. My happy endings are normally based on my feelings. The things that I wish would happen to me."

Aliyah smiles and says, "I knew it! You want a girl like Marcella don't you?"

He stares at Aliyah as her similarity to his character takes his breath away. He stutters, "Yes."

Aliyah says, "It's Robyn isn't it? She makes you feel the way Marcella made Glen feel right?"

Tim stares at Aliyah speaking about his feeling about her without her knowing, "Not even close. Robyn doesn't make me feel anywhere as near as Marcella does. Or would. Robyn is my Mai."

Aliyah becomes disappointed wanting to hear a happy ending, "Oh. Well do you think you'll ever find your Marcella? Has anyone ever made you feel the way she made Glen feel?"

Tim stares at her, "I don't know if I'll ever find her."

Aliyah looks away dissatisfied. She becomes surprised to hear him say, "But yeah, someone has made me feel like that recently."

Aliyah becomes excited saying, "Oh my gosh who?? She's the luckiest girl on Earth Tim. You have to tell her. Who, who? Snow's pretty cute and poetic. Is it her?"

Tim stares into her beautiful and innocent eyes as she moves his soul with her earth-shattering smile. He struggles to breathe as she repeats, "Come on tell me. Who?"

Tim struggles to speak. Aliyah says, "I'm sorry it's none of my business." She gets up.

Tim says, "Aliyah wait. It's…"

She stops him saying, "No it's fine. I'm being too nosey."

She turns away. She thinks.

"So he's already found that special girl. I figured someone would catch his eye sooner or later. I can't compete with a Marcella. Robyn was right. I wouldn't be enough for him…"

Tim gets her attention, "Hey Ms. Conrad."

She looks back to see him smirking. She becomes puzzled saying, "What?"

"I'm glad you came to me today. You saved me the trouble of searching this gigantic school to find you."

Aliyah becomes confused, and says, "Find me for what?"

Tim gets up and says, "Let's get out of here. There's something I want to show you."

Aliyah says, "But it's school hours."

He grabs her hand and leads her towards the door. His touch dazes her for a moment as she follows. She gains her senses as she panics saying, "Tim wait we'll get in trouble!"

Tim tells her, "Relax." He walks with her to the secretary. The secretary looks up as he says, "Hey can you cover for me? Tell Kurt that I went to buy copy paper and lunch."

The secretary teases, "Ok Tim. Have fun with your girlfriend."

Tim says, "Thanks. But she isn't my…"

He looks at Aliyah. She finishes for him, "Girlfriend?"

Tim says, "Yeah, my girlfriend."

T.Edward Redd   **154**

They walk with each other. As they walk down the hall, comfort begins to fill each of the voids in their hearts. Both let out a relieving sigh. They look at one another hearing the synchronized sigh and laugh. It's as if they can understand each other's wordless expressions.

Enjoying the silence as they walk outside, they stroll to Tim's car. It's been repainted and its tires have been replaced.

Aliyah says, "Hey you got new tires!

"Yup. It's pretty hard to drive with just three."

He opens the door for her. She stops to ask, "So where are we going?" Tim smiles. She repeats, "Tim where are we going?"

He says, "Just shut up and ride ok? We'll be there in a minute. Don't worry. I have it all under control. Relax and have some fun."

Aliyah smiles at him as she gets inside. He gently closes the door for her once she's seated. After he gets inside, he begins driving. They drive for a few miles.

Their peaceful quietness keeps them both pleased as they ride. Aliyah looks at Tim who no longer has his laid back and non-caring attitude, but free and happy as he smiles.

After a few more miles they arrive at an expensive restaurant. The place looks like a mansion with beautiful trees surrounding the outside. Aliyah looks at a dreamlike wish fountain in front of the eating-place.

They get out. Aliyah stares in shock saying, "Wow..."

Tim holds her hand and leads her towards the building. Aliyah stops and looks at the wish fountain. She looks at the hundreds of coins in the water. Patting her pockets, she becomes disappointed realizing she left her purse in her locker at school.

Tim holds a coin to her saying, "Here."

She smiles and takes the coin. She stares for a moment to make a wish. The penny flickers across the air and into the body of water. She smiles in awe as the coin splashes once it hits the surface. She looks back at him saying, "Thanks for the coin. That was cool. But hey, aren't you going to make a wish?"

Tim replies, "I don't have another coin. My wish is that your wish comes true."

She smiles, "You're not supposed to tell me your wish! It's bad luck."

Tim takes hold of her hand smiling as he guides her towards the restaurant. She follows as they walk inside. She becomes astonished to see the gorgeous scenery. It's like walking into the eatery of a princess. She stares at the many waiters elegantly carrying trays to tables.

She says, "This place is Heaven. Tim why are *we* here?"

Tim guides her and says, "Be patient. Just follow me. Let's find our table."

She mutters, "Our table?"

Tim leads her to a table with a reserved sigh on it. Tim offers her to sit. Aliyah panics not wanting to get into trouble saying, "No Tim. We can't sit here Tim. It's reserved for someone!"

Tim laughs and says, "I'm pretty sure I have to know how to read in order to write. Come on. I thought I was the boring one here. Relax and sit Aliyah."

Aliyah looks confused as she slowly sits first. She watches in confusion as Tim reads the menu. Her eyes widen as she sees the pricey dishes.

"This stuff is really expensive Tim. If you're trying to pay me back it's ok. Let's go back?"

T.Edward Redd   **156**

Tim reads as he says, "Aliyah, seriously. Stop asking questions and enjoy yourself. Everything is on me."

A waiter walks to them and greets Tim as if he's a good friend, "Mr. Derr, it's nice to see you again."

Aliyah becomes confused as she mutters, "Again?"

Tim smiles and says, "Kevin. It's a pleasure to see you too. How are you?"

Kevin replies, "I'm doing well Mr. Derr. So I take it that this is the birthday girl?"

Aliyah looks at Kevin saying, "Birthday?"

She looks at Tim. He smirks cunningly as he winks, "Don't say anything yet. The best part hasn't come. Just order anything you'd like."

Aliyah smiles and says, "Ok. Ha, um," she reads the menu. She says, "I would like to try the famous pasta dinner with a coke please."

Tim says in disappointment, "What? That's all you want? Come on. I was looking forward to you burning a hole through my wallet. You can do better than that can't you birthday girl?"

Aliyah says, "But Tim, this stuff is very expensive."

Tim playfully says, "Hey take it easy. You're making it sound like I'm poor or something. Order what you want."

Aliyah gets excited and says, "Ok, ok I'll get more just relax. Um." Her eyes scan the menu as she tries to decide what to order. She says, "Ok, I would like a salad and some fries along with what I just ordered."

Tim smiles and says, "Is that all you've got birthday girl?"

Aliyah smiles at his playful tease and challenging smirk. She asks, "Can I get a strawberry and banana smoothie too?"

HERO'S ROMANCE

Tim adds, "With whipped cream?"

Aliyah smiles as she says, "Yes please."

Tim smiles and says, "Go for it. Today is all about you."

Aliyah smiles happily as she looks at Kevin asking, "Could I get that please sir?

Kevin replies, "I've already wrote it down. I'll be back with your food shortly."

He walks away to another table.

Aliyah becomes alarmed as she looks at Tim saying, "Oh wait! You didn't get to order your meal!"

She looks back to call for Kevin but Tim stops her as he gently places his hand on hers saying, "Hey relax. I ordered the day I planned all of this."

Aliyah says, "Why did you do all of this? "

Tim says, "Don't you dare ask if I have some sort of dark motive."

Aliyah smiles out of embarrassment as she squeezes his hand reassuringly saying, "No. I wasn't thinking that at all Tim. I know you're too sweet for that. This is really special. I just don't understand. Why for *me*? I don't deserve any of this."

Tim says, "Yeah I know. You deserve a lot more. But this fits my budget so this will have to do for now ok?" Aliyah laughs. He smiles and says, "But more seriously, you made me experience a great day last week. So I wanted to help you have a happy birthday. Even though it's late."

Aliyah smiles as she blushes, "Awe, Tim. Thank you. That means a lot."

They begin to enjoy the moment as they gaze at each other.

"I'm speechless. I never would have imagined anyone doing something like this for me. He's sweet. I had forgotten all about my gloomy birthday. But it's been on his mind all week. I wish this feeling I have could last forever."

CHAPTER FOURTEEN

Tim and Aliyah share a conversation as they wait for their food to arrive. Tim watches as Aliyah cheerfully talks.

"But the best part, the absolute best part was when Thomas held Samantha so gently as he embraced her. Ugh, I could faint just thinking about it."

Tim says, "What about the fact that she's a demon though? You don't find that creepy?"

Aliyah counters, "That's the best part! Everyone fears her yet they don't know what she really is. It's like the souls of their heart can tell that she's this monster. But Thomas sees right through it all. He sees *her*. When he discovers who she really is, he accepts her anyway. That's true love." She blushes as she thinks.

Tim replies, "Wow I had no idea you were into romance novels so much. I thought you were a cheerleader."

Aliyah replies, "I used to love it. But I guess as I grew up, I got more into reading. I don't like cheer anywhere as near as I like reading a good book or seeing a nice romantic movie. My friends don't get me at all anymore. I doubt they ever did."

Tim listens. She stops to look at him saying, "I'm sorry. I'm talking your ear off and I didn't even give you a chance to talk."

Tim kindly says, "Oh no it's fine. It's just I like to listen to you talk you know? You seem really happy and I'm glad about that. So I let the moment just take its course. I prefer this over seeing water in your eyes."

Aliyah smiles, "Well aren't you sweet. Thank you Mr. Derr."

Tim asks, "How are things at home?"

Aliyah says, "Hey stop worrying about me ok? This is my birthday remember? I'm supposed to be happy. No more sad talk."

Tim says, "You're right Aliyah. I guess I'm just a little worried."

Aliyah smiles at his kindness. She says, "Well what about you? Everyone keeps talking about football. Especially Robyn. But you obviously love writing and you're amazing at it. What happened to you and football?"

Tim replies, "I liked it a lot at first. But I've always been more into writing. It's just I kept it secret until last year. Writing helps me release all of the bottled up emotions inside of me. It just feels amazing. I never get bored when I write. I could do it for days. You probably think I'm the weirdest guy right now."

Aliyah says, "You're really sensitive."

Tim becomes slightly uncomfortable, as he feels insulted.

Aliyah continues, "And deep. No, I don't think you're weird at all Tim. You're a kind-hearted and a gentle person. I can see through that silence of yours. You act very laid back and casual.

"But underneath it lies this gentle, yet so strong person. You hide it with your silence. You don't want the world to see you, because you don't think they would understand."

Tim listens. Her words slowly calm the violent oceans in his heart as she touches his hand.

She says, "But Tim, I think I do understand. If I don't fully get you, I somewhat understand you, even when you're quiet. You need to know that you're a special person. There needs to be more guys like you. I'm glad I had the unlikely privilege to be around you. You help me feel so, happy."

Tim's heart races as her words move him. He looks at her hand resting on his hand. Her soft and welcoming touch begins to drive his feelings rampant. She pulls her hand away as she notices him staring at it. She says, "Oh I'm sorry."

Tim gently grabs her hand saying, "You have really soft hands. They're comforting."

They look into each other's eyes as the mood begins to heat up. The moment is interrupted as Kevin brings the food saying, "Your meals have arrived."

Tim and Aliyah look up as their hands separate. Aliyah says, "Oh my goodness. It smells so good."

Kevin places an order of: steak, mashed-potatoes and green vegetables in front of Tim. Aliyah becomes even more surprised as Kevin places her meal of: pasta with red sauce, French fries and a Caesar salad in front of her.

He places a strawberry smoothie in front of her, completing the wonderful meal. Aliyah stares in awe. Kevin says, "Enjoy." He walks away.

She stares at the mouth watering meal saying, "Oh my gosh Tim this is great. I didn't have breakfast either so I'm starving."

Tim smiles as he begins to cut his steak and says, "Happy birthday Aliyah. I hope you enjoy it."

They begin to eat their meals pleasingly. Tim watches as Aliyah elegantly eats like a queen. Not a single drop of food gets on her clothing or her cheeks. She politely eats but is obviously enjoying the dreamy occasion. She gently wipes her mouth and takes a sip of her smoothie.

Tim smiles asking, "How does it taste."

She offers the drink to him with a smile that says, "It's great try it!"

Tim politely declines, "Oh no I can't."

Aliyah smiles as she says "Come on try it."

Tim protests, "No it's yours. Enjoy it."

She begs, "Just try it. Please? For the birthday girl?"

Tim smiles as she holds the straw to the drink, close to his mouth. He takes a greedy sip as the smoothie satisfies his taste buds. He smiles relieved saying, "That was great."

Aliyah says, "Yeah I know. Thanks Tim. Thanks for all of this. It's special."

Tim humbly says, "No problem Aliyah. Happy birthday."

She blushes as she begins to smile. Tim stares.

"She's so graceful," he thinks. "I can't find anything damaging or destructive about her. She's polite and modest. She's caring by nature and she has this warm aura. When I'm by her I can't help but to smile."

Aliyah teases, "So do you smile this much when I'm not around? Or is it just a good month?"

Tim says, "I've been happy lately."

Aliyah smiles as she flirts, "Because of me?"

He playfully teases her, "No it's just a good month."

They laugh as Aliyah says, "Stop copying me Mr. Derr. If I see that in one of your books I'll sue you. Just kidding."

They enjoy the moment as Tim thinks deeply. His thoughts about her begin to change as he develops stronger feelings for this wonder before him.

"I can't blame her for what's happened to her. She's a normal person just like me. Imagining someone hurt something so delicate brings me to tears. I can't let her stay in an abusive life. I don't want her to be mistreated. I know I wouldn't hurt her. It's wrong for me to assume she wouldn't know how to react to being treated the way she deserves to be treated. It's not her fault things turned out this way for her."

Aliyah finishes her meal and lets out a satisfying sigh. She lies down saying, "Oh my gosh I'm so full."

Tim says, "Hey get up. You'll miss the best part."

She laughs, "There's more?"

Waiters come out with a birthday cake as they sing her happy birthday.

T.Edward Redd

She sits up with shock and awe as they approach the table singing. She becomes touched as they place a green cake in front of her. The cake reads: *A special cake, for a special girl, on her special day. Happy Birthday Aliyah.*

She sees a smiley face similar to the one Tim put on her card when they first met. She becomes teary eyed, as she says, "No. Why are you being so great to me? It's my favorite color green. Thank you so much." She wipes her eyes as people in the restaurant watch.

Tim holds her hand saying, "Hey don't cry Aliyah."

He wipes her face gently with a napkin as he says, "No being sad remember? It's your big day. Now make a wish."

She smiles as she looks at the cake. She looks at Tim for a moment then back at the cake. She blows out the candles. People around them clap in awe as they share a moment.

Tim says, "What did you wish for?"

Aliyah cuts his words short as she wraps him in her arms tightly, hugging him saying, "Thank you Tim. I haven't been this happy in a long time. My mom was the last person to make me feel this way. Thank you I love-"

She stops herself as she realizes what she almost says. Tim holds her as he says, "What?"

Aliyah blushes saying, "I'm really sorry I-"

Tim insists, "No say it."

They stare at each other as their heartbeats match one another. Aliyah doubtfully looks away. Tim becomes disappointed.

"Just as I thought. She's scared. But...it's not her fault. And right now, I can't help myself."

She looks to him as he says her name. He kisses her. She briefly becomes surprised but instantly kisses him back passionately. They hold each other as if they were holding back their feelings the entire time. They stop.

Aliyah becomes frantic as she says, "Oh my gosh, no!" Tim becomes surprised as she says, "I have a boyfriend!"

Tim tries to rationalize as he says, "Aliyah I thought that-"

She stops him saying, "No, no, no! This is all wrong. I'm so sorry. We can't do this Tim."

Tim tries to comfort her, "Aliyah it's ok. I like-"

She interrupts again in a panic saying, "It's not ok! You're with Robyn and I'm with Regan! All of this is wrong!"

She gets up. Tim says, "Aliyah wait!"

She looks back at him. He holds a wrapped gift towards her. She takes the gift. He gets up and confesses, "Aliyah I care about you. I care more than a lot. I think that I-" He hesitates to follow his heart.

Aliyah says, "This was nice Tim. But I can't do this. I'm not a cheater. I'm sorry. Look I'll call a cab ok? We shouldn't keep doing this. It's just you've helped me become so happy lately.

Tim says, "I know! You've made me happy too. It doesn't make any sense! I've been fighting these slowly growing feelings."

"I don't even feel what I used to with Robyn anymore. She doesn't help me get to that special place anymore. The person that does that for me is you Aliyah. *You're* my Marcella."

Aliyah stares lost for words, "Um. Look I should get back to school. The lunch period will end soon. We'll get in trouble. Let's not drive together ok? I'll call a cab. I'm sorry Tim."

She quickly walks away. Tim watches as she flees the eatery. He sits down in disappointment. He stares at her birthday cake and lets out a big sigh. He begins to eat the cake as the feeling of defeat joins him.

CHAPTER FIFTEEN

Aliyah lies in her bed staring at the ceiling with deep thought. She looks to a clock on her dresser to see it is 5p.m. She holds the wrapped gift she received from Tim earlier.

"Today was amazing. No one has ever done that before. My mom used to do stuff like that for me. It was incredible. I couldn't stop thinking about Regan. Why can't he be like that? When he kissed me it was amazing. It took my breath away. I felt as if I was in new world. No one could see us. It was just me and Timothy Derr."

She sits up and stares at her present. Slowly, her fingers begin to open it. She becomes intrigued to see two books written by Timothy Derr. She holds a recognizable book *Hero's Wake* and a new one, *Hero's Romance.* She smiles to see both books are autographed. She looks at *Hero's Romance* with curiosity.

"Is this a new one," she says out loud.

She opens the book and reads out loud, "'I've never written anything like this before. All it is are journal entries written out into a book. I think this book will help my readers understand who I am and where I get my inspiration.'"

She flips through the book and says, "He published his journal?"

She reads out loud, *"'I cry myself to sleep every night, hoping the screaming will stop.*

"'The constant drama that woman puts this family through. All of the lies she makes up to make my father look like this horrible person. I hate her for it.'"

Aliyah thinks, "He must be talking about his mom."

She flips a page and continues, "'Today was my 16th birthday. I was excited because this was the day I got to get my license. The sooner I get my license the sooner I have more freedom away from her. She didn't care that today was my birthday. I hate her. She tried to get my father to cancel my birthday plans so she could go out of town.'"

Aliyah begins to think about Tim as he flips through the book. She closes it.

"The closer I get to him, the more I feel as if I belong. I'm scared though. He's not like anyone I've been with. His warmth reminds me of my mom's love. His mannerisms and fun attitude remind me of Liel. He hasn't had the best life.

"Like me he's been hurt. His mother left him just like Regan's did. At the same age and a similar relationship. But Tim doesn't have any visible traces of anger or hatred. He's sweet and gentle."

She stares in the mirror at herself. She sits at her dresser and puts her head down.

"I don't know what to do. I keep messing up around Timothy. I'm not even good enough for my own father."

"I couldn't even get Regan to feel what I feel for him. If I can't get my own father to love me, how can I expect someone like Tim to stay with me? I'm not enough and that's my reality. I don't want to waste his time."

She notices a text from Regan.

"Besides Regan needs me. I can't give up on him."

She reads the text: **Come over.**

"I still believe in him. I love him."

She begins combing her hair in the mirror. She looks at the bruise on her face and stops combing for a while. She places her hand on it.

"Regan didn't even notice. I can't believe he hit me at the drive-in."

She looks at the copy of *Hero's Wake.*

"I never finished it. Why am I so hesitant to end it? It's just a novel. Is it because the more I read the more I understand him? Or is it because the more I read it the more I imagine myself as Marcella. Rescuing him from the sadness and isolation left for him by Mai or Robyn."

She looks at her diary and reads her past entries.

"For so long I've written about this person I dream about meeting. It's a person that can understand my pain and take it away. My hero. Then out of the blue I meet someone like him. It's too much to take in."

She leaves her room. She walks downstairs and looks around. No one is home.

"My dad is out with my brother Liel. He's trying to win him over with gifts now so he forgets about me. I wonder if Liel would like Tim. I bet he's good with children."

She drives to Regan's mansion. She parks and stares at the mansion.

"Regan is horrible with Liel. He treats him like a pest. Liel dreads spending time with him. I would never leave him alone with Regan. I imagine Regan turning out a lot like my father. He'll drink a lot to ignore his problems. He'll push his children away and neglect me as his wife."

She walks to the mansion and knocks on the front door.

"Tim would be the complete opposite. He'd be a lot like my mother but I imagine he'd be more fatherly and protective. The type of guy that would carry me over rain puddles. He'd never lay his hands on me in a harmful manner. He'd always be gentle but a man at the same time."

"Even when we argue he'd be calm and gentle. He'd interrupt our fights with a kiss. We would hold each other and forget why we were arguing. Most importantly, he'd be amazing with our children. He'd never yell or call them names. He'd make his son out to be the perfect gentleman. He'd be especially protective of his daughter. He'd treat her like a princess and spoil her. He'd be everything a woman could want in a man."

Regan opens the door smiling as he says, "Babe!"

Aliyah doesn't become excited like she normally would as he hugs her. She becomes annoyed as he kisses her, "Hey Regan? What's wrong?"

He smiles and says, "I missed you!"

Aliyah blankly says, "*You* missed *me*?"

Regan says, "Yeah! Come inside beautiful!"

He holds her hand as he guides her inside. Aliyah asks, "Are you feeling well?"

Regan says, "Of course!"

He leads her to the dining room. She sees a well-cooked meal.

Aliyah is unimpressed as she says, "Regan wow. Is this for me?"

He happily sings, "Of course. Happy birthday."

Aliyah sits at the plate with the most food. Regan walks to her saying, "No, no babe. That's my plate. That's your plate." He points to a poorly made salad with a glass of water.

Aliyah says, "Regan, that's just a salad and water."

Regan says, "Yeah I know babe. Aren't you watching your figure for cheerleading? Plus I know how much you like Caesar salad."

Aliyah sits by the plate and looks at the embarrassing dish. She says, "But this isn't even a Caesar's salad. It's just lettuce with ranch."

Regan simply says, "Well I got what I could find in the fridge. You know I hate cooking. I hope you like it babe. Happy birthday."

Aliyah sarcastically says, "Gee thanks. You're the best."

Time passes as she watches in boredom as Regan eats. He looks at her taking note that her plate hasn't been touched.

He says, "You haven't touched your food babe. What's wrong?"

Aliyah says, "I'm not hungry. I already ate."

He replies, "Where? I didn't see you at lunch."

She replies, "I went out to eat."

Regan becomes suspicious asking, "During school hours? With who?"

Aliyah becomes irritated, "Why are you asking me that? I took myself."

"With what money?"

Aliyah says, "Why?"

Regan replies, "I know you don't have any that's why. Who took you out to eat? Was it Tim? I didn't see him in the office during lunch. Robyn told me you were with him the other night."

Aliyah slightly gets angered at his controlling behavior, "I can spend time with whoever I want. You don't own me Regan."

He puts his fork down in frustration saying, "Damn it Aliyah. I told you to leave that loser alone."

Aliyah barely responds to his anger as if used to it. She doesn't even flinch. She slouches and casually says, "Sorry I guess."

Regan calms down, "I hate yelling at you. I just wish you would behave. How was your day?"

Aliyah smiles mockingly, "It was peachy perfect as always."

He walks over to her and begins to hold her saying, "I missed you."

He strokes her arm and grabs her breasts. Aliyah pulls away as she shouts, "Stop!"

Regan stares in confusion, "What's wrong?"

Aliyah calms her slowly erupting anger down, as she politely says, "Not now ok?"

Regan smiles saying "It's fine babe. Come on let's go sit on the couch and watch TV."

They walk his living room and sit. Regan turns on the television. Aliyah watches blankly with a defeated look. The more Regan smiles the more she becomes annoyed with his presence. She starts to dislike everything about him.

"What's wrong with me? I used to love being around Regan. Today I don't feel that way. I have a bothered feeling around him now. My feelings for him aren't as strong as they were the other day."

Regan puts his arm around her and she stops him. "What am I doing wrong," he asks.

Aliyah replies, "Nothing. I just don't want to lie on your arm. The couch feels nice."

Regan smirks and says, "Do you want to lie on it?"

Aliyah firmly says, "No."

She becomes uncomfortable as he holds her hand and gets close.

He says, "I care about you."

Aliyah struggles but says, "I don't believe that. The other day you told me you didn't love me."

Regan becomes impatient, "But I will! That's why I did all of this today!"

Aliyah shouts, "Regan love isn't something you show through materialistic things. You show it through genuine thought and care about someone. My birthday was last week. This was the worst birthday present anyone could ever think of! You made me watch you eat a wonderful meal and gave me that sorry excuse for a salad! It wasn't even a salad. It's just green leaves and dressing. At least you were a gentleman and put the faucet water in a glass."

Regan says, "You're so ungrateful! I missed your birthday. So I'm making up for it. Sorry that I have a life."

Aliyah turns away fed up. Regan holds her saying, "Look I'm sorry."

He touches her face and kisses her on the lips. Aliyah pulls away as she says, "No Regan."

He ignores her as he kisses her on her neck and rubs her inner thighs. She pulls away shouting, "Regan I said no!"

Regan pulls her arm as he says, "Stop being so difficult! Come here!"

He gropes her and is halted with a scratch to the face as Aliyah shouts, "STOP!"

Aliyah becomes fearful as blood pours from the wound she dealt.

Regan looks at her infuriated. She tries to apologize only to be fiercely grabbed. She fights him shouting, "Regan no! Stop!"

Out of desperation she grabs a beer bottle on a table near the couch and slams it hard onto his face. The glass shatters on impact. Regan flinches back in agony as he screams. Aliyah quickly gets up and flees the house in a tearful fear. She races to her car, looking back to see if Regan is behind her. He's nowhere to be seen.

She gets into her car and locks the doors as she begins to cry fearfully. She lets out a scream of anger and sorrow as she hugs the wheel in pain. She starts the car and quickly drives away not wanting to give Regan time to recover.

CHAPTER SIXTEEN

Tim sits in the school office working efficiently as he types a paper with his laptop. Principal Frawgs walks out of his office and sees Tim working and being abnormally productive.

He walks to him saying, "You're working harder than usual. Are you alright?"

Tim says, "I'm fine. I'm just being diligent for once."

Frawgs watches as Tim wears his typical *I hate the world* expression as he types. Frawgs becomes confused. Recently Tim has been a lot more cheery than he usually is. But today, he's back to his normal quiet and serious mood.

He asks, "Are you sure? How are things with Robyn? Is she still giving you trouble? Come on Tim what happened? You were happier than I've ever seen you when that girl came in the other day. What was her name? Aliyah? Yeah, she's senior class president. She's quite the scholar."

Tim says, "It's nothing."

Frawgs replies, "You know I can tell when you're lying right? You've been working in here since late last year. Tell me what's on your mind. I was looking forward to seeing you beat my high score."

Tim laughs as he looks back at him. He says, "Well alright."

Frawgs sits on the desk and listens as Tim says, "Have you ever liked someone but you knew it wouldn't work? But you spent more and more time with them. Then you developed feelings for them?"

Frawgs smiles saying, "Yeah, I knew a girl like that in college. She was out of my league. She modeled and came from a wealthy family. I was normal. I grew up in a home where my mother struggled to feed us every day. I knew it would never work."

Tim smirks believing his feeling of doubt is absolute saying, "So you let it go right? It would have never worked so that's the logical thing to do. You ignore the silly feelings and move on?"

Frawgs shakes his head no to Tim's surprise. He becomes confused asking, "What did you do?"

Frawgs simply replies, "I ended up marrying her."

Tim becomes dumbfounded saying, "What? I don't understand. You just said it would have never worked. So why marry her?"

Frawgs explains, "Sometimes your heart is right where your mind is wrong Tim. Though I thought it wouldn't have worked. I liked her to the point of not caring. I took a risk for her."

Tim looks not knowing how to respond as his logic has been thwarted.

Frawgs continues, "I don't know Aliyah well Tim. But if you like her enough to spend hours thinking about her, why not risk it?"

He pats Tim on the back. He walks away saying, "Go to class Tim. You only have thirty minutes left." Tim packs his things and walks out. He walks down the hallway in deep thought.

"Yesterday was so surreal. I know why she ran away. She got overwhelmed and panicked." He sits in his science class, towards the back, as he watches Aliyah.

"If she really is afraid what can I do? I can't force her into taking a risk."

Aliyah looks back at him. He looks at her and smiles slightly as he prepares to wave. She gives him a serious look and turns around. his smile fades as he puts his hand down. He takes out a copy of *Hero's Wake*. He opens it towards the end.

He continues from where Aliyah stopped and reads to himself, *"'Marcella stared at him with passion in her eyes as if hearing words from the heavens as Glen continued, "Mai doesn't have your love to offer. Only your love feels the void in my heart Marcella. I need it."*

Glen kissed Marcella. Marcella let go of his hands and held his face as he held her waist.'"

He turns the page and continues, *"'She lied in Glen's arms as he brushed her hair with his hands. She held his hand and said, "Glen we can't keep doing this. You can't keep doing this to Mai. We don't belong together."*

Glen held her and looked her in the eye and said, 'Then why did all of this happen? Why did we meet and experience all of these happy moments with each other? All of this has happened for a reason. I don't love Mai. I love you.'"

The school bell rings and Tim stops reading. He looks up at Aliyah as she gets her things and leaves.

He follows her slowly and hesitantly. He struggles to speak as other students come out of the classrooms. As he calls out her name, the sound of students drown out his voice as the halls become crowded. He loses sight of her.

"I don't know. I always know and this bothers me. I have to know what if. Why is she so similar to a character I wrote long before I knew her? I can't go back to Robyn knowing something deeper lies ahead. I need to see who Aliyah Conrad is really."

He pushes through the crowd. Once he regains sight of her he smiles, but it fades as Regan approaches her. She turns from Regan as he tries to talk her. Tim takes note of bandages on the left side of Regan's face.

Tim watches in confusion as she violently pushes him away. She yells at him as she slams her locker shut and storms away. A blonde headed girl walks to Regan. He holds her and walks away.

"What just happened? She looks really upset."

Tim watches as Aliyah walks out of the school. He walks after her. Robyn walks out of a restroom and waves at him as he passes her. She watches as he walks after Aliyah. Tim sees Aliyah at her car. He calls for her as she opens the car door.

She looks back and sees him. He approaches her as she says, "Tim?"

He replies, "Hey Aliyah."

"Hey Tim," she says.

There's a moment of awkward silence. Tim breaks the ice saying, "Are you alright? I saw you in the hallway a moment ago."

Aliyah says, "Tim I'm fine."

Tim asks, "Are you sure? What happened to Regan's face?"

Aliyah becomes annoyed saying, "Tim I'm in a rough mood okay?"

He looks around as he becomes more and more uncomfortable. He says, "I'll just go then."

He turns away but pauses. Aliyah stares at him as she tries to find out his motives. Why hasn't he left yet? She can't figure out why he seems to care so much when no one else ever has.

He thinks, "Why can't I walk away? I want to say so much to her. Yet I want to just walk away and not risk the hurt. But I can't. I can't walk away from her. But I can't say what I want to say.

He looks to her and says, "Aliyah listen."

She says, "What Tim?"

He slowly walks to her saying, "There's something I need to say. The other day when we kissed."

Her face turns red and she looks away, "Oh, that."

Tim quickly shoots, "I mean I wanted to know how you were. At home I mean."

Aliyah barks, "I said I was fine! Stop asking me!"

Tim shouts back, "I'm just seeing if you're ok! Is that such a crime?"

Aliyah counters with hurt and sorrow in her voice, "Who are you and why do you care so much? Why are you so nice to me when everyone else treats me like I'm nothing? Why are you so different? Why can't you just be a disappointment like the rest of them?"

Tim yells, "I don't know! It confuses the life out of me too! Why do I care about you so much? I can't make any sense out of it! You're not the only person who has it bad you know."

Aliyah's face softens as she sees the frustration in his face as he struggles to fight his emotions. She slowly steps towards him as he continues.

He says, "All I know is that there's this feeling I get when you're around. From day one, I've been getting this fuzzy, warm and happy feeling around you. You take the pain away. You remind me so much of Marcella. It makes no sense."

He feels her soft hand as it wraps around his. He looks back at her. They stare into each other's eyes as if they can feel one another's pain. She lays her head on his chest as she slowly holds him.

He says, "Aliyah."

She replies, "Just hold me please…no talking."

He holds her as she begins to cry silently. Silently, he comforts her as he runs his fingers through her beautiful brown hair. She tugs on his shirt as she cries softly. He sympathizes as he slowly begins to understand her familiar pain.

She feels his warm arms hold her as she finds comfort and cuddles his chest. Her tears slowly cease. The silence lengthens as they sit on the front end of her car. She rests in Tim's arms. He understands her silence and allows her time to herself. But he keeps his arms wrapped around her, letting her know she is safe. A quarter of an hour's worth of quietness passes.

Aliyah softly says, "That fuzzy feeling you were talking about." Tim looks at her as she continues, "I've felt it for a long time also. I feel it right now."

She rubs her face on his toned chest as she says, "When I'm with you, I feel so happy and safe. I feel like nothing can go wrong. Being around you helps me be free. You make breathing so easy yet so hard. You told me I'm always bubbly. But I only get like that around you, Mr. Derr."

She looks at him. He watches her as she says, "I care about you more than a lot too." Tim remains silent as she gazes him. She says, "Well, aren't you going to say something?"

"You told me no talking," he says.

Aliyah laughs at him. He laughs along as she says, "Well say something."

Tim says, "I don't have any good lines. You bested me. Here I thought I was the deep one."

They laugh with each other. Aliyah playfully pushes him saying, "This isn't exactly an appropriate time to be goofy, Mr. Derr."

He teasingly pokes her saying, "I'm being serious, Ms. Conrad."

He lies back on the car. Aliyah crawls beside him and lies close looking at him. He closes his eyes as he says, "Thank you, Aliyah."

Aliyah asks, "For what?"

He replies, "You wipe the negativity away. It's like a dirty window. The sun can't shine through because of all of the grime and dirt. Happiness couldn't make its way to my heart with all of the despair and pain blocking it. But like a rag cleans the window, letting the sun shine through, you wiped those negative emotions away and allowed happiness to make its way into my heart again. Thank you. You make breathing a breeze, yet a struggle too, Ms. Conrad."

Aliyah smiles. He looks at her and says, "How's that for a response?"

She replies, "It was beautiful Tim. I love it. You're really deep."

Tim smiles as he stares at the sky peacefully.

Aliyah says, "Hey I want you to meet me at the park."

He says, "Today?"

She says, "Meet me at the park by the restaurant I took you that one day. Meet me in an hour."

They both get off of the car. Tim watches her as she gets into the car. She repeats, "One hour ok? At the park and don't be late Mr. Derr."

Tim says, "You got it Ms. Conrad."

Tim watches as she drives away. He begins to walk away from the school. His thoughts flutter as he walks around for a half hour just thinking. He heads towards the park. He sits on a bench once he arrives, thinking as he stares into the distance.

"What if things go the way I want them to? What if she turns out to be my Marcella? Part of me wants this more than anything. Then another part of me I... I just can't believe in this. So many people have said these amazing things. I love you and promises, that turn into lies and hurt. Why should she be any different? Who is this girl? I barely know her."

Aliyah's car pulls up. She parks the car and steps out. Tim looks up as she looks towards his direction.

"Yet I want to take a risk."

Aliyah walks to Tim. He asks, "Why are we meeting here."

She replies, "I want you to meet someone I love very dearly. He means the world to me."

Tim becomes hurt and insulted saying, "Oh that's what this is? I can take a hint. No thanks."

He gets up and begins walking away. Aliyah says, "Are you sure you want to walk away without meeting him first Timothy?"

He says, "Why do you want me to meet this person? I get it. He's the world to you. I wouldn't want to intrude." He looks at the car and sees a little boy sitting in the car. Confusion spreads across his face. Quickly he puts the pieces together.

He looks at Aliyah and says, "It's your little brother isn't it?"

Aliyah smiles as she signals for Liel to come out. He steps out the car nervously.

Aliyah encourages Liel, "Hey don't be shy. He's nice I promise."

Liel slowly walks towards Tim. Tim looks at Aliyah saying, "You wanted me to meet him?"

She says, "He's shy. So please be nice to him. Do you like kids?"

Tim watches, as Liel gets closer. He stands a few feet away from Tim. He watches as Aliyah kneels to Liel saying, "This is the boy I've been telling you about Liel."

Liel stares at Tim. His face lightens up as he waves at Liel and says, "Hey buddy!"

Liel curiously looks at Tim's skin as he says, "Your skin is brown."

Tim looks at his skin smiling as he casually says, "I guess it is huh? Pretty cool huh?" He winks.

Liel smiles and says, "Yeah!"

He races to Tim and takes his hand. Aliyah becomes embarrassed saying, "Liel stop that!"

Liel looks back in confusion as he says, "What did I do?"

Tim smiles reassuringly as he says, "Yeah Aliyah, he just wants to see my hand."

Aliyah walks to the two as Liel examines Tim's soft and brown skin. Liel says, "It's so warm."

Aliyah looks to Tim and says, "I'm really sorry."

Tim says, "For what? He's just curious. All kids are. Aliyah relax. I'm not easily offended. I take it he hasn't been around too many black people?"

Aliyah says, "I'm not sure actually. He goes to a small school. I don't think there are any black students there. I've never hung around a lot of black people. Just you now that I think of it."

Tim says, "I feel special now. I'll make the best impression for him then."

He kneels down to Liel and kindly says, "Your sister talks about you all of the time kiddo. You're really important to her you know."

Liel smiles and says, "Li, Li was right about you. She said you were really nice."

Liel looks at Tim's short and curly hair saying, "Your hair looks really cool. Can I touch it?" Aliyah watches as the two quickly bond as if they are brothers. Tim allows Liel to touch his hair, "Wow it's really curly."

Tim smiles as Liel gets up saying, "Hey! I bet you can't catch me Tim."

Liel taps him on the head and quickly runs away saying, "Tag you're it!"

Tim says, "Hey don't talk too soon. I'm pretty fast kiddo."

Aliyah observes as Tim chases Liel. She shakes her head yes as if confirming something. She smiles peacefully.

CHAPTER SEVENTEEN

Aliyah watches Tim play with Liel on the playground goofily as if they are siblings. Liel teases Tim as he runs around the playground and laughs as he chases.

"I've never seen Liel this happy with anyone besides me. He never opens up to anyone. He's so shy. Regan was the first guy he opened up around besides dad. Regan treated him like such a pest so he went into a shell. But with Tim..."

She watches Tim carry Liel on his back as he runs around. Liel holds his hands out freely as if he's a plane while Tim carries him. They laugh cheerfully.

"...It's like they're brothers. It's just like I thought. Tim is perfect with Liel."

She watches as Liel races to the swings. He trips and falls. Aliyah panics calling for him. Tim walks to Liel but doesn't baby him. He allows the child to get up on his own but is there if he needs a hand. He looks up as Aliyah comes in a panic.

She frights, "Ah! Liel!"

As Liel gets up, Tim asks, "Are you alright buddy?"

Liel shakes his head smiling. Tim dusts Liel off. Aliyah runs to them.

Aliyah worries, "Liel are you alright?"

Tim confidently says, "He's fine. He was just a little excited about riding on the swing." He pats Liel on the head.

Liel smiles asking Aliyah, "Can Tim push me on the swing Li, Li? Pleeease?"

Aliyah says, "I'm not sure." She looks to Tim asking, "Can you Mr. Derr?"

Tim says, "Of course I can. I would love to. Come on buddy."

Aliyah watches as Tim helps Liel onto the swing. Tim pushes Liel back and forth. She watches as Liel laughs and swings.

"He's so...I don't know, amazing. He acts as if Liel is his own brother or son even. He looks as if he's really having fun. They're a lot alike."

She sits in the grass and watches as Liel giggles and plays with Tim. Liel and Tim look at Aliyah. Aliyah looks at Tim.

"He looks so happy."

They smile at each other. Aliyah looks at the sunset.

"I hadn't realized how much time had passed since we've been here. Tim barely knows Liel. Yet he has such a way with him. It's really amazing. He's so benevolent yet strong at the same time. He wouldn't harm a fly but if that fly were to ever hurt his loved ones, he'd know how to deal with it."

She gets up and walks to Liel and Tim. Liel shouts, "Tim you should come over!"

Tim smiles and says, "Heh, well I'd love to buddy. But you know, I have a bedtime."

Liel whines, "No. Please? Just for a little while?" He looks at

Aliyah with eyes of a puppy as he begs, "Please Li, Li? Tell him he can come over."

Aliyah has trouble saying no as Liel's innocence pleases her.

Tim says, "Liel I would love to come over. But I can't tonight."

Liel becomes worried, as he whines more, "No, Please?"

Aliyah smiles at Liel. Tim and Aliyah gaze at each other and smirk. She smiles saying, "He's gotten attached. I'm jealous."

Tim pats Liel's head playfully as he says, "Don't be. He's great. He's crazy about you Aliyah."

Aliyah becomes shy as she bites her lip slightly as she says, "Tim. Are you hungry?"

He says, "Actually I am."

Aliyah says, "I don't want to see him cry. Come over for dinner?"

They stare into each other's eyes smitten by one another. Tim says, "That sounds nice. What time Ms. Conrad?"

She says, "8 p.m. Mr. Derr. Be early." She stares at him feeling the chemistry between them grow. She thinks.

"I can't stop thinking. Thinking about how he held me. How he kissed me. How he made me feel so breathless yet so alive. His touch was so warm and comforting. He's calm yet so full of passion."

Tim says, "I'm going to go home and get ready."

She replies, "Same."

Tim stands up and begins to walk away. Aliyah watches as he begins to walk. She realizes he's walking towards the road and not a car.

She yells, "Hey! Where's your car? Don't tell me you walked again."

He replies, "I did. It's a small town. It's fine. Gas money you know?"

She becomes concerned saying, "Tim it's sunset, ride with me."

Tim replies, "No it's fine."

Aliyah worryingly says, "Timothy come on. I don't want you walking alone at night. I hate that you walk like this. Please come on?"

Liel insists, "Come on Timmy!"

Tim smiles and walks towards them. Aliyah, Tim and Liel begin riding in the car. She looks at Tim as he stares out the window.

Aliyah says, "Um, what do you want for dinner?"

He looks at her saying, "You're asking me?"

"Well yeah. You're my guest," she says.

Tim replies, "I like meatloaf with mashed potatoes and macaroni."

Aliyah smiles, "Alright Tim."

They drive a few miles and pull into a neighborhood. Tim pays close attention in suspense as he waits to arrive to Aliyah's house. He expects to see a house similar to Regan's, only more elegant and higher classed. He slowly begins to become nervous. His assumptions shatter into glass pieces of ignorance as they pull into a house around the same size as his.

There is no mansion, expensive cars and not even a white picket fence. The neighborhood and house is nice and plain, nothing poverty stricken, but nothing extraordinary.

He stares in confusion, not being able to understand how his logic has once again been cancelled out by reality. Aliyah turns off the car. They get out. She becomes nervous to see her dad's car in the driveway. She thinks.

"I was so absorbed into the moment that I forgot about my father! Tim makes everything feel so in place. As if nothing will go wrong. But not here. My father won't like him." She looks at Tim's skin color then her own.

Tim says, "This is a pretty nice house. It's a lot different from what I thought it would be like though." He begins walking towards the house with Liel.

Aliyah panics shouting, "Hey wait!"

Tim looks back in confusion saying, "What's up?"

Aliyah says, "I mean are you sure you want to eat *here*? I can't cook very well. Let's go to a diner. I will pay this time."

Tim says, "It's fine Aliyah. I'm not a picky eater."

Aliyah looks at Liel as he tugs Tim's shirt and leads him to the house. Aliyah follows. She becomes increasingly nervous as they get close to the front door.

Tim notices and asks, "Hey what's wrong?"

She tensely smiles, "Well nothing I just um I uh. I think it's nice that you're so good with Liel."

Tim pats Liel on the head and says, "How couldn't I be? He's awesome!"

Liel says, "Thanks Tim! Aliyah he's so cool!"

Aliyah smiles as she puts a key into the door's lock.

"This won't go well. I already know what's going to happen. My father is going to make sure Tim is as uncomfortable as possible. Tim won't want to be around me anymore after this. Maybe this is for the best then. At least I'll know that him and I are a bad idea."

She unlocks the door and hesitates to open the door.

"But I don't want this to be the last time. I mean..."

She looks at Tim doubtfully.

He says, "What's wrong?"

Aliyah frights, "This is a bad idea. My dad, he's horrible. I don't want you to stop seeing me after you meet him!"

Tim steps close to her and places his hand on the knob. He makes her feel safe saying, "It's fine Aliyah." He opens the door for her as he offers, "After you Ms. Conrad."

She looks at him for a moment.

"He's so relaxed and confident. Fine then."

She smiles, "Ok Tim." She opens the door and leads them into the house.

CHAPTER EIGHTEEN

Tim walks behind Aliyah as she guides him inside. He looks around and notices the house isn't huge nor is it overly fancy. He looks to his left and notices beer bottles on a table in the living room, in front of a widescreen television. He looks forward to see a table littered with papers and a few more beer bottles. He watches Aliyah immediately start to collect the bottles.

She says, "I'm sorry."

He begins to help her as he says, "Don't be. It's fine."

They throw the bottles away. Tim takes a moment to further examine the house as Aliyah begins cleaning up the surrounding area. He thinks.

"The house is different from what I thought it would be. It's nothing like I imagined."

He looks into the kitchen. He notices it's very clean and organized. He sees several empty beer boxes by the trashcan. He looks out the kitchen and sees Aliyah walking around as if looking for someone.

"She's looking for her dad. Is she really that nervous about him meeting me? She seems so alert. Is she afraid of him?"

He watches as she walks to the stairs and looks up.

"He's hit her. Of course she's afraid of him to some degree. No girl should ever have to go through that kind of pain and stress. It's her father for crying out loud. He's supposed to make her feel safe, not afraid. I want to meet this coward. I want to see this sorry excuse of a man."

He walks to Aliyah and holds her hand protectively. She looks at him as he says, "It's ok. Please relax." She looks away in shame. He gently squeezes her hand saying, "Hey."

She looks at him as he supports her says, "Stop worrying. I'll be fine and so will you. Nothing will happen to you. Not while I'm here. Just trust me."

She becomes touched by his words as he says, "Ok?"

Aliyah smiles and blushes. His bravery and confidence moves her. She says, "I should, I should go start dinner."

She begins to walk away but Tim doesn't let go. She looks back as he gazes her with deep care. She says, "Thank you Timothy. You wanted meatloaf right?"

Tim nods saying, "Yeah. Meatloaf sounds good. "

Aliyah stutters, "Ok."

She walks to the kitchen swept away by his charm. Clumsily, she stumbles as she walks into the kitchen. She looks back and smiles at him embarrassingly as her face becomes redder and redder. Tim sits at the table and watches as Aliyah begins preparing the cooking tools.

"How can someone justify harming something so delicate?"

He looks at Aliyah as she takes out the food.

"She doesn't deserve to be abused. It upsets me that she has lived through this for God knows how long."

He balls his fist and becomes angered as he becomes protective towards Aliyah. Liel sits beside him. Tim opens his eyes and snaps out of anger. He relaxes his fist as Liel says, "You want to see my room? It's really cool."

Tim smiles at Liel saying, "That sounds fine Liel."

He gets up and follows Liel. The toddler goes to his sister asking, "Li, Li can Tim come play video games with me?"

Aliyah cooks as she says, "Go ahead. It's fine."

She smiles at Tim. Tim smiles back saying, "Don't overdo it ok?"

Aliyah says, "Hey, hasn't anyone ever told you not to disturb a woman while she's cooking? Go play, Mr. Derr. Out of the kitchen."

Tim teases as he steps in and out of the kitchen. She laughs saying, "Out!"

Tim smiles as he backs out slowly saying, "Alright, alright."

He walks out of the kitchen and follows Liel to his room. Tim watches as he plays a shooting game.

"This game is pretty violent. This kid is only five and his dad doesn't mind him playing stuff like this? My dad would never let me play this stuff at his age. Even now my dad doesn't like me playing games like this."

Tim smiles at Liel saying, "This is a pretty fun game huh kiddo?"

Liel says, "Yeah, Aliyah hates it though."

Tim smiles saying, "I can imagine why."

Liel says, "She tried to take it from me. But my daddy wouldn't let her."

Tim asks, "So your dad is pretty cool huh?"

Liel shrugs his shoulder as he becomes slightly annoyed hearing about his dad. He says, "I don't know."

Tim hesitates to dig further, "Well um, is he mean?

Liel says, "Not to me," he beats Tim and shouts, "Yeah! Do you want to play again?"

Tim shakes his head yes, "Yeah, but hey you got lucky that time."

Liel starts a new game. Tim continues the conversation, "So what do you mean he's not mean to you? Who is he mean to?"

Liel becomes upset saying, "He's really mean to Li, Li. He hurts her and makes her cry all the time! He calls her mean things and hits her a lot. It scares me. Li, Li said that daddy hurt mommy and made her leave forever."

Liel looks at Tim and continues, "I don't want my sissy to leave me by myself. I'll be alone. I don't want daddy to make her leave like mommy did."

Tim looks empathetic for Liel. He says, "Don't worry she won't leave."

Liel pauses the game and looks at him with hope asking, "How do you know?"

Tim says, "Well because I'm here. I won't let him hurt her. Your sister isn't going to leave."

Liel excitingly says, "Really? You really mean that? You'll protect her?"

Tim replies with a smile, "I *promise* kid."

Liel says, "Li, Li said that my mommy wanted me to protect someone I really care about and to never hurt them. I care a lot about Li, Li but my daddy is bigger than me! Can you protect Li, Li for me? Please?"

Tim places his hand on Liel's head as he says, "Don't be afraid of anyone Liel. Not even your father. You're her brother so you have to be brave for her and look out for her. Never hurt her either. She loves you more than anything. I won't let anyone hurt her but I can never take your place as her brother."

Liel surprises Tim as he hugs him tight saying, "You're super cool Tim, Tim. You're like my big brother now!"

Tim loses his words as he awes silently being moved by Liel's words. He mouths, "Thank, thank you Liel."

Liel says, "Why don't you ever come over? You're way cooler than Regan."

Tim says, "Huh?"

Liel explains, "The guy Li, Li always brings over. He's mean! I don't like him. He calls me names and makes Li, Li cry."

Tim becomes upset saying, "You've got to be kidding me. He makes her cry too? I thought Regan was, well, perfect."

Liel continues, "She's always in her room crying because Regan doesn't talk to her! She says he cheated too!"

Tim becomes astonished, as he says, "No way. Regan has cheated on her?"

Liel continues, "Yeah but it was weird. I didn't know Li, Li liked videogames."

Tim stares at Liel thinking.

"I had no idea Aliyah had it so awful. She goes through this daily. I feel awful. I've completely misjudged her. I was wrong about literally everything."

T.Edward Redd   **198**

He checks his phone for the time to see it's 7:55 p.m.

He says, "Let's go see if your sister if finished cooking."

Liel says, "Ok."

They walk downstairs. Tim smells the air and becomes hungry as the delicious aroma of a home cooked meal frenzies his appetite. He says, "Wow." As he steps into the kitchen, Aliyah looks back at him.

He halts in place saying, "Hey I can leave. Just don't yell again. The food smells so first-class that my nose drug me here."

Aliyah says, "No, no this is perfect! Come here and try this please."

Tim walks over to her and sees meatloaf, mashed potatoes and green beans on the stove. He looks in the pot, Aliyah wants him to try and sees macaroni.

He says, "Aliyah this is amazing. It smells great. Is it ready?"

She becomes flattered, as she giggles, "Not yet. I have to make sure this macaroni is perfect for you. I made green beans too.

I'm not sure if you eat them, but I try to get Liel to eat vegetables every day."

Tim says, "No it's perfect. I'll have some."

Aliyah dips a stirrer in the macaroni and takes a spoon full out and holds it to Tim's mouth.

She says, "Try it. Tell me how it tastes. Please be honest."

Tim opens his mouth as Aliyah puts the spoon full of macaroni in his mouth. He eats the macaroni with satisfaction.

Aliyah says, "I'm sorry I didn't know what you liked so…."

Tim hugs her saying, "It's flawless!" He looks at her, "It tastes mind-blowing Aliyah."

She smiles saying, "I'm glad you like it."

They stare at each other passionately. He leans towards her and she leans towards him. The front door opens and they stop to look back. Alvin walks in the house with a young blonde woman.

The blond woman says, "Wow it smells amazing in here."

Tim looks at Aliyah's father as he steps through the door. Tim looks at Alvin as he looks at him. Aliyah's father rudely says, "Who are you?"

Tim observes without any fear or nervousness, but absolute readiness for whatever is about to occur.

"So that's her father," he mutters softly.

Aliyah nervously says, "Oh um, dad this is Timothy Derr. He's our dinner guest for tonight."

He replies, "Do you know he's black? "

Tim smirks as Aliyah shouts, "DAD!"

Tim says, "It's fine Aliyah."

Liel shouts, "Daddy he's really cool!"

Alvin asks, "Is he? We'll see."

He walks to Tim and offers his hand saying, "Alvin Conrad."

Tim introduces himself and says, "Nice to meet you."

Aliyah nervously says, "I'll set the table."

Alvin says. "No, no. You two sit down and I will make the table."

Aliyah says in surprise, "You'll what?"

Alvin looks to his lady friend saying, "Come on Andy. Help me set the table." Andy smiles and follows him into the kitchen.

Aliyah and Tim sit down next to each other. Aliyah watches her father suspiciously wondering what he's planning. Tim looks to Aliyah saying, "See I told you. That wasn't bad at all."

She says, "Give him five minutes. He's acting weird. It might be because you're here."

Tim says, "Stop worrying so much." He playfully pinches her arm. She smiles and leans on him asking, "Why are you so calm? Aren't you nervous?"

Tim brushes her hair out of her eyes and behind her ear as he says, "Nope."

Alvin comes into the room with plates and silverware. Andy brings out the food. Alvin passes the plates and silverware as she places the food on the table. They sit across from Tim and Aliyah. Liel sits on the corner by Aliyah.

An awkward silence fills the room. Tim casually eats as Aliyah watches her father, nervously waiting for disaster to erupt from him. Alvin looks at Tim bluntly asking, "So how do you know my daughter Timothy?"

Tim looks up saying, "We go to the same school."

Alvin asks, "So what do you do in school? Do you play any sports like basketball or football?"

Aliyah gets an embarrassed look on her face. Tim replies, "I used to play football."

Alvin becomes excited asking, "Oh really? Were you good?

Tim says unexcitedly, "I was the star running back."

Alvin jumps in shock as he says, "Wait a minute. You're that kid from last year? You were the lead scorer! I thought you looked familiar."

Tim smiles nonchalantly as he fiddles with his fork saying, "That's me. I couldn't finish last game though."

Alvin says, "Yeah you guys lost didn't you?"

"Yeah, *they* did," Tim says.

Aliyah joins, "Tim writes his own novels and he's really good."

Andy asks, "What kind?"

Tim says, "Mostly romance. I've written some horror too. Generally I'm pretty well rounded with genres."

Alvin becomes appalled asking, "Wait, what about football? Did you quit for writing?"

Tim proudly smiles as he says, "Yup."

Andy becomes impressed saying, "I think it's impressive that he's a writer. He's so young."

Alvin mockingly says, "Yeah but does he make money off of it?"

Aliyah boldly defends Tim saying, "Well, actually he published a novel last summer called *Hero's Wake*. It's on shelves at stores for how much?"

Tim replies, "Twelve ninety-five. "

Andy says, "Wow how many copies have you sold?"

Tim modestly answers, "Not that much maybe close to a thousand. It's not as popular as I thought it would be but it's my first novel. I think I did well."

Andy obsesses, "Wow one thousand?"

Alvin asks, "So you make a lot of money huh?"

Tim says, "Yeah kind of. I put a lot of the royalties towards other books I'm making so I can continue investing. My books help me make money while I sleep."

He explains, "See I have three separate accounts: Primary checking, Spending and Savings. The royalty money goes into my primary checking. That's for investing and business purposes. My spend account is for personal expenses like clothing, food, and other stuff. Then my savings won't be touched for years."

Alvin becomes annoyed at how successful Tim is as he's just a high school kid. Andy and Aliyah stare in amazement.

Aliyah says, "No wonder you could afford to take me to that restaurant. You never told me any of that."

Tim says, "I don't normally tell anyone but my dad about my finances. But this is a special occasion. So I made an exception."

Aliyah smiles and looks to Alvin and says, "Isn't he mind-blowing? He gave me an autographed copy of *Hero's Wake* for my birthday and a new novel called *Hero's Romance*.

Alvin says, "That is pretty impressive."

Andy smiles saying, "I bet your parents are proud huh?"

Tim says, "*Parent* and yeah."

Andy replies, "Oh you only live with one?"

"Yes," he says patiently,

Alvin says, "Yeah fathers can suck sometimes. My father left me too."

Tim looks at Alvin as he say, "I have a father."

Alvin replies, "Well everyone *has* a father. I was talking about them sticking around."

Tim doesn't get fazed as he says, "So was I. I live with my dad."

Alvin acts overly surprised as he says, "What?"

Tim smirks, seeing exactly what Alvin is trying to do. He smirks at the challenge he knows he won't lose, as he's far too intelligent to fall for such obvious bait.

Aliyah says, "Dad stop it! Tim I am so sorry."

Tim smiles saying, "No Aliyah it's fine. There was no way he would have known. But no my mom left when I was sixteen. My dad has been by my side since birth."

Alvin asks, "Does he know you're dating a white girl?"

Tim mocks Alvin's comment as he looks to Aliyah playfully saying, "Wait you're white? You should've told me!"

Aliyah laughs as she covers her face in embarrassment at the situation. Tim laughs as he picks up a green vegetable with his fork.

He says, "No my father doesn't mind. All he cares about is me finding someone who treats me well and he makes sure I do the same."

Andy agrees, "I don't think it should matter as long as they like each other."

Liel shouts, "I think Tim is awesome!"

Alvin says, "Does Regan think he's awesome?"

Tim almost becomes hurt but Aliyah says, "I dumped that low-life."

Tim slowly begins to smile as he looks at his plate, quietly muttering, "Bingo." Aliyah smiles at him knowing about his quiet verbal celebration.

Alvin becomes alarmed saying, "Why? He was perfect! Don't tell him you left him for this kid!"

Aliyah raises her voice saying, "Regan was horrible to me. I can't be with him anymore. I did myself a favor. I'm not dealing with him anymore."

T.Edward Redd   **204**

Alvin says, "You're so ungrateful. He's going to be a star and you'll miss out hanging out with this joker. No offense to you, Tim."

Tim politely smiles, goading him, as he says, "None taken."

Alvin begins his assault on Tim saying, "Must be difficult being a writer. You have to write based on personal experiences for inspiration. People get tired of reading about death, drugs and murder."

Tim holds his polite smile, not letting the effect of Alvin's words show on the outside.

He thinks, *"He's pushing buttons. But I can't show it. He's trying to get me to cause a scene. He's trying to make me crack, so he has a reason for me not to hang out with Aliyah. That's too bad for him though because I'm an intellectual. He's going to have to try a little harder if he wants to beat me."*

He looks at Alvin as he smiles and says, "You'd be surprised at what I've been through."

Alvin bluffs saying, "Enlighten me."

Tim calls the bluff, "I'd hate to be a spoiler. But if you're so interested, buy the novel. It's worth the small amount of money you'd have to spend."

Alvin rejects, "Thanks, but no. I prefer intellectual type novels."

Tim smirks in annoyance. Aliyah becomes more and more nervous as the two go to war with each other, trying to make the other break while keeping their composure. Tim struggles to keep smiling as Alvin politely insults him.

Tim speaks out loud, "Hmm, well besides a thousand others. Your daughter seems to think it's pretty good."

Aliyah tries to stop the mind duel as she interrupts, "SO! Dad, tell us about the woman you brought to dinner."

Andy says, "Oh I'm sorry. I'm Andy I'm your father's new..."

Alvin cuts her sentence short as he deals Tim one last but fatal insult, "Well you know Tim, kids don't always know what's best for them. She dropped the star quarter back like it was nothing. I can't see a brother like you..."

His racial insult gets halted as Andy shouts, "I was talking!"

Alvin and Tim stare each other down. Tim focuses on Alvin. Andy gets frustrated as Alvin ignores her. She shouts, "Hey!"

Alvin looks at her as she says, "I was introducing myself and you cut me off!"

Alvin rudely says, "Ok talk."

She gets up and walks out of the house. He gets up and walks after her. Tim watches as he leaves the house. Tim looks to Aliyah and jokingly says, "I definitely won that staring contest. He totally blinked. Am I right?"

She laughs as she says, "Tim I am so sorry. I told you he was horrible. Look if you don't want to come back I understand."

He says, "It's fine Aliyah. I'm here for you, not your father. Just relax."

Aliyah says, "I envy your courage so much. That took a lot of bravery. You didn't even frown. How do you stay so calm all of the time? Nothing bothers you."

Tim says, "No, things bother me. I'm just really smart. I do that emotional stuff behind closed doors." He checks his watch to see it's 9:00 p.m, "Well, it's getting late. I should go. I'm sure you have a curfew."

She says, "Yeah I can't have company after 9:30 on school nights."

T.Edward Redd   **206**

Liel becomes sad, "Are you leaving?"

Tim replies, "Yeah, buddy. It's past my bedtime."

Liel says, "Sleep here! You can! Li, Li will let you stay with her. Sleep in her room!"

Tim looks at Aliyah. He gazes her as he thinks.

"I've never slept with anyone before. The thought of being beside her or holding her while I sleep is soothing. I can't fight this feeling. I'm developing feelings for her. I care about her."

He looks away as he says, "Um well I mean I don't really want to go."

Aliyah blushes and smiles as she says, "What? You want to stay the night with me?"

Tim panics, thinking she's offended, "Uh! No, that's not what I meant!"

Aliyah says, "There's no way I can do that! Not with my dad here. He would kill you. I don't want him to hurt you."

He says, "Wait you're not mad that I want to stay the night with you? You always ask if I have dark motives."

Aliyah says, "But I know you don't now. I trust you. Of course I'm not mad. Being in your arms while I slept would be beyond amazing. I feel so safe with you. Maybe we'll experience that one day."

Tim smiles at her peacefully, "Yeah. Alright Aliyah I'll get going before he comes yelling for me to leave."

Aliyah says, "Hey let me walk you to your car."

They walk outside holding hands. They walk towards Aliyah's car. Tim says, "You did a really good job with dinner tonight. You doubt your skills too fast."

She replies, "I'm sorry I lied. I just didn't want you to come over. I knew my dad would have attacked you like he did. I'm really sorry."

He says, "You worry way too much. Aliyah I'm great these days all because of you. Nothing bothers me. So don't let anything bother you ok? I'm here for you."

Aliyah smiles, "You and your words. Do you do that on purpose or are you just deep like that?"

Tim smiles and leaves her to wonder as they walk. He looks around for his car. He says, "Wait, you drove me here."

Aliyah says, "Oh yeah that's right! Ugh, it's so late. My dad will yell at me for this but come on. I'm driving you home."

Tim says, "No, I'll walk."

Aliyah says, "Tim it's dark out."

He replies, "I can handle myself. It's a small town and I'll be fine. I don't want you to upset your father. I like your face. It's healing pretty well."

He rubs her cheek. She holds his hand to her cheek as if being healed. She says in a worried tone, "Please be safe. You're so brave."

Tim says, "Don't be afraid ok?"

She looks as him saying, "Huh?"

Tim says, "Don't be afraid of your father. It's ok. You aren't alone. I'll see you around," he kisses her softly, yet it dazes her.

She holds his hand as he tries to leave. She says, "I want to see you again, Mr. Derr."

He says, "I'll see you at school Aliyah. Maybe I'll cook you dinner next time around. Goodnight, Ms. Conrad. Sleep well."

Aliyah says, "Goodnight, Mr.Derr. Please be safe on your way home! If you need anything call me ok? Stay on the street. Don't go walking in any dark allies or secluded areas okay?"

Tim looks back at her smiling as he says, "Stop worrying and go to bed beautiful. Don't be troubled so much about me. I can take care of myself. I promise to see you tomorrow. Sweet dreams, Ms. Conrad."

He blows her a kiss. She pretends to catch it and holds it to her chest. She waves him goodbye. Tim walks backwards for a while not wanting to leave her presence. She watches until he blends with the night. He smiles as she walks inside her house. He turns around and continues his walk home.

CHAPTER NINETEEN

Aliyah sits in her room happily early in the morning. She cheerfully reads *Hero's Romance* as she sits at her dresser. She's dressed in a green t-shirt and blue jeans. She's been up since 6a.m wanting to read Tim's new novel before going to school.

She flips a page as she reads, *"'A lot has happened since I wrote in this thing. My mom left today. I honestly don't feel anything. I don't feel sad at all. She made me carry her bags to her truck before she left. It made me angry but at the same time relieved. She's gone. Maybe now there will be peace in this house.'"*

Aliyah checks her cell phone for the time and see it's 7:35 a.m. She closes the book and thinks.

"Yesterday has left me with mixed feelings. It was amazing. Tim was great with Liel. Liel never stops talking about Tim now. It's good for him."

She walks downstairs into the dining room area.

"My dad has taken Liel to school already. It's obvious my dad doesn't like Tim. He was horribly rude to Tim. Tim stayed calm and never attacked him though. I can't stop thinking about what he told me about how I didn't have to be afraid and that I'm not alone. He makes me feel secure. I'm starting to fall deeply for him."

She holds *Hero's Romance* and looks at it.

She goes to school. During her classes, she reads Tim's novel as the day speeds by. A bell rings starting the one hour lunch period.

She begins to walk down the halls. Her thoughts drown the noisy movements and chatter of students out as she continues towards the auditorium. She doesn't bother getting dressed for cheer practice as she sits on the bleachers. She begins to read more of *Hero's Romance*.

She begins to smiles as she reads some cheerful things he's written in the past:

November 25th, 2009

Since I last wrote, a lot has happened. Thanksgiving was good. I went to Peru, Indiana and saw family. My cousin John had a kid. I saw him and his girlfriend at my Aunt Tammy's house. I think John is really cool, I always have. I've always admired his confidence and humorous side. Although I've never had a brother, I've always imagined if I did, the way I am around him would be what it feels like to have one.

Aliyah continues to read. Robyn, Snow and 3 other cheerleaders; Catherine, Jodi and Yasmine, walk into the gym from the locker rooms chatting.

Robyn says, "Okay, so I have this new cheer routine. If Aliyah doesn't show up, then we'll practice that instead of the boring one we've been doing."

Yasmine an attractive Hispanic girl with long black hair asks, "What's been up with Aliyah? She barely shows up to practice now."

Robyn says, "I don't know. But it doesn't matter. While she's gone, I'm head cheerleader."

Catherine twirls her wavy blond hair with her finger as she chews bubblegum. She blows a bubble as she sees Aliyah sitting and reading. Snow says, "Robyn it doesn't feel right without Aliyah."

211

Yasmine replies, "I like Robyn's routines more. They're hotter than the one's Aliyah comes up with."

Catherine points to Aliyah as she says, "Quiet or she'll hear you."

Robyn becomes jealous to see Aliyah sitting and reading. Robyn's spotlight has been stolen. The girls run to Aliyah with excitement.

Catherine smiles saying, "You're here today!"

Jodi who has delicate freckles and brown hair as long and wavy like a princess says, "Where have you been? You've missed a lot."

Aliyah says, "Oh it's okay girls. It's so close to the end of the school year. I guess I'm getting a little lazy."

Robyn walks to them as she stares down her rival saying, "Where are your cheer clothes?"

Aliyah reads as she says, "We don't need them unless we're at an actual event. I've said that a thousand times. I want you girls to wear whatever makes you comfortable."

Robyn argues, "How are you going to move around in those tight jeans. You need your cheer uniform."

Aliyah says, "Don't worry. The routine is really simple. I can do it in jeans."

Snow asks, "Aliyah are you leading today? Robyn had a new routine she wanted to try."

Yasmine adds, "Yeah it's a little more up to date."

Aliyah says, "No. I'm leading. We're going to do my cheer."

Robyn complains, "But that routine is boring! Let me show you my routine. It's way better."

Aliyah says, "We're not doing any slutty dancing. You know I'm against it. I'm cheer captain. We're going to do my moves. If you don't like it, leave."

Robyn shoots her an evil stare. Aliyah misses it as she keeps reading. Jodi says, "I like Aliyah's routine. They're classy and still keep the crowds going. So let's just do what she says. Aliyah, are you ready?"

Aliyah reads as she says, "Yes. Hold on."

Snow says, "Come on Aliyah. You can finish your silly book later."

Robyn stares at the book cover suspiciously as Aliyah says, "It's not silly."

She walks towards Aliyah as she recognizes the cover asking, "Hey can I look at that?"

Aliyah looks up, as she says, "Um actually no I was…"

Robyn quickly grabs the book. She looks at the title: *Hero's Romance* by Timothy Derr.

Robyn becomes annoyed saying, "So I was right. Tim wrote this. Look at that he even signed it for you."

Aliyah says, "Yes but those are actually mine this time. They're really good."

Robyn becomes slightly calm as she says, "Oh, so you bought these. Good."

Aliyah corrects her saying, "He gave those to me for my birthday."

Robyn's nerves spike as Snow says, "Why would he give you gifts?"

Yasmine adds, "Yeah isn't Tim with Robyn?"

Robyn snaps at Aliyah, "Yes! He is."

213

Aliyah looks up in utter shock saying, "What?"

Catherine confirms, "Robyn and Tim are together Aliyah."

Robyn says, "I told you that already. Why are you still seeing him?"

Jodi smiles with excitement. Not realizing the situation she dumbly asks, "Aliyah do you like Timothy?"

Aliyah becomes caught off guard and quickly nervous.

Robyn angrily says, "You're becoming too friendly with my boyfriend! We already talked about this. Maybe I should go talk to Regan about this."

Aliyah looks at the book hurt as she has developed feelings for Tim. She thinks.

"Tim never said anything about still being with her. Did he think I was still with Regan? What was the point of last night? He said those things for what? So he can have me and her?"

She takes *Hero's Romance* from Robyn as she says, "I broke up with Regan. Don't worry I won't be talking to Tim anymore. It's time for practice. Line up."

Robyn overrides Aliyah's order as she halts everyone. She says, "Tell me the truth. Do you like Tim or not?"

Aliyah ignores her, "Get to the center of the gym or I'll make the whole team do laps and I'll put *you* in the mascot costume."

Everyone but Robyn follows Aliyah to the center of the gym. She becomes furious and walks in front of Aliyah.

Robyn shouts, "Answer my question!"

Aliyah shouts back, "Robyn, get out of my face!"

Snow tries to calm the two down saying, "Girls, relax! Aliyah, just answer her question."

Aliyah says, "Tim is with you. That's all that should matter to you."

T.Edward Redd

Robyn shouts, "Just answer the question! Stop dodging it!"

Aliyah nervously fidgets with the novel as she struggles not to confess. Robyn snatches the novel and slams it on the ground and shouts, "Answer the damn question!"

Aliyah shouts, "Stop!" She kneels to get the novel and Robyn steps on it. Aliyah aggressively pushes Robyn off the book and picks it up. She wipes the book off saying, "Why would you treat something he wrote so poorly?"

Robyn yells, "It's just a stupid book!"

Aliyah says, "No it's not! It's more than that. He puts his heart and emotion into it. When I read it's as if he's with me. I can feel what he feels through his writing. I understand how he feels. It's amazing and you should be proud of him. How can you love him but not understand him? You don't understand who he *really* is. Not like I do."

Robyn shouts, "I DO UNDERSTAND HIM!"

Aliyah says, "No. No you don't. He's not this all-star football player you want him to be so badly. You don't understand Tim. Not at all. You like him yet you would literally step on his dream."

Robyn angrily says, "How would you know any of that? You think you understand him?"

Aliyah stares at the novel with deep thought saying, "Yes. I do. I understand him a lot more than you. And, well, I think he understands me too..." she stares at the book.

Catherine says, "Aliyah, you sound like you're in love with him."

Aliyah loses her breath hearing Catherine's words, realizing that it's more than just feelings she holds for Tim. He's the first person besides her mother to show genuine thought and care. It hits her that Tim is more than just some boy.

Robyn viciously shouts, "Tim doesn't understand you! Look at you! There isn't anything great about you! Tim isn't into emotionally damaged girls. Especially not the ones who date people like Regan."

Aliyah looks at Robyn with tears in her eyes. Robyn breathes heavily, enraged as she struggles not to attack Aliyah.

Snow says, "Girls that's enough. Everyone just take a breather."

Robyn shouts, "No! I won't let this bitch steal Tim from me!"

Aliyah cries, "I don't have to steal him! He comes to me! I don't have to beg him to spend time with me. He comforts me when I'm hurt. He makes me feel safe. He sees me. He understands me. You will never understand Tim the way I do. You're manipulative and selfish! You treat him like an object or some award."

Robyn shouts, "You don't know anything! If you understand him so much, tell me something. Has he ever told you about the time he tried to kill himself? How about the time he ran away?"

Aliyah loses her breath, "What are you talking about? He tried to kill himself?"

Robyn shouts, "He may fill your head with all of his cheap lines but he tells me the things that actually matter! All he wants is your attention! He doesn't actually like you!"

Aliyah looks away hurt. She thinks, "So he used me? But, why? Was the birthday surprise and being good with my brother just apart of some plan. So when he said I wasn't alone was he talking about himself? How could I be so dumb? I knew this was a bad idea." She gets up and begins to walk out of the gym.

Snow shouts, "Hey! What about practice?"

Aliyah keeps walking, as she says, "I quit. I'm done with cheerleading," she says to Robyn, "You win."

Robyn shouts, "Leave my BOYFRIEND alone!"

Aliyah says, "Don't worry. I will never speak to him again."

She walks out of the gym.

Her eyes leak tears but her face expresses no emotion as if her heart and mind have disconnected. People ask her what's wrong as she walks towards the café. She ignores them as she walks in. She gets her lunch. She sits alone from the other students. She becomes depressed as she eats pasta and fish in isolation.

"Lies...lies...lies...lies. He seemed so perfect. I'm such an idiot."

She looks up and sees Regan. He's eating lunch with a girl laughing with friends. Aliyah looks sad. Her appetite dies as she wipes her tears and gets up. She doesn't bother to grab her tray as she rushes towards the café exit. She bumps into someone.

She looks up and becomes filled with pain to see Tim. He smiles and says, "Hey I've been looking for you! How are you?"

She glares at him as if trying to kill him with her stare.

He says, "Whoa. Hey, what's the matter?"

He tries to grab her hand. She pulls away heartbroken screaming, "GET OFF!" The entire room stops and becomes silent as they stare.

Tim says, "Aliyah what's the matter? What did I do?"

She cries, "How can you still be with her?" He stares with confusion as she weeps, "How could you lie to me like this? I was starting to trust you! I thought that maybe you actually were different. But you aren't. You're just another person who hurt me! Why?"

Tim says, "Aliyah please calm down and breathe. I have no idea what you're talking about. Come here."

She shouts, "No! You're a liar! Just leave me alone!"

Tim stares in complete confusion not knowing how to resolve the situation. Robyn walks in, grinning at Aliyah behind Tim's back. Aliyah stares at both of them with hate and sorrow.

Tim pleads softly, "Aliyah. Please, I don't know what's going on. Just talk to me."

He tries to hold her. She violently slaps him across the face shouting, "Both of you can go to Hell!"

Tim stands in confusion as Aliyah storms away. He looks back to call for her but gets caught by surprise to see Robyn. She walks to him and holds him.

"Finally. She's gone."

Tim says, "Gone? What do you mean?"

She says, "Tim this charade needs to end. You had your fun with Aliyah, now it's time we got more serious. We need to start talking about our future. School will end in a couple of months. So I was thinking you and I needed to start talking about our plans."

Tim says, "Our future? Wait, so it was you who made Aliyah cry. Robyn, what did you say?"

Robyn says, "Huh?"

Tim shouts, "Why was she crying?"

Robyn plainly says, "Tim come on. I did you a favor. She's starting to think you actually care about her. You love me don't you?"

Tim shouts, "No!"

Robyn gets annoyed saying, "Tim please. Be serious for once in your life and stop playing these games."

Tim shouts, "Get it through your head Robyn. I will NEVER be the Tim you want me to be! He's gone. Get over it! You don't love me and I don't love you. I don't think I ever did."

He starts to come to a realization as he continues, "I wanted to be in love with someone. I thought if I had someone I wouldn't feel so alone and weak all of the time. So I forced myself into believing what we had was real. As if you and I were meant to be. Even if that meant being someone I wasn't. But then I found someone who truly admired me, just for being me."

Robyn argues, "Tim you can't really like Aliyah. How can someone like her ever please you? Please you the way I did."

Tim says, "I need to go." He begins walking out of the café.

Robyn shouts for him, "Tim, get back here! TIM!" He ignores her and walks towards the exits.

"I've never turned my back on Robyn. But, seeing Aliyah cry like that. It made me feel this familiar feeling. Am I making a mistake?"

He runs out of the school calling for Aliyah. As he looks around, he sees her at the school park, sitting on a bench as she cries. He walks to her. She looks back as he approaches and turns away from him saying, "I don't want to talk to you ever again. Go away."

He sits beside her saying, "Fine. I'll sit here quietly until you do."

She scoots away from him. He sits trying to think of a way to speak to her. As she pouts, he can't help but smile. He can't help but scoot closer. He places his hand on hers.

She whimpers, "Stop. Just go away."

Tim says, "Please Aliyah. Stop crying."

He tries to hold her but she pulls away saying, "Tim, leave!"

"Aliyah," he says.

She gets up as she turns to him shouting, "I can't believe myself. You're just like everyone else! Why didn't you tell me you were still with her? Here I am head over feet for someone I barely know and you've been stringing me along this whole time from day one!"

Tim says, "Aliyah I'm not with her!"

Aliyah cries, "You're a liar! You're a liar! Robyn told me you loved her! She told me everything! Just leave me alone!"

She tries to walk away but Tim grabs her hand pleading, "Aliyah wait! Just let me talk."

She turns back crying, "You're such a jerk! I started caring about you! You gave me butterflies! You made me feel as if everything would be ok. You made me feel as if I actually mattered. I stayed awake at night thinking about you. Then you tricked me into thinking you were good with Liel. How can you still be in love with Robyn? I was right to think you were too good to be true!"

Tim gets up saying, "That's the exact same attitude I was afraid of. You're afraid! Well so am I Aliyah! I've been wrong about everything when it comes to you and it scares me! I'm never wrong about anything. But you contradict everything I think of."

He explains, "You're not snobby. You're sweet and kind. You're not a spoiled rich girl. You've been hurt and left alone just like I have. You're this innocent little girl who just wants to be seen and held on the inside. You understand me more than I understand myself. That's the scariest thing I've ever come across."

Aliyah says, "Just go away!"

He walks to her, softening her heart with each step. She weakly steps back but struggles. Tim continues, "Aliyah, I don't love Robyn..."

She cries, "Just leave me alone. I don't want to be hurt. I won't let you win me over with your unworldly and perfect words. Just, just go."

She turns away. Tim shouts, "Listen to me damn it! Stop running away!" She turns back as he continues, "I care about you a lot a Aliyah. Since that day we first spent time together, I never stopped thinking about you. My feelings for Robyn faded the more we spent time with each other."

She shouts, "Lies! Then why did she say you loved her?"

Tim replies, "The first time I said it, I forced myself to say it. But the second time...I didn't say I love her..."

Aliyah asks, "Then what did you say? You wanted to love her?"

His heart pounds at his chest as if trying to be let out. He bravely but hesitantly says, "I said, 'I love you too, *Aliyah*'."

221

Aliyah looks back with shock.

He explains, "We were about to have sex. It was going to be my first time sleeping the night with anyone. When I was holding her, all I could think about was your smile and warmth. How we were at the playground and how I was on top of you. All I could think about, was how badly I wanted it to be you. When Robyn said she loved me that night. I said, that I love you too, *Aliyah*."

Aliyah blushes and becomes stunned for words. She fights her emotions as she weakly speaks, "Stop...stop lying to me."

Tim gets less than a foot away as she stares at him. Their hearts thunder as their eyes connect.

Tim holds her hand, "None of it makes sense. We're going against our thoughts. The opposite of what we expect constantly throws us off balance. We can't help but smile and laugh. Even when there's nothing but silence between us we can understand each other. Aliyah, I'm not lying."

She slowly takes his other hand. She looks at it and slowly looks to him. She stares into his war brown eyes with restrained passion in her eyes as he says, "Aliyah."

She shushes him softly, "No. No more talking, Mr. Derr."

He stares back deeply as he says, "Ok, Ms. Conrad."

They slowly get close as their bodies press gently against each other. Aliyah bites her lip softly as she hesitantly moves in and out. Tim does the same not wanting to make her angry. They both lose patience as they grab one another and kiss passionately.

Aliyah holds his face as he holds her sides. Tim runs his hands through her graceful hair as she feels his warm and strong arms. They kiss as sparks of love fly in their hearts.

They slowly stop as they gain their senses. Aliyah holds his face as she slowly pulls her lips away. She places her head onto his chest as she clings to his shirt.

Tim keeps his hands placed on her sides as he says, "You wouldn't have gotten so upset if you didn't feel the same. This isn't like me. I'm saying things and doing things that nothing but this thing inside of me can understand. I know we're both afraid, but I still want to try."

Aliyah slowly wraps her arms around his waist, hugging him, as she says, "I do too...it's really nerve shaking though. You know?"

Tim rubs her back soothingly, "Yeah. But try not to worry. It'll be all right. We have to help each other feel okay. If we want a future, we can't let the past have a bad effect on us."

Aliyah smiles as she says, "You need to stop doing that."

Tim asks, "Doing what?"

She replies, "Stop being so poetic. It always makes me smile."

He laughs, "I'm sorry. I promise it's not on purpose. The words just flow out of me. I speak from the heart. I guess since I'm smart and articulate that-"

Aliyah interrupts him as she puts her finger to his lips smiling, "Now you're rambling." They laugh as they hold each other. Aliyah sighs, "Take me away Tim."

He says, "Where?"

She replies, "Anywhere. Just take me away from everything. All of the chaos and sad things."

Tim replies "Let me then. Don't be afraid."

Aliyah says in a soft pleading tone, "I want to and it's not easy to *just* let go. To let go of all of these hurt feelings is hard. I've been hurt a lot. Not by you. But you know, people."

Tim replies, "I know, Aliyah. I have them too. But I want to try. I want to try for you." They kiss each other. They share a moment of silence as they hold each other.

She says, "Let's hangout again."

Tim says, "Ok that sounds fine."

Aliyah adds, "But this time let's go to your house."

Tim looks at her as he says, "What?"

She smiles saying, "You heard me. I want to meet your dad. You got to meet mine. Now it's my turn to meet yours."

Tim says in a sarcastic tone, "Should I cook you dinner too?"

She replies, "Nope. I just want you to introduce me to him. If you want to though, you can cook for me. My favorite is baked fish with fries and a Caesar salad."

Tim counters, "My dad doesn't get home until late."

Aliyah smirks saying, " It's a good thing it's a Friday then."

Tim says, "Fine. You win Aliyah. You're meeting my dad today. Come by my house at 7 p.m."

Aliyah says, "No, no, let's do things your way today. You walked here right? So I'll walk you to walk me to your home."

Tim says, "Hey are you sure?"

Aliyah says, "How hard can it be. If you can do it all year, I'm sure I can survive one day. So we're walking together to your house today. Deal?"

Tim caringly asks, "Are you sure?"

Aliyah smiles saying, "Stop asking so many questions. Pick me up at 3:30 homeroom. Don't be late, Mr. Derr."

She begins walking away back to the school building with a smile of red. Tim calls her saying, "Hey wait! We don't have the same homeroom on Fridays!"

Aliyah keeps walking as she says, "School doesn't end at 3:30 either. It ends at 3. Pick me up at 3:30. I'll be waiting for you. I know you'll find me somehow."

He watches as she walks into the school. Peacefully he sighs as he begins walking in behind her. They smile at each other as they part ways.

Tim makes his way to the office. Once he arrives he begins going through the school's class schedules list. He looks at Aliyah Conrad's Friday schedule. Her last period is Philosophy, room 514.

Time speeds by as he plays computer games on his laptop. The end of the day bell rings. He packs his things and makes his way out as he waves the office staff goodbye. Students begin to come out of the classrooms and fill the hallways. Tim tries to avoid Robyn who comes out of a classroom. She sees him and walks to him. He ignores her calls as he makes it to the Philosophy room.

Robyn says, "Ugh. Talk to me!"

"There's nothing to talk about Robyn," he says.

She shouts, "Why are you acting like this? Just last month you were all over me! Just talk to me!"

Tim says, "We have talked. We have the same talk every time. I don't want to do this anymore."

Aliyah opens the philosophy room's door and sees Tim. She says, "Oh hey! How long have you been standing there? You're early."

Robyn gets annoyed saying, "You're meeting *her*? But Tim why? Is she your girlfriend now? I had you first!" She stomps the ground.

225

Tim says, "Robyn stop, you're causing a scene."

Aliyah says, "Hey I should go."

Tim says, "No *we* should go. Come on."

Tim and Aliyah begin to walk away. Robyn shouts, "I don't care what you say Tim. She can't have you!"

Tim and Aliyah leave the building. They begin walking down along the school park, away from school. They head west. There's an awkward silence as they walk down the street for a few minutes.

Tim says, "Don't mind Robyn, Aliyah."

She replies, "Oh gosh no. I'm not worried about her."

He says, "But you're so quiet."

Aliyah plays with her hair as she says, "Well I guess I'm a bit nervous."

Tim laughs, "About meeting my dad? Don't be Aliyah. This won't be anything like it was when I met your dad. My dad will love you."

She looks at her skin then Tim's as she says, "Yeah but still, I'm nervous. I mean. I'm not like *you*."

Tim asks, "What do you mean?"

She flips her hair as she struggles to get her words out. She says, "I um, I sunburn easily."

Tim says, "So?"

She holds her arm to his face saying, "I'm *different*. Get it now?"

Tim says, "You smell nicer?"

Aliyah gets frustrated, "Ugh! No. Look at *me* then look at *you*. What's the difference?"

Tim says, "What? You're a girl? Aliyah that's good my dad wants me to be with girls."

Aliyah says, "Are you seriously this dense about what I'm talking about?"

Tim says, "Honestly? Yes."

Aliyah bluntly says, "Look at your skin. Then look at mine! What's the difference?"

Tim examines his arm then Aliyah's as he says, "Well, your arm is a lot less hairy than mine and smoother. You smell nicer?"

Aliyah gives up shouting, "No, I'M WHITE!"

Tim says, "Huh? Oh," he catches on, "OOH!"

Aliyah blushes as she stresses, explaining, "What if he doesn't accept me? I've never been with a black guy before…"

Tim smiles as he hugs her, "You worry too much about the small things Aliyah. You shouldn't be worried about that. My dad doesn't mind. He liked Robyn and she was destructive. But you, well you're not."

Aliyah becomes less worried and smiles at his wordplay. She says, "Whatever. You have a way with words don't you, Mr. Derr?"

He answers, "I have a way with telling the truth. I don't try to flatter or charm people. I tell them what I believe and feel. That's what writers do. They write what they think and feel."

Aliyah smiles and says, "That could be why you're so good at it then."

"Maybe," he says with a smile.

Aliyah sighs in relief saying, "Finally. It's been a while since I've seen you smile like that."

"Like what?"

She replies, "I've noticed that when you genuinely smile your eyes kind of brighten and your teeth show. It's a nice smile Tim. You close your eyes when the smile is fake."

Tim says, "I've had a lot of reasons to smile lately is all."

Aliyah smiles saying, "I wonder why."

He pulls her close saying, "Can you guess for me?"

She playfully says, "I would like to buy a vowel please."

"I'll give you three. Two A's and one I," she says.

Aliyah says, "Sometimes Y?"

They laugh at their corny humor. Tim reassures her, "My dad will like you Aliyah."

She replies, "I hope so."

CHAPTER TWENTY

Aliyah and Tim walk close together on the sidewalk. She looks at him as he walks. He looks happy and confident. She looks away and smiles.

"He's so different. He doesn't try to impress me at all. He just does. There is no gloating or showing off. He's not smug or overconfident. He's sure of himself. How does he do that?"

She holds his hand and leans on him as they walk. She says, "Tim."

He looks at her as she asks, "You asked why I chose Regan. Well I have to ask now. Why Robyn? I mean you aren't like a lot of guys. You're really sweet and polite. You're gentle, yet not afraid to protect yourself or others. Don't laugh at me. But you're like the hero."

Tim feels charmed as she explains, "You have all of these strengths and good characteristics. Yet you don't use them for dark purposes. Instead you help others and humble yourself. A guy like you ends up with the princess."

Tim begins to feel flattered. He laughs and says, "I don't know about that one."

Aliyah says, "Don't you know any fairytales or action movies? Where the hero gets the damsel in distress? The hero goes through a journey, a long one. He faces many dangers and obstacles just to rescue this girl. At the end he always saves her. That's the type of guy you are. Come on, you're a writer. You should know this. You're the hero," she smiles.

Tim smiles stunned for words saying, "Aliyah that was amazing. I'm speechless."

She says, "So I have to know. Why Robyn? She just isn't right for you. She's not the princess. Robyn is self-centered and mean. She doesn't see *you*. She can't even see what a great writer you are. Someone like her could never understand let alone appreciate someone like the hero. Not like the princess can. The princess likes, no she loves the hero for both his imperfections and strength. In fact it's his imperfections that draw her the closest to him.

"Every hero has an obstacle he has to face before saving the princess. The obstacle is always stronger than the hero in some way, shape or form. Despite all of that, the hero faces his fears and disregards any weaknesses he may have within him, in order to overcome the obstacle.

"The princess sees that. She admires him for it. Having the will to overcome the fiercest and most horrible forces just to be by her side. It's the most honorable thing any man could do for a woman. Robyn will never be like that. She can't even take one hour to read a book her boyfriend wrote."

Tim replies, "Robyn meant well. Not everyone will like my novels. The woman of my dreams might hate them."

Aliyah holds him as she says in a serious tone, "You're wrong. You're right not everyone will like them. But your princess will love your novels. She will push you to go above and beyond. She will help you out best your work every time. Tell me why you chose Robyn."

Tim stares at her as she holds his hand waiting for his response. He thinks, *"She's really thought this through. This hero and princess stuff sounds a lot like the things I write about. What I feel. She's had these thoughts about hero's way before we met. I can tell by the way she just described them."*

He speaks, "Well I don't know. I mean, of course now I see how bad she was for me. But when we were together there were times where we shared good moments. Times that made me feel loved and happy you know? It's hard. It's hard to let someone go after they've made you feel those kinds of feelings. In the beginning it was amazing. I thought I'd be with her forever. I loved her. After I stop playing football she changed.

"She didn't even care about my novels. She was obsessed with football and me. I didn't answer your question yet did I? I guess I chose her because I wanted to feel that love again. It's hard to let go when you've already experienced so much love with a person. It's hard to grasp. Why would they do this? What happened to *I love you*?"

Aliyah listens and watches as she thinks, "I know exactly how he feels. I felt the same way about Regan. It was so amazing in the beginning. He said he'd always be there. But time passed and he changed. It hurt and I didn't want to accept it."

Tim explains, "You can't grasp the sudden change. You ask yourself, 'Why have they changed?' So you refuse to accept it. You trick yourself into believing the person you fell in love with will eventually come back. That's what I did. I chose the girl I fell in love with. After she faded away, I chose to wait until she came back."

Aliyah replies, "I know what you mean, Tim. But you're better than that. You were settling. Don't ever settle for less than what you deserve. What you deserve is a princess. The hero always ends up with the princess. Do I need to tell you about the princess?"

Tim smiles saying, "She's a lot like you I'm assuming?"

Aliyah blushes as she says, "That was sweet. Thanks Tim. She'll support you in everything you do. She won't hate your novels. She will love them."

Tim smiles as they keep walking. Aliyah smiles and checks her to see it is 5:01 p.m. Aliyah becomes surprised saying, "My gosh. It's been over an hour since we started walking. You walk this long every day? With all of those heavy books?" Tim smiles as he nods his head yes.

She becomes upset with him saying, "That's not good for your back. You shouldn't walk this far every single day."

He says, "It eats the time away. I spend a lot of time home alone. I hate it there. It's like a prison. No it's worse. In a prison there's people to interact with. But there it's different. There's just an empty house and me. My so-called friends now hate me. I have no one Aliyah and it hurts. I'd rather walk far then-"

Aliyah becomes upset with his self-pity as she shouts, "Stop!" He becomes silent as she walks behind him and opens his backpack. He looks back as she begins removing a few books from his bag.

She softly but soothingly says, "You aren't that person anymore. You aren't alone. You have *me* now. So stop torturing yourself ok? From now on, we drive to school together. I can pick you up or you can pick me up. If I catch you walking home again, I will hurt you. Ok, I'll carry these books. How does your bag feel? Is it less stressful on your back?"

Tim smiles saying, "Yes. Thanks, Aliyah."

Aliyah smiles saying, "Don't worry about it Tim. You worry about me all the time. So I get to worry about you too. We're like a duo. We help one another."

They continue to converse as they walk a few more blocks. They walk into a gated neighborhood filled with impressive houses. Each house's grass is healthily green and finely cut. Aliyah stares in awe.

She says,, "Whoa. I guess I didn't notice how beautiful it was out here at nighttime. This is really elegant."

She begins to feel more and more nervous as she begins to compare her plain neighborhood to Tim's seemingly exclusive neighborhood. She starts playing with her hair as she unknowingly bites her nails.

They arrive at Tim's house. It's about the same size as Aliyah with a more impressive landscape. She stares at the many beautiful flowers, trees and bushes around his neighborhood.

A few rabbits hop in and out of the yards. They begin walking on the driveway towards the house. She notices three cars in the driveway and becomes even more nervous. Tim continues to walk. He stops to notice Aliyah is no longer by his side. He looks back to see her staring at him. Her face is as red as a tomato.

He says, "Aliyah what's wrong?"

She whispers loudly, "I'm even more nervous than I was before! I had no idea you lived in this high-class neighborhood. I would've worn a dress!"

Tim looks around and says, "Oh yeah. I do live in a fancy area. But I guess I didn't think it was a big deal. So I never told you. But look my dad isn't a snob or anything. He's not going to ask you math or political questions. We're normal people. We just live in a costly area. Please don't let that affect anything. I really like you."

Aliyah looks around as she tries to calm herself down.

Tim walks to her and grabs her hand as he says, "Aliyah, none of this material stuff matters. Notice, that I don't where fancy clothing. I favor V-necks and nice jeans. I like you and I want you to meet my dad. So come on."

She smiles as he guides her to the front door. He takes out his keys and begins to open the door. He turns the knob. Suddenly Aliyah stops him and says, "Wait. Tim, how do I look?"

He opens the door and offers her to enter first as he says, "Like a princess. Welcome in, Aliyah."

She kisses him on the cheek as she steps inside. She walks in and smells baked fish and fries in the air. Closing her eyes, she tastes the air. She becomes famished and her appetite ripples.

Her stomach growls as she says, "That smells so good." She looks around and notices the house is spotless. The carpets are very clean and stainless as if they were just cleaned.

"Do I need to take off my shoes?? This house is nice. Ooh, I'm too nervous," she asks.

Tim holds her saying, "Just relax. Aliyah it's fine."

He lightheartedly laughs at how jumpy she's getting. She looks at him asking, "What's so funny? Is something in my teeth or hair?" She takes out a mirror and begins looking into it.

Tim holds the mirror saying, "Aliyah you're perfect. Seriously relax. You'll creep my father out if you're so tense. Just calm down ok?" He hugs her.

She says, "Ok. I'll try. Thanks, Tim. you're really sweet."

Robert walks in and sees them hugging. He sees Tim happy and smiles. He says, "Oh you guys are early!"

Aliyah looks back. She sees a muscular middle-aged man walking out of the kitchen with an apron and cooking gloves on. He gives off a warm and welcoming vibe.

"That's his father?"

Robert says, "You must be Aliyah. Tim never stops talking about you."

Tim becomes embarrassed, "Awe come on dad. Don't tell her stuff like that. We just started getting close."

Robert walks to his son proudly smiling as he says, "Loosen up son. If she agreed to meet me, she must like you already. I'm sure she doesn't mind." He offers a handshake to Aliyah. Welcomingly, he says, "It's nice to meet you. I'm Tim's father, Robert Derr."

Aliyah shakes his hand saying, "Thank you sir. My name is Aliyah Conrad. It's a pleasure. Thank you for having me."

Robert replies, "The pleasure is ours, Aliyah. Tim told me what you liked to eat. So I made baked fish, fries and a Caesar salad just for you."

Aliyah smiles with awe saying, "Oh thank you sir. That's really nice. Thank you."

He kindly says, "Please Aliyah, call me Robert. Anyone who my son chooses to be around wins my respect. He's a good kid. I know if he likes you, you must be pretty amazing. Welcome to our home."

Aliyah becomes happy as both Tim and Robert's kind energy make her feel safe and welcome.

"He's very welcoming. He's nothing like I imagined. Even though he's muscular he's really welcoming. Just by looking at him you can tell he's kind natured."

Robert says, "Well since you two are here do you want dinner? I made it early since I have to hurry and get to bed. I have to leave for work around 12."

Aliyah looks to Tim asking, "Are you hungry?"

He smiles at her thoughtfulness as he says, "Aliyah, you're the guest."

She embarrassingly laughs as she says, "Dinner sounds great. I didn't have lunch."

Robert looks to Tim saying, "Tim show her to the dining area and I'll bring you your plates."

Aliyah asks, "Excuse me Robert? Did you want me to take my shoes off before I walk on your carpet?"

He says, "Oh no you're fine, Aliyah. Just enjoy yourself."

Robert walks to the kitchen as Tim leads Aliyah to the dining area. She looks at the house as she walks through the home. She sees family portraits, nice furniture and vases.

"It's so nice here. I feel awful. My house was a mess. All of those beer bottles my dad left out. I doubt his dad even drinks. I'm starting to feel out did...how can I live up to this?"

Tim pulls out a seat for Aliyah formally saying, "For you, Ms. Conrad."

Aliyah elegantly sits as she plays along saying, "Very lovely Mr. Derr. Thank you."

Tim helps his father set the table. Robert brings out Aliyah's specially made plate and sits it in front of her. Tim brings out the other two plates and sits them on the table. He sits by Aliyah. Robert sits across from them. They all begin to eat.

Tim smiles as he watches Aliyah eat her salad. She notices him watching. She becomes self-conscious and stops eating. She asks, "What's wrong?"

Tim says, "I think it's cute how you always save your tomatoes for last."

She offers to feed him one. He politely eats it. Aliyah smiles as he says, "Wow that's better than the fancy food place we went to."

She says, "I know! Your dad is a really good cook. Thank you Robert."

Robert says, "I was glad to do it. So Aliyah, tell me about yourself. What school do you go to and what do you do."

She replies, "Tiger Southeast High School."

Robert says, "Oh you go to the same school as Tim?"

She replies, "Yes. I'm a head cheerleader. Well until I quit today. I'm also the senior class president. When I get out of high school, I want to go to college to become a nurse. I want to help deliver babies."

Tim asks, "You quit cheerleading?"

Aliyah replies, "Yes. I got into an argument with Robyn. It's fine. I don't like cheer as much as I did when I first started anyway. I'm more into reading and focusing on school."

Robert says, "You sound very smart, Aliyah. Tim has a few achievements as well. Did you know he's an author?"

Aliyah becomes excited saying, "Oh yes! I have two of his novels. Your son is very talented."

Robert says, "All he ever does is type his stories. When he published his first book, I was so proud. He did it all on his own."

Aliyah says, "Isn't he impressive? I'm betting by the time he's a junior in college he'll be well known. If he works hard he might become a hit as a sophomore."

Tim interrupts, "Guys I'm flattered. But tonight isn't about me. It's about you, Aliyah. Put me on the backburner for a while and talk about yourself. You're pretty remarkable too."

She smiles at him saying, "Ok, ok. What would you like to know Robert? I'm pretty bad at selling myself but I'm great at answering questions."

Robert asks, "Tell me a little about your family."

Aliyah becomes slightly uncomfortable as she says, "Oh, *my* family?"

He smiles eagerly saying, "Yes tell me about them. You seem well brought up. You must have really great parents."

Aliyah's confidence lowers as she says, "Well I live with my dad and my little brother. My mom died a few years ago."

Robert becomes mournful as he says, "Oh I'm sorry."

She looks at her plate as she says, "No you're fine."

"Who am I kidding," she thinks. *"Robyn was right. I won't be enough for him. My family is a complete mess. My father is abusive and my mom died. I've only been here for half an hour and I can tell that Robert is a great father. It's no wonder why Tim turned out so well. I just got lucky. My mom saved me before she died. Tim is clearly the hero. But I'm not the princess."*

She looks at Tim as he holds her hand saying, "Hey, it's alright."

She smiles weakly saying, "Thank you."

Robert says, "I apologize Aliyah. I didn't mean to offend you.

"It's fine," she says with a weak smile.

Tim smiles as he gets an idea, "Hey tell us about Liel." He looks to his dad saying, "Her brother is the best. You'd love him!"

Robert smiles saying, "Oh please share."

Aliyah smiles saying, "Oh, he's five. He turns five next month. He's a really bright kid. Since mom died I've been raising him. He reminds me so much of her."

Robert smiles saying, "That's great. What about your father?"

Tim blurts out, "DAD!"

He looks at Tim in confusion. Tim calms down as he tries to fix his tone, "I mean, don't you think you're being a little forward?"

Robert replies, "I want to know about the young lady my son is dating. That's all. Aliyah, don't answer anything you don't feel comfortable answering. I can be very blunt sometimes. But I mean no harm."

Aliyah says, "No it's fine. My father and I don't get along very much. Since my mom died our relationship kind of just faded. We don't really talk to each other like a father and daughter should. We barely have a relationship."

Robert says, "Oh. Well I'm sorry to hear that, Aliyah. You're welcome here anytime. I hope things get better for you."

She becomes touched and thanks him. Robert stands up from the table as he says, "Well this was nice. You're obviously a well-put young lady. I don't see anything bad about you. As I said before, welcome to our home. You're welcome here anytime. Tim, be respectful."

Tim smiles saying, "I will dad. Come on you're embarrassing me."

Robert yawns saying, "Well it's 7 p.m. I have to leave for Illinois around 12 a.m. So I'm heading to bed. Goodnight you two. It was nice to meet you, Aliyah."

Aliyah replies, "Thank you very much Robert. I enjoyed dinner. Thank you for welcoming me."

Robert says, "No problem, Aliyah."

Aliyah watches as he goes upstairs.

She thinks, *"There's a very contrast difference between Tim's life and my own. Tim comes from a well put home and family. I don't. Tim's dad is a hardworking father. My dad is an alcoholic. He got laid off before my mom died because of the economy. Tim has actually published some of his work. He's on his way to reaching his dreams."*

"I'll be lucky if I make it to a good college. My grades are perfect but without a scholarship, college will be impossible for me. Even if I do manage to get into a good college, who will take care of Liel? All of this is a lot to take in. How am I supposed to live up to all of this? How am I supposed to be enough?"

She stops her thoughts hearing Tim's voice, "Aliyah, are you ok? You look a bit sad. I'm sorry. He didn't know."

Aliyah smiles doubtfully as she says, "No it was fun. You're just, you're really special Tim. A lot more special than me."

Tim becomes firm saying, "Stop it. Don't you dare."

Aliyah begins to get emotional saying, "Oh come on. Look at how different our homes are. Your house is beautiful! There isn't any beer bottles or caps on the tables or floors. Your dad probably doesn't even drink does he?"

Tim tries to calm her saying, "Aliyah please."

She continues, "Your carpets look brand new. The walls are freshly painted but my walls are cracked and ruined from my dad punching them!"

She starts crying as she says, "But do you know what the golden part was? The golden part was your dad. He's amazing. He cooked for his son's girlfriend and made her feel at home! My father didn't even care enough about me to celebrate my birthday. My father insulted you! He compared you to my ex who hit me."

Tim remains quiet as she finishes, "I can see why you turned out so perfect. But look at me. I'm worthless. How can I be enough for you when I was never enough for ANYONE? Not Regan, not my friends and not even my own father! I'm nothing but a waste of space. You're wasting your time on me. I'm not- I'm not the princess you belong with. I'm not the..."

Tim stops her with a kiss. She barely struggles as she begins to melt in his comforting arms. Their breathing speeds up as they kiss passionately. Aliyah let's go of her destructive feelings as Tim caresses her. They stop for a moment of silence as they catch their breath.

Tim says, "I was going to wait for you to finish. But you were taking way too long. Aliyah none of that stuff matters to me and it shouldn't matter to you either."

Aliyah pleads, "Tim you're making a huge mistake, taking me under your aid. My life is a mess. You have a bright future. Don't go and ruin it by taking in a basket-case like me."

Tim becomes serious as he says, "Would you stop attacking yourself? I don't know how you got it in your head that something is wrong with you because there's not. But it has got to stop. You're an exceptional and lovely person Aliyah. Who says you're not the princess? Who says you're a waste of space? Who says you're a waste of time? I never said any of those things. It's not your fault that there's bad in your life. You can't control others and you can't control who your parents are. But what you do control is your heart.

"Aliyah you have a beautiful one. It's so beautiful that I finally see the beauty of my heart. I used to be so depressed and down on myself. It wasn't until I met you that I realized how pitiful I was. In life people will try to tear you down and try to stop you from reaching your full potential because they can't do it. You have to protect your heart. You taught me that Aliyah."

Tim waits for Aliyah's response. There's a moment of silence as she stares at him blankly. He says, "Was that too long again?"

Aliyah becomes overly dramatic letting out a sigh as she pretends to faint in Tim's arms. She says, "Gosh, your words. They drive me rowdy. They're so breathtaking and motivating. Ooh why are you so good to me? I feel so girly around you, like a fan girl or something."

Tim smiles as he holds her in his arms. She cuddles against his face, feeling its warmth with her face like a mammal. She settles against his chest as she holds him. She sighs peacefully and closes her eyes.

Tim rubs her back, "Give yourself a break ok? You can't control other people or the way they treat you. You know how you told me about heroes earlier. You told me about how heroes go to Hell and back for the princess. But didn't you ever notice that the princess was always in danger? How she went through all of these things until the hero showed up? You're the princess in the castle, waiting for me to come rescue you."

Aliyah smiles as she keeps her eyes shut, holding him. She says, "Don't stop talking. Please say more."

He smiles as he continues, "I hurt too Aliyah. But I'm fighting it. I believe I can be happy with you. So I'm fighting all of my rationality and following my heart. It says *Aliyah Conrad.* I need you to follow your heart for me. Try for me."

Aliyah looks at him saying, "Ok Mr. Derr. I'll try my best. I promise."

She kisses him. She smiles as she thinks, *"He makes everything feel better. I didn't feel like I was enough. But he makes me feel like I am. He makes me feel beautiful. He's my hero and I'm his princess."*

She confides in him, "You're amazing Tim. You're not like anyone I've known or met. I feel as though I've known you all of this time. I was just waiting for you to appear."

He smiles saying, "I'm sorry for being so late."

Aliyah playfully replies, "It's ok. I know you'll make up for it somehow."

She hugs him tightly. He holds her as he says, "So, I have a question."

She looks at him saying, "Yes?"

He smiles as he looks away nervously, "Earlier my dad said you and I were dating. You didn't correct him. Then you said you were my girlfriend. So are we together?"

Aliyah blushes, "Mr. Derr, are you asking me to be your girlfriend?"

He confidently looks back to her and holds her close, "Yes, Ms. Conrad. I am asking you to be my girlfriend."

She proudly says, "Mr. Derr, I would love to be your girlfriend. Be my boyfriend."

They kiss. They finish eating as time passes. After eating, Tim guides her to his room. She watches as he walks to his laptop and sits down. She lies on his bed, flipping through a portfolio of drawings. She sees many different cartoon characters with names and numbers.

She says, "I didn't know you drew. Did you make all of these up?"

Tim types on the computer at a fast pace replying, "Yes. That's a graphic novel I'm working on. It's my longest and first project. The story is 400 chapters long."

Aliyah says, "This is amazing. I never knew you were an artist. Draw me?"

Tim smiles at her, slightly distracted as he focuses on typing. Aliyah smiles at his diligence. She gets up and walks to him. She stares in excitement saying, "Wow. So this is where all your masterpieces are conceived huh?"

He replies, "Yup. I love doing this. I never realize how much time passes."

Aliyah examines a bookshelf. She picks up a novel. The cover reads: *Butterfly* By: Timothy Derr.

She stares in astonishment realizing, that the books on the shelf are written by Tim.

She says, "Whoa. Tim, are all of these published?"

He saves his work on his computer as he finishes typing. He closes the laptop as he looks back to say, "Soon to be." He gets up and walks to the bookshelf.

He says, "After I finish a story I like to take it and get it made into a book like that. Then I place it on this middle row. I put them there to remind myself of my dream to be a well-known writer. Plus it makes me feel professional to have my work in book form, ready to read. This top shelf is for the published books. It's just *Hero's Wake* and *Hero's Romance* but it's a start."

Aliyah picks a book from the middle row titled: *Dead Awakened.* She asks, "Is this about zombies?"

Tim replies, "Yeah but not just zombies. It's about these two people helping each other through an apocalyptic era. The story is deeper than the typical zombie story. I try to portray the influence of an amorous connection between two people and how powerful love alone, can drive even the weakest individuals, to find their way through something as horrifying as an era where the dead walk amongst the living."

Aliyah smiles in excitement as she giggles, "This is so cool Tim. You're so gifted."

She picks up another novel: *Temptress.*

She gasps at the beautiful cover saying, "Whoa. Tim did you do the artwork for this one?"

He says, "Yes. That's actually one of my favorite covers. I do the artwork for all of the book covers. It saves me money."

Aliyah sits on his bed as she flips through the book as she says, "Hey do you know what would be really cool? You should let me read all of your rough copies. You know, so you can get someone's opinion before you decide to publish? I could be like your personal reader or maybe assistant! Don't worry though. I don't want any commission."

Tim smiles as he sits beside her, "I'd love it if you read my rough copies Aliyah. Thanks for asking. You don't know how great it feels to have someone who likes what I do."

Aliyah says, "Well how could I not like it? One, I love to read and two you're a pretty good writer. I loved *Hero's Wake*. I'm going to read this one next." She turns to the first page of *Dead Awakened* and begins reading.

Tim says, "Every story can be followed back to my life. Experiences, memories, even my desires. They all inspire my novels."

Aliyah walks to the bookshelf and picks up *Hero's Romance*. She looks at it less excitingly as she asks, "Even this one?"

Tim replies, "Especially that one. Everything in that journal is true."

She walks to him holding the novel. She sits beside him as she looks at the novel with sorrow.

Tim asks, "Did you read it already? How'd you like it?"

She softly says, "I don't like reading it. I've read a few entries but not all of them."

Tim says, "What didn't you like?"

Aliyah says, "Well...it's really sad. It's like I can experience the pain you've went through when I read it. It's dreadful, not the book but the things I read. Tim, do you really hate your mom? I just can't imagine ever hating my mom. I'd do anything to have her with me. You really hate her?"

Tim looks away saying, "You don't understand. You weren't there all of those years."

Aliyah holds his hand saying, "Help me understand. Talk to me about it. I want to understand that part of you. I care about you. Don't feel judged or anything. I don't agree with this hatred you hold for your mom. But I know you aren't a bad person. There's a reason you write and say these things about her."

Tim struggles to stay hardened as he replies, "I never had a good relationship with her. It's hard ok?"

Aliyah says, "Tim it's fine. I'm not judging you. Talk to me about it. You're holding things inside of you. Open up to me. Help me understand. I'm here for you."

Tim begins to explain, "My mom would always yell at me when I was little. I never got the affection I needed from her as a child. I remember crying at the end of school every day in middle school. I would see all of my friends excited to see their moms. Their moms hugged them and smiled. I wanted that. My mom wasn't like that with me."

Aliyah asks, "How did that desire for affection become hate Tim? Why didn't you just tell her how you felt? Were you afraid of her?"

He continues, "I had my father. Although I didn't have the affection I needed from her. I had my dad. My dad has always been a good parent. Even as a baby, I clanged to him more than my mom. So as I grew up my bond with him grew. But with my mom, we never had a strong bond. My mom used to treat my dad horribly and she did it right in front of me. That made me begin to resent her."

Aliyah says, "I think I understand. You never bonded with your mom but you did bond with your dad. So as you grew up seeing her mistreat your father, you became hateful towards her. But at the same time she's still your mom and you still long for that affection you never got."

Tim laughs at his own pain as he says, "You always say how I'm good with words. You're pretty smart too, Aliyah."

He becomes surprised as a tear drops from his face. He tries to hide his tears as he laughs weakly, pretending something is in his eye. Aliyah gently moves his hand from his face as she wipes his tears.

She says, "You always try to act so tough. Don't be ashamed to cry in front of me. It's ok. You always comfort me and hold me when I cry. I want to do the same for you. Come here."

She holds and comforts him as he hugs her. She says, "You don't hate your mom Tim. You're just hurt."

Tim argues, "She left me and I hate her for it."

Aliyah keeps her arms wrapped around him as she tries to relax his nerves by rubbing his back. She says, "No Tim you don't hate your mom. You love her. You have mixed emotions. You're frustrated that she isn't here and that she left. But you're only frustrated because you love her. You want your mom's love. I think that's why you stayed with Robyn for so long. You were trying to fill this hole you have inside of you with love from Robyn."

He cries silently. Aliyah eases his shame with her warmth as she says, "And Tim that's ok. You're hurt and you're doing things you think will heal you. There's nothing wrong with wanting to be loved."

She kisses him on the cheek. She continues, "But no girl can fill the void you're trying to fill Tim. Not like your mama can. Not even me."

They hold each other for a moment. She holds him comfortingly as she lets him slowly relax. They hear a car engine start. Tim looks out the window and sees his dad leaving.

Tim says, "My dad left for work."

Aliyah becomes alarmed asking, "What time is it?"

He says, "Midnight."

Aliyah panics, "Oh gosh. I have to go home!" She gets up and Tim holds her hand. She looks back at him asking, "What's wrong?"

He says, "Stay."

She blushes and says, "What?"

Tim repeats, "Stay the night."

"You want me to spend the night," she asks.

Tim shakes his head yes as he holds her hands as he says, "I don't want to sleep alone tonight. I mean I sleep alone every night. But I want to be with you tonight."

He gently pulls her close and holds her. Aliyah strokes his broad shoulders as she says, "My dad would kill me, Mr. Derr."

Tim replies, "Tell him you stayed over a friend's house, Ms.Conrad."

Aliyah counters, "Your dad would kill you."

Tim says, "He won't be back until late tomorrow."

Aliyah waits a few seconds to answer as she thinks. She gets closer saying, "I'll stay under one condition. I want to lay in your arms and cuddle with you."

He scoots back and welcomes her onto the bed. She gets on the bed and crawls to him. They sit on the bed staring at each other. The awkward silence makes them laugh at each other nervously. They hesitate but slowly begin to kiss as they hold each other.

Aliyah places her hands on his shoulders as he holds her sides. They slowly begin to lie down as they hold each other kissing. Tim kisses her on the neck. She giggles as she slightly scratches his back with excitement. They remove each other's shirts as they continue to caress one another's body.

Aliyah runs her hands down his chest and feels his smooth and hard abs as he kisses her behind the ears and down her neck. She lets out a soft and pleasing moan as he squeezes her breasts. Slightly, she digs her nails into his skin unknowingly as his soft moist lips excite her delicate body.

She removes her pants as he kisses her. Tim stops to look at her white and green-striped panties and her green decorative bra. She blushes at him as she says, "Don't stare. I'm a shy girl."

She lies beside him as he begins to rub on her body. She kisses him as he rubs her legs and thighs. She giggles and moans as he softly squeezes her soft and ample butt.

She softly says, "Hey. Take off your pants."

Tim stares at her for a moment. He hesitates but removes his pants. Aliyah holds him close as she begins to kiss him with infatuation. He kisses her back in the same manner. Aliyah gets on all fours and teases Tim with her butt as she pulls the covers back. She crawls to the front of the bed and motions him to follow.

He crawls to her as she invites him to lie on top of him. She opens her legs, as he gets close. He holds himself over her in a semi pushup position. He stares at her.

Aliyah whispers, "Hey have you had sex before?"

Tim replies, "Yes."

She smiles saying, "Well come on. This is the part where we remove our underwear and well, you know the rest."

Tim says, "Yeah, I know but."

Aliyah asks, "Hey what's wrong? Do you not want to?"

Tim quickly replies, "No! I mean yes!"

Aliyah becomes confused, "So you do?"

Tim replies, "I do want to do it. But not now."

She says, "What do you mean? I'm sorry. I was too aggressive wasn't I?"

Tim says, "No, no! Aliyah you're perfect. You have the most arousing body ever. I could never put in writing how much you're turning me on. It's just..."

Aliyah says, "What is it? Come on tell me. If it's me you can just say so."

Tim says, "No Aliyah it's not you. See I don't know how to say this without you feeling like it's you."

Aliyah replies, "Tell me what? Tim if you don't want to have sex it's fine. I shouldn't have come on so strong."

Tim says, "But that's the thing. You didn't do anything wrong. You set my body on fire and all I want to do is have you all night. But..."

She becomes annoyed and says, "But what? What's wrong? You keep saying you want to have sex, but you don't want to have sex. I don't understand. If you want to have sex with me, why aren't we having sex?"

Tim softly says, "Because…because I'm pretty sure that I love you."

She stares breathlessly as he looks at her deeply. He continues, "I've had sex before. I always did it because I thought I was in love. But none of my relationships have lasted. When Robyn and I had sex I thought it was love. But after a while it just became disgusting and lustful. There wasn't any passion. Aliyah I have these strong feelings for you and I care so much for you.

"But I just don't want to ruin this. I want to wait a while before we have sex. There's nothing you did wrong I promise. I just care about you. I want us to form a strong bond and grow on each other before we have sex. I don't want sex to trick us, into thinking, that just because we have sex, we're in love. I want us to learn more about each other and let our love continue to grow. So when we finally do have sex, it's not sex at all. It'll be love."

He stops as he's finished talking. He looks at Aliyah who's staring at him with a confused look on her face. Tim becomes doubtful as he looks away saying, "I know it's weird."

She says, "I'm just trying to figure out how and why on Earth did I find someone so perfect. Tim, that has to be the sweetest thing I have ever heard let alone have those words directed towards me. That was so beautiful."

"You're putting off sex because you love me and want to wait until we're both ready? Tim, that's so charming. Most girls give it up because they're afraid to lose the guy. But you're choosing to save it, because you don't want to lose *me*. There needs to be more guys who think like you."

Tim smiles as she says, "But you're all mine!" She hugs him tightly. He holds her in relief.

253

She says, "I love you too Tim. Of course I'll wait. I agree with you. A lot of people have sex thinking it's love. Then they have sex again and again trying to force it to be love. I'm guilty of that too. It actually does ruin the relationship. The relationship starts to orbit around sex. I don't think I'm ready to have sex yet again either. I want to wait for you too."

Tim smiles and kisses her. He says, "You're amazing Aliyah. I feel like I can be myself around you. We have this mental connection."

She replies saying, "Same here. Hey, can we still cuddle? I like cuddling with you."

Tim smiles and says, "That's what I was going to say."

They lie beside each other and hold one another. Aliyah pulls the covers over them as they hold and kiss each other. They cuddle each other for a while, enjoying one another's warmth. They stare at each other as they become quiet.

Aliyah whispers, "Hey."

Tim whispers back, "Yeah."

She says, "You're still in your underwear and I'm still in my bra and panties. Should we put our clothes back on?"

Tim replies, "I sleep in my underwear. I can put my clothes on if it makes you uncomfortable."

She whispers, "No I don' mind. I sleep like this too. I just didn't want to make you uncomfortable either."

Tim holds her hips, as he gets closer. She turns her back to him as he wraps his arms around her.

Tim whispers, "How's that?"

She whispers back, "Perfect. Whoa, is that your…"

He whispers, "Sorry. Even though we agreed to wait, you still excite me. It'll go down eventually."

T.Edward Redd   **254**

They laugh together as they snuggle. Aliyah whispers, "You're still exciting me too. I know how you feel."

Tim whispers, "Can I ask you something?"

She says, "What's up, Mr.Derr?"

Tim asks, "Why are we whispering?"

Aliyah laughs, "I don't know. I guess because we're half naked, under your covers at 1 a.m. But I forgot your dad isn't here."

Tim replies, "I like it though. Let's keep whispering. Let's do this every time we sleep together ok? It'll be like our thing."

Aliyah says, "I like that idea. It'll be unique to us because we're unique."

He whispers, "We're not unique."

She asks, "We're not?"

Tim says, "No, we're awesome."

She replies, "Oh, yeah you're right. My bad."

They laugh as they continue their conversation of whispers. They become tired as they yawn. Tim says, "I'm getting sleepy."

Aliyah replies, "Me too. It has to be like 2 at the least. Let's go to sleep."

Tim says, "Ok. Goodnight Aliyah."

Aliyah says, "Goodnight, Timothy. Hey, Tim?"

Tim asks, "Yeah?"

She says, "I love you."

Tim smiles saying, "I love you too."

They smile as they slowly fall asleep, holding each other.

CHAPTER TWENTY-ONE

Tim sleeps soundly in his bed, early in the morning. Aliyah lies beside him watching and waiting for him to wake up. She gently pokes his face as she says in a soft tone, "Hey."

He doesn't wake. She continues to slowly poke him. He swats her hand away as he sleeps. She begins to poke his forehead. He opens his eyes quick but calmly. Aliyah blushes and smiles. Tim looks at her quietly for a moment.

She whispers, "Hi."

Tim smiles as he whispers back, "Hey."

She says, "It's morning. I thought you were going to sleep forever."

He asks, "What time is it? Wait are we late for school?"

She replies, "It's only 7:30 a.m. But we don't have school anyway. Yesterday was Friday, remember?"

Tim says, "It's so early for a Saturday. Do you get up this early every day?"

She answers, "Yes. I wake up around 7a.m every day."

Tim smiles as he asks, "Have you been watching me sleep this whole time?"

She says, "No, I got up to use the restroom like ten minutes ago. Then I looked around for the remote but I couldn't find it. So I tried turning on your TV. Then I looked at it and went wait, this TV doesn't have any buttons. That's when I came back to bed. I couldn't fall back to sleep. So I started playing with your face. Hey, you're really beautiful."

Tim becomes offended repeating, "Beautiful?"

Aliyah gets close as she says, "Yeah. You sleep so peacefully. All I could do was smile when I looked at you."

Tim says, "But beautiful?"

Aliyah replies, "Yeah. What's wrong with that?"

Tim says, "It feels weird. That's such a feminine word."

Aliyah argues playfully as she smiles, "No it's not. You can call anything beautiful. I think you're beautiful so I called you it. Don't be a wimp about it."

He sticks his tongue out at her. She teasingly pinches him. He pinches her side and she flinches as she giggles. Tim begins to tickle her sides and stomach. She wrestles as she giggles playfully. She falls out of the bed on accident. Tim sits up and looks to her trying not to laugh, "Hey. Are you alright?"

She bursts out laughing. Tim joins her as he offers his hand. She pulls him out of the bed and he falls down to her. They laugh joyfully until their stomachs hurt as they lie beside each other on the carpet. They settle down but cling to their smiles as they hold hands close together.

Aliyah says, "This is just like it was at the park. It's nothing but clean fun and joy. I can't remember the last time I laughed so hard. I feel like a little kid."

Tim joins, "Yeah, I feel the same way. We have such a good time when we're together. I love it. Being around you makes me realize there's so much to smile about. It makes me regret wasting so much time being sad and alone."

Aliyah says, "I regret wasting so much time doing things that I either didn't like or things that hurt me. I'm glad we met that day. It's so weird too. No one remembered my birthday then out of the blue you showed up. It was so random."

Tim replies, "Yeah. It was funny because I couldn't figure out who you were. The computers were down so I had to ask around about you and what you looked like. You just so happened to be in the same class. You're right, it was random."

There's a moment of silence. They stare at the ceiling for a few seconds waiting for the other to speak. Aliyah looks at Tim as he stares at her.

She says, "What?"

Tim teases, "Nice bra and underwear."

Aliyah blushes and becomes embarrassed as she says, "Shut up! Don't stare like that." She laughs as she jumps into his bed and covers up with a sheet. She watches him as he gets up smiling. He casually walks to his desk.

She whines jokingly, "No don't start typing yet. Come hold me please."

Tim smiles as he grabs a remote from a drawer under his desk as he says, "Relax."

He turns the television on as he walks to the side of the bed. He flips through the stations as Aliyah stares at his body. She takes note of his exceptional muscle tone and flawless skin.

"Hey you know, for a writer, you're pretty built."

He sits on the bed saying, "I like to lift weights. I try not to get bulky so I do a lot of high reps to stay toned once I gain size."

Aliyah hugs and holds him from behind. She wraps her legs around him playfully as she kisses his cheek. He plays with her long brown hair as it dangles past his face, while he keeps flipping the stations.

Aliyah says, "Hey turn to 311."

Tim turns to 311. Aliyah smiles to see her favorite sitcom is on, "I love this show. Can we watch it please?"

Tim hands her the remote as he lies back happily. She lies beside him and snuggles in his arm as he holds her. They watch TV for a while having a few laughs every now and then. Aliyah looks at Tim for a moment as she thinks. She looks at the TV as she hesitates to say, "Hey, Robyn told me something really personal that I want to ask you about."

Tim replies, "She probably lied. But go ahead.

She nervously asks, "So, did you really try to kill yourself?"

His facial expression turns to regret, "Oh, that."

Aliyah whimpers, "But why Tim?"

He looks at her feeling the shame as he says, "I'm not proud of it."

Aliyah looks tearful, "Why did you try it?"

He explains, "It was in my darker times. I felt hopeless and worthless. I felt alone and miserable. All of those emotions kept building up. I started cutting. Eventually I committed or tried to commit suicide. It was unbearable."

"I took three shots of very powerful nighttime medicine. At first it didn't do anything so I stopped. I decided suicide wasn't what I wanted. So I went to bed. Then I woke up late night with a drowsy feeling. My entire body was aching and I was very cold."

Aliyah stares in sorrow and holds Tim's hand as he continues his unsettling story, "I felt awful. All I can remember is calling for my dad. I got up from bed and my body was numb. I dropped to my knees and I called for him. My voice was so weak. I didn't think I could be heard. I crawled to his room. But he had already left for work.

"It was ironic. The reason I tried to die was because the feeling of being alone was too much. Now I was going to die alone. I wanted to live. I forgot why I wanted to die. All I could think about were the things I never got to do and what I was leaving. I regret trying to kill myself more than anything."

Aliyah snaps at him in a serious tone, "Well, you should regret it. Don't EVER do that again!" She hugs him tight as she mournfully kisses his cheek. She says, "Imagine how things would be if you would have died. We wouldn't have experienced each other. We wouldn't be here. I'm glad you lived Tim. I've learned so much from just being around you. You're so warm and uplifting."

Tim replies, "Thank you Aliyah."

She slowly massages his shoulders comfortingly as she says, "You're not alone anymore. So don't hurt yourself again. It's like you said last night. We have to stop attacking ourselves. There isn't anything wrong with us. Sometimes it rains when we least expect it. That's when we have to protect our hearts and be strong enough to survive the storm, and if the rain doesn't stop put on your biggest smile and dance in it."

"Tim we've both helped each other to learn how to dance in the rain instead of letting the storm ruin our life. We can help each other survive. I believe us meeting was more than just chance. I think we were supposed to meet. So far we've helped each other come out of that destructive part of our heart. We always smile and laugh when we're together."

She stops as Tim stares at her. She brushes her hair back saying, "What?"

Tim smiles as he replies, "Am I rubbing off on you? Since when are you poetic?

She replies, "I probably read your books too much. Yes you've rubbed off on me. I'm sure I've rubbed off on you too. You're not as quiet as you used to be and you smile a lot more when I'm with you."

She kisses his cheek as she plays with his hair. Tim peacefully smiles as she holds him. She says, "I love you, Mr. Derr."

He replies, "I love you too, Ms. Conrad."

She blushes as she asks, "So I'm the first girl you've ever spent a night with?"

Tim laughs saying, "Yes."

Aliyah says, "Do you want to know something funny? You're the first guy that I've spent the night with."

Tim becomes surprised as he asks, "But what about Regan?"

She replies, "He was my first. But he never spent the night. He never even asked me to stay the night. Even though you and I haven't had sex yet, sleeping with you was better than sex. I felt so safe and comfortable. I'm a little afraid of the dark so I always let the moonlight shine in my room. But last night I didn't care. You were here."

Tim asks, "So wait, I'm you're second? Or your potential second?"

She replies, "Yeah, why?"

He says, "You're my possible second too."

Aliyah smiles as she says, "Let's just clean the slate. We're each other's first real anything. You made me feel really comfortable asking to wait. I know because we chose to wait, that we will grow strongly on each other. We'll be close like best friends. Once we're ready, it'll be beyond anything we've ever experienced."

Tim replies, "It's like you can read my mind."

She smiles as he playfully lies back on top of her. She wrestles to get from beneath him. He begins teasing her as he playfully pins her down. She manages to break his grip and get on top of him. She holds his arms down laughing as she says, "Gotcha!"

They both breathe heavily. They become startled as Tim's stomach growls. Both laugh hysterically. Aliyah says, "Somebody is hungry. Do you want me to make you breakfast? I'm pretty hungry too."

Tim replies, "I have a better idea. How about we cook together?"

Aliyah smiles as she says, "Ok but don't burn anything," she laughs. "But we should get dressed first."

T.Edward Redd   **262**

They get out of bed and get dressed. Tim puts on a royal blue graphic t-shirt and black pants. Aliyah puts back on her green t-shirt and blue jeans. They walk downstairs. They begin preparing cooking tools.

Aliyah asks, "Hey what are we eating?"

Tim sits a skillet on the stove as he takes out pancake batter. He walks to the refrigerator and takes out eggs, sausage and blueberries. Aliyah helps him by taking the bag of blueberries as he carries the carton of eggs and sausage.

He says, "Have you ever made blueberry pancakes? Let's have eggs and sausage with pancakes?"

Aliyah smiles saying, "Yes, that sounds great. I make all kinds of pancakes for Liel all of the time. So I'm a veteran at this. You can cook the meat and eggs. I'll make the pancakes."

They smile at each other as they begin taking care of their tasks. After preparing the breakfast, they share a plate. They sit at the dining room table and begin to eat. Aliyah feeds Tim. He smiles as he enjoys the satisfying and savoring blueberries in his mouth. He takes the fork from her and feeds her in the same manner.

Aliyah asks, "Do you like it?"

Tim kisses her as he says, "It's amazing. I love doing these types of things with you. We should go out tonight. It can be our first actual date."

Aliyah becomes excited as she says, "I'd love that! Hey how about a movie?"

Tim says, "No not for the first date. That's too cliché. I like being playful like we were at the park. How about we have dinner. Then play laser tag or even bowling."

Aliyah becomes thrilled as she says, "I've always wanted to go laser tagging. Let's do that instead. We can always rent a movie and watch it at your house or mine. Don't worry about my dad. He won't actually do anything to you. He might harass you though. But you handle him pretty well don't you my amazing hero?"

She holds his face gently with one hand as she kisses him. He holds her side as they kiss. Aliyah's phone sounds. Tim watches as she looks at a text message she's received from her work. The message reads:

Aliyah, don't forget to take the dogs out for exercise today. You're doing a great job with Sammy. He seems to be more behaved these days. I won't be in today so I'm leaving the shop under your supervision. Don't disappoint me.

Aliyah becomes alarmed as she says, "Oh no, I forgot! It's almost 10 a.m.! Tim I have to be somewhere at 11a.m. Can you drive me home please?"

He becomes confused as he replies, "You're leaving? But it's so early."

She gets up and rushes upstairs. Tim watches and listens as she moves around upstairs.

"Who just messaged her? She was just worried about me and now she's in a rush to leave. It doesn't make sense."

Aliyah comes down the stairs with her purse saying, "I have to get home Tim. I'm in a rush."

He doesn't question her as he grabs his keys and leads her outside to his car. She quickly hops into the passenger seat and starts combing her hair. Tim gets in as he begins speculating what she's preparing for. His thoughts begin to race as he becomes suspicious.

"Why is she rushing? Who is she getting ready to see?"

He asks, "Is your dad upset?"

Aliyah replies, "No, he thinks I spent the night over Snow's house. Are you ok? You seem bothered."

Tim doubtfully says, "It's just, I don't know. You're leaving so early."

Aliyah smiles saying, "I spent the whole day and night with you Tim."

He replies, "Yeah I know but why are you leaving so early and in a hurry? You got a text from someone and suddenly started rushing."

She says, "I work at a dog kennel on Saturdays. I got a text from my manager reminding me to take the dogs out today. I know it seems like I'm rushing but I forgot. I'm not bailing on you I promise. I want to spend more time with my boyfriend." She kisses him on the cheek reassuringly.

He smiles in belief saying, "Alright."

They arrive at Aliyah's house. Alvin's car is gone to her relief. They look at each other for a moment.

Aliyah says, "Alright. I have to go. I'll miss you hero."

Tim replies, "I'll miss you too princess."

They kiss as Aliyah gets out of the car. She shuts the door.

She says, "Call me ok Mr. Derr? I should be free at 7p.m. be early."

Tim replies, "You bet."

He watches her she walks into her house. He drives away.

"It's hard not to trust her. There's this vibe you get with her. Even though you're doubtful, you just know she's genuine. I'll try not to worry too much. Aliyah isn't a liar. I'll occupy myself so I don't think too much."

He drives to his school, walks inside and goes to the office. Discreetly, he sneaks in not wanting to be caught working after 11 on a Saturday by Frawgs. He goes to his desk and begins working on paperwork. He works for 30 minutes while still thinking about Aliyah.

"Maybe I should go see her at work. It'll be a surprise. No, that's a little obsessive. I need to just relax. I need to not think so much and just trust her. Alright it's time for a snack."

He gets up to stretch. As he turns around, he becomes surprised to see Robyn. She's behind him crying silently, "Robyn? What are you doing here," he says.

She gasps for air as answers, "Tim, we need to talk."

Tim becomes frustrated as he says, "Robyn, come on. Not again."

She pleads, "Tim please."

Tim argues, "Robyn I'm at work. You can't do this here."

Robyn pleads in tears, "We're at school and they don't even pay you. I need to talk to you. Please."

CHAPTER TWENTY-TWO

Aliyah comforts Liel as he cries. She kneels to him, trying to calm him down.

She says, "Liel it's ok. I'm here. Where is dad?"

Liel replies, "I don't know. He left last night. I was scared!"

Aliyah becomes alarmed as she asks, "He left last night?"

Liel cries, "Why didn't you come home? You left me."

Aliyah begins to feel guilty. She hugs him and says, "No Liel! I never would do that. I thought dad would be here. I would never leave you by yourself."

Liel repeats, "Where were you? I needed you and you weren't here."

She pleads, "Liel, I'm so sorry. I didn't know but I'm not leaving you. Please don't think that. I thought dad was going to be here with you, since he picked you up from school."

They look back as they hear the door open. Aliyah becomes fumed as Alvin walks in with another woman.

Alvin says, "Oh good you're here. I need you to watch him. I'm going out for a while."

Aliyah shouts, "Are you crazy? You left this little boy home alone at night! What's wrong with you? You're his father!"

Alvin replies casually, "It was like 4 a.m. He was asleep when I left. He's fine."

Aliyah shouts, "Look at him, he's crying! It doesn't matter when you left! You don't leave a five year old home alone EVER!"

Alvin becomes slightly angered as she shouts. He says in a daunting tone, "Lower your tone Aliyah. Don't forget whose house you live in. Speaking of which where were you last night?"

She counters, "I told you last night. I told you I was staying over Snow's house."

Alvin says, "I don't remember that. You were supposed to be here to watch him, so I could go out."

Aliyah becomes confused, as she replies, "No, You never told me that. I would have come here and watched him if I knew that."

Alvin casually says, "I must have been drunk. Whatever, he's fine."

Aliyah becomes annoyed, "Drunk, oh what a surprise."

Alvin harshly replies, "Stop trying to lecture me, child. Since you weren't here to watch your brother last night, watch him now."

Aliyah says, "Watch him? I can't do that. I have work and I'm already late. Melissa has trusted me to watch the shop by myself today. I can't mess this up. She might promote me if I do a good job. You know I need college money."

Alvin says, "Just like your mother. What college would accept you? Don't they look down on little girls who slut around at night? Stay here and watch your brother."

Aliyah shouts, "I'm not a slut and neither was my mom! Stop saying that. It hurts. Why do you hate me so much? What did I ever do to deserve this from my own father? Tell me!"

She prepares to cry, but her newly found courage stops the river and lets but a single tear fall. She realizes this and wonders, was it because of Tim that she's gained this novel bravery? No longer backing down like a weak girl, but standing tall like a strong woman. Alvin stops and looks somewhat affected. He halts his attack as he places money on the table saying, "Just watch your brother."

He leaves with the woman as Aliyah stares in sorrow. She wipes her face as she calms down. She looks to Liel and finds a reason to smile asking, "Hey do you want to go see the puppies?"

He shakes his head excitingly. Aliyah takes him with her to the dog shelter. She sighs in relief to see it's an hour before opening. She opens the shop and let's her brother inside.

She speaks, "I have so much to do in so little time. It's 11:30 a.m. I'll just have to work fast. Hey Liel go sit at that counter for me ok? I have to clean and take care of the dogs. But when I'm done I'll let you play with the puppies ok buddy?"

He smiles and races to the counter. Aliyah begins to clean out dog cages after she sweeps the floor. She takes out a few dogs to get exercise. Liel helps out by feeding and watering the puppies. An hour passes by. Aliyah manages to finish her tasks before it's time to open the store. She lets out a relieving sigh.

She looks to Liel and says, "Ok. Let's go play with the puppies."

Liel gets excited shouting, "Yay! Can I play with Sammy? Please Aliyah?"

She says, "Sure buddy. Come on."

She takes him in the back of the store. She lets out a small black Labrador retriever and sits it on the ground. It happily runs back and forth around the store wagging its tail. It races to Liel begging to be pet. Liel smiles and holds the puppy.

He says, "Li, Li why can't we take Sammy home? He likes us a lot. Don't you think he would like living with us?"

Aliyah replies, "I'd love to take Sammy home. But dad won't let us have pets remember?"

He says, "Yeah I know. Sister, I'm sorry daddy calls you mean names."

She pats him on the head, "It's not your fault. It's ok Liel."

"Sis, I wish mommy were here. She would let us take Sammy home wouldn't she?"

Aliyah smiles, "Yes. Mommy loved animals. She's the reason why I work here. She got me this job."

A familiar voice says, "Hey. How about I buy the dog so Liel can come over and play with him anytime he wants?"

Aliyah becomes alarmed as she looks back. Regan stands holding a bouquet of flowers. She becomes unwelcoming asking, "Why are you here?"

Regan replies, "I decided to visit my amazing girlfriend at work. I even got you flowers."

She becomes annoyed, "Regan I'm not your girlfriend and I'm not taking flowers from you."

He says, "I know I messed up Aliyah. I'm sorry but I need you in my life. I can't sleep at night. I haven't been doing well with football. I've lost my drive since you left."

Aliyah firmly says, "You pushed me away Regan. When I begged you, you ignored me. It's too late for apologies. We are never getting back together."

T.Edward Redd   270

Regan begs, "Aliyah please I'm sorry. Can we please talk?"

She says, "I'm clearly at work. A customer might come in at any time. And Liel is right here. I won't argue in front of him. You need to leave."

Regan kneels to Liel, "Hey, kid. What do you think about me buying that dog for you, so you can come over and play with him any time you'd like?"

Liel says hopefully, "Really?"

Regan replies, "Yeah. Aliyah could bring you over and I'd let you see him whenever."

Aliyah interrupts "Stop it Regan. I'm not letting you use my little brother to persuade me. Get out."

Regan says, "Aliyah come on. I'm trying here. Give me a chance!"

Aliyah shouts, "Don't you get it? I don't want you in my life anymore. I'm so sick of everyone in my life mistreating me. You treat me like I'm some object that can be won over with your money and gifts. When it works you start treating me like trash. I finally get how wrong you were for me. Get out, now."

Regan says, "Here, I got you these flowers."

Aliyah snatches the flowers. She walks to a trashcan and tosses them inside it. She says, "There, I put them in a special place. Now go home, Regan."

He shouts, "Why are you acting like this? Aliyah I miss you! I need you in my life. I think about you all of the time!"

Aliyah becomes more frustrated as he continues, "I regret mistreating you. I was dumb for always putting you last. Nothing makes sense without you. I don't even play football as well now. The scouts didn't like my performance and it doesn't look like I'll be playing college ball. I have to start looking into a career plan now. Aliyah I'm sorry I hurt you. I'm sorry I didn't say I love you back, because I do." He walks to her and holds her.

Aliyah says, "Regan, I'm sorry you're having such a rough time."

He holds her as he says, "It's ok, and I know it'll get better with you around."

He becomes shocked as she gently pushes away from him, "I'm sorry things are so rough for you. But you'll have to get over it, without me. My heart isn't yours anymore. I finally see how wrong it is to be mistreated every single day by people you love. I know what it's like to be treated right. I refuse to go back to hurt. Leave."

Regan cries, "What are you saying? Aliyah please, I'm begging you!"

Aliyah says, "Regan don't you get it yet? I have moved on."

Liel plays with Sammy and says, "Hey Li, Li, maybe Tim can take Sammy!"

Regan becomes disgusted and infuriated as he says, "Tim? You're with the reject?"

Aliyah defends Tim, "Stop calling him that! You know, Tim takes a lot of crap from you. But I never hear him talk down about you. He broke your nose, but you deserved it. You were way out of line that night."

T.Edward Redd   272

Regan shouts "Why him of all people? You can do better than that loser reject!"

Aliyah shouts, "SHUT UP! He is better. Better than you!"

Regan argues, "Wha-what? How is he better than me? He doesn't have money and he's not a football player. He has nothing to offer you. He'll drag you down with him and his worthlessness."

Aliyah proudly says, "You don't know anything about him. He's successful and he's going somewhere with his life. But I don't care about that stuff. The most important thing he has is his genuine love. That's more than enough for me. I love him and I won't let you or anyone else bad mouth him. Especially not behind his back!"

Regan shouts, "How can you say you love that reject?"

Aliyah replies, "Do you really want to know? Fine, Tim makes me happy. He gives me butterflies and he makes me feel so girly. He makes me feel safe and warm in his arms. He's my hero."

Regan becomes angered, "Did you two have sex? Is that what this is about?"

She laughs softly to herself as she thinks about the night she spent with Tim. She smiles peacefully as the memories move her. Regan becomes jealous, "What's funny? Are you trying to say he's better than me in bed?"

Aliyah smiles as she says, "Way, way better. You have no idea. We didn't even have sex."

Regan laughs as he mocks Tim, "I guess he's not man enough."

Aliyah smiles to herself, "Regan, you could never understand this. Tim and I slept together but we didn't have sex. He's so sweet and charming."

Regan says, "You slept with him and didn't have sex? He has to be gay. I told you he was a reject."

Aliyah shakes her head with pity, "I think it's funny you call him a reject. No one actually rejected him. But he rejected you, Robyn and everything else that didn't support him. He rejected football to follow his dream. You're the reject Regan. Now I'm rejecting you. Leave."

Regan says, "Fine whatever. Have fun with the loser, slut." Aliyah watches as Regan leaves. She thinks to herself.

"It's strange how similar Tim and Regan's lives are. They both didn't get their mother's affection. Regan's mom cheated on his father and walked out on them when he was 7. His father is abusive. Regan started football in order to win his attention. It barely works. All his father sees is a football player now. But he can't see his son."

Liel tugs on Aliyah's shirt. She looks at him as he says, "Are you okay?"

She smiles saying, "I'm fine Liel. I'm going to go and watch for customers while I read a book Tim let me borrow. Be safe with Sammy ok?"

Liel smiles happily as she walks to the front of the store. She sits at the counter and digs into her purse to pull out *Dead Awakened.* She spends a few minutes reading, stopping to help a customer every now and then. As she gets further into the story, it begins to move her and take her away to another world. She starts to see herself in the setting, watching and hearing the characters and their actions.

T.Edward Redd

"Wow, I thought *Hero's Wake* was good. This is well written too. He has a gift. He really knows how to make the reader feel what he feels as he tells his stories."

She bookmarks the page and closes the book. She takes out *Hero's Romance.*

"This is my least favorite so far. I really don't like reading about his bad times. He's so good with words that when he writes about sad and shocking things, it actually makes you feel the pain of his experiences. There are good memories in here. But still."

She opens to a random journal entry.

It reads: *August 28, 2009*

Today was pretty bad. I did something I'll probably regret. I hung out with Karissa and her friends. Karissa wasn't being herself around them. She wouldn't let me hold her or kiss her. I guess she was uncomfortable doing that in front of them. It hurt me though. I felt as if she was embarrassed by me. How can you say you love someone yet fear what others think about the one you love?

One of her guy friends rode with us. They slept with each other apparently. She even talked about it in front of me. I was uncomfortable and felt as if I was going to have to fight for her attention. We rode to a park to smoke. I initially wasn't going to smoke. I wanted to spend time with Karissa. But she wasn't being the way she normally was when we were alone. I hated that.

My emotions got the best of me and I smoked. I got high and my emotions got worse. I opened up to her and she basically brushed me off. I know I shouldn't have gotten high but I was coping with my emotions. I mean is it horrible to want your girlfriend to show that she loves you and not just say it? Why couldn't she see I was hurting? Does it make me weak that I even care about that stuff? All I know is that today I lost to myself. She had to drive me home. I was too messed up. Today I lost. I don't deserve Karissa.

Aliyah stares at the entry as she says, "No Tim. She wasn't right for *you*."

Time passes by moderately as she continues to read. She begins to close shop around 6p.m. After she finishes she walks to Liel who is on the floor sleep with Sammy.

"Liel is so sweet. He loves that dog. I wish dad would let him have it. I wonder if Tim likes dog. Liel's birthday is coming up soon. It would be a really nice gift but Sammy couldn't stay at our house. Maybe Tim would like to take Sammy in. I bet he's great with animals."

She wakes Liel up gently, "Liel, it's time to go buddy."

He replies, "Awe, but I don't want to leave Sammy."

Aliyah says, "I know, it's just for now. Hey, let's go see Tim. He might like to adopt Sammy."

Liel becomes excited, "Oh yeah. Tim! Tim is super cool. I know he'd be really good with Sammy! Come on Li, Li. We have to hurry!"

Aliyah smiles as Liel puts Sammy in his cage.

Liel says, "Don't worry boy. Tim is my best friend. I know he'll take you in," says Liel.

Aliyah smiles as Liel walks to her and takes her hand. They walk towards the exit. She cuts off the store lights and leaves the store. She locks the door from the outside and leads Liel to her car.

CHAPTER TWENTY-THREE

Tim and Robyn argue in the office as Frawgs walks in drinking coffee. He becomes slightly annoyed to see Tim at a desk filled with papers. He sighs and walks towards Tim and Robyn.

Tim calmly says, "Robyn go home."

Robyn refuses saying, "Stop treating me like a pest! I still love you."

Tim argues, "No you don't!"

Frawgs interrupts, "Ok, ok you two, simmer down. Timothy, it's close to noon and your desk is filled with paperwork. We talked about this last Saturday."

Tim says, "Kurt, I have a really good reason to be here. I'm occupying myself to pass time so I don't stress myself out worrying."

Frawgs looks at Robyn who has tears on her face. He asks, "What's wrong with you?"

Robyn says, "Tim is a jerk. That's what's wrong! Tim, we need to talk now!"

Tim tries to stop Robyn from pouting as her whining disturbs the office. Frawgs says, "Tim here's an idea. Go talk to her, outside."

Tim says, "What? No! She won't leave me alone. She's obsessed!"

Robyn shouts, "I'm not obsessed! You were all over me until Aliyah came along! Now you act as if I don't even exist! You jerk!"

He mutters, "Why do these girls keep calling me a jerk? That's so out of my character."

Frawgs says, "Alright I have a solution. Follow me you two. Come on. We're going to work this out."

He grabs his keys and walks towards the office door. Tim becomes puzzled as he and Robyn follows Frawgs out the office. They step into the hallway.

Frawgs points to a spot in the hall as he stands by the door saying, "You two stand right there." Tim and Robyn walk to the spot he points out as they stare in confusion.

Frawgs says, "Now stand right there."

He quickly walks into the office and closes the door. Tim becomes shocked as he runs to the door yelling, "Kurt!"

Frawgs smiles as he locks the door saying, "Have a nice weekend Tim. See you Monday, don't be late."

Tim scoffs in annoyance as he looks back at Robyn. Her arms are crossed as she looks away. Tim rolls his eyes and begins walking towards the exits. Robyn follows shouting, "Hey wait!"

Tim ignores her as she walks behind him. He walks outside towards his car. Robyn catches up to him and snatches his car keys away. He looks back demanding, "Give them back Robyn."

Robyn sticks her tongue out playfully, "Take them."

Tim tries to grab the keys but she moves them away. He grabs her gently trying not to hurt her as he tries to take the keys. She playfully pins him against the car and puts the keys in his hands. Tim becomes irritated saying, "Gosh, you're so annoying."

Robyn replies, "Are you going to cry about it?"

279

Tim says, "Robyn what do you want?"

She grabs his hand as she says, "Please just listen ok? I've done a lot of thinking. I was wrong to you Tim. I regret not realizing how cruel I was. Please, Tim just a few minutes?"

He says, "Ok we're going to talk. Don't get your hopes up because this is our last talk. I'm going to help you understand that it's over ok?"

Robyn looks away doubtfully as she says, "Just walk with me and stop talking." They begin to walk. Tim remains quiet as they begin walking towards the school park. Robyn hesitates but speaks, "So I realize that I've been a pretty bad girlfriend this past month."

Tim sarcastically replies, "You mean this past year."

Robyn becomes guilty, "Ok, I deserved that. Tim I regret it. Words can't express how sorry I am. I stay awake at night thinking about you."

Tim hardens saying, "I spent months thinking about you. I wasted tears, stress and sleep wondering. Wondering if the girl I fell in love with would ever come back. These past few weeks have made me realize she never existed."

Robyn panics, as Tim shows no signs of wanting her back. She pleads, "No! Tim I'm her! I'm sorry I made a lot of mistakes. But Tim I'm still the girl you fell in love with last year. The girl you fell in love with still loves you. Don't you love her?"

She lays her head on his chest and holds him. Tim gently pushes her off saying, "Robyn, I'm with someone."

She cries, "You can leave her now! I'm sorry! You can't be in love with her, Tim. This is just you using her to make me jealous right? I had you first. We belong together Tim."

He unknowingly becomes lyrical saying, "Robyn I don't feel the way I used to about you. My love for you has faded into the abyss."

Robyn argues, "In five freaking weeks!? Your love for me has disappeared in one damn month? Now you're so in love with Aliyah?"

Tim sasses her, "Actually, I haven't been in love with you in five months. Aliyah made me realize I was clinging onto the past. I realized that I stayed with you hoping you would change into something you weren't. Just like you were trying to make me something I'm not. Robyn we're not right for each other."

Robyn rolls her eyes in annoyance as she cries, "How can you say that! You're being such a jerk! I'm pouring my heart out to you! I'm SORRY! I'm not perfect but I'm trying for you! I can change Tim."

Tim's heart doesn't soften as he says, "You're expecting me to feel sorry for you. Well I don't. You did this to me. You hurt me so many times and now you're finally waking up. Well now it's too late Robyn."

She grabs and kisses him. He tries to resist but slowly kisses her back. She holds him but he gains his senses as he pushes her away.

"Robyn! No! I'm with..." He becomes shocked to see Aliyah in the distance, watching from outside her car. He calls for her but she gets into her car and drives away. He watches with guilt.

Robyn grabs his hand saying, "Just forget about her, Tim. We can be together now. We can be an actual couple."

Tim shouts, "Robyn! We are never ever, EVER, getting back together!"

Robyn whimpers, "Tim I love you..."

Tim shouts, "No you don't! You're jealous and immature! You hate the fact that I'm with someone who can appreciate me. You hate the fact that I'm with someone else instead of being all over you when you treat me like garbage! You hate the fact that you lost! Now you want to ruin what I have with her!"

Robyn stares in tears as he calls Aliyah with his cell phone. She waits silently not knowing what else to do. Tim gets upset as the call gets sent to voicemail. He calls again. Robyn takes the phone. Tim shouts, "ROBYN!"

Robyn cries, "IT HURTS! You can stop cutting me now ok? I get it. I messed up. Just stop trying to hurt me so badly. It's too much to take all at once."

Tim becomes slightly empathetic as she weeps on his chest, numbed by his words. She holds him tight as if trying to ease her pain by squeezing him. Tim can't help but to feel sorry for a woman crying her eyes out on his chest. He slowly holds her as his soft feelings get the best of him.

He comforts her as he says, "Robyn, come on. I'm sorry. That was a bit harsh."

She catches her breath and says, "No I deserved it."

Tim replies, "Robyn."

She begs, "Take me back Tim. Please I've learned my lesson. Make this nightmare end and wake me up. You don't need her. I've changed. I promise. You're right, I am jealous. I see you two doing all the things you and I did first. You're taking her to every restaurant and everywhere we went. Seriously?"

"I'm jealous because I love you. I want to read your novels. I want to be the one that gets them for my birthday. I want to be in your life. I want you back. I love you. I don't care about football anymore. I just want to be with you."

Tim says nothing not wanting to hurt her more but not wanting to take her back either. He follows her blindly as she holds his hand. She leads him to his car as she says, "Let's get out of her babe. Come on."

Tim thinks deeply as they get into his car. They drive to his house. He holds her hand but his mind continually orbits around the memories he's shared with Aliyah. Robyn gets his attention saying, "Hey."

He replies, "Huh?"

She says, "Aren't you going to open the door?"

He says, "Oh. Yeah, the door."

He opens the door. They walk to his room. He becomes more and more depressed with each step as he notices Aliyah's absence. It's cold and quiet now that she's gone, even though he's not physically alone.

He lies on his bed as he stares blankly at the ceiling. Robyn walks to his desk and sees a picture of him and Aliyah. She rolls her eyes and picks up the original *Hero's Romance*.

She says, "Ooh one of your novels. Hero's Romance huh? I bet I can guess what this is about without even reading it."

She walks to him as she smiles saying, "It's obviously a story that talks about this hero who tells his stories of love, bravery and adventure. He gives the reader an awesome story about how he became a well-known hero and marries so hot princess in the end."

Her ignorance of his work makes him even more depressed, as he knows Aliyah would have took the time to read the novel. She wouldn't try to guess. She would be too interested in the book to care about guessing. She loves his books.

She says, "Was I right?"

Tim lies, "You nailed it. Good work."

She puts the book back and picks up the ripped version of *Hero's Wake.* She becomes alarmed saying, "Hey you ripped this? Why babe? You're such a talented writer. You shouldn't tear up something so delicate."

Tim replies trying to hold his feelings in, "Aliyah's father did that."

Robyn sighs in frustration. She calmly says, "Stop worrying about her." She sits the novel down. She walks to him smiling, "I know what will relax you."

She removes her shirt and sits beside him, beginning to kiss on his face and neck seductively. Tim's mind continues to drift as he thinks about Aliyah. He thinks about the night he spent with Aliyah. He smiles remembering him and her whispering to each other underneath the covers.

Robyn gets on top of him and kisses him. She kisses on his face and neck. Tim says, "Robyn this doesn't feel right. Let's wait ok?"

Robyn continues kissing him, as she says, "No baby I want you *now*. Just relax ok? I'll take care of you. Don't worry."

He stares at the ceiling in deep thought as she kisses him.

"All those things Robyn just told me and yet I can't stop thinking about Aliyah. I can only imagine how much she's hurting right now. Aliyah...I love her...I love her! "

T.Edward Redd   **284**

He becomes surprised. He stops Robyn as she begins to unbuckle his belt. He says, "Robyn stop! I can't do this. I'm in love with Aliyah!"

She argues, "Tim you don't love her!"

He sits up as he says with excitement, "No I actually do! I can't stop thinking about how I can't do this to her! She needs someone. She needs me and I need her! I have to go get her!"

He gets up and grabs his car keys. Robyn stares in confusion as he rushes out the room. She puts her shirt back on as she chases him.

She shouts, "No Tim. I need you! Where are you going?"

Tim smiles with enthusiasm as he answers, "To talk to my girlfriend!"

He begins to dig into his wallet as he continues, "I can't hurt her. No way. This is that moment in the story where I run to her and confess my true feelings. She'll yell at me. But in the end we'll have a happy ending. If you read one of my books or any for that matter, you'd know that. Look here's some money."

He hands her one hundred dollars, more or less. She stares in confusion asking, "What's this for?"

Tim says, "I need you to lock the door behind you and call a cab ok?"

Robyn stares, utterly confused, "A cab? Tim what's wrong with you?"

He smiles and shouts, "I'm in love with Aliyah Conrad!"

She stares not knowing what to say as he dashes out of the house. She leaves the house in defeat as he drives away. Tim drives to Aliyah's house. He forgets to turn the car off as he parks and quickly gets out. He gets confident as he runs past her car. His energy gets thrown off, as the door slams open.

He watches as Alvin storms out of the house dragging Liel with him. Alvin shoots Tim an evil glare as he walks past him towards his car. Aliyah comes out crying with a bruise on her face.

She shouts, "Dad!"

Alvin opens the car door and forces Liel inside. Aliyah cries for them as they drive off. She cries, "Bring back my brother!"

She drops to her knees crying. Tim rushes to her saying, "Hey what happened?" She cries as he kneels to her. He holds her face and stares at her new bruise. "Oh no. What did he do to you?"

She quickly hugs him tightly as she cries. He holds her and rubs her back as she holds him, seeking comfort.

He helps her up as he says, "It's ok. I'm here. Come on let's go inside."

He leads her into the house. He closes the door and says, "Aliyah what happened?" She cries as she sits at the dining room table. He sits beside her and repeats, "What happened?"

In a worked up tone she cries, "We were arguing and he hit me then Liel tried to fight him then he-", she stops and shoots Tim a hateful look.

Tim says, "Then he what?"

She becomes hostile saying, "You think I forgot don't you? You kissed Robyn!" Tim becomes weak as she shouts, "Why? After last night and you still kiss that conniving wretch! How can you of all people let me down? I need you!"

Tim replies, "I know! That's why I raced over here!"

She interrupts angrily, "Then why would you kiss her?"

Tim shouts, "Aliyah, she kissed me! I'll admit I didn't pull away. I thought maybe I wasn't over her. But, Aliyah you're all I think about. All I thought about when I was with Robyn was all the silly things you and I do."

He continues, "I couldn't stop thinking about your smile, your long brown hair, your giggle and all of the things you do to make me laugh and smile. Aliyah I love you."

He grabs her up and kisses her intensely. She holds him and embraces him as if she was waiting. They caress each other as their feelings lighten the moment. They stop kissing but continue to cuddle silently like animals in the wild. They don't need words to understand one another's love.

Tim runs his fingers through her long brown hair as she rubs his arms. They share the moment of romantic silence. After a moment of silence they look at each other and smile. Aliyah says, "How do you always make every bad moment a good one?"

He replies, "That's what I was going to ask you. Aliyah, I love you. Robyn isn't a part of my life anymore."

She kisses him and says, "I love you too."

Tim stares into her beautiful grey eyes. She holds his soothing hand to her face as if his touch takes the pain away.

"You make everything better. Thank you Tim," she says.

He rubs her face as he says, "This can't go on, Aliyah. We can't keep letting him hurt you like this. We need to start a rebellion. By rebellion I mean tell the authorities."

Aliyah laughs at his goofy humor, "Shut-up. I'm not supposed to be laughing. This isn't funny, Mr.Derr."

He tries to stop smiling saying, "Right. I am sorry, Ms. Conrad." He says in an overly professional like manner, "Tell me what happened, please."

She looks at him in annoyance, as she tries not to laugh too.

Tim says, "Ok I'm sorry. Go on."

She explains, "I came home and I guess I forgot to turn the stove off. My dad was in the kitchen letting the smoke out. He started yelling at me but his speech was slurred. I asked him if he was drunk and he slapped me across the face."

She lets out a heavy sigh as she holds her head and continues, "Why does he hate me so much? I never did anything to deserve this. I'm his daughter and he hates me."

She begins to sob. Tim holds her saying, "He doesn't hate you ,Aliyah."

She shouts, crying, "HE DOES HATE ME! HE SAYS IT ALL THE TIME! Every day he calls me a slut. He thinks I'm trashy! I've only had sex with one person! Maybe he's right though. Maybe I am worthless. If I weren't, everyone I know wouldn't hurt me like they do."

She looks at Tim, as he holds her shoulder, "No, I'm not going to let you do that to yourself, Aliyah. I know you don't really mean that."

She wipes her face, as she weakly says, "Why shouldn't I? Everyone else does."

He says, "Who cares about everyone else. Who needs them? You've got me and I've got you. Your opinion is the only one that matters to me Aliyah. People will try to make you hate yourself just like they learned to hate themselves. You have to be stronger than them."

"Look at you. You're everything a guy could ask for, everything a person could ask for in a friend. You're a great daughter and sister. Aliyah I love the person I see when I look at you. You're beautiful inside and out. You're so beautiful yet you don't let your looks define you. You're so effing hot."

She blushes as she giggles. She hugs him tightly and kisses him on the cheek saying, "You're so effing corny!"

Tim says, "Ok I shouldn't have said effing. You never curse and I don't want you to start. And no I'm not!"

Aliyah laughs at him saying, "I was teasing you! Stop being so sensitive!"

She pinches his side. He lifts her off the ground and puts her over his shoulder. She laughs happily as he carries her into the living room. He playfully slams her onto the couch and wrestles with her. Their play fighting evolves into romantic touching and kissing. They cuddle lightheartedly as they fight for couch space, laughing.

Aliyah says, "I love you."

Tim says, "I love you more."

Aliyah says, "Well I love you more plus one."

Tim counters, "Well I love you infinity plus one. Bam. Can you top that?"

Aliyah says, "How about I love you infinity times infinity? Uh oh, trouble."

Tim humors her as he gasps in shock. She laughs and holds him. He notices her crying and says, "Hey what's wrong? You're crying."

She smiles saying, "I'm not crying because I'm sad. I'm really happy right now. I started crying but I'm not sad at all. Not anymore. You're my guardian angel Tim."

She kisses his cheek. She lays on him and places her head on his chest. Tim looks at her asking, "You believe in angels?"

She cheerfully replies, "I'm looking at one. Of course I do."

He says, "What about God?"

Aliyah proudly replies, "Definitely. Don't you?"

Tim says nothing as she looks at him.

She becomes slightly unmoved as she asks, "Wait, do you?"

Tim replies, "I used to. But now, I'm not so sure."

Aliyah becomes worried saying, "Tim why? Everyone should believe in something."

He argues, "What kind of God would watch its creations suffer the way we do? It's supposed to be this high and mighty being that created everything from nothing. It has the power to do anything. Doesn't that mean it causes our suffering? Even if it doesn't shouldn't it intervene and stop our suffering?"

Aliyah says, "He works in mysterious ways Tim. I know how you feel. But he's not as bad as you're making him out to be. He's made things easier for me. He sent you and led me to you."

Tim looks at her for a moment as he thinks.

"I never thought about it like that. All this time I've begged God for someone. She's been here this whole time. It's taken me my entire high school career to see it."

Aliyah continues, "My life isn't perfect at all. But it could be much worse you know? I think that God wants us to do things on our own with the power he's blessed us with, instead of us always expecting him to just make things happen out of thin air. He wants to see his creations make their own miracles happen and thank him for the power he's blessed us with."

Tim looks at her with amazement as he says, "That makes a lot of sense. Aliyah I had no idea you were so religious. I didn't get bored from hearing you say it either. You should consider preaching."

She laughs in flattery as she says, "I'm not that religious. I just read my bible a lot and have a very strong belief in God. There has to be a God. Sometimes it feels like he's forgotten about us. But he never does Tim. He doesn't forget about anyone. Not even you. He helps us when we need it. But until we need his help, we need to use the power we already have."

Tim smiles at her as he says, "Thanks, Aliyah. Maybe you're right. He did lead me to you. Maybe he is out there."

They hold each other as they fall asleep.

CHAPTER TWENTY-FOUR

Tim and Aliyah sleep as they hold each other lovingly. Aliyah wakes up as her cell phone vibrates on her nightstand. She blinks her eyes as she tries to wake herself up.

"Oh, we must have fallen asleep. I feel like I've been asleep for years." She looks to Tim, *"He makes it so cozy."*

She smiles as Tim rest beside her. She looks to her dresser and sees her phone vibrating, *"What time is it? Who would be calling this late?"*

She gets up and walks to her dresser. She checks her phone to see her father is calling her. She looks puzzled.

"Dad never calls me." She answers the phone and says, "Dad?"

She listens for a moment. Her face turns from plain to shocked as she says, "You what?"

Alvin interrupts her, as he speaks. She becomes frantic and horrid as she begins panicking. Tim slowly wakes up to the commotion as Aliyah argues with her father on the phone.

She says, "Oh my gosh. I can't believe this is happening! I'm on my way." She ends the call. She looks back to see Tim watching.

He says, "Are you ok?"

She replies, "Yes but you need to leave. I need to drive somewhere. It's an emergency."

Tim becomes worried as he sees worry in her eyes, "What happened? You look like you're going to cry."

She tries to remain calm, "Tim please, you have to leave. I need to go. There's an emergency."

Tim gets out of bed, "What's the emergency? I'll go with you."

"Tim! Seriously! I need to be alone! Go home and I will call later. I need to go," she says.

Tim puts his shoes on as he stares at her in confusion. She struggles and tries not to cry. He walks to her saying, "Aliyah please talk to me. What happened?"

She hugs him tightly, and begins crying slowly. She says, "It's probably nothing. But I need to go. I don't want to worry you with this ok? You go home and get some sleep. I will talk to you in the morning."

She let's go of him. He stands not wanting to go but agrees to leave.

He says, "Whatever happened, I hope it gets better. I'm here for you, Aliyah. I'll check up on you later tonight."

He begins to walk away. Aliyah rushes to him and hugs him tightly from behind, as she cries, "Please don't change, Tim I love you. Promise me you won't change. Promise me."

Tim turns to her. He kisses her and comforts her, "I promise, Aliyah. Please call me if you need anything."

She watches as he leaves the house and drives home. She grabs her diary and writes in it for a few minutes as she cries. She opens her dresser and places the diary inside. She leaves the house.

She drives down the road for a few minutes. The road is empty and dark without any cars in sight. She starts to feel a horrid feeling turning in the pit of her stomach as it begins to rain. As if a foreshadowing for what's to come as she drives.

She begins to see a traffic jam as she drives. More and more fearful, she becomes, as she starts to see blue and red flashes of light as she joins the traffic jam. Cop cars, news vans and ambulances surround three crashed vehicles. Aliyah becomes petrified to see her father's car is one of the vehicles in the crash site. It's totaled.

She begins to shed a few tears as she says, "Oh God. Please, no." She parks her car in the middle of the traffic jam. A car frightens her with a loud honk as she steps out in front of slowly moving vehicles.

In a panic she yells, "Sorry!"

She looks towards the crash site. Her heartbeat speed up as she walks slowly towards the accident. She enters a crowd and begins to fidget with her hair as she sees medics running around a stretcher. Her heartbeat drowns out the noise of everything else. She gets closer in suspense to see whose body lies on the stretcher.

She becomes anxious and begins pushing through the crowd, not being able to take any more suspense. A police officer blocks her path saying, "Ma'me, please stay back!"

Aliyah pleads, "I need to see," her sentence comes to an end as she sees whose body is on the stretcher. Liel lies on it unconscious, covered in scratches and bruises, hooked up to a breathing machine.

Aliyah screams in terror, "No! LIEL!"

She cries, as she breaks free from the officer's grip. She rushes to her baby brother screaming. She runs to the stretcher, leans on it screaming and begging for Liel to wake up. The medics try to pull her away but she refuses to leave his side.

She pleads, "Liel! Liel say something! Your big sister is here Liel, please talk to me!" She stares in horror, as Liel doesn't move, let alone respond.

A medic sorrowfully says, "Sorry, we were too late."

Aliyah holds her head as her pain and sadness, peaks "No, no, no, no, NO!" She lets out a horrifyingly loud scream of anger and sorrow. The crowd watches with grief as she begins to cry over Liel's body and screams. The rain begins to pour down harder.

Alvin pushes through the crowd. His face fills with hurt as he sees Aliyah crying over Liel's body. He runs to her calling for her. She instantly opens her eyes as she hears his voice but doesn't turn her back. She stands, as he gets close. She begins hitting him in a rage right before he tries to hug her. She claws him across the face.

She shouts, "How did this happen? What have you done? What have you done to him!"

Alvin falls to the ground as he stares at her in shock and sorrow. Aliyah cries, "What did you do to my baby brother? I hate you! I *HATE* YOU!"

She tries to attack him again but the medics hold her back. Alvin watches in sorrow. She shouts at him, "First my mom and now my brother! Damn you! Damn you! You monster! YOU MONSTER!"

She stops as the medics place the stretcher in the ambulance. She looks back. She pleads, "No! Liel! Don't leave me! I need you! Liel!"

She screams in sorrow as police officers gently hold her back as the ambulance prepares to drive off. Alvin walks to her and says, "Come on, we're going to follow them to the hospital. We need to go as a family. I don't think it's safe for you to drive right now. I'll drive your car ok?"

She doesn't react as he opens the door for her. She slowly gets inside. They begin to drive. Alvin follows the ambulance. He looks to see Aliyah crying next to him.

"Aliyah," he says softly.

Aliyah shouts, "Pay attention to the road! Or do you want to kill me too? You'd love that wouldn't you? I bet you wish it were me instead!"

He cries, "No Aliyah! I don't! I'm sorry!"

Aliyah shouts, "Can it, monster! I can never forgive you for what you've done. I never want to speak to you again! You killed mom and now you've killed Liel! I HATE YOU. YOU'RE DEAD TO ME!!"

Alvin begins to cry silently as they begin to approach the hospital. He drives to the emergency wing entrance and parks. Aliyah quickly unfastens her seatbelt. Alvin tries to talk to her only to have the door slammed into his face. He puts his head down on the steering wheel and slams his fist on the dashboard as he cries.

Aliyah races through the hospital after getting Liel's room number. She finds the room but is told to sit and wait until the medics are ready. Her sit last for half an hour as she pulls on her hair nervously.

"They could've made a mistake. It happens all the time. Miracles can happen. Liel isn't going to die. He can't die. He's all I have left."

Her phone vibrates. She checks it and sees that Tim is calling. She puts it away.

"I can't worry him with this. There's nothing to worry about. My brother is fine."

A doctor comes out of the Liel's room. Aliyah stares in fear.

He asks, "Are you the mother of Liel Conrad?"

Aliyah replies, "No. His mother died a few years ago. I'm the closest thing to a mother he's got though. I'm his sister."

He says, "Where is his father?"

She says, "How is Liel? Does he want something to eat or some toys?"

Her eyes fill with tears as he sits beside her saying, "Aliyah your brother passed away."

Aliyah cries, "That can't be right. You have to check again! Doctors make these mistakes all the time. There has to be something you can do. You guys didn't try hard enough! Check again!"

He empathetically says, "Liel was dead before he reached the patient room, miss. There was nothing we could do. I'm so sorry."

She says, "His birthday was in a few weeks. This can't be real. He was only five."

The doctor tries to comfort her, "I know. I hate telling people this kind of news. If I could, I'd do everything I could to bring him back. I'm sorry Aliyah. Is there anything I can get for you?"

She shakes her head, "No, no it's fine. I just need to be alone."

The doctor allows her some time alone. She spends a few moments in silence, occasionally looking at her phone. She thinks about calling Tim but doesn't. As Alvin walks towards her from down the hall, she becomes enraged. He walks to her and instantly notices the bruise.

He looks sad as he says, "Your face..." Aliyah glares as he says, "Aliyah I'm so sorry. I shouldn't have hit you. I'm..."

She finishes his sentence, "A bad father? Don't worry. *Everyone* but you knows that. It's not big news at all."

Alvin sadly says, "Yes. I'm a bad father. I was a bad husband and I lost my wife and now I've lost my son. You're all I have left."

Aliyah barks, "Wrong! You lost me a long time ago!"

Alvin cries, "Aliyah."

Aliyah coldly says, "You have robbed me of literally, everything I've ever loved. I can never forgive you for what you've done. I don't pity you at all. I hope you live with this feeling for the rest of your miserable and meaningless life. I want nothing to do with you. After I graduate I'm leaving and I never want to see you again. Not even at your funeral."

She gets up and begins walking away. Alvin stares at the floor crying as Aliyah walks toward the exits crying.

CHAPTER TWENTY-FIVE

Tim sits in his room folding laundry. He looks plainly as he begins folding his whites. Since Aliyah left that night, he hasn't stopped thinking about her. It feels as though she has vanished from the face of the Earth.

"It's been almost a whole week since I've heard from Aliyah. I have no idea what happened. The last time I saw her she looked really worried. What if something happened to her?"

He puts his whites into his dresser drawers. His mind continues to ponder on what may have possibly happened. In order to stop the thoughts, he begins reorganizing his bookshelf. He can't help but to glance at his cell phone lying on his bed.

"She hasn't returned any of my calls. It's as if she has completely vanished. Was it something I did? She told me everything was ok. But why would she start ignoring me like this? I've sent 12 messages and she hasn't replied to any of them. Maybe she's mad at me for the other day. When she saw Robyn and I kissing. So, maybe she doesn't want anything to do with me now."

He gets on his computer and begins working on a story in order to occupy his mind. His heart begs his mind to listen as he struggles to type.

After deleting a whole paragraph, he stops to find focus.

"What should I do? If she's upset all I can do is try to talk to her. But if she doesn't even respond to my calls or texts how can I get through to her?"

He begins typing on the computer but stops to look around his room. The room used to be his haven. But now it's just like the rest of the house. There is nothing but silence and warm air. Though he is used to silence. This silence is a bit different. It's the silence of absence, not loneliness.

He stops typing and deletes what he typed. His writing doesn't satisfy him as he tries again. Again he deletes his writing, then again. He writes from his heart, but at the moment, his heart is disturbed. It's as if it can hear the cries of Aliyah's heart as it tries to tell hiss mind, something is wrong. Eventually, he takes a break.

"I can't think clearly with her on my mind. Did I mess things up? What if she's gone back to Regan? He's not right for her at all! I can understand me messing up. But she can't leave me for him. She deserves better."

He begins typing a text on his phone. He deletes his draft and closes his phone.

"I don't want to fill her phone up with messages. She'll think I'm being annoying like Robyn did. This is exactly how things were right before Robyn broke up with me the first time. What can I do? Should I just try to move on and forget about her?"

Tim leaves his house in the middle of the day. Not in a driving mood, he decides to take a walk in the nice neighborhood. He looks deep with thought as he stares at the ground as he walks. A young woman with freckles and shoulder length red hair walks in his path and he looks at her.

She smiles at him. Tim keeps his deep thought expression, slowly crawling into his abandoned shell. The woman gets an annoyed expression and walks passed him. He stops to realize how depressing he was before he met Aliyah. He looks back at the woman and calls, "Excuse me miss." She looks back as he says, "You look really nice."

She smiles, "Thank you. I'm Jane."

Tim replies, "It's nice to meet you. I'm Tim. Do you want to walk with me for a while Jane?"

She smiles saying, "Sure." They begin to walk with each other down the neighborhood. Jane looks at Tim, as he remains quiet.

She says, "You're really quiet Tim. You must be the shy type huh? It's ok. I like shy guys. It says something when a girl makes a shy guy talk."

Tim replies, "I used to be somewhat of a loner. But recently, I've found out that I don't really like being a loner. I like being around people. Someone close to me, showed me that people aren't as scary as I make them out to be."

He thinks about his first encounter with Aliyah and how his first thoughts about her were wrong. He smiles as he thinks about her more and more.

Jane replies, "Oh I see. I used to be pretty quiet too. This was my last year of high school. I decided that I don't want to be quiet for another 4 years. So are you in college?"

Tim replies, "I will be this upcoming year."

Jane smiles saying, "Nice! We'll both be freshmen. What major do you think you want to pursue?"

Tim replies, "English Major and Accounting."

She becomes excited, saying, "No way! I want to be an English Major too! I guess the next thing you'll say, is you're going to publish books too."

Tim becomes embarrassed as he smiles at her, "Actually I've already published two."

She becomes hysterical and gasps, "No way! That's so cool. You're not even in college yet! Wow, I'm so jealous. What books have you written?"

Tim replies, "Well I doubt you've read the latest one since it's not on shelves yet. But I released *Hero's Wake* last summer. That one is somewhat popular."

She becomes shocked saying, "Wait I've read that. A boy has trouble staying faithful to his girlfriend after she starts ignoring him. Then a new girl shows up in his life and makes things tempting for him?"

Tim smiles saying, "So you've read it?"

Jane shouts, "I loved that book! I'm a hopeless romantic so it's my kind of book. Wait a minute… you're Timothy Derr aren't you!?" Tim smiles as she becomes star struck, "I can't believe it's you! I loved *Hero's Wake*! This is so cool. How old are you?"

Tim replies, "I'm 18."

Jane becomes dumbfounded, "Whoa! You must be a genius. That's really cool! I bet by the time you're twenty you'll be really amazing. I mean you're already amazing now. But, you know what I mean."

Tim smiles as he stays humble asking, "So what do you write about?"

Jane replies nervously, "Me? Oh um well I used to write a lot of romance but I was never able to hold my reader's attention. I'm obviously light years behind you." She puts her hand on his saying, "Hey, maybe you could give me some pointers?" She blushes.

Tim politely pulls his hand away saying, "Sure it's not hard at all."

She pulls her hand away, embarrassed and looks away smiling and blushing.

Tim asks, "Are you alright?"

She replies embarrassed, "I am," she giggles, "It's just meeting you in person. I never would have imagined that I'd get the chance. Your novel is so amazing. I fall in love with your words."

Tim smiles kindly, saying, "Thank you, I'm flattered."

She holds her face franticly, "This is so embarrassing. Am I blushing? Sorry. I've always had this *crush* on you. I know that's weird since we've never met. But the way you write, it's so heavenly. I know as a writer if you can write it, you've felt it. You're so deep and romantic. It's a lot to take in. I'm just nervous."

Tim replies, "Haha, I've never met such a big fan before."

He thinks, *"This girl is perfect. Where did she even come from? We have so much in common. Still, I can't take my mind off of Aliyah. Aliyah, she's beyond perfect. Something has happened. I can feel it. Aliyah wouldn't just ignore me like this."*

Jane leans on him and touches his arm, "You know, Tim. I can be more than a fan. I'm not obsessed or anything. I just admire your work. But I want to get to know who *you* are."

She holds his hand. She kisses him on the lips. He pulls away. She panics, "Oh no. I'm so sorry. I just thought that…"

Tim replies, "No. Jane you're fine. That was sweet. Everything you said and the kiss. You're a really nice girl. It's just I'm with someone. Someone I really care about."

Jane becomes surprised saying, "Oh I can get that. Well she's a very lucky girl Mr. Derr. I should get going. Um can I have your autograph?" She hands him a book and pen. Tim gladly takes the book. He looks at the cover.

He says, "*Lost in Tears*? Did you write this?"

She replies, "Yes, I hope to publish it soon. Meeting you has inspired me greatly. I'll take the signature as motivation to someday reach my dreams like you are."

Tim signs the cover, wishing her good luck on her writing: *I'm glad I could inspire you. Good luck Jane.*

Jane says, "Thank you. It was nice to meet you, Mr. Derr. Take care of her. She has to be very special if she's with you."

They wave each other bye. Tim watches her as she walks away. He thinks deeply about Aliyah.

"That girl was great. But Aliyah, she's more than just some girl to me. I need to find out why she isn't responding to me. Something is wrong and I can feel it."

He calls her but she doesn't answer. He continues walking around for half an hour. He tries to come up with possible reasons why she would be ignoring him. Eventually, he arrives at his school and goes inside out of boredom. He begins to recount the times he has seen Aliyah before actually knowing her. He begins walking to her locker as if he's reliving the first time they met. Dozens of get better notes and letters lie stuck to her locker to his surprise. He takes off a note to read it.

The letter reads: ***Hope you're doing better. Keep your head up.***

Tim becomes confused, not knowing what has happened. He turns around and sees Regan standing with a card. He glares at Tim as he places the card on Aliyah's locker. Regan walks away.

"What's going on? Is she sick or something?"

He walks to the sports hall where Aliyah normally leads the cheer team's practice sessions. He sees Snow walk around from a corner, towards him.

He says, "Snow! Where's Aliyah? Have you seen her?"

Snow walks to him as she says, "Huh?"

He replies, "Aliyah has been ignoring me for five days. I haven't seen her around here either. What's happened? I saw her locker."

Snow empathetically replies, "Her little brother died in a car accident."

Tim gasps in shock, "What?"

She says, "Yeah last week her father and brother got into an accident. Her father came out with a few scratches and bruises. But her brother didn't make it. She didn't come to school after. I don't blame her. I can't imagine losing my brother."

Tim stammers with disbelief, "Liel is… dead?"

Snow replies, "Don't you watch the news? It's been on all week now. No one has even seen Aliyah. I can only imagine how she's feeling right now. She probably didn't want you to worry."

He replies, "But I am worried! She should've told me! Thanks Snow I need to go." He turns around and runs to the exits. As if he's a running back, he races full sprint to Aliyah's house. Stopping at the driveway, he catches his breath.

He smiles as he sees her car in the driveway. Breathing heavily, he walks to the door and knocks. He becomes slightly intimidated when Alvin opens the door. He notices a scratch across Alvin's face.

Tears are in Alvin's eyes but Tim doesn't notice as he says, "Hey, can I see Aliyah?"

Tim becomes annoyed thinking Alvin is lying when he says, "She's not here."

Tim turn away saying, "Ok. I'll just come by later."

As he walks away Alvin cries, "She's been missing for 3 days." Tim looks back with shock as he continues, "Can you help me find her? She's all I have left. I don't know what I'll do if something happened to her too."

Tim walks to Alvin as he says, "It's going to be alright Mr. Conrad. I'll help you find her. Let's go inside."

Tim sits on the couch in Alvin's living. He waits for Alvin *patiently.*

"This can't be good. I've heard so many bad things about him. To see him cry like this. It makes me fear for Aliyah's safety. Shoot, I shouldn't have been so passive that night. I was so worried about not annoying her that I let it go. I feel horrible."

Alvin walks into the living room with two beers. Tim watches with discomfort, as Alvin is already halfway finished with his beer. He sits the beers down as he sits by Tim.

He says, "I'm a horrible father. I lost Elena because I was a horrible husband. I lost Liel and now I've lost Aliyah because I'm a horrible father. Everything is my fault." He takes a big gulp of beer.

Tim looks mournful. He looks around the house. Broken beer bottle glass rests on the floor throughout the house. Tim's tone angers as he asks, "That scar on your face and this broken glass on the floor. Did you two get into a fight? Did you hurt her?"

Alvin replies with shame, "Not this time. I wanted to talk to her. I wanted to try and be her father and just try and comfort her. She kept asking if I was drunk when I crashed the car. I swear to you, I wasn't drunk. I was trying to comfort Liel. He kept screaming for his sister. I took my eye off the road for a split second. That's all I remember."

Tim's anger dies out as his heart softens to the tears of another human being, "I wake up on a stretcher. My first thought is, 'where is Liel?' Then I see him dead on a stretcher! I didn't mean for any of this to happen. It should be me that's dead. I deserve it. I'm a worthless father."

Tim says, "Don't say that. You don't deserve to be dead. But you do need to be a better father for Aliyah. She needs you. You're all she has left."

Alvin finishes his beer. Tim looks with pity as Alvin sits the beer down. He looks at the other one on the table and says, "That one is for you. I'm sorry for the other night. I hope you can forgive me."

Tim replies, "It's fine sir and I don't drink. You shouldn't either. At least not this much."

Alvin says, "It helps me get relaxed. I'm so frustrated and sad. Alcohol helps me cope with everything. I lost my wife, I lost my job, I've lost my son and now I'm losing Aliyah."

He reaches for the beer but Tim becomes angry and stops him saying, "No. Beer isn't helping you relax. It's making things worse. She tells me all of the things you say and do to her.

"She's told me you hit her, that you call her names and the worst that you hate her and that she disgusts you! No child needs to hear that from its only parent! She counts on you for safety and comfort. Do you realize how bad you're damaging her?"

He stops himself as he sees Alvin shed a single tear as his lip quivers. Tim becomes guilty and says, "I'm...I'm sorry. I didn't mean to come off so harsh and mild-toned it's just..."

Alvin smiles sadly saying, "No. Let me have it. I deserve it. You're really good with your words. I can see how you would sell so many books. You think I'm a monster don't you?"

Tim explains, "I don't think that at all. I think you miss your wife. You're angry with yourself. You blame yourself for her death and take your rage out on Aliyah. I think you're a great father. You're just going through so much and you don't know how to deal with it properly."

Alvin says, "You're a pretty good kid Tim. Aliyah talks about you all of the time. You care about her don't you?"

Tim smiles to himself as he replies, "Very much so, yes."

Alvin replies, "I'm glad she has you. I can tell you care deeply about her. To add to that, I can also tell you're a pretty good kid. She cares a lot about you too. I'm really sorry for how I was when we met for the first time."

T.Edward Redd

Tim replies, "Don't worry about that, Mr. Conrad. We need to focus on finding Aliyah. Where is she?"

Alvin replies, "I don't know. She won't answer my phone calls. I can't lose my baby girl, Tim. I know you'll be able to find her. She hates *me* right now."

Tim says, "What did she say before she left?"

Alvin says, "She blamed me for her mother's death. She threw all my beer bottles on the ground and blamed my drinking for Liel's death. Maybe you'll find something in her room."

He walks to the kitchen as he tosses the other beer into the trash. Tim stands up and walks to Aliyah's room. He sits on her bed and thinks hard about where she could be.

"I can only imagine how she's feeling right now. Liel, was her everything. Without him she might feel hopeless. It's like I can hear her cries...feel her tears. Aliyah let me help you please."

He looks around her room and he fixes his eyes on her dresser. He walks to the dresser as he sees a pink journal.

"I didn't know she wrote." He opens the diary and begins reading:

Life is so strange...things seemed to be going so much...better. Father hasn't changed at all. But I was happier. Since Timothy entered my life I've felt so free. He makes me feel alive. As if I matter. Just when life gives me my dream it takes away my hope...Liel was everything to me. With him gone I just don't see the point in anything anymore. I used to think I was enough. Now I don't feel enough for anyone. I'm worthless. I'm an empty shell with no purpose...I don't want to live anymore. Timothy deserves someone stronger. Mother I wish you were here...

My final entry.

"I might know where she is," Tim says.

T.Edward Redd **310**

CHAPTER TWENTY-SIX

*Life is so strange...things seemed to be going so much...better.
Father hasn't changed at all. But I was happier. Since Timothy
entered my life I've felt so free. He makes me feel alive. As if I
matter. Just when life gives me my dream it takes away my
hope...Liel was everything to me. With him gone I just don't see
the point in anything anymore. I used to think I was enough.
Now I don't feel enough for anyone. I'm worthless. I'm an empty
shell with no purpose...I don't want to live anymore. Timothy
deserves someone stronger. Mother I wish you were here...*

My final entry.

Aliyah sits at a graveyard as it lightly rains. She sits in front
of a tombstone. It read: *Elena Scott.*

Aliyah sheds a tear, "Hey mom. It's me. I haven't been doing
too well. Everything has fallen apart since you left. I tried my
best to take care of Liel. I tried to raise him well. I really did."
She snivels as she struggles to confess, "There was an accident
and Liel, well, he died," she chokes

"I'm so sorry mom," she cries, "I wish you were here. I miss
you so much. None of it's fair. This is too much to bear on my
own. Why did you have to go so early, huh," she cries, "you
really thought I could take care of this family by myself? I feel
so worthless and alone. I know you're probably disappointed in
me."

She takes out a bottle of aspirin and eats a pill, "You know, there's this boy, Timothy Derr. He's really great mom. You would love him. His heart is just like yours. He's been really good to me. But mom, how can I ever be enough for him? He's this successful writer. He's sweet and family oriented. I don't deserve someone like that. Look at me, I let this family fall apart and I failed you miserably."

She takes another pill as she sheds a tear, "Mom, I'm sorry. I've failed you. I'm too weak and I just can't stand feeling so worthless and sad ALL of the time. Please forgive me, mother. I know that I probably won't meet you and Liel after I do this, but this is too much to endure. I hope you two are somewhere smiling and safe. Goodbye."

She begins to pour several aspirin into her hand. She becomes alarmed as someone grabs her hand, making her drop the aspirin into the wet and muddied grass.

"Aliyah! What are you doing?" She looks back in shock to see Tim holding her hand as he continues, "You're going to kill yourself now? After everything you've been through! You're just going to end it now?"

Aliyah cries in pain, "Tim it hurts too much! I can't deal with this pain!"

She reaches for the bottle of aspirin saying, "Aliyah, give me the pills."

Aliyah shouts, "No! I want to die! Just leave me alone and go away!"

Tim wrestles her for the bottle of pain pills as she screams and cries. He breaks her grip and snatches the aspirin away. Aliyah gives up on fighting for the bottle as she breaks down in tears. Tim hugs her tightly as if protecting her.

T.Edward Redd   **312**

He pleads, "Aliyah your mom doesn't want you to kill yourself. I can only imagine how painful it is for you right now, but you absolutely cannot kill yourself. You're not worthless ok? You're NOT. It's ok to hurt and it's ok to cry. But don't you dare give up. None of this makes you worthless."

Aliyah holds him as she sobs, "It hurts so much Tim. I let, Liel die. I let that monster take him away and now he's dead."

Tim holds her, "Don't blame yourself, Aliyah. Why did you try to deal with this alone? You ignored me for five days. What about me, huh? If you would have killed yourself, think how bad I would be hurting. I love you. You can't go like that Aliyah," he hugs her tight.

She holds him "I didn't want you to worry, Tim."

He says, "Well you did. Don't be afraid to come to me for anything ok? Stop saying you're not good enough. You're beyond perfect."

Aliyah starts to feel secure as she says, "Thank you, Tim. I really needed that."

They hold each other in the wet grass as it continues to rain. Tim looks at Elena's grave. He asks, "Is this your mother's grave?"

Aliyah shakes her head yes as she asks, "How did you know where to find me?"

He answers, "Your diary. You write a lot about your mom. It just so happened she was buried here. We can stay as long as you want. But I'm not letting you walk home alone. It's getting pretty late."

Aliyah says, "I'm not going back home. Not to him."

Tim says, "Aliyah your father is worried."

Aliyah shouts, "He doesn't care about me!"

Tim calmly says, "He does Aliyah. He wants you to come back."

She cries, "Why? So he can hit on me some more and call me a slut or whore? I HATE him!"

Tim says, "Aliyah you don't mean that."

She becomes angry and coldly says, "No Tim you don't understand. I *hate* him. I cannot stand him. Everything he's done to me and everything he's taken from me. The only thing that was keeping me from expressing my hate was Liel. But he killed him with his drinking habit. I wish it were dad that died!"

Tim holds her hand soothingly, saying, "You don't mean that. Your dad regrets the things he's said and done. He doesn't hate you, he loves you."

Aliyah shouts, "I'm sorry. I didn't realize *you* lost your brother!" Tim remains silent as she shouts, "You don't know how I feel! Your father is perfect. He deserves a father of the century award. Your father doesn't hit you! He doesn't try to break you down with his words every chance he gets. Your father actually cares about you."

Tim replies, "I do know how you feel. Or did you forget that I hate my mom?"

Aliyah says, "And now I know what you meant. I know what you meant when you said you couldn't stand her. I feel the same way!"

Tim replies, "Only except you were right."

Aliyah becomes confused, "What?"

He says, "You were right when I said I didn't hate her. I hate the fact that she isn't in my life. I miss her and I hate that I never felt her love. Now I know what *you* meant when you said I didn't mean what I said. You hate that your dad doesn't show the love a daughter needs from her father. You love your father and you wish he would show he loves you."

Aliyah shouts, "I'm not going home! I don't care what you say to me."

Tim holds her close as she looks away. He kisses her on the cheek saying, "Aliyah, let's go to my house and figure something out. We need to get out of this harsh weather or we'll both catch colds."

They hold hands as they walk. Aliyah looks back at her mother's grave as if saying goodbye. They walk for what seems like ages as they approach Tim's house. Tim smiles trying to lighten the moment, "Hey, I thought you was against long walks."

She softly says, "This time was different. Is your dad ever home? It's almost 8p.m and I don't see his car."

Tim replies, "Yeah, he should be here any time now."

He opens the door for her and let's her walk in first. She yawns restlessly as she walks to the living room and lies down on the couch.

"Would you hold me please," she asks.

He sits beside her. She scoots close as she wraps her arms around his stomach, lying down. She snuggles as she slowly finds comfort in his hold.

Tim rubs her back saying, "Do you have a place to stay Aliyah? Look I know you're upset with your father but he really does mean well. You should talk to him. I'll go with you ok?"

He looks to see she has fallen asleep, finally calming down for the moment. He kisses on her forehead as he gets up. Under her head, he places a pillow and a blanket over her body. He begins to take her shoes off of her feet.

"She's had a rough week. I'll let her sleep peacefully."

He walks to his room. For a while, he cleans. After reorganizing his bookshelf once again, he sits at his desk and turns on his computer. He begins to edit a book, *Hoi de Space*. For almost an hour, he works. He becomes startled as someone makes noise on his bed. He flinches and looks back.

Aliyah sits up saying, "I'm sorry. I didn't mean to scare you. I woke up by myself downstairs. I want to be by you."

Tim says, "No you didn't scare me. You weren't sleep too long. How are you holding up?"

He walks to her as she begins to shake her head no as she sheds a tear. She begins to cry softly in his arms as he holds her. He pats her back as she struggles to breathe. A few minutes pass as Tim gives her time to relax.

She weakly says, "The funeral is tomorrow. Why did it have to be my brother? He was so young. He would be six next week."

Tim replies, "Life is strange like that sometimes. I'm sorry Aliyah. You can relax and heal here all night ok? Do you want anything?"

She shakes her head no saying, "Just you." She kisses him on the cheek, "I love you, Tim. You're so amazing and comforting. I would've been dead right now, if it wasn't for you."

Tim replies, "I know how it feels to want to die. I was lucky enough to survive my suicide attempt. I didn't want you to try and not get lucky like I did. Aliyah I love you too. Please don't leave like that."

She says, "I feel bad about it. I was so worked up and emotional. It just got hard to handle. But I don't really want to die. Tim, can I stay here with you?"

He replies, "The whole night?"

Aliyah smiles and says, "Yeah. Don't you think it was fun sleeping with each other? It felt so pleasing and safe to be in your arms. I don't want to be alone tonight and I have nowhere to go. But you ease my pain. I need you."

Tim becomes nervous knowing his dad will be home soon. He says, "Aliyah what about my dad?"

She replies, "You're dad is just as nice as you. He won't mind. Besides you just told me I could stay here all night so I could heal and relax. I can't do it alone though. Please, Tim?"

Tim smiles saying, "Ok, Aliyah. You can stay. I'll figure something out."

She hugs him tight saying, "You're so good to me, Mr. Derr. You spoil me rotten."

Tim rubs her back saying, "You haven't been spoiled enough, Ms. Conrad."

They kiss as they hold each other. Tim playfully tickles her and makes her giggle. She tries to tickle him back as they begin playfully wrestling on the bed. Aliyah harmlessly hits him with a pillow. Tim pins her down and begins to playfully lick her face. She flinches away giggling. They lie besides each other laughing.

Aliyah wipes her face saying, "That's exactly why I need to be here tonight."

Tim looks at her smiling, "Why? For saliva?"

She laughs saying, "No. You make me smile and laugh. Even at a time like this. You make it easier for me to smile. Thank you."

Tim smiles and says, "Well you know. I love you, so it's the least I can do. Don't forget how great you are too. You make me smile and laugh too. Ok, it's time to get back to work."

He sits up and says, "Are you ok with me being ten feet away? I need to edit this story and work on book formats for about two hours."

Aliyah replies, "That's fine, Tim. I'll just watch until I fall asleep. You're really dedicated aren't you?"

He gets up and says, "Yeah. It's the dream that I love living." He sits at his computer and begins typing.

Aliyah says, "Don't ever give up Tim. You're a really good writer. Always try to do better than your best. I know you will."

Tim says, "Thank you. That means a lot, Aliyah. Hey, I bet you're hungry aren't you? I'm going to make dinner."

She replies, "That's fine Tim. Do you need help?"

He kindly says, "No, no. You stay here and relax. Come down if you need anything."

Aliyah shakes her head yes as Tim walks out of his room, down the stairs and towards the kitchen. He takes out pots, pans then food as he prepares to cook. After cooking for a quarter of an hour his father walks into the house.

He looks back as his dad sniffs the air saying, "Wow, it smells great in here. You must be starving if you're cooking. Sorry I'm home so late. The load took longer than usual."

T.Edward Redd   **318**

Tim replies, "It's fine. Dad I need to talk to you about something."

Before he can speak Aliyah comes down the stairs saying, "Hey Tim? Do you mind if I use your shower?"

Tim and Robert look back as she reaches the bottom of the stairs. She becomes nervous as she sees Robert.

Robert says, "Aliyah, hey! How are you?"

She tries to smile but can't, saying, "Not too well. My brother died. So I'm just, coping."

He says, "Oh my gosh. I'm so sorry. How's your father? Shouldn't you be with him right?"

Tim gently taps his dad's shoulder saying, "She has a bad relationship with her father. He hits her. She wanted to get away with the accident and all. I told her she could stay."

Robert replies, "That's good that you did that. You're a good person, Tim. Let her have your room for the night and sleep on the couch. We'll figure things out with her father later. Make yourself at home, Aliyah. Our towels are in the closet by the bathroom. You'll have to use Tim's bathroom though. I need to shower and get ready for bed."

They watch as Robert leaves the kitchen towards his room. Tim turns off the stove and grabs a plate. He looks to Aliyah asking, "Are you hungry?"

She replies, "Not really. But I know it's because I'm sad. So I'll eat anyway."

They walk to the dining area and begin to eat. Tim watches as Aliyah fiddles with her food with her fork. She stares at the pasta and garlic bread and begins to lose her appetite. She places her fork down in frustration and covers her face with her hands, sighing.

319   *HERO'S ROMANCE*

Tim says, "It'll get better. I promise, Aliyah."

She replies, "I'm just going to go take a shower then sleep. I'm sorry I didn't finish this."

Tim smiles kindly saying, "It's ok, Aliyah. Let me know if you need anything."

His smile fades as she gets up shaking her head yes. She walks away without returning his smile and goes to his room. Tim watches not knowing how to react or help.

"This is the most horrible thing that could've happened to her. Liel was her everything. I could never imagine what it's like to have that taken away so suddenly. I barely know what to do for her. I'll just let her have some time to herself."

He goes to the living room and sits on the couch thinking for a while. He lies down and stares at the ceiling.

"Even though it's not my brother. Seeing her so sad makes me sad too. It feels like a rainy day."

After a couple of hours Robert comes down the stairs. Tim wakes up from his unexpected slumber to see his father dressed for work. Robert says, "Alright son. I'm off to work. How's she doing?"

Tim replies, "Not so good. I don't even know how to help her. It's usually really easy to connect with Aliyah on a mental level. But now I can barely do that. She's there, but she's far out."

Robert explains, "The best thing you can do for her is be there for her. Let her know you care and just listen to her. If she asks for answers do your best to give her one. But for now just comfort her and make her feel loved. You should go to the funeral with her. I'm sure it would make her feel better. Death isn't easy for anyone Tim. Don't expect to make her feel completely better. She lost her brother."

Tim replies, "Ok dad. Thanks."

Before Robert leaves he adds, "Just do your best to be there for her. Let her know she isn't alone. Have a good night son."

Tim watches as the door closes. The time is 1 a.m. He gets up to walk to his room. To his surprise, Aliyah is sitting at his window wide-awake. She cries silently as she stares out of the window. Looking back, she sees Tim standing behind her. She embraces him as he welcomes her with opened arms. He rubs her back and let's her cry for a moment before saying, "It's alright. I'm here for you."

She cries, "I don't want to sleep alone. Not tonight."

Tim sit with her on the bed as he says, "I won't leave you alone tonight. It's ok."

She hugs him saying, "Thank you Tim. Thank you for being different and being here for me. You mean a lot to me."

She hugs him as he asks, "Aliyah, do you need anything?"

She replies, "You. All I want is you. I don't really have an appetite. I just want to lie down and relax. Lay with me for a while. At least until I fall asleep?"

Tim holds her as she turns her back to him. They lie down and hold each other for a while. Aliyah struggles to fall asleep, as her mind is too unsettled. An hour passes.

She whispers, "Hey? Are you still up?"

Tim says, "Yeah. What's wrong? Do you want something to drink?"

She says, "No. I just can't sleep. I won't be able to for hours. I'm too stressed."

Tim replies, "That's fine. I'll try to get you relaxed."

She replies, "Thank you Tim. You're really sweet.

"I can't believe Alvin would do this," she says.

Tim becomes confused for a moment, "Alvin? Oh, you mean your dad?"

Aliyah becomes cold saying, "That monster is *not* my father. I want nothing to do with him. He killed my brother."

Tim mournfully says her name. She argues, "No! He's a monster! I hate him more than anything right now. I wish it were him instead of Liel that died. We'd be better off. I wish he were like your father. Our parents got with the wrong spouses. What do you think about my dad?"

She continues, "Do you think you could ever forgive your mom? I can honestly say I know how you feel about her now. I feel so much hate for my dad. I'm sorry I tried to tell you how you felt without knowing. Do you think you'd be ever to forgive your mom?"

Tim begins to feel horrible as he sees his behavior towards his mom from the outside. He starts to feel guilty as he realizes his past statements towards her are encouraging Aliyah's.

Not wanting to upset her he replies, "I'm…I'm not sure. Let's not talk about my mom ok?"

Aliyah kisses him on the cheek saying, "Ok babe. I understand. I'm going to sleep. Goodnight."

Tim replies, "Goodnight."

CHAPTER TWENTY-SEVEN

Aliyah sits in bed beside Tim early in the morning. Tim is sleeping heavily but she is looks wide awake with a mellow look. She checks the time to see it's 9:50 a.m. She turns the alarm clock she set for 10 a.m. off.

"Another day of waking up and hoping it was all a dream. Just to realize he's really gone. I barely got any sleep last night. I couldn't stop thinking about today. The day of the funeral."

She begins putting on her day clothes. Today she wear's a black t-shirt with dark-blue jeans. She doesn't bother to brush her hair. Slowly, she begins to creep towards the door, not wanting to wake Tim. She drops her purse as she grabs the door handle.

As she begins to bend down to pick up her purse, she becomes startled to hear, "Oh no. Are we late?"

She looks back to see Tim sitting up in bed as he rubs his eyes. She replies, "Late?"

Tim says, "Yes. The funeral is today. What time is it?"

Aliyah says, "It's close to 10 a.m. You're coming?"

He replies as he gets dressed, "Of course I am, Aliyah."

She says, "Tim you don't have to."

He walks to her and holds her hand saying, "I know. But I want to be there for you."

She hugs him saying in relief, "Thank you."

He begins guiding her out the door as he says, "Come on. We need to be at the airport soon or we'll miss the flight."

Aliyah looks to Tim in confusion saying, "The flight?"

Tim leads her down the stairs saying, "Yes. The funeral is in Florida. We have to catch this plane."

She replies, "I never told you it was in Florida. How do you know that?" She gasps, "You talked to my dad!"

Tim says, "Aliyah, please calm down."

They reach the door as Aliyah becomes angered pulling away. She repeats, "Why did you talk to him? Don't tell me to calm down! He killed my brother and you know I hate him! Why would you talk to him behind my back?"

Tim calmly says, "Aliyah your father has been calling all week. He's worried about you. Yesterday I found out you were missing from him. I told him you were okay yesterday and that you were staying with me."

She becomes defensive, arguing, "You told him I was staying *here*?" She panics, "Are you out of your mind? He'll come here and fine me!"

Tim holds her and says, "Aliyah please, calm down. You're going to stress yourself out."

She pulls away as she cries, "I'm not going back to him! I'm not going to let him hurt me anymore. I'm not letting *anyone* hurt me ever again! And you can't make me!"

Tim holds her as she cries, "Aliyah he's not coming here. Relax and breathe. I'm not letting anyone lay a hand on you."

She whimpers, "Don't let him hurt me again, Tim. Please don't make me go back."

He holds her saying, "Come on. You know me better than that don't you?" He wipes her tears as she looks at him.

He says, "Aliyah I won't let him or anyone else harm you ok. I love you. We need to get going to the airport. Your father will be there with our tickets. I need you to be strong and trust me. He won't hurt you ever again."

Aliyah replies, "You always know the right things to say to me at the right moments. Thank you, Tim."

Tim says, "Don't worry about it. Come on. Let's go."

She takes his hand as he leads her out of the house. They take a quiet but short drive to an airport on the west side of Indianapolis. At the airport, they walk amongst many busy travelers, towards a food court at a higher level. Aliyah becomes astonished to see the many people, food places and stores.

She says, "This is so cool. I've never been on a plane before. We usually drive."

Tim replies, "It'll be a first for us both then huh?"

She smiles as she walks close to him. Tim looks around as if searching for someone. Aliyah notices that he's looking at someone. She looks back to see Alvin sitting at a table with two bags of food.

Tim says, "There he is."

Aliyah becomes upset as they walk towards him. Alvin waves, as they get close. "Hey kids. How've you been," he says.

Tim smiles and says, "We've been-"

Aliyah cuts him off saying, "You killed my brother. I've been horrible."

Alvin becomes guilty. He quickly takes out two tickets and offers them to Aliyah. He says, "They're first class. I got coach but it's fine. I just want you two to ride comfortably. Here dear."

Aliyah glares at him for a moment and looks away.

Tim takes the tickets saying, "Thank you."

Alvin stares at Aliyah who refuses to make eye contact with him. Tim watches with pity not knowing how to intervene. Alvin looks to the bags of food on the table and smiles.

His face brightens, "Oh! Hey I got you two food. Aliyah, I bought your favorite. It's a Caesar salad, fish and fries with bottled water. Tim I bought you something too."

Tim smiles as he happily takes the bag, "Thanks. I'm starved."

Alvin says, "Aliyah aren't you hungry dear?"

Aliyah rolls her eyes and looks to Tim, "Can we board the plane already?"

Tim begins to feel nervous as Aliyah places him in between her and Alvin. He says, "Um yeah, if you're ready."

He grabs the bag Alvin bought for her and hands it to her. She quickly tosses it into a trashcan in front of her father and grabs Tim's hand. She begins walking toward the terminals.

Alvin says, "Hey Aliyah. When you two get to Florida go to grandma's house. That's where everyone is meeting. Do you remember how to get there?"

She stops to look back at him with a fierce and cold gaze.

Her stare staggers his heart. In defeat he says, "Tim, just call me if you need directions ok?"

Tim shakes his head yes, comforting Alvin slightly as he watches them walk towards the terminals. Tim struggles to match Aliyah's pace as she drags him. She stops.

He looks at her with concern as she says, "Which terminal?"

He replies, "Aliyah do you want to talk about anything? It's okay."

T.Edward Redd

Aliyah holds back her tears saying, "I just want to get on the plane! Why is that such a battle right now? Let's go!"

Tim holds her close saying, "Alright. Come on. The ticket says, terminal 5. Is there anything you want to get to eat before we leave?"

She nods and points to a fish restaurant. After they get a meal they board the plane. They sit comfortably in soft and luxurious chairs. Tim sighs in relief, "Wow. Your dad gave us the royal treatment huh?"

He watches as she ignores him and pulls her food out. She sits a Caesar salad and bottled water on a tray built into the seat. Then she begins eating fish and fries. Tim becomes more and more concerned as she begins eating as if trying to wash out her pain with the food.

She stops eating and looks at Tim, "What?"

Tim replies, "Didn't your dad buy that same exact meal?"

She scoffs, "I honestly don't care."

Tim says, "Never mind. Wow, it was pretty nice for your dad to get us first class huh?"

She arrogantly remarks, "It's the very least he could have done. He owes it to me and a whole lot more."

She stops eating as she sees Tim looking at her with deep worry. She puts her fork down saying in annoyance, "I know what you're thinking and what you're about to say. He may have bought *you* over with this petty charade. But it's going to take a whole lot more than plane tickets and food to get even an ounce of my pity. I hope he lives with the shame he feels until he dies."

Tim replies, "I just don't want you to let your hurt feelings keep you from seeing that your father is trying. He knows he's messed up, Aliyah. Nothing he says or does can ever bring Liel back. He has to live with that until he dies. Every time he looks at you, he has to face what he's done in the past. He had to see that bruise he put on your face and eat up the shame. It's killing him Aliyah."

She smiles as her eyes begin to water, "Perfect! Let it. He deserves it! He's made his choices in the past. He chose to call me a slut. He chose to hit me all of those times. He chose to hurt mom and push her to her death! He chose to take away Liel. Now he has to face everything by himself! I'm done with him. He's dead to me!"

Tim hugs her comfortingly. She holds him as she begins to cry silently. Tim softly speaks, "I know you don't mean that. You're very angry and sad right now. We're going to get through this."

She replies, "Thank you."

A couple of hours pass as the two spend time talking and occasionally, playfully flirting. Tim eventually calms her down. She falls asleep for a while. After a few hours pass they arrive in Florida. Tim leads her off the plane and heads towards the rental car station.

Tim looks to Aliyah asking, "Do you know how to get to your grandmother's house?"

She replies, "Yes. Don't worry about what they'll think of you. They'll love you. They aren't like Alvin."

He says, "Ok. Well it's 2 p.m. and the funeral starts at 3. Let's take our stuff to her house and head to the funeral."

Aliyah smiles saying, "Ok."

She holds his hand and walks close to him as they walk to the rental car. She says, "Thank you Tim, for everything. I'm really glad you came."

He replies, "Don't worry about it."

He opens the car door for her. She gets inside and takes her bag. Tim gets into the driver's side. They begin driving east towards Aliyah's grandmother's house.

CHAPTER TWENTY-EIGHT

Tim and Aliyah stand beside each other at the burial ceremony of Liel. Aliyah looks deeply saddened as the pastor speaks, "Did anyone have any last words that they would like to share before we bury the body?" She becomes disgusted as her father stands with a piece of paper.

He says, "Yes sir. I have a few words I'd like to share. I've written down some of my feelings." He struggles to speak as he sighs sadly, "I loved my boy. No matter what happened he always kept a smile on his face. I'm not the best father.

He stops as a laugh erupts from the listeners. Everyone looks back to see Aliyah laughing to herself. Tim gets her to quiet down as Alvin continues as he begins to cry.

"Well I wasn't always there for him but he was always there for me no matter what happened. When Liel died he took a part of me with him. Part of me died that day. I miss him so much. I know I've done a lot of bad things. Things I'll have to live with for the rest of my life. I regret those things." He looks at Aliyah and says, "I'm sorry. I'm so, so sorry."

He begins to breakdown in tears. Tim looks sorrowful as Alvin continues his speech. Aliyah bursts out laughing. Tim grabs her hand whispering, "Aliyah stop!"

Everyone looks back as she shouts, "Sorry? You're not sorry! You're a monster! You're a horrible father and I HATE YOU!"

Tim grabs her hand and gets up saying, "Come on."

T.Edward Redd   **330**

He struggles to escort her away as she shouts, "It should be you in that casket! You MONSTER!"

The pastor comforts Alvin as he cries. He cries to himself as Tim takes Aliyah away from the burial site. He lets her go as they reach the parking lot. She begins to walk back and forth in a rage as Tim watches, wanting to let her get her stress out.

Aliyah's rage continues to build as she says, "Can you believe all of those people? He's reading them those pathetic lines and they were just eating up! I hate him so MUCH!" She picks up a stone and screams as she throws it at Alvin's rental car.

Tim grabs her hand shouting, "Aliyah!"

She looks back viciously saying, "What?"

He replies, "Aliyah you're losing yourself through this. Can you see yourself right now? Do you realize what you just did?"

She barks, "Yeah I do! I told that bastard off in front of everyone!"

Tim counters, "Aliyah this is your *brother's* funeral! Would you really want your brother see you act this way?"

Aliyah cries as she shouts, "What are you talking about? This is MY fault! If I would've acted this way before, he might still be alive! Someone could have stopped him. *I* should have stopped him! This is my fault. I never said anything. I've been too quiet and scared! This is all of my fault."

Tim holds her tightly as she cries in his arms, "It's not your fault Aliyah. Don't blame yourself for his death."

She cries, "It hurts, Tim. It hurts so much."

He holds her saying, "I know sweetheart I know. I'm going to help you through this. Let's go for a walk."

Aliyah smiles slightly saying, "I forgot you like to walk around a lot."

They walk with each other along a sidewalk. Tim notices how small the town is. He says, "I have a question. Why did they choose to burry Liel here? Why not at home with his mom?"

Aliyah replies, "It was my dad's request. *He's* from Florida, that bastard."

Tim looks at her with worry as he comments, "You curse a lot lately."

She says, "Yeah. So?"

He replies, "I don't know it's just, not *you*. Aliyah I can get you're angry with your father and that you're sad that Liel has died. But you can't let any of this change you. You've been very spiteful these last couple of days."

Aliyah becomes shocked and defensive, "Spiteful? How can you say that? You actually feel sorry for that piece of crap, sorry excuse for a human being? You're *my* boyfriends and you're supposed to be on my side!"

Tim pleads, "I am on your side! I love you and seeing you act so hurtful is hard for me. I don't want you to change."

She shouts, "I haven't changed!"

He explains, "The woman that I know never curses and she never tries to purposely hurt people. Your father bought you lunch today and you threw it away in his face. Then you bought the same exact stuff he bought you right after. To top it off, you laughed at him and told him off in front of everyone at the funeral, after he apologized to you in tears."

Aliyah begins to cry, "You're making me sound like a horrible person! What about the things he's done huh? What he's done to me all of these years is so much worse! So what if I'm spiteful for two damn days. He deserves it!"

T.Edward Redd   **332**

Tim holds her, calmly saying, "Aliyah you're not a horrible person. I love you. That's why I'm worrying about you. I don't want your anger to take control of you and change you into the bitter person your father is or was."

She whimpers, "I'm not trying to change babe but it hurts so much ok? I don't know how to deal with my anger. When I was quiet and afraid, things only got worse. But now that Liel is gone I have no reason to hold back my feelings. I don't like being spiteful but I'm hurting, Tim."

He hugs her tight and kisses her head, "I know, Aliyah and I'm here for you. I won't leave your side. Don't let your anger change you. Instead learn to respect your father as a person. He's bitter and hateful. You can see it in his eyes that something is wrong with him. Something probably happened when he was your age. Maybe he was abused too and he never learned how to handle it. Now he's passed that life onto you.

"Now his son is gone and you're all he has left. That's why he cried at the burial today. He's finally realized the wrong he's done to you. He can't take any of it back. He can't take that bruise back and he can't take his words back. When he sees you he'll have to swallow the shame and let it bottle up inside him, silently, for the rest of his life.

"You don't have to caste vengeance on him, Aliyah. He's caused his own undoing. If anything you should pity him. Pity him for what he's been through and what he has to live with until he dies. He's cursed himself. Don't let him pass that curse onto you. Learn how to deal with your pain so your children don't go through this."

Aliyah becomes enlightened saying, "Timothy I love you so much. You should really consider being a public speaker. Don't worry I don't plan on turning out like him at all. You're right I shouldn't let any of this change me. Thank you, Tim."

He replies, "No problem, Aliyah."

She kisses him. They hold hands as Aliyah leads Tim to her grandmother's house. Time passes and they begin to have dinner with Aliyah's grandmother Jiliet, her aunt Wendy and her husband Sampson, her uncle Fredrick and lastly her two cousins, Amanda and Joline.

Jiliet is an elderly woman in her late 60's. Her hair is grey from age and her skin is slightly wrinkled but not noticeably wrinkled. She smiles cheerfully as she watches Tim and Aliyah show obvious signs of affection for one another.

She says, "It was nice of you to come out with, Aliyah today, Timothy. Liel was very special to all of us."

Tim replies, "I was glad to come out for Aliyah."

Wendy, a woman in her mid-thirties with shoulder length brown hair smiles at her niece as she says, "How long have you two been dating?"

Aliyah blushes saying, "Close to a month but we were talking and hanging out before then. He's so sweet you guys. Give him five minutes. You're not going to want him to leave."

Wendy's husband, Sampson rubs his black silky hair back as he says, "I hope you aren't like the last guy she was with. Typical football jock. I didn't like him at all."

Aliyah becomes excited, "Tim doesn't play sports anymore. Can you guys guess what he does? He's kind of famous."

Tim smiles out of embarrassment as Wendy says, "Whoa really? What do you do?"

T.Edward Redd   **334**

Sampson guesses, "Do you write music?"

Aliyah smiles saying, "That's kind of close!"

A blonde girl at age 18 with long wavy hair; Joline joins the conversation saying, "Please don't tell me he's a rapper."

Tim laughs out loud as Aliyah corrects her, "Haha no. He writes novels!"

A girl with shoulder length black hair and freckles; Amanda laughs with them. She's only a year older than Aliyah.

"I was kind of thinking the same thing as Joline. I didn't want to offend you or anything," she adds.

Tim kindly says, "No way. You all are great."

Fredrick, smiles as the group begins to talk to Tim. His hair is short and brown. He says, "What do you write about Tim? You got any horror or suspense? I'm a writer too and that's what I write."

Wendy rolls her eyes saying, "Oh please. You haven't written in months."

They laugh amongst each other. Tim smiles peacefully, seeing Aliyah genuinely smile again. She reaches into her purse and pulls out her copy of *Hero's Wake*. She hands it to her grandmother, Jiliet.

She says, "This is my favorite. He wrote it."

Jiliet examines the book as she flips through the pages. Everyone begins to crowd around her as they try to see. Tim can't help but to smile as people new to his work, begin to fancy his book.

Joline becomes intrigued asking, "Hey is this published?"

Tim replies, "Yes. It's my very first one. It sold over one thousand copies."

Everyone looks at him and becomes impressed. Jiliet looks to Tim saying, "That's really amazing Timothy."

Joline asks, "Grandma can I see it?"

Jiliet hands Joline the book. Amanda joins her as she begins to read the novel. Tim hands Fredrick his copy of *Dead Awakened*.

He says, "Here you go. That's the closest I have to a horror story, besides this one."

He pulls out another book titled; *Tales of the Red Abyss*. Fredrick holds both books in his hands and gives *Tales of the Red Abyss* to Wendy as he begins flipping through *Dead Awakened*. Amanda and Joline begin to whisper to each other and look at Tim as they smile to each other.

Amanda smiles and says, "He's the romantic type isn't he Aliyah?"

Joline slightly blushes as she reads and says, "Yes, this novel is very, intense. Can we have this?"

Aliyah smiles as she says, "Nope that one is mine. See how he autographed it? He gave it to me for my birthday. But you can buy one from the bookstore."

They all look at Tim as Joline asks, "Wait you sell these?"

Tim nods saying, "Yes but just that one. But I hope to start selling them all eventually."

Wendy reads his novel as she says, "Whoa, Aliyah. Now this one is a keeper. You hit the gold mine. He's respectful, well educated…"

Fredrick becomes excited as he reads *Dead Awakened*.

He interrupts Wendy saying, "And he has a career going and he's not even in college yet! This kid is amazing. Hey if you ever need an editor talk to me. I can even get you in contact with more publishers."

Wendy says, "Leave her boyfriend alone, Fred. He doesn't want you as his editor."

Fredrick argues, "How would you know?"

Tim smiles at Aliyah saying, "They're amazing, Aliyah."

She replies, "Yeah I knew they'd like you. They're a lot more welcoming than my dad."

Everyone stops as Sampson says in shock, "You met Alvin? Face to face? In his house?"

Jiliet holds her head with embarrassment saying, "Oh, gosh. How did that go, dear?"

Aliyah becomes upset, "Horrible, grandma. He was rude the whole time."

Sampson replies, "Yeah I can imagine how Alvin would react. We didn't grow up around too many black people. So he's a bit closed-minded. We aren't like that though. So don't be nervous or anything."

Joline blushes saying, "I don't know why he doesn't like black people. I like black guys. Speaking of which, Tim do you have any brothers?"

Aliyah smiles out of embarrassment shouting, "Joline!"

Tim laughs saying, "No. Just a sister."

Joline says, "Aliyah if he's lying let me know." Everyone laughs and she adds, "I'm serious! Does he have a brother?"

Aliyah smiles and laughs shaking her head no. Jiliet says, "Timothy we don't care what color your skin is," she points to Aliyah as she continues, "as long as you keep that girl happy and never lay a hand on her in a harmful way you're welcome here anytime."

Aliyah hugs and kisses Tim on his cheek as he says, "I promise Ms.Conrad."

Aliyah says, "Grandma he would never hurt me. He's amazing. You guys should hear him talk. He's really deep! Say something deep babe."

Everyone pauses and waits for Tim's response.

Tim smiles saying, "Ok, if I found an eagle that broke its wing, I would help heal it so it could flutter the skies once again. If I found a friend with a shattered soul, I would help heal it so they could fly the heavens as if they had always had wings."

The room grows silent as they stare at him. Aliyah smiles at him excited and then at her relatives. Wendy smiles, as her eyes brighten. She says, "That was lovely Tim."

Aliyah adds, "See? I told you!"

Amanda says, "That was amazing. You can do that out of the blue like that whenever?"

Tim answers, "Most of the time yeah. That was a little something I remembered. It's my favorite quote."

Fredrick says, "He's only 18! He's going to be so amazing once he's aged and gotten more experience. Wow."

Aliyah hugs Tim tight as she leans on his shoulder saying, "That isn't even the best part. The best part is his heart. He's so warm and comforting. He makes life at home bearable."

She becomes surprised as she stops to realize what she just blurted. Everyone looks at her.

Wendy says, "What do you mean by that?"

Aliyah buries her face into Tim's chest, trying to hide her bruise as she replies, "Huh?"

Sampson adds, "Yeah how have you been Aliyah? Is everything ok at home? What was that all about earlier at the burial?"

She becomes nervous saying, "I was just upset. That's all."

She looks at Tim nervously as if trying to tell him not to tell with her silence. Tim rejects with his own silence as if telling her to tell them.

Their mental discussion is broken as Jiliet says, "Li, Li how is your father? He's keeping his drinking under control right? Last time you were down here, you showed us bruises."

Aliyah looks to Tim as if asking for advice. He shakes his head yes as if telling her it's ok. Fredrick sees the telepathic conversation.

He says, "You don't have to lie for him, Aliyah. We want you to be safe. Tim, has her father hurt her at all?"

Tim looks at him and acts coy saying, "What do you mean?"

Jiliet explains, "Alvin has a drinking problem. Before her mom died he used to hit on her. We found out he used to hit on Li, Li too when we went down for the funeral. He's on probation. Has he hit my granddaughter?"

Tim looks at Aliyah. She becomes teary eyed as she looks at him realizing she has to confess on her own.

Tim holds her quietly saying, "It's alright sweetheart. Don't be afraid. You wanted to get your feelings out of you. Here's your chance to do it in a non-destructive way. It's alright. No one will hurt you."

Aliyah holds him tight and he kisses her cheek. She slowly swallows her fear as she stands up and wipes her makeup off. The bruise appears on her face. She begins to cry as her relatives become alarmed.

Jiliet places her face in her hands with great disappointment saying, "Damn it, Alvin."

339

Wendy and Sampson walk to Aliyah. Wendy hugs Aliyah saying, "It's alright honey come here."

Aliyah cries, "This is my fault. If I would've said something they would've taken him away and Liel would still be alive."

Fredrick and Wendy comfort her. Wendy says, "No don't think like that Li, Li. This isn't your fault at all."

Fredrick looks to Tim asking, "Is she staying with him, Tim?"

Tim answers, "Yes but not since yesterday. She's been at my house. My dad agreed to let her stay. I gave her my room."

Amanda asks, "When did he hit you Aliyah?"

Aliyah sadly answers, "He's been hitting me for a while now. But I got this bruise last week."

Wendy holds her saying, "I'm so sorry, Aliyah."

Aliyah adds, "Tim has been by my side the whole time so it's been easier. He's the only one who remembered my birthday."

Wendy says, "Well you can't go back home with you father. We have to deal with this before it gets worse. We'll clear a room for you here."

Aliyah quickly holds Tim's hand as she says, "Huh? No, I can't stay.

Wendy becomes confused, "Aliyah you have too."

Sampson adds, "It's too dangerous, Aliyah. If we knew Alvin was still hitting you, you wouldn't be there now."

Joline notices Aliyah looking at Tim as she holds his hand, not wanting to let go. She says, "She wants to be with Tim you guys."

Aliyah adds, "She's right. I don't want to leave Indiana. I want to stay there with him. Plus I have to finish school and start college in the fall."

Tim looks at her and says, "Aliyah, are you sure? This could be a better option."

She says, "No. I want to go back with you Tim. You're the only person who's been by my side. You make me feel good and happy. I can stay with you right? At least until college starts?"

Wendy asks Tim, "Who do you live with? Do they care about her staying?"

Tim replies, "I live with my dad. He doesn't mind. He wants her safe too."

Aliyah says to Wendy, "Auntie his dad is the most amazing dad I've ever met. He made me dinner the first time Tim brought me over. He was very welcoming."

Everyone pauses as they hear the front door open. They look back to see Alvin walk in. He smiles and greets everyone only to be given glares of shame and anger. Jiliet says with a stressed tone, "Come sit, Alvin."

He sees Aliyah's bruised and sad face. He quickly understands what's going on and becomes fearful. He walks to the table and sits by his mother; Jiliet. He looks to Aliyah who covers her face, trying to hide her tears.

Sampson says, "She told us you're hitting her, Alvin. Are you hitting your first child and only daughter?

Alvin quickly confesses as he cries, "I regret doing it!"

Wendy shouts, "WHAT'S WRONG WITH YOU?"

Joline adds, "How can you hit a child? Look at her face!"

Alvin looks down in shame as they continue to scold him.

Fredrick says, "Al you need to get help. You can't keep hitting on her like this. It's gotten out of control."

Sampson adds, "We need to just call the authorities."

Alvin panics, "No! No I've changed I promise. I've been hurting all week. Liel died and it woke me up. I'm a horrible father. I was a horrible husband but I know I can be a better father. I just need another chance."

Wendy says, "No you've had your chances Alvin. Aliyah doesn't need to be put through this. There isn't any excuse for laying your hands on a woman let alone your own child."

Alvin pleads, "I want to change! I mean it. I'm sorry, Aliyah!" She looks away as she cries in Tim's arms. Alvin looks to his mother. He pleads, "Mom I can change. You know I can. Mom?"

She holds her head and closes her eyes, shamed at her son. She says, "Alvin I can't even look at you right now. I've never been so disappointed in you. The way you treated Elena. That woman was a beauty, nothing but joy. She was God's gift to you and you treated her so poorly. Now you're doing it to her child."

Alvin cries, "I'm sorry. I really am. I want to get help. I want to be in her life."

Sampson says, "Alvin it's too late. You're already on probation."

Wendy angrily adds, "There's no excuse for what you've done. You should be ashamed! I'm going to call the cops. You need to be put away."

Jiliet shouts, "Everyone sit!"

Everyone becomes quiet as they look at her. Wendy slowly sits down in confusion and says, "But mother."

Jiliet says, "Wendy it's ok. I'm not happy with your brother either. But we're not sending him away. Alvin we're getting you help, today. Do you understand?"

He replies, "Yes mom."

T.Edward Redd   **342**

Jiliet looks to Aliyah saying, "You're going back to Indiana with Tim ok? You're going to stay with him for a while. Tim, call your father to make sure it's ok."

Tim and Aliyah both say, "Yes ma'me."

She breathes deeply as she brings herself to look at Alvin saying, "Son you need to promise me that you'll get help as soon as you get home. I don't want to see you get put away. You're my son. But you can't keep doing this. You need help dear. Promise you'll get it."

Alvin desperately agrees, "Yes mom. I promise."

Jiliet looks to Tim, "Protect my granddaughter ok? Make sure he gets help before she goes near him by herself. If he doesn't get help you call me ok? Call us if you need anything, Aliyah."

Tim and Aliyah agree as they begin to discuss arrangements.

CHAPTER TWENTY-NINE

A couple of months pass. Tim and Aliyah continue to grow and bond with each other as the school year starts coming to a close. Alvin admits himself into rehabilitation in hopes of breaking his drinking habits. Tim has been checking with him weekly to monitor his progress upon Jilliet's request. Aliyah hasn't spoken to or seen him since the day of Liel's funeral.

Tim lies in bed asleep as an alarm clock sounds off. He covers his head with a pillow not wanting to get up. Aliyah sits up beside him as she rubs her head. She leans over him to turn the clock off.

She gently shakes Tim, "Hey babe, wake up. We're going to be late."

Tim opens his eyes as Aliyah gets out of the bed. He watches her as she walks to a mirror she's placed in his room. She smiles to see her face is bruise free.

Combing her hair she smiles, "How did you sleep, Mr. Derr?"

Tim sits up and lets out a yawn as he says, "Great. How about you Ms. Conrad?"

Aliyah looks back at him and smiles. She sits on the bed and hugs him saying, "I slept like a baby. I'm ready to start and finish our last day of school."

She gets up, walks to the restroom and says, "I'll get dressed first. I'll be quick don't worry." She shuts the door.

Tim smiles as he stands up. He removes his tank top and sweatpants. He puts on a white V-neck and black-wash jeans. He walks to his computer and opens a PDF file of *Hero's Romance*.

Aliyah walks out of the bathroom and sneaks up behind him. She surprises him with a quick hug from behind saying, "What's up?"

He holds her arm gently as if he knew she was going to do that saying, "It's just *Hero's Romance*. How does it look?"

She looks and becomes amazed saying, "This is finished isn't it? Are you sure you're ready to publish it? Any lines you want to add or take out?"

He said, "I decided not to publish this one. I want more time with it. I'm redoing it. The first version is out but I want to redo it." He types.

Aliyah replies, "What will your publisher think? Did you give him the heads up? You're meeting with him today aren't you?"

Tim replies, "Yes."

Aliyah becomes confused, "But this is your baby. It's all you talk about. Are you sure?"

He smirks as he opens the finished version of *Dead Awakened*, "This is what's getting published instead," he says.

Aliyah gasps with shock as she smiles. She takes out the draft version saying, "Oh my gosh. Babe! You never told me this. That's my favorite book. I liked *Hero's Wake* but this one is more intense and I like the suspense too. You sly devil. You did this on purpose."

Tim smiles saying, "I knew you'd like this idea. This version has added dialogue and a more detailed story. Some things were changed."

Aliyah says, "Wow, Mr. Derr." You're so motivated. Hey I might get that internship for nursing today. I have to check with my guidance counselor."

Tim stands up saying, "I'm sure you'll get it. You've worked so hard. I'm really proud of you."

Aliyah blushes as they kiss. They leave the house and walk to Tim's car. The car is freshly painted with a new coat.

Aliyah says, "Wow it still looks so shiny. I love the red. It looks new."

Tim replies, "I finally had time to get those scratches out of it. The paint job looks legendary. Do you want to drive it?"

She looks at him, "Are you sure?" She looks back at the car. He hands her the keys and gets into the passenger side. She becomes excited as she gets into the driver's seat. She puts the key in the ignition and starts the car.

Tim says, "Ok do you remember what I showed you? This is a stick shift, so it's not like your car."

Aliyah shifts into gear, "Sweetie, don't worry. I remember." After backing out, she puts the car into drive and slowly drives away, slightly nervous. With it being her first time driving without his help, Tim's nerves rattle as they approach a road.

He says, "Don't be afraid to give it some gas. Just remember it's fast." Aliyah stops the car in annoyance and looks at Tim, "Fine, fine. I'll be quiet," he says.

Aliyah says, "Thank you sweetie. Sit back. I don't want to make you late for your card games, so I'm going to go a little fast."

They laugh with each other as she drives to the school. As they drive they begin talking to one another.

Tim says, "Aliyah, Your father has been in anger management for a while and he's been getting help for his drinking. He should be done with grief counseling by now. He's made a dramatic change."

Aliyah politely says, "I know where you're going with this and my answer is no."

He says, "But Aliyah it's been two months. He's changed and he really misses you."

Aliyah gets annoyed, "I'm not going to see him. I never want to see him again. It's been 3 months since Liel died and I just started getting better. After today you and I will be out of high school and we'll be able to live with each other."

He says, "But Aliyah, he's still your father. You can't just avoid him for the rest of your life. You're suppressing your emotions."

She parks the car and says, "It's not for the rest of my life. It's for the rest of his, babe. Now I'm not going to argue with you about this. Let's have a good last day ok? Alright, I'm going to class. Good luck on today hon. I love you."

"I love you too, Aliyah," he says.

Tim walks Aliyah into the school. They part ways as one heads to the office, while the other goes to a classroom. He begins working on paper work.

"Aliyah hasn't talked to her father since Liel's funeral. She gets upset every time I bring him up. The way she acts towards him is really cruel. I know Alvin isn't the best person and he's made his mistakes. But he's still a person with feelings just like us. The way she talks about him reminds me of how I use to act towards my mom. Was I that cruel to my mom?

"The way Alvin was crying and the look of pain in his eyes. I could feel it and it was horrible. The thought of putting my mother through that kind of pain...it makes my stomach twist and turn."

He stops working to take a deep breath.

"Did mother cry when I said the things I said or when I did the things I did? I haven't talked to my mom in almost 3 years. Does she miss me?"

He continues to type. Time passes and it gets close to the end of the day. Principle Frawgs approaches Tim with an envelope.

"Hey Tim," he says.

Tim looks as Frawgs hands him the envelope, "Hey Kurt. What is this?"

Frawgs smiles saying, "Just a little something for helping out in the office all of these years. I'll miss you kid."

T.Edward Redd   **348**

Tim replies, "Thanks, Principal Kurt. I'll visit from time to time you know?"

Frawgs says, "Yeah. But it won't be the same. Who will beat my score at that game when you leave?" He laughs, "Did you get into the college you applied to?"

"Yeah. Aliyah and I applied to Anderson and we both got in. So it should be good."

Frawgs smiles saying, "You never cease to amaze, Tim. How's publishing coming along?"

Tim says, "I have a meeting today. I made enough money off of my last publish to pay my way through the first couple years of college and hopefully enough left over for an apartment for me and Aliyah."

Frawgs replies, "Looks like you've got it all figured off. Well, Tim it's almost 3 p.m. You're free to go. Good luck."

They shake hands. Tim waves everyone his final goodbye as he leaves the office. He walks to an Ap Chemistry classroom. He peeks in the window to see Aliyah reading peacefully as class proceeds. The end of the day bell rings and she packs her things. Tim walks into the classroom.

Students rush towards the door as the two smile at each other. They walk towards one another and hug as they celebrate the end of their high school career.

Aliyah joyfully says, "Ah! We finally finished babe. Now we just have to do four years of college. Can we go see the apartment in Anderson after you meet with your publisher?"

Tim smiles saying, "Of course. Are you going to see your dad?"

Aliyah apathetically says, "Ugh, gosh no. Haha, why would I waste time going to see him when I can be looking at a place to live with my amazing boyfriend?"

"Because Aliyah, he's your father," he replies.

She rolls her eyes, but smiles saying, "Tim I understand what you're doing. You're trying to keep me from turning out like he did. I don't have any negative feelings towards him whatsoever."

Tim says with concern, "But now it's like you aren't feeling anything towards him at all."

She smiles and replies, "Exactly, because I *don't* babe. Come on let's get out of here."

Tim stares at her with shock as she holds his hand and leads him to the door. They walk to Aliyah's locker and begin to clean it out.

"I'm glad I never had a lot of stuff in here like everyone else does in their lockers," she says.

She waves her goodbyes to a few friends that pass her as she finishes packing. She puts her bag over her shoulder and looks at Tim. He looks at her with worry. She becomes worried as she holds his hand.

Softly, she says, "Hey what's wrong? Are you going to miss being here?"

Tim replies, "Aliyah, I need you to go see him today."

She becomes slightly annoyed saying, "Tim we've already talked about this. I'm not going to see my dad. Not today, not tomorrow and not ever."

With a concerned tone, he says, "Aliyah please. I know you can't stand him right now. But you're burying your feelings. That's not good at all."

She replies reluctantly, "Ok Tim, ok. I'll go see him. Just stop looking so depressed. Pick me up after you finish with your meeting ok?"

Tim replies, "Don't worry about that. I rescheduled it, so I could go with you. We can go now."

Aliyah scoffs as they get outside the building. They walk to Tim's car. She gets to the door and waits impatiently. He grabs his keys as he stands by her door. He offers her the keys.

She says, "I don't want to drive."

Tim says," Are you ok?"

She lies, "I just want to sit. My feet hurt. Could you open the door?"

He opens the door for her. They get into the car and begin to drive away. Aliyah becomes more and more irritated with Tim the longer they drive, feeling forced to see someone who hurt her, by the one she has fallen for. She becomes annoyed as she stares at him. Tim doesn't notice as he focuses on the road. She looks away huffing.

"It's been three amazing months and now he's going to ruin them by forcing me to go see this monster? The thought of being in the same building let alone in front of that man makes my blood boil. Six years of abuse. Six years of being told I'm a worthless slut!

"Six years of being hit. I'm finally free and now he's trying to make me go back to that monster. What the hell is wrong with Tim right now? Does he not understand what I'm feeling? Can he not understand that Alvin is a monster? Can he not see that he will NEVER change?

"I thought you understood me, Tim..."

She looks to see the car approaching a rehab center. She looks at Tim with distress in her eyes as they park. Slowly, she takes her seatbelt off as he gets out of the car. He walks to her side and opens the door.

He smiles asking, "Are you ready to see the new, Alvin Conrad?"

She says, "Tim. I appreciate this. Really, I do. But I don't want to do this. I can't. I don't want to see him."

Tim replies, "You're afraid that he hasn't changed. But Aliyah, he might surprise you. I'll be right there with you. No one is going to touch you I promise. Let's just see how he's doing. We can leave whenever you want."

She says, "Fine, let's leave now."

Tim replies, "You know what I meant babe."

She gets out of the car and softly shuts the door. They hold hands as they get close to the building. She gets close to him as she becomes fearful and nervous.

She starts to panic as she thinks, *"I can't do this. I can't go back to him. I can never go back. I won't let anyone hurt me again. No one will ever hurt me again. I refuse to go back to hurt. It's pretty here without the abuse. No one can make me go back."*

T. Edward Redd   **352**

As they enter the building they see families sitting in a waiting area. She sees a boy and a girl with their mother. Aliyah's fear becomes anger as she begins reminiscing the past where she had a mother and a brother.

They walk to a secretary. Tim asks about Alvin. She gives him room info and allows them to walk towards the room. Aliyah becomes angrier as they approach room 201. Knowing how it feels to be treated kindly, her panic fades as rage begins to engulf her. She refuses to be a prisoner to pain and will no longer back down in fear.

Tim says, "Alright. We're here."

Aliyah barks, "Obviously I can read the sign, Tim. I'm not stupid."

Tim says, "I never said you were stupid. Aliyah what's wrong?"

She replies in a spiteful tone, "I told you the problem outside. You forced me to come in here anyway knowing I didn't want to."

He tries to appease, "Ok. I'm sorry. We can leave Aliyah."

She sasses, "Don't gain a conscious *now*. You've already drug me into this hellhole. Since I love you, I'm going to see him like *you* begged me to. After we see that he's the same sorry excuse for a man he was the last time we saw him, we're leaving. Clear?"

Tim replies slightly annoyed with her attitude, "Crystal."

She rolls her eyes, "Just open the door, Timothy. I want to hurry so we can go see our lovely home."

Tim opens the door and they walk in. They look around the room. The room is neatly furnished and the bed is made. There isn't a TV, just a bookshelf. They see Alvin sitting at a table wearing reading glasses. He sips a cup of tea as he reads.

He says, "Don't worry. I've already made the bed. Thanks though." Aliyah looks with utter confusion saying in anger, "What the hell is this?"

Alvin becomes surprised recognizing his daughter's voice. He looks behind and becomes happy as he gets out of his seat.

Overjoyed he says, "Oh my goodness! This is an amazing surprise! I didn't know you two were coming to see me," he says gleefully.

He hugs Aliyah cheerfully but she doesn't hug him saying, "Hey...how's it going..."

Tim sees her get more and more annoyed as Alvin hugs her. He becomes nervous realizing Aliyah is barely holding her hate and anger back.

Alvin smiles as he looks at Aliyah saying, "Thank you so much dear! I've thought about you this whole time. I've been doing great. I haven't drunk in 2 months.

Aliyah starkly replies, "Well *Tim* here was just dying to see you."

Alvin smiles saying, "Hey look at this!" He walks to his desk and holds up 5 books, "I've read all of these. They're amazing dear. I told them not to give me a TV. I wanted to start reading. These books are amazing!"

Aliyah gets more upset as she can't find a beer bottle, not even a cap in sight. The fresh air of his room begins to make her blood boil. He isn't in pain like she wishes he were.

She thinks, *"Why the hell is he so happy? He should be suffering and miserable. He's walking around smiling as if nothing has happened! He's on a damn vacation!"*

Alvin hands her a book saying, "Look at that. It's amazing! You'll love it, Aliyah. Tim you should read some too. You might get inspired." Tim smiles and takes a peek at the book.

Aliyah smirks asking, "So how many times have you relapsed? We all know you can't go five minutes without touching a bottle." Tim becomes shocked and looks at her saying, "Aliyah!"

Alvin laughs playfully as Aliyah searches every possible hiding place in the room. She looks under a pillow, then his bed. She stands and becomes frustrated. She looks at Tim who's watching her.

She says in annoyance, "What now?"

He replies, "Aliyah come on. Take it easy."

She replies with hate, *"Easy?"*

Alvin laughs saying, "You kids are great for each other, arguing like a married couple already. Haha, well I won't lie and say this has been easy. The first month was torture."

Aliyah balls her fists and her rage rises, as his story gets better.

He says, "But I hung in there and it just got easy over time. These books make it easier too. I don't really like drinking now. I'd pretty much rather read and drink tea. Who knew I'd have such a deep interest in reading right?"

355　　　　　　　　　*HERO'S ROMANCE*

Tim laughs with him saying, "Yeah I hear you."

Aliyah shouts, "Tim, shut-up!"

Tim stops laughing, surprised at her outburst.

Alvin laughs thinking they're just being playful lovers. He says, "Man you two are great."

Aliyah moans in annoyance and shouts to Alvin, "Stop fucking laughing and smiling like that!" Alvin quickly stops and looks to her.

She continues, "None of this is funny! You're laughing and joking around like nothing has happened! You've got your glasses on and your stupid books. You're acting like nothing has happened at all!"

Alvin becomes distressed saying, "Aliyah I'm sorry. I've been trying really, really hard. I know I messed up ok?"

He nervously removes his glasses as he becomes teary-eyed. He says, "But I'm trying to get better for you sweetheart. I want us to be a family again. I want my daughter back."

Aliyah shouts, "Stop acting so delusional and open your eyes Alvin. We haven't been a family since mom died!"

Alvin starts sweating and biting his nails. He struggles to remain calm saying, "Um, um look let's drink some tea and relax dear? Let's just have some tea."

He pours her a cup and offers her the tea. She smacks the cup out of his hand shouting, "I don't want any of your stupid, fucking tea!"

It smashes against the floor and gets on his feet. He flinches in pain as the hot tea scolds his toes. Tim becomes shocked saying, "Aliyah! I'm sorry sir, are you ok? Let me help."

Tim prepares to help pick up the broken cup pieces. Aliyah stops him saying, "If you do that we're through. Step back. This has nothing to do with you. You wanted me to deal with my anger so I'm doing it. Get back, *now*."

Tim struggles not wanting to upset her further. He looks at Alvin with concern. He looks away from Alvin as he steps back. Aliyah steps to her father.

She says, "I've been quiet for far too long. Yeah, this is great. Now I can say what I've wanted to all of these years. I'm not the weak little girl you used to smack around anymore. Thanks to him," she looks to Tim, then her father, "I'm strong enough to face you. I'll take back what you've stolen Alvin. My mother and brother are dead because of you. I wish they could see this."

Tim watches in horror. Aliyah's persona has changed completely. The sweet and caring woman he knows has been replaced with a cold and dark one. Her grin isn't a happy one. It's full of hate and cruel intentions. He can see the thirst for vengeance in her eyes.

She speaks coldly, "Look at you. You've got your tea and glasses on as if you're this high-class businessman. Well guess what. Alvin, you are a drunk and a shameless father. I won't even consider you my mother's husband."

Alvin cries silently as she continues to coldly yet calmly speak, "You can smile and pretend like nothing has happened all you want. But you can't undo the wrong you've done to me. You can't bring mom or Liel back. You have no one to blame for their deaths but yourself."

Alvin begins to have a panic attack as he holds his ear, "Stop it please, stop it. Let's just drink some tea and relax. Let's just relax!"

"Aliyah he's had enough," Tim pleads.

Aliyah smiles finally seeing her father suffer. She says, He pleads, "No this is great Tim. You were right. I needed this."

He pleads, "No! You misunderstood me. This is *not* what I meant. I never said attack him Aliyah. He's been through enough as it is."

She responds, "He's had enough when I decide he's suffered enough. You stand over there and be quiet. You're supposed to be on my side."

Tim says, "Aliyah I am! But this isn't the way! He's hurting!"

She shouts, "Hurting! What do you know about hurt, huh?"

Tim argues, "My mother left me! I do know hurt!"

Aliyah shouts, "That's child's play compared to what I've been through! You have both of your parents and sister. You don't know anything. You're a spoiled brat compared to me!"

Tim looks away as she shouts with rage, "Spend most of *your* life watching your mother be beaten for years on in! Watch the one you're supposed to call father beat your hero down with his words and fist! Watch until she leaves, then dies! Become his prisoner now that your hero is gone and have his words kill your insides day by day! Stand defenselessly as he robs you of your pride, your joy and your desire to live!

"Let's see *you* go through all of that then have him rob you of the one thing you had left to live for! Go through all of that then. Only then can you tell me what HURT REALLY IS! He has stolen from me, everything that I've ever loved, AND HIS DEBTS WILL BE PAID!"

Tim stares at her in shock as she stands over Alvin who cowers away at her mercy.

She shouts in tears, "No! I won't take it easy! You've had it easy for six years. Well now it's my turn. I refuse to be afraid and I refuse to stay quiet! This is my liberation and you will pay for everything you've done! Does it hurt yet? Huh *father*? How does it feel to know that the only person left in your life hates you?"

Alvin begins to weep as he covers his ears crying, "I'm sorry! I'm sorry! I'm fucking sorry!"

Tim steps to Aliyah and gently holds her as she begins crying as she shouts. He guides her to the door as she cries and laughs, "Take a good look, Alvin! It's last time you'll ever see me!"

Alvin watches as Tim takes her out of the room. He panics as he sits on the bed rocking as he panics saying, "Breathe...just breathe..."

He begins to breakdown in tears of haunting shame as he cries, "I'm sorry Aliyah! I need you! Please come back!"

Aliyah storms out of the building. Tim walks out of the building behind her holding his head, in stressed out fashion, "I made a huge mistake doing this. I shouldn't have forced her to do this. I thought I was helping."

He walks to her and tries to hold her but she slaps him across the face shouting, "How dare you! How dare you obligate me to go see that sorry excuse for a man!"

359

"Aliyah I'm so sorry. I was trying to help," he pleads.

She angrily says, "How dare he smile and laugh after everything he's done! He should be in there rotting!"

She slams her fist on the hood of Tim's car. He tries to comfort her, only to be pushed away as she says, "Get off of me! I'm upset with you right now! You're supposed to be on my side! You were in there laughing with him! I thought you understood me. I thought you cared about me!"

He sympathizes, "Aliyah I do! I love you. I was only trying to help. I'm sorry."

She utters, "Let's just go to Anderson. Jesus."

She opens the car door and gets in. Tim takes a deep breath and gets in. He looks at Aliyah who shoots him a look of annoyance.

She says, "Tim, start the car and let's go. We aren't going to argue about this. I came like you asked and it pissed me off. Deal with it and take me home."

Tim becomes confused as he starts the car. He becomes nervous but asks, "Do you mean *your* actual house or the other house?"

She sighs in annoyance and laughs slightly. Even at a time like this, he makes her laugh. She speaks, "Our home is in Anderson, sweetheart."

Tim begins to drive to Anderson. They drive for a half hour. Aliyah stares out the window filled with bitterness as they approach an apartment complex. Tim parks in front of an apartment and turns the car off. Aliyah takes her belt off and quickly gets out. They walk to the front door of their apartment.

T.Edward Redd   **360**

Tim thinks, *"I've never seen her so upset before. I thought if she went and saw how much improvement her dad had made, maybe she'd start caring again. But that only made things worse."*

He takes out his keys and begins flipping through them. He uses the wrong key, "Which one is it?"

Aliyah snatches the keys away and opens the door saying in a mild tone, "You take too long."

Tim walks in as he slams the door shouting, "Hey!"

She looks back upset as he walks to her seemingly angered. She shouts, "What now, Tim?"

He grabs and kisses her softly. He slowly kills her anger with his gentle touches and soft kisses, "Take it easy with that temper ok? I'm sorry I made you do that. You weren't ready. Aliyah I love you and I just worry about you."

She sheds a tear and holds him saying, "I'm so sorry I hit you. I was angry. I wasn't even mad at you. I was just frustrated with everything I've been through with him. But I didn't need to take it out on your face. Timothy I'm sorry for being so cruel and yelling at you."

She covers her face in embarrassment saying, "I can't believe I hit you. I'm so stupid."

Tim takes her hands smiling as he kisses her. He hugs her saying, "That's the Aliyah I know."

She replies, "I never went anywhere babe. I'm just upset. Why did you make me go there today? You know how much I hate him."

Tim says, "I didn't like the change I was seeing in you."

She becomes confused, saying, "Change? I haven't changed."

Tim says, "Before your brother died you would cry and wonder why your father treated you so badly. You wanted his love and you cared about him a lot. But after your brother died you started hating him. Your hate is so strong and dark. I didn't want it to become a part of you. I want my princess."

She becomes guilty saying, "Baby it's hard."

He says, "But the way you're dealing with your anger. Aliyah this isn't the way. I know you feel like you have every right to make him feel as much hurt as possible right now but Aliyah it's changing you and I don't like it."

Aliyah says, "Tim I'm sorry. It's hard."

He holds her saying, "It's ok babe. We'll get through this I promise. Just be strong and don't let your anger change you. I want us to have a happy life together up here. "

Aliyah replies, "We will babe I promise. I'll try to deal with my anger better." She kisses him on the cheek. They get on a couch in the house and cuddle as they begin to fall to sleep.

CHAPTER THIRTY

A month passes as Tim and Aliyah settle in their new home in Anderson. Two weeks have passed since they moved the rest of their things from Fishers. The two are set to start college in a month.

Aliyah stands in a lovely kitchen as she cooks. She cleans off counters as she turns off the oven. From the oven, she takes out meatloaf and places it on top of the stove. Tim walks into the house with a box. He smells the air and looks to the kitchen as he says, "Oh man I'm late aren't I? I was supposed to cook."

Aliyah looks back and smiles saying, "Hey, babe."

He walks in saying, "Wow this smells great honey."

He sits his box on a couch as he walks towards Aliyah. They hug and kiss. Aliyah looks to see the box on the nicely decorated couch. She points saying, "Babe, the couch."

He smiles saying, "Sorry I forgot. Hey come sit with me. I want to show you this."

They sit on the couch as he places the box on a table in front of them. Aliyah says, "These are copies of the book aren't they?"

Tim opens the box and pulls out a book saying, "Yup."

Aliyah becomes surprised as she sees the title. She says, "Blue Owl! You used my idea!"

Tim smiles, "Yes. I think it's catchy."

She hugs him saying, "Oh my gosh, that's so cool. I bet you're starving from carrying that heavy box. Come eat baby. Put this down for now. We'll admire your work later. Let's eat."

They go to a medium sized table, in a dining area, near the kitchen. Tim stares at the white cloth covering the table and the candle light dinner in front of him. Aliyah places a single rose in a vase, in the middle of the table. She sits down as she smiles with delight.

She says, "Perfect. It's just how I pictured it in my mind. Let's eat. Hey, what's the matter? You look bummed out. Did I cook this wrong?"

Tim replies, "Nothing it's just I was supposed to do this stuff for you. I was supposed to cook tonight but time got away from me."

Aliyah blushes and smiles as she says, "Hey don't worry about that sweetheart. I like cooking for you. Plus your writing career is what's feeding us and paying the rent right now. I don't mind at all babe. I like that you're successful. It motivates me to work hard towards my nursing career. I was so glad when I got that internship."

Tim says, "I'm really proud of your hard work, Aliyah. You inspire me too. You're going to be a great nurse."

Aliyah blushes as she thanks him. She looks around the house and smiles. Soft white furniture, clean carpets and nicely made drapes on the windows of the apartment make up the apartment's setting.

She knows this isn't her dream home and that eventually they'll move into an actual house. But this scenery is a lot more peaceful from what she came from. She feels proud and at peace.

T.Edward Redd

She looks to Tim and says, "I love it here. How do you like it?"

He replies, "I love it. I think we made a good choice with the white and navy blue color scheme. It's relaxing."

Aliyah replies, "Tim I was thinking. I know that this probably won't be our first home. I mean who wants to live in an apartment forever right?"

Tim looks at her as he says, "Yeah I know that. What's on your mind?"

She replies, "I don't have a job and I don't pay for anything here. Sometimes I feel like I'm no help."

Tim soothes her saying, "Aliyah, don't think about stuff like that. I don't work either. Well I kind of do but that's with my books. I'm here all the time just like you are. Besides we need to focus on school so we can get our careers, not jobs. Aliyah you're my motivation. You give me that extra boost I need to keep typing even when I'm super tired. You're helpful."

She replies, "Yeah I know. But when I finish my internship and become a nurse, I'm going to help you buy our next home. I don't want you to do everything. I want to help, you know?"

Tim says, "I understand, Aliyah. You're amazing dear. I love you. Fine, the next place we get will be purchased with our money, not my money."

Aliyah smiles as she says, "Deal. It was a pleasure doing business with you Mr. Derr."

Tim replies, "The pleasure was mine, Ms. Conrad."

They laugh at each other as they continue to eat. Aliyah thinks for a while and says, "Oh, speaking of money, your dad sent money for the cable bill. I don't think we need it but he insisted. So I took it. I didn't know what you wanted to do with it. I set the cable up earlier so it's working now."

Tim gets excited saying, "Sweet, so do we have on demand now?"

She replies, "Yes I got the package you wanted. I also added a few romantic stations too. You know I love soap operas. Do you want me to send the money your dad gave us as the payment?"

Tim says, "No we'll put that back for emergency money. I'll pay for the cable. Wow you've gotten so much accomplished since we moved here. You got the house decorated, you went out and got kitchen stuff, you bought groceries and you helped me move everything out here."

She replies, "Yes don't remind me. Wow, those car rides back and forth to Fishers were tiring. Unpacking is finally finished. We can rest for a year or two at the least. How did you like supper?"

He answers with a smile, "I loved it. You did great princess."

She playfully says, "Well it was the least that I could do, my lovely knight."

Tim says in a heroic tone, "However will I repay, my fine royal gemstone?"

She flips her hair elegantly replying in a laid-back tone, "Well sir knight, I fancy a nice cuddle along with a thousand kisses beneath our fine sheets as we watch shows on our royal screen of storytelling."

Tim stands up and walks to her. She stands up and begins to laugh as he lifts her and carries her to the couch. He places her on the couch as he begins to playfully kiss her. She giggles as she becomes ticklish.

She laughs saying, "Tim wait, I have to do the dishes."

Tim kisses her saying, "Forget about doing dishes tonight. I'll do them. I was supposed to cook so I'll wash plates instead."

She kisses him back and hugs him, "Grrr stop being so perfect. What are we doing tonight?"

He says, "I'm not sure. Do you want to go out again?"

She answers, "Eh, no it's too hot out. Let's just lay with each other and watch a movie. You can choose tonight, nothing scary though."

Tim kisses her. She kisses him back as he caresses her back. He gently squeezes her breasts. She lets out a soft moan. She pulls him close as he kisses her.

She stops him saying, "Wait, wait babe. I thought we agreed on no sex before marriage. We can't get each other excited like this or we might break our vow."

Tim calms himself down and lies beside her saying, "Yeah I know. It's really hard though."

She turns to him smiling, "This was your idea Mr. Derr. I'm just helping us reach our goal remember?"

He kisses her replying, "I know. Thanks, you're perfect. Yes, we're waiting until marriage. It's really hard when you're so fiery though."

She seductively replies, "Well I'll help you resist the urge hon. I know that we both are waiting for something more deep and meaningful to happen. I'll do whatever it takes to make it happen. It's hard for me too."

Tim holds her saying, "You're great, Aliyah. I feel like we're starting to connect on a mental level. We can understand each other better than ever."

She snuggles him saying, "We spend practically all of our time together. I'd be pretty disappointed if we didn't get as close as we are now. I'll be sad when classes start. We won't be able to share the entire day with each other like we are now."

Tim replies, "We'll still live together though babe. Don't worry about stuff like that. We need to focus on getting our degrees so we can be successful together."

She smiles saying, "You're so smart. With you selling so many books you probably won't even need a degree."

He says, "You never know. Besides, I think the experience I'll get with getting a degree in English will help me become a better writer."

He begins to dig into the couch around her thighs. She looks at him in confusion as she says, "Are you getting frisky?"

He laughs as he gets the remote from beneath her. He hands her the remote and holds her as she turns her back to him. She begins flipping through the TV stations. She turns to a commercial. They laugh as they watch.

A woman begins talking to her father, "Your drinking has gotten out of control!"

The man shouts, "Shut-up!"

Aliyah rolls her eyes saying, "Why does she even bother? He won't change no matter how many times she screams."

The man looks at the beer in his hand saying, "You have ruined my life. I want my family back. You can't be in my life anymore."

He throws the bottle against a wall and it shatters. The commercial ends with the ad saying: "Alcohol ruins lives...put the bottle down and start living".

Tim says, "You spoke to soon, babe."

Aliyah counters, "It's Hollywood. That stuff isn't real. People don't just change."

Tim asks, "Are you talking about your dad?"

She sasses, "If by dad you mean Alvin yes. That's exactly who I'm talking about. Don't do it Tim. We're having a good night.

Tim replies, "So you really don't think he's improved? Come on we both saw it. He was sober."

Aliyah says, "Two months, big deal. Maybe you should give him a medal since you're so proud of him. And the arguing starts yet again, oh boy."

Tim counters, "Aliyah two months was probably Hell for him considering the fact that he's been drinking for years now."

She smirks, "That's good. It's too bad he did all that other stuff to me though. You know, the physical and verbal abuse? Or did you forget he blacked my eye? It'll take more than a few months to clear that slate."

Tim sighs. Aliyah becomes irritated saying, "Don't you dare feel sorry for him. Stop worrying about Alvin and start worrying about your emotional scarred girlfriend. Ugh! Don't you love me?"

Tim appeases, "Baby yes! Of course I love you. That's why I'm so worried!"

She cries in annoyance, "Worried about what? I am fine! Stop worrying about me like I'm a defenseless child!"

Tim replies, "Aliyah you are not fine. You're bottling up your emotions and the jar is so full that your sorrow and anger are leaking out of it. Before your brother died I never heard you curse and I never saw you intentionally try to hurt someone. You were gentle and kind. You're burying your pain and emotions. It isn't healthy, Aliyah. Do you remember how you used to tell me that I didn't hate my mom?"

She says, "That was before I knew what it was like!"

Tim replies, "But now I'm starting to think hate is love. Hate is love gone sour. If we didn't care about our parents we wouldn't say these hurtful things towards them. We wouldn't try to hurt them if we didn't feel anything at all. I know you still love your dad Aliyah."

Aliyah says, "Ok, let's just watch a movie."

Tim tries to get her to be serious saying, "Aliyah, come on."

She raises her tone, "What do you want from me? You know I hate talking about this. It's my father and you're more worried than I am! Why won't you just drop it? We're living together. We should be happy. Why do you always ruin it with talks about my dad?"

Tim says, "Because now that I see myself from the outside it hurts me. It makes me regret the way I was towards my mom all those years. The way you are towards your dad now is the exact way I was towards my mom. Even though our parents wronged us, they're still our parents. I don't want my mom to pass away one day and all I have are these horrible memories of her. I know you don't want that either, Aliyah. If your dad died tonight could you handle it?"

Aliyah fights her feelings, "Tim, stop. Just let it go."

Tim continues, "Aliyah we both have resentment towards our parents. I want us to resolve the issues we have with our parents as soon as we can. We need to try."

Aliyah looks back at him in confusion, "Our parents? *We* need to try? What are you saying?"

He takes a deep breath and exhales saying, "I want to go see my mom."

She looks at him, surprised as she says, "Sweetheart. Wow, are you sure?"

He replies, "I am. I want to get all of my negative emotions out and resolve things with her. I feel like I need this for myself and I think in the long run it will improve my relationship with you."

She sits up and holds his hand asking, "Do you want me to come with you?"

Tim shakes his head yes, "I want you to see what this does for me and how doing the same with your dad will be good for you. I want us both to resolve the problems we have with our parents, together. I won't force you to face your dad. I'll let you come with me though. If you choose to go see your dad after I do this I'll go."

Aliyah hugs Tim as she sheds a tear saying, "Where have you been all of these years. You're so strong and brave. I love you, Tim. If you're willing to face your mom, I guess I can warm up to the idea of facing my dad too. Yes, I'll go with you. I love you."

Tim kisses her saying, "I love you too.

They hold each other as they kiss. Eventually they fall asleep as they watch TV. Morning soon approaches. Aliyah sits at a table in a blue t-shirt and black jeans. She watches as Tim walks in the kitchen dressed in a royal blue V-neck and blue jeans. He holds a pencil to his chin as he stares at a pad of paper in his other hand.

Aliyah asks, "What's that?"

He replies, "I wrote down all the things I've been mad at my mom for. I wrote down the main reason why I've been hurting so long."

Aliyah says, "You wrote a list?"

He answers, "Yeah. It's not really a long list. But I have a good idea of what I'm going to say. I made sure I wrote this in a way that doesn't make me sound like I'm attacking her too."

Aliyah says, "That's a really good idea. You know you're very intellectual. Especially when it comes to writing. It's really attractive, Tim."

Tim replies with a smile, "Thanks babe. I think it would be a good idea if you did this too." He hands her the pad and pen as he continues, "Writing is a good release."

Aliyah replies, "I write in my diary every day. I should just read that. But I want to read it in a way that doesn't attack him like you mentioned. When do you want to go see her?"

Tim studies his writing saying, "Today."

Aliyah becomes surprised asking in a caring tone, "Today? Do you even know where she even lives?"

He shakes his head saying, "Mhm, she lives in Brownsburg."

Aliyah stares in confusion, "Wait, she lives here in Indiana? I thought she moved to another state or something."

Tim explains, "No, she lives in Brownsburg. My sister goes to see her all of the time. But I haven't seen or spoken to her since I was 16"

She says, "So you think you're ready?"

He answers, "Kind of. I am slightly nervous."

Aliyah adds, "Me too kind of. It's not like you can warn her that I'm white or anything."

Tim says, "That won't bother her, Aliyah. We have white people in our family. Well, on her side anyway."

She replies, "Well then, I'm ready when you are babe. "I can write my thoughts on paper on the way there and back."

Tim gets up and looks at what he wrote. He looks nervous. He thinks to himself.

"Am I really doing this? It's been at least 3 years since I even talked to my mom. What if this goes badly? What if my mom doesn't even..."

His thoughts get brought to an end as Aliyah gets his attention with a gentle nudge to the shoulder. She says, "You were just standing there staring into space. Are you ok? Don't be nervous Tim. I'll be right there with you ok?"

Tim becomes motivated as he thanks her. They ready themselves and leave towards Brownsburg. Tim begins to thinks deeply as he drives.

"This is my chance to clear everything with my mom. All of these years of silence and the reason why I've felt this empty void. It's because she left me when I needed her the most. Why would she do that? Am I not enough? Even when she was here, I never felt her love. She was awful."

Aliyah notices his facial expression becoming tense as he becomes infuriated, "Tim, baby what's wrong? Talk to me."

373

He speaks, "Aliyah she was horrible. I can't believe that I'm actually reviving these bad memories. I've become so much stronger and more mature. Now I'm taking steps back."

She tries to calm him down, "Tim relax baby. It's ok."

He disagrees, "It's not ok. All of those years, watching her mistreat my father and all of the abuse. Then she has the nerve to leave? She's the reason why I'm so messed up now."

Aliyah firmly says, "Tim pull the car over."

He pulls to the side of the highway. Aliyah steps out of the car and motions him to get out. He gets out and walks to her. She gives him a comforting hug.

She says, "Take a deep breath and breathe. Your feelings are starting to overwhelm you. We both harbor negative emotions. This is why you're going to meet with her, to resolve the bad relationship you have with her."

Tim asks, "What if things don't go the way I want them to?"

She says, "What you're doing is very mature. Instead of continuing to hate your mom you're trying to build a healthy relationship with her. I'm proud of you for that. You're trying and that's what's important."

Tim smiles as he holds her close, "Thank you, Aliyah. You're great. God I love, you."

She says, "We help each other. You've helped me mature so much. I want to help you too, babe. I'll be here with you whenever you need me. Now come on. We're already half way there."

He kisses her as he thanks her again. They get into the car and continue driving to Brownsburg.

CHAPTER THIRTY-ONE

Aliyah watches Tim as he drives. She looks around to see that they are exiting the highway as they enter Brownsburg. Several cars pass them as they drive into an apartment complex. Tim looks at his GPS with confusion.

He says, "This is the place?"

Aliyah replies, "Yeah babe. The address is right there on the building. What, you don't think we're at the right place?"

Tim gets out of the car saying, "I just didn't think she lived in an apartment. I guess we got the better end of the deal."

Aliyah becomes confused repeating, "Better end of the deal?"

He replies, "Yeah, she walked out on my father and I. Now she lives in an apartment. I bet she can barely afford to live here."

Aliyah holds his hand saying, "Don't make this about revenge ok? You came here for closure and comfort with your mom. Don't compare your life to hers."

He replies, "Thanks, Aliyah. You're right."

They walk to the apartment and enter. Tim stares at a staircase as they stop walking. Aliyah says, "Okay so it's apartment 3B. I think it's up there babe. Come on."

Aliyah allows him to lead the way as she watches him.

She thinks, *"He looks so nervous. I've never seen him get like this about anything. When Regan and his friends beat him up, he was calm. When he met my dad, he was calm. But now, it's so clear that he's troubled. He's so brave for doing this."*

Tim walks to a door with the letter and number 3B. Aliyah stands beside him as she waits for him to knock or ring the bell. Tim stares at the door as he thinks.

Aliyah says, "Baby?"

He says, "Just a minute. I'm thinking."

She politely says, "Ok" as she waits quietly beside him. She holds his hand as she gets close to him. Tim finds comfort and motivation in her warm and gentle grasp as he knocks on the door. They wait in suspense as they stare at the door. Aliyah watches Tim.

Seconds seems like hours as she watches him slowly become more and more anxious. They hear soft footsteps as someone presses against the door. Aliyah watches the door as they hear the rattling of security locks and bolts. She feels Tim slightly squeeze her hand as the doorknob turns.

Aliyah watches as a short woman with long black hair, peek from behind the door. Her skin complexion is similar to Tim's but slightly lighter. She looks to be in her late thirties or early forties. She becomes confused to see Aliyah and says, "Can I help you?"

Aliyah becomes surprised, not knowing what to say. She looks at Tim. Tim's mother looks to see who Aliyah is looking at. He looks her in the eye with a somewhat serious face. Not a look of anger or even sorrow, but a look of waiting. She becomes more shocked to see her son who's grown a lot since she last saw him.

"Tim," utters.

He replies, "Mom."

She quickly hugs him. Aliyah takes a soft step back as Tim's mother embraces him. He stands motionless not knowing how to react. His mother stops to look at him.

She says, "Wow, you've grown so much. You look just like your father, Timothy. Who is the girl you brought with you?" She smiles slyly as she whispers to him, "Is she your girlfriend? She's pretty Tim."

He remains serious as Aliyah starts to smile at his mother's affection. He says, "Yes, she is."

She looks to Aliyah and smiles saying, "Hi, how are you? I'm Amber."

Aliyah smiles as she speaks, "Hi, I'm Aliyah."

Amber shakes her hand welcomingly. She welcomes them inside. Aliyah holds Tim's hand as he guides her. She observes nice leathered furniture and clean wooden flooring.

Aliyah says, "It looks pretty nice in here doesn't it, babe?"

Tim's thoughts mute her as he looks around, observing the lovely interior of the home. He notices a small bookshelf as they walk into a living area. Aliyah walks to a widescreen TV and sees two theater-like chairs behind her.

She says, "Haha, Tim look. This one doesn't have buttons either. I'll never be able to figure out this new technology. It's so fancy in here. Babe?"

She looks at Tim who still ignores her unknowingly. He stands at the bookshelf looking at a novel. Aliyah walks to him.

"What book is that hon," she says. She gets close to see a copy of "Blue Owl" in Tim's hand. She says, "It's one of your books?"

Tim replies, "Not just one."

He points to the top row of the bookshelf. Aliyah becomes amazed to see every copy of the books he's published, neatly stacked. She picks up a copy of *Hero's Wake.*

She says, "Wow, she has every single one of your books. Well, the one's you've published."

Tim picks up a copy of *Hero's Romance* and becomes shamefaced as he sees a bookmark towards the end.

"You're a very talented writer sweetheart. I never knew you were so gifted with writing. I remember how much you loved to draw."

They look back to see Amber coming out of a kitchen holding two cups. She hands them to Tim and Aliyah. He says, "You collect my books? How did you know I published any?"

She replies, "Your sister told me. She comes by every so often with her schooling and all. But she told me you were publishing a book a couple of years ago. I kind of keep tabs of you."

She continues, "There's a bookstore down the street. I've been checking for new books written by you for a while now every month. I buy and read each one. They're good, Tim."

She gently takes *Hero's Romance.* Aliyah watches as Tim struggles to look at his mother as she flips through the book. She holds no looks of sorrow, but pride in her son's work.

She says, "I'm glad that you came by son. It's been so long. I wanted to see you. I know that we haven't exactly had the best connection. I never knew you thought the things that you've thought."

He says, "I shouldn't have published this. Mom I'm sorry."

She replies, "Timothy don't be ashamed of your work. This is good. Writers write what they feel and think. You focused all of your emotions in a healthy way and birthed this great skill. I'm glad that I was at least able to understand how you were feeling through your books. Son I'm sorry. I know it must have been hard for you when you were so young. I'm sure you know by now what was going on."

Tim says, "I do. That's why I came here today. I wanted to talk about everything. I hold a lot inside and there were things I didn't understand until I was older. But by then, you were..."

She finishes sorrowfully, "Gone. I know son. I'm sorry."

Aliyah watches as Tim sees the regret in his mother's eyes. He hesitates to speak from his feelings of pain. He slowly let's go as he says, "I just wanted to come here and catch up with you. There's a lot I need to fill you in on in my life. It's not too late for us to form that special mother and son bond."

Aliyah watches as Amber hugs Tim tight with relief. She watches as he shares a long awaited moment with his mother. After a while they sit in the living room as Tim begins to talk about his high school years. His mother listens with interest as she smiles and laughs. Aliyah watches, politely adding commentary when she feels it's appropriate. She watches as she begins to admire Tim more and more.

"He's so brave and strong. Everything he does is admirable. He used to speak so poorly about her. After all that has happened, he would drop all of the pain just to start over fresh with her. That's very manly of him. It's motivating me to do the same with my father too. Timothy did all of this in order to get rid of any pain that's within him. So he can truly give himself to me."

379   *HERO'S ROMANCE*

She watches as his mother begins to show him her favorite quotes from his books. They begin to look like a mother and son bonding happily.

"If he can forgive her so easily and restart so he can give himself to me, I need to at least try to do the same with my father."

She watches as Tim and his mother bond for a couple of hours. She joins in on the conversations they have occasionally. Tim's mother begins to ask about college and where Tim stays. She says, "You two are living together?"

Tim replies, "Yes, Aliyah and I are both attending Anderson University this semester. She's pursuing a degree in nursing and I'm going for an English degree. Everything is fine with our housing. My books help pay for everything. Dad also helps."

She smiles proudly, "You've grown up to be a very independent young man Timothy. I'm proud of you, my son."

Tim replies smiling, "Thank you mom." He looks back at Aliyah saying, "It's getting pretty late. Are you ready to go home sweetheart?"

She replies, "Are you? We can go whenever you want. I'm fine, sweetheart."

Amber says, "She's a sweet girl, Timothy. Don't let go of her. You should go. Anderson is kind of far away. I don't want you to be out driving too late."

Tim holds Aliyah's hand as they stand. Amber walks them to the door. Tim hugs her one last time before they say their goodbyes. Finally, he feels the approval and love he'd longed for years as he steps back.

He says, "Thank you, mom. I love you. I'll visit again sometime."

T.Edward Redd   **380**

She replies, "Please do, Timothy. Be safe on your way home. Timothy I expect grandchildren."

Tim and Aliyah look at each other as they blush embarrassingly. They laugh slightly.

"But not too soon you two," she adds.

They continue to blush and laugh with embarrassment. The two have never had sex with one another. Hearing other people talk about their non-existent sex life tickles them. They know it's one of the big things that have allowed them to get so close. The day they have sex, will be beautiful.

Tim replies, "Don't worry mom. Take care. I'll call soon."

Tim and Aliyah walk away as Amber watches them out, to make sure they get to the car safely. Aliyah walks closely to Tim, under the night sky as they approach the passenger's side.

Tim says, "Alright sweetheart, let's go home."

She surprises him as she hugs him very tightly. She places her head on his chest as she hugs him.

"Aliyah, what's wrong," he asks.

She looks at him smiling with admiration, "I love you so much, Tim. You're so encouraging and brave. Up until now you've never had one nice thing to say about her. But you didn't even bring any of your pain. It's like you started over."

He replies, "I just saw the regret in her eyes. I couldn't bring myself to let out my pain and make her cry. I decided to just, let it all go. I want to just move on and build a relationship with my mother. No more despair."

She says, "Tim, I love you."

He replies, "I love you too, sweetheart. Let's get home."

He opens the door for her and let's her into the car. After he gets into the car, they begin to drive home. After an hour they approach the house. The moon shines brightly as Tim parks. He gets out of the car. Aliyah watches as he comes to her side to open the door. She stays seated, thinking deeply as he opens the door.

He says, "Come on sweetheart. I bet this long day has made you really tired. Thank you for coming with me Aliyah. Come on, you've earned a nice foot massage."

She takes his hand and steps out of the car. He guides her into the house and up a brown staircase. She watches Tim as he leads her into a bedroom. They sit as he removes his shoes. She sits back as he removes hers. Tim begins to massage Aliyah's soft and delicate feet. She let's out a relieving sigh as she lays back to relax.

Tim looks back at her. He smiles, pleased to see his beautiful companion relaxed. He says, "You're pretty tired huh, Aliyah?"

She replies with her eyes shut, "Yeah, today was pretty long baby. I'm really proud of you."

He replies, "You're proud of me?"

She says, "Yes dear. What you did today was very mature and so manly. I'm so turned on right now. What's more, you've encouraged me to resolve my issues too."

Tim rubs her feet saying, "So you've decided to see your father? I hope you don't feel pressured."

She sits up, "No babe, I'm motivated. I know that this is the right way to deal with things, before you and I start this new chapter of our lives. We can't turn the page until every detail has been schemed thoroughly."

T.Edward Redd   **382**

"You handled things with your mother and now it's time for me to handle things with my father. We'll be able to live happily with each other without any despair in our hearts. So when we have children, they won't inherit our pain."

Tim smiles at her, "I see I've been rubbing off on you. That sounds like something I would say. You've become really eloquent these past few months."

Aliyah blushes saying, "I think the way you speak with intelligence and smoothness is cool and sexy. I've been reading more and looking new words up so I can do it too. I like it a lot, babe. I get most of my vocabulary from your writing though."

She scoots close and wraps her arms around him as she kisses him. He holds her as he lies down with her. She lets out a laugh as he begins to kiss and tickle her neck. They lie beside each other.

Aliyah says, "Your mother wants grandkids. I think that's so funny. We have never had sex."

Tim replies, "Do you want kids in your future?"

She answers, "Well yeah. I always wanted a nice sized family. Do you want kids?"

He says, "I do. I've always wanted a little girl since I held my niece when she was really small. But I don't want children until I'm married."

Aliyah replies, "I agree with you, Tim. It's been a pretty long day, honey. Let's get some sleep. Let's let the future decide what happens. Go with the flow."

Tim agrees as he kisses her goodnight. They go to sleep.

CHAPTER THIRTY-TWO

A few years pass as Tim and Aliyah continue their relationship. As time passes, their lives slowly become one. They continue through their schooling. Tim successfully graduates college early and his writing career begins to blossom. Aliyah begins to catch up on Tim and starts to gain her own success as she advances through nursing school.

A woman screams in a hospital's patient room. A nurse tries to calm her down, saying, "Ma'am please, I need you to try and relax."

She says, "It hurts so much! Get this baby out of me!"

Her husband stands beside her panicking, "Just breathe, Jayne. Remember your breathing."

Jayne becomes frustrated as she grabs him by the collar shouting, "I am breathing! I've been breathing for the past 9 months! Get this baby out!"

The nurse looks to another nurse saying, "Conrad, where is Dr. Rim?"

Aliyah stands beside the nurse dressed in pink scrubs. Her brown hair is noticeably longer and she looks more like a woman and less like a teenager. She grabs a pair of gloves and places them on.

The other nurse says, "Conrad what are you doing?"

She answers, "We have to help her get the baby out. Dr. Rim is taking too long."

He panics saying, "Conrad, just follow procedure! We aren't qualified."

Aliyah disagrees, "I get my degree soon, therefore I am qualified. We've seen enough childbirths to do this without the doctor. That baby needs help out before she either faints or goes into shock. Do you want to lose the baby?"

The man becomes nervous saying, "Well no but..."

Aliyah cuts him off, "Then stop stuttering, man up and help me deliver this baby. We have everything we need right here. This isn't impossible for us. Go get the warm water and towels and hurry!"

He follows her instructions. Aliyah holds the woman's hand saying, "Miss, I know it hurts. But I need you to push ok? The doctor is taking longer than we expected. But I'm very experienced in this field. I'm going to deliver this baby and I need your help in aiding your baby boy out. He's in there and he's healthy. But I need you to push ok? How are you feeling?"

Jayne says, "I'm scared and I'm in so much pain. This isn't anything like I thought it would be. I knew it would hurt but not this much. I just want to see my baby boy. You're saying you can deliver the baby? You look so young. How old are you?"

Aliyah kindly answers, "I will be 22 in a month. I'm qualified to do this. This is what I went to school for four years and I'm getting my degree very soon. I know that this must be very nerve wreaking with me not being a doctor, but please trust me."

She takes the lady's hand, "Breathe deeply with me and try to relax. Follow the pace of my breathing and it will help you calm down. Let's deliver this baby Jayne."

Jayne nods and begins to follow Aliyah's lead in breathing. Aliyah places pillows behind the lady's back as she helps her get into a relaxed position. The other nurse stands and watches not knowing what or how to react without the actual doctor present.

Jayne's husband says to Aliyah, "Hey, how can I help miss?"

Aliyah says, "Help her stay calm. Try rubbing her back and talking to her. She needs to be relaxed. If she panics during delivery it will hurt her even more and she could harm the newborn."

The man holds his wife's hand and begins to comfort her. Aliyah places a cool washrag on the lady's forehead. The other nurse brings Aliyah several towels and a bucket of water. He asks nervously, "What now?"

Aliyah looks at the lady and watches as she tries to stay calm but her contractions begin to hit more and more. Aliyah says, "She's ready to give birth. I can tell. I'll guide her through this."

The man asks what he should do but Aliyah doesn't hear him as she becomes focused on the lady. This is one of the moments she's been waiting for. She wants to prove herself. She strives to be successful, like her boyfriend.

She says, "Ok Jayne, I want you to lie on your back and bend your knees. Sir, help her get comfortable. We're going to begin the delivery. Try to stay calm and breathe."

Aliyah kneels down to see how dilated Jayne is. She says, "1o centimeters...she's ready. Ok, I've seen this done at least one thousand times. I can do this."

She looks to Jayne saying, "Ok, I want you to start pushing. When you feel an unstoppable urge, push hard. Take rests between contractions so you don't lose all of your energy. Sir, I need you to hold her hand. Nurse, go get an ice pack."

Jayne's husband begins to worry, "Ice packet? For what?"

The lady begins to moan in pain as Aliyah says, "Ok push!"

Jayne grunts and screams as she pushes. She squeezes her husband's hand hard. He screams in pain with her as she unknowingly crushes his hand. The lady stops to catch her breath. Aliyah stares at the lady's vaginal opening. She stares in awe as the baby's head begins to crown.

She says, "I...I can see it!"

Jayne begins to moan and yell in pain as she squeezes her husband's hand fiercely. He starts to scream in pain with her again. Aliyah begins to see the baby's head. She becomes slightly surprised and moved.

"Oh my gosh...I can see it. Hey! Where's that towel and water at," she says.

Jayne says, "You see him? Is he ok??"

Aliyah says, "He's fine. Jayne I need you to help him out and I'll guide him. Keep doing what you've been doing. Sir she needs your hand again, I promise we'll patch it up for you. It's helping her fight the pain."

Jayne moans once more as a contraction hits. She pushes as she screams loudly. The baby begins to come out as Aliyah guides it gently. The nurse stares with amazement as he watches Aliyah deliver the baby as if she's a doctor.

Dr. Rim rushes into the room but stops as he sees Aliyah cut the umbilical cord. The baby begins to cry slightly as the other nurse begins to help Aliyah clean it. The doctor stands and watches Aliyah as he becomes intrigued with her performance.

She takes a moment to look at the baby. Slightly, she becomes attached, but gives him to his mother. She wraps both the baby and mother in clean towels. She looks to the other nurse, saying, "See, I told you we could do it."

The nurse becomes edgy as he stares at the doctor behind Aliyah. She looks back to see him watching her with his hand to his chin as he watches her.

She says, "Doctor I'm sorry. But the lady was having her contractions and she was dilating. I had to deliver it. We didn't know where you were. Doctor Rim I'm sorry. Please don't end my internship. I've worked so hard and..."

He stops her as he says, "Miss Conrad, I have to end your internship."

Aliyah panics as she says, "But sir! I didn't know what else to do. But look the baby is fine and so is the lady."

Doctor Rim walks to the lady and her husband. He watches as the lady bonds with her newborn son. He asks the lady how she's feeling.

She says, "I'm fine. She was great, doctor. She did everything. She knew what she was doing. Thank you, Miss Conrad"

Aliyah says, "Please don't end my internship. I need my degree so I can become a nurse. I've worked so hard sir. Please. My boyfriend, he..."

Doctor Rim says, "Miss Conrad I need you to gather your things from the intern labs. Your internship has ended early."

T.Edward Redd   **388**

Aliyah becomes teary eyed as she struggles not to cry, "Sir I am begging you. My boyfriend will be beyond disappointed and I've put so much time and effort into this. So much relies on me graduating. I'll never do this again. Please, I promise. I thought I was doing the right thing. Give me another chance, I beg you."

Doctor Rim says, "Conrad get your things and move them into my office. I'm giving you a part-time job as my assistant nurse. Your internship is over. I want to put you on commission, you graduate today."

Aliyah's tears cease as she says, "What? Your assistant? Me?"

Doctor Rim says, "You've shown remarkable talent these past couple of months, Conrad. Your grades in your classes are excellent and your knowledge about the work here is almost as keen as some of the doctors here. I'm offering you a part-time job as my assistant nurse. If you keep impressing me, I will give you a fulltime position."

Aliyah becomes surprised saying, "OH MY GOSH!! YES! YES! YES!" She becomes excited as she hugs the other nurse uncontrollably. She stops to ask, "When do I start sir? Of course I'll take it. This is my dream!"

He replies, "Well you were scheduled to start next week. But this performance you did tonight will count towards your work. I want you to take the rest of the week to relax. You've earned it. You start Monday at 6a.m."

Aliyah says, "Thank you sir. Thank you so much! I'll go move my things right now. Did you need me here?"

He shakes his head no, "You pretty much did everything here. You're good to go. Oh, your boyfriend is here too."

She smiles happily saying, "Tim?"

He says, "Yes, he's waiting to take you home. You should hurry."

She thanks the doctor and quickly walks out of the room. As she walks to the front desk of the floor, she sees Tim sitting in a chair. Slightly her cheeks blush as she sees him dressed in a striking black dress-suit as he works on a tablet. He looks up to see her and smiles.

She says, "Baby! Ah, come here."

Tim stands as she hugs him tightly. She kisses him happily as he holds her. He says, "Hey sweetheart. Haha you seem really happy. How was your day?"

She says, "Baby I just delivered my first baby! It was beyond amazing."

He replies with confusion, "Don't you deliver them every day?"

She answers, "I *help* deliver every day. But today I actually delivered! It was great baby you should've saw me. It was so amazing! And the baby, he was adorable. I can't describe it. Baby it was amazing. But that's not the best part. Guess what."

Tim rubs her shoulders as he smiles, "Hey relax, sweetheart. Tell me all about that stuff over dinner. We have a date tonight remember?"

She holds her head and says, "Oh gosh, I forgot all about that! I need to go get ready. Oh no, I overlooked the fact that I need to go get all of my stuff from the labs. Can you help me?"

Tim hugs her and says, "Haha yes, dear. Don't worry I made reservations for 11p.m. I know how busy you get. Let's go take care of the lab stuff so we can jet."

They hold hands as they walk down the hospital halls. Walking close and flirting like a newly made couple, they stroll into the labs. Tim begins to help her pack her things. He becomes confused as to why they're moving her things out of her workspace.

He looks up asking, "Wait a minute. Why are we packing your things again? I thought this stuff was supposed to stay here for your nursing."

Aliyah replies with a smile, "I'm no longer an intern. It ended early."

Tim says, "Oh no. Aliyah I'm sorry. I'm going to go give that man a piece of my mind. What happened?"

She says gleefully, "Oh nothing too special. I just got a part-time job as an assistant nurse is all."

Tim becomes shocked as he says, "Whoa no way. Really sweetheart?"

He hugs her as she smiles. Joy spreads throughout her whole body, feeling how proud Tim is with her. She hugs him back happily. Tim says, "Aliyah that's amazing. I'm so proud of you. This is your dream. You've worked your brains out for this."

She says, "I know. Now we both are living our dreams."

Tim says, "Oh! That reminds me. We have to hurry because it'll take half an hour for us to get there."

She says, "Half an hour? Where are we eating, baby?"

Tim smiles as he gathers Aliyah's nursing tools and supplies. He says, "It's a surprise. But I've been dying to do this for you. Come on let's go."

She smiles saying, "Mr. Derr, you know I hate surprises."

He replies, "Make an exception, just this once, Miss Conrad."

She blushes as she follows him. After they move her things to her new workspace they leave. As they drive Aliyah watches Tim, trying to figure out what he's got up his sleeve.

They begin to arrive in Indianapolis. Aliyah begins recognizing the area saying, "Babe why are we in Hoosier Ville? You picked out an eatery here? You know there's places close to home right?"

Tim says, "Not like this one."

Aliyah looks to see them arriving at a familiar expensive restaurant.

She says, "Oh wow. It's the place you took me for my 17th birthday. We were seniors back then and no one even remembered my birthday. But my hero did. Didn't you handsome?"

Tim smiles and says, "Yes, this is a special occasion."

He parks the car in the same spot he parked on their first unofficial date. He turns the car off and steps out. Aliyah smiles as he opens the door for her. She takes his hand and steps out of the car. They begin walking towards the restaurant as they hold hands. Aliyah looks at the wish fountain.

She says, "Wow, Tim it looks just like it did four years ago. It looks even prettier at night. Oh honey, you're perfect."

Tim takes out a coin and offers it to her. She smiles saying, "Not this time dear. I won't tell you what I wished for back then." She squeezes his hand gently as she hints, "But it came true. You make a wish this time."

Tim smiles as he looks at the coin. Closing his eyes, he flicks the coin into the fountain. Aliyah smiles as she kisses him on the cheek. He passes her a smile as he gently squeezes her hand lovingly.

T.Edward Redd

He opens the door for her and bows saying, "For you royal princess."

She smiles and bows to him as she enters, "Why thank-you, Sir Derr."

As they walk inside they observe the fine dining area. Aliyah stares at the marble flooring as they enter the eating area. She lifts her dress slightly to keep it from dragging. Tim guides her to a reserved table. They sit.

She looks at him saying, "Everything is just like it was back then. I feel like I'm 17 all over again. Haha."

Tim smiles saying, "Don't you turn 22 next month?"

She teasingly replies, "You mean you have to ask?"

He winks at her, "Not really sweetheart. How could I ever forget the first day we met? March 7th, 2011. It was sometime between 8 and 9a.m. And of course, it was your birthday."

She smiles at him as a waiter with curly red hair and glasses arrives at their table. He hands them menus nervously, saying, "Do you want a few minutes to decide on your meal tonight?"

Aliyah looks to Tim, "I'll just share with you. Does this place have couple sized meals like the place we go to in Anderson?"

Tim answers, "Let's just get two separate meals and share with each other. Steak or fish?"

She says, "I'll get fish and you get steak. We can have both. I'll get a side of fries and you can get vegetables like you usually do."

Tim replies, "Alright that sounds great. Sir, we would like the smothered steak dinner and…"

Aliyah finishes, "The fish dinner with extra fries. He can eat a plate full so we might need extra."

The waiter shakes his head as he walks away. Aliyah looks around and says, "Where is the guy who took our order last time?"

Tim replies, "That was over 4 years ago, sweetheart. I asked about it and he's in school. That's a new waiter. So he's kind of nervous with people."

Aliyah says, "That makes a lot of sense. That doesn't matter though. This is great, Tim."

Tim looks nervous as he looks at her.

She says, "So you have a surprise?"

He replies saying, "I do."

She smiles asking, "What is it? You're making me nervous."

Tim says, "Tell me about this new job you got, sweetheart. Did you graduate today?"

Aliyah gets excited saying, "Yes. I was supposed to graduate at the end of this semester but I guess after he saw my performance today, he decided to give me an official job. I'm so excited. Do you want to hear about the delivery?"

Tim stares nervously wanting to say something but doesn't as he shakes his head yes. He stares into her eyes deeply yet peacefully as she speaks.

She says, "So Dr. Rim left the patient's room for a really long time. The woman's contractions got closer and closer. I had to help. So there I was with Adam. Haha, he was acting like such a baby! Ironic huh? But I knew what to do and delivered the baby confidently."

Tim holds a thoughtful look as he stares at her. While watching her gracefully explain her day, he takes a moment to admire every aspect of her beauty. First looks, then mind and lastly, soul. His feelings deepen as he holds in his words.

T.Edward Redd   **394**

She continues, "Tim the baby was so adorable with its little cry and its tiny arms. Baby do you think I could be a good mother?"

Tim answers, "Aliyah, you would make an excellent mother."

She blushes and smiles. Her smile fades as she starts to notice Tim's not so excited mood. She says, "Tim what's the matter? Am I talking too much?"

He becomes startled comfortingly saying, "Aliyah no, you're perfect."

She replies, "But you look distressed. What's the matter dear?"

Tim says, "It's the…the surprise."

She becomes concerned, "Did the waiter do something wrong? Baby, it's ok. I love this."

He says, "No, you don't understand. The waiter doesn't have the surprise this time. I do."

She says, "Well what is it baby? Are you afraid I won't like it? Honey you're starting to worry me. Please talk to me."

Tim adjusts his tie nervously as he coughs. He wipes sweat off of his head saying, "Heh, wow. I wasn't this nervous when we first met and now I'm shaking like a little boy. Man, this is rough. Get it together, Tim. You can do this."

Aliyah watches in confusion and worry, "Do what honey? Just tell me already. You surprise me all of the time. You've never failed to impress me. Why would this be different?"

He says, "You're right, Aliyah. Look."

He stands up and bumps into the waiter as he brings their meal. Aliyah watches with shock as the two fall down. Food and drinks fall on to Tim's head and suit. Everyone begins to watch as Tim rubs his head in embarrassment.

"Ah, shoot. Sir, I'm so sorry," he says.

Aliyah stands to help, "Timothy are you ok? Here let me help you. You're acting so strange. What's on your mind?"

He grabs her hand as she helps him up. The waiter begins to clean the mess politely. Tim says, "Sorry, I'm so nervous. Can you feel me shaking?"

Aliyah shakes her head yes, "Why are you nervous sweetheart? Please just tell me what you're thinking about."

Tim looks at her deeply as he says, "You."

She says, "What about me is making you this nervous? Honey we've lived together for almost five years now. You sleep with me every night. I shouldn't make you nervous anymore."

Tim takes both of her hands saying, "I want us to live together much longer than five years."

Aliyah says, "We will baby."

He says, "No, you're not understanding. Aliyah I've been planning this moment for a year now. I needed the right time, place and setting. It's nerve wreaking. Ok breathe Tim. Just speak from the heart."

Aliyah watches deeply as he continues, "Aliyah, these past four or five years have been wonderful. We've helped each other grow so much. Each day we get closer and our love is as new as it was the first time we held one another. I was successful when we first got together. Now you're starting to rise like the star you are. I'm so proud of you. You're my world."

Aliyah forgets to breathe as his words move her. She gasps as he takes her breath away and says, "Tim, oh my god...are you going to..."

T.Edward Redd

He interrupts, "I want more years with you. I want all of my years with you. You're my home. Everything I've accomplished, it's because of this light your love has placed inside of me. I need you in my life. I want to live long with you. I want to travel with you. I want to settle down and raise a family with you. Aliyah…"

Her eyes begin to water as he kneels before her. He takes her left hand as he takes out a small black box. Aliyah sheds a tear as she holds her face with her free hand. She says his name softly as he speaks.

He says, "Aliyah, you and I met out of the blue. We both never imagined that day, that in four years we would be where we are. We changed each other's life for the better and we've grown alongside each other. Even though I was already publishing books when we met, I have always seen you as an equal, my equal."

He continues, "Aliyah you make me whole. Separate, you and I are great. But together, nothing stops us. I want that for the rest of my life. Aliyah I want to marry you and have you become my husband. No, I mean I want to be your wife."

Aliyah let's out a giggle mixed with tears as she listens to him mix his words up. He says, "Aliyah I want you to take my hand in marriage. Marry me, Aliyah."

Aliyah stares at him for a moment as she holds her hand to her face. She can't help but to cry.

Tim watches as she cries, "Oh my god, oh my god, no this isn't happening. It can't be no. It seems so perfect and dreamlike. No, Tim you're beyond perfect. Gosh, no way this is happening."

Tim becomes confused, "You don't want to?"

Aliyah says, "No! I mean yes! I mean no to your question."

Tim says, "You don't want to marry me?"

Aliyah becomes frustrated, "Yes!"

Tim becomes frustrated, "Aliyah this was hard to pull off and it's very emotional for me. You're confusing me and…"

She cuts him off as she pulls him up. Wrapping her arms around him, she kisses him lovingly. Tim holds her sides as he kisses her back. She gently pulls away and holds her face close to his.

She says, "Yes, I will marry you, Timothy Derr. I would be honored to be your bride. Please put the ring on my finger. I want to marry you, Timothy Edward Derr."

He wipes a single tear from his eye as he places the ring on her left ring finger. They stop to look as the people of the restaurant applaud their affection as a couple of people cheer for Tim. Aliyah hugs him tightly.

She says, "Timothy Derr, I've been dying to hear those words from you since the day we moved to Anderson. I knew that you were the one the moment we settled in. I just had to be patient and wait. You make me feel so safe and temperate when you hold me. I've been dreaming of this day since I was a little girl. It's so perfect and special. I love you."

Tim cuddles her saying, "I love you too, Aliyah."

Aliyah removes an onion bit out of his hair as she smiles at him. Tim looks behind him as the waiter finishes cleaning the mess. Tim says, "I'm sorry about that, sir."

Another waiter brings out a new meal for them as the waiter says, "It's alright. If you give me your autograph, we can give you that one for free. Sir, my girlfriend loves your books. If I get your signature she would be head over feet for me."

T.Edward Redd   **398**

Tim smiles saying, "Sure, ha, ha thanks."

The waiter stands as Tim and Aliyah sit close to each other as they prepare to eat.

Tim says, "This calls for some wine. What do you think, sweetheart?"

She says, "I'd like a little bit of wine. That sounds like a good idea."

The waiter stands saying, "I can get you a free bottle. I'll be back, Mr. Derr."

They watch as the waiter rushes to the back. Tim and Aliyah begin to eat their food happily. After half of an hour they finish their meal and wine as they begin dessert. They have chocolate cherry cake with whipped cream. Aliyah feeds Tim saying, "So you want children too honey?"

He says, "I hear about you helping with childbirth so much lately. It just got me thinking. I do want a baby or two, maybe even three if you want. I've always wanted a daughter."

Aliyah smiles saying, "That's a very big possibility. I have a lot of women on my mother's side. I want sons too but we'll be happy with whatever we get I'm sure. We can start after we marry. It'll be our first time having sex with each other."

Tim replies, "Yes I know. I have to sleep next to that gorgeous body every day since we graduated. I have no idea how we managed to abstain for so long."

Aliyah replies, "Things are usually easier with teams. We make a very good team. You're my drive too dear. Every time I took an exam or had to help deliver a baby, I thought about you. I thought about how much I wanted to help out with the house and be an equal to you. I've worked hard just so we can have a great life together."

Tim says, "And Aliyah, I'm proud of how far you've came. You reconciled with your father. You worked hard through college and now you're about to live your dream. Even though I got my degree, writing is my dream. When I graduated early I didn't feel complete until I was home with you. I work hard for you too."

Aliyah kisses Tim on the cheek as she hugs him. He hugs her back and they begin to cuddle like they did in high school. Aliyah playfully puts cake on Tim's cheek. He laughs and does the same to her. They laugh happily as they begin to play fight and tickle one another. They laugh until their stomachs hurt and lie down on the comfy booth's furniture.

Tim leans against the cozy seat and allows Aliyah to lie on him comfortably. She says, "Tim this is great. It's just like it was on my 17th birthday, only except I didn't flee. I came to you without any fears or worry. This is amazing."

Tim replies, "I'm glad you liked it sweetheart. Wow, I think we're the only ones here. Look, everyone is either gone or leaving."

She sits up saying, "It's close to 1a.m, baby. I think this place is about to close. Are you sober enough to drive or should I do it?"

Tim yawns as he holds her, "Let's call a cab. I'm too tired to sleep. I mean I'm too tired to drive. Let's get a hotel for the night. Besides we're going house hunting in Fishers later today."

She becomes excited, saying, "House hunting? Really, baby? Not an apartment but an actual house for a family?"

Tim rubs the top of her head playfully, "Yes, sweetheart. We're finished with school. I don't think there's any reason for us to keep that apartment. Your job is only 30 minutes away from Fishers. You could manage that right?"

She eagerly says, "Yes I could! Baby when are we going? Do you already have houses picked out? Are they fenced? You know I love the gated fences and then we have to worry about location. I want the house close but not in the city. I want it to be slightly exclusive. Oh and there needs to be a lot of trees. Then we need a dog and a backyard because…"

Tim says, "Whoa princess, slow down there. Haha, save that energy for later when we're hunting. Don't worry sweetheart, my publisher knows a real estate agent who has quite a few nice houses. You know, indoor pools, a balcony, hot tubs, secret spots in the house so when we have kids you and I can you know."

Aliyah smiles and grabs his hand, "Come on we have to go get some sleep! Today is going to be really busy. Well this entire week will be busy. We have to pick out the house, plan the wedding, decide who can come and then we have your book signing on Friday. Let's go honey. I'll pay for the cab ok? You've passed your spending money on Aliyah limit for the week."

Tim gets up as he holds her hand saying, "I don't like that rule very much."

They hold each other as they walk to the exits. Outside they stand on a curb, waiting for a cab. Aliyah keeps warm as Tim wraps his arms around her.

She says softly, "Jesus, I could fall asleep right here honey. You're so warm."

401   *HERO'S ROMANCE*

Tim asks, "Can I please pay for the cab?"

She shakes her head no with her eyes shut as she snuggles in his arms.

She says, "You know the rules sweetheart. You spend on me for three days and then I spend on you for three days and on the seventh we divide the balance and pay together. I like doing this, Tim. I like being a team. I know you want to be a man and pay for your woman. But I want to be a woman and take care of my man too. We're a team. I'm paying for the cab and that's the end of it."

Tim nibbles and kisses her neck playfully as he holds her. She yawns and begins to stagger. Tim catches her, saying, "Whoa, are you ok?"

She laughs saying, "Just slightly drunk mixed with sleepiness. Don't let me fall please. These heels are impossible for me right now."

He holds her, "I won't Aliyah," he laughs, "you're such a lightweight, dear."

He holds her as the cab arrives. It parks in front of them. Tim helps Aliyah into the cab and gets in after her. She takes off her dress shoes as she lies beside Tim closely. Slightly drunk, she begins kissing him on the neck as she touches his chest.

"Tim I want you," she says.

Tim laughs as he holds her, "Take it easy, sweetheart. Relax and breathe ok?"

She kisses him fiercely on the lips as she grabs his tie. He runs his hands through her long and graceful hair as he holds her. The cab driver looks at them through the rearview mirror saying, "Are you two lovebirds going to tell me where I'm taking you?"

Tim gently pushes Aliyah away as he says, "Take us to the M Hotel. Go slow please. She gets motion sickness easily when she's drunk. I'll give you the extra money."

As he digs into his pocket Aliyah places her hand on his as she leans towards him, "No, no, I'm paying buddy. You aren't slick. The only thing you're going to give tonight is your…"

Tim covers her mouth as he laughs saying, "Aliyah!"

She licks his hand and bites it in a goofy manner as she leans over him. He laughs at her drunkenness as she gets on top of him. He tries to kindly nudge her off but she pins both of his arms against the seat as she kisses him. Tim kisses her back as she holds his face. He slowly wraps his arms around her.

She whispers, "Tim I want it tonight. I want it now."

Tim whispers back, "Aliyah take it easy, you're drunk. Come here and lie down. We're almost there."

She lies down on his legs as he supports her head. Not a moment sooner after he relaxes his hands, she grins and gets up to kiss him. She tackles him as she places his face into her chest and caresses his head gently.

She says, "We've been taking it easy for four years. Baby I'm ready and so are you. I'm sitting on it and I feel it." She bounces up and down.

Tim becomes tense as she slowly rubs her rear against his thighs. He tries to sit up to stop her but only excites her even more. She lets out a soft moan as she giggles. He manages to seat her beside him, only to be tackled by her again.

He gently holds her back with both hands as she playfully tries to bite at him. As she lets out a small drunken hiccup he laughs. She smiles as she hugs him. Tim begins to notice the cab driver watching.

403   *HERO'S ROMANCE*

Tim shouts, "Hey! How long have you been watching us?"

He says, "Kid I haven't had any action in years. Look, we're at the hotel."

Tim looks back to see they're at the M Hotel. He tries to get money from his pocket but Aliyah stops him, "No baby, I got it. You're giving me something else when we get our room."

She hiccups as she takes out the incorrect amount of money. She goofily tosses the money at the cab driver. He becomes surprised to see several twenties and a couple of fifty-dollar bills.

Tim guides Aliyah out as he laughs and says, "That's your tip I guess. Thanks for putting up with us. Have a good night sir. Come on, sweetheart."

The cab driver says, "I'm sure your night is going to be better than mine will."

Aliyah giggles as the cab driver rides away.

She holds him saying, "So we're going to have a good night?"

She kisses on his neck and reaches for his pants. He stops her. He says, "Alright let's get you to bed. You've reached your limit, Miss Conrad."

She jumps onto him. He catches her as she wraps her legs around him. She says, "I'm Mrs. Derr now, sweetheart. See the ring? Take me and make love to me now, my knight."

He carries her as she playfully kisses on his face and neck. They enter the hotel. The doors slide open as he carries her inside. To his relief, the lobby is empty with only a receptionist available. He holds Aliyah as he walks to the desk to order a room.

He says, "We need a one night room please."

The lady watches as Aliyah nibbles on Tim's face playfully.

He says, "She's just a little drunk. I'm too tired to drive."

Aliyah blurts out, "I'm too turned on to drive! Haha, take me Timothy, you bad boy!"

The lady raises her eyebrow as she looks at Tim. He jokingly says, "I'm the good one here. I'm completely sober. She's clearly the bad one."

Aliyah says in a drunken tone, "We're getting married and having like twenty-three babies. I already have the names. Hey miss, do you want to hear the names? Samantha, Violet, Edward, Lyssa, Thome," she drags on.

The receptionist becomes annoyed and says, "I'm assuming you only need one bed then?"

Tim says, "She's my fiancée. It's not like what you're thinking. We just need a room so we can rest. Do you have anything?"

She answers, "Guest room 508 on the 5th floor. It's a one king with a city view. Enjoy your night with your bad boy miss."

Aliyah takes the ticket saying, "Oh I will. Won't I, Tim?"

Tim says playfully, "Don't encourage her. Haha, have a good night miss. Come on Aliyah, let's get you to bed."

Tim thanks the lady once more, as he carries Aliyah to an elevator. They walk inside after waiting a couple of minutes and ride the elevator to the 5th floor. They step out and walk to room. Aliyah opens the door as Tim holds her. He carries her inside.

He stares in amazement as he sees the neatly organized hotel room. The cool breeze from the room's air conditioning welcomes them.

"Aliyah, are you okay to walk," he asks.

She replies, "Yes handsome. Thank you."

She places her legs down and falls to the ground. Her knee hits a table in front of the bed. She moans in pain as Tim kneels to her. He picks her up as she whines softly.

"Alright come on. Bedtime," he says caringly.

She says, "Sleep with me please."

He gently places her on the bed. She lies on her back as he sits towards the front of the bed. He removes his tie and starts to remove his shoes. Aliyah begins to remove her dress but notices her dress shoes are missing.

She whines, "No! My dress shoes are gone!"

Tim looks back, "Oh, we must have forgotten them in the cab. I'll get you another pair. Those are history."

She whines more, "But those were my favorite. I want my dress shoes. They made me feel like Cinderella. How can I be your princess now?"

As she begins to drunkenly cry, Tim holds her and rubs her back. He says, "You don't need those things to be my princess, sweetheart. All you need is that special thing inside your chest."

He smiles at her while she stares at him blankly. The alcohol makes her very emotional, wild and her attention span reduces to that of a child. She can't make sense of what he just said.

She hiccups saying, "My chest?"

She looks at her chest and smiles at her breasts. Quickly she takes off her dress. Tim laughs as he turns back to ignore her drunkenness.

He says, "You can't have any more alcohol miss. You're such a lightweight. I guess that's good. At least you aren't an alcoholic I guess. Wow, today was pretty long huh? It's going on 2a.m."

He feels Aliyah's hair fall down his shoulders as she leans towards him. He looks back to see her in a black bra and laced panties. She blushes as he turns to her.

She whispers, "I want you tonight."

Tim laughs and says, "Aliyah you're drunk."

She pulls him close and kisses him as she removes his shirt. She lies down and holds him close. Tim stops her as she begins to remove her bra.

He says, "Aliyah we're waiting until marriage and I won't have sex with you when you're drunk."

She says, "We are married see," she shows him the ring, "we've waited long enough now give it to me, Mr. Derr."

Her hand drops and she passes outs. Tim stares at her for a moment. He checks to see if she's breathing. He lies beside her as he sighs in relief. He places covers over her.

He says, "I want it too, sweetheart. But we're so close to the finish line. Let's not ruin what we have."

He lies beside her and eventually falls to sleep.

CHAPTER THIRTY-THREE

A few weeks pass as Tim and Aliyah spend time with one another. They pick out a house in Fishers, close to Geist. Aliyah cleans a spacious kitchen in her nursing outfit. She looks around to see not a spot in sight. She smiles peacefully as she constantly checks the kitchen clock.

"Where are they? I hope they can find the house," she says.

She walks out of the kitchen and into a living room. The house is spacious but it's obvious the move was recent. There are few pieces of furniture and a couple of tables. She walks to the front door and opens it. As she walks outside onto a long driveway, she puts her hand over her eyes to block the sun as she looks for someone.

She says, "They must be running late. I'll give it five more minutes before I call."

She looks back to adore the beautiful house and smiles as she sees the large home surrounded by a breathtaking lawn and its landscape. The house seemingly shines as the sun beams brightly on its pearly white paint. She looks back as a car honks. She becomes happy to see her aunt Wendy and her cousins Joline and Amanda in the car.

She waves as they park. The three women step out of the car. They stare with amazement at the house. Joline says, "Whoa, Aliyah is living the life out here. This house is gorgeous."

Wendy says, "It had better be. It took us an hour to find it."

Aliyah walks to them happily saying, "You're here!"

They hug her gleefully as they greet one another.

Aliyah says, "I haven't seen you all since Aunt Madison's wedding."

Joline smiles saying, "Only one year. I see it made you decide to tie the knot with Tim. Congratulations, Aliyah."

Aliyah blushes saying, "Thank you. Timothy was the one who proposed. He was so moving when he did and beyond nervous. He even made the waiter drop our food. Come on we can talk about it inside. The sun is too hot and I don't want a tan," she laughs.

They follow Aliyah inside. They walk into the house and into the living room. The house is a bit vacant as they see one couch and a wide screen TV.

Amanda says, "It's a little empty in here isn't it?"

Aliyah says, "Yes, Tim paid for the mortgage and it was pricy. I don't let him spend a lot of money without me spending some of mine too. We waited until I got my paycheck. He's out picking up some furniture right now. Should be back soon. Do any of you want lemonade? I made some earlier. I was bored," she laughs.

They kindly shake their heads yes as they follow her into the kitchen. They walk on the yellow and white tiled flooring as Aliyah walks to chestnut brown cabinets above a silver and black stove. She hands them each a glass and walks to a sink. To allow sunlight into the room, she opens yellow silk blinds. She walks to a large and silver refrigerator beside a white freezer.

Wendy says, "Tim must be doing pretty well with his writing if he paid for the mortgage by himself huh?"

Aliyah gets a look of disappointment on her face as she pours them strawberry lemonade.

She says, "Yes, he is. He paid for the mortgage by himself. I felt pretty bad about it. That's why I'm paying for the furniture. I bought almost everything in here except the freezer and curtains. I bought the kitchen and dinnerware. I just started working as a RN nurse and I only make 55 dollars an hour. So I only make close to four thousand every two weeks."

She sits with the group as she takes a sip of the lemonade and continues, "Tim never fails to amaze his readers. He's been doing a great job with providing for us these past four years. He even helped with my tuition. I want to help him too and provide for him. That's why I paid for the furniture he's going to get. Once I've been working for a while, things will even out."

Amanda says, "I think it's so cool you get to deliver babies. I'm getting a teacher's license soon. I'll be teaching pre-k."

Aliyah smiles saying, "That's amazing, Amanda."

Wendy says, "So Aliyah, you were talking about the wedding plans when we spoke over the phone?"

Aliyah replies, "Oh! Yes, I wanted help planning the wedding. Hold on." She gets up from her seat and runs into the living room. Tim walks in the living room carrying a tiny puppy. As Aliyah walks, she blindly bumps into Tim and causes the puppy to yelp.

She becomes surprised as she focuses.

Tim says, "Hey, don't go scaring her like that, sweetheart. She's really shy. Hey I got the furniture on a huge truck. We can take our time getting it off though. I rented it for about six hours. Hey did I hear voices earlier?"

T. Edward Redd   410

Aliyah stares at the black Labrador retriever pup in Tim's arms. She asks, "Tim, why do you have an adorable puppy? Was it outside lost?"

Tim says, "Haha, no dear, she's yours. Here, happy birthday sweetheart. Be gentle with her. She's very nervy."

He holds the puppy towards Aliyah. It wags its tail as it licks her nose. Aliyah instantly becomes attached as she gently holds the puppy.

She says, "Awe, Tim she's adorable! You know my birthday is tomorrow right?"

He answers, "Yeah but I didn't think she would be at the pet store tomorrow. She's really adorable and a lot of people were looking at her. I thought with the new house and us becoming a family, a dog would be nice for us."

Aliyah holds the pup saying, "Tim I love her. You're amazing honey. You should name it."

Tim jokingly says, "Nallie-Boo."

Aliyah laughs saying, "No."

Wendy, Joline and Amanda walk in. Amanda becomes excited to see a puppy as she walks to pet it.

Tim says, "Oh hey ladies. How's it going in Florida?"

Joline smiles and says, "Hot and rainy. Nothing too normal. We heard that you made quite the proposal last month."

Tim laughs embarrassingly, "She told you that?"

Amanda says, "Tim everyone is talking about *Tears*. I read it maybe two or three times. I really like it."

Aliyah smiles and says, "Tim based it on our summer in California back in 2012. He added some fantasy with the mythical creatures but most of the book was based on summer break."

411   *HERO'S ROMANCE*

Tim adds, "Yeah everyone is starting to recognize my name because of that book. It's pretty popular. The book signing was packed. I'm glad Aliyah came to help that day."

He kisses her on the cheek, "Hey I need to set up this new computer. Where was I going to put it? I remember you saying you like when I work in the open."

Aliyah says, "Yes sweetheart. Set it up in the lounge area, down the hall. That way I can join you in your silence sometimes but you'll still have quiet time when we have kids. I just didn't want you to work in a closed off area so you get disconnected from us."

Tim replies, "Yeah I get what you're saying. I like that idea. I have my laptop so I can work pretty much anywhere. But the lounge will be my workspace."

Aliyah looks back at her cousins and says, "Oh we're supposed to be wedding planning. Ok Tim we're going back into the kitchen. Here take the pup."

He slyly steps away saying, "Hey I can't help if she's attached to you, sweetheart. Plus I need both hands to set this computer up."

Aliyah smiles saying, "Be careful, Tim."

She sits with her relatives in the kitchen as she holds the puppy. They begin to discuss wedding plans as she takes out a notebook, pen and a wedding planner.

She says, "Ok so Tim and I want to marry May the 1st. This is all I have planned so far. We have down who we want to invite like friends and family. Then we have the theme and color scheme. What I needed were bridesmaids. I called you three out here for a weekend, so you can help me come up with a plan to make all of this work."

T.Edward Redd   **412**

Wendy says, "Wow, the 1st of May? Are you sure? That's pretty close."

Aliyah flips though her wedding planner saying, "Tim and I have been together for almost five years now. I can't see myself with anyone else and I know he feels the same. With us out of school, marriage is ideal for us. We want to settle down, maybe travel a couple of summers then we want to start a family. I know this is what we want.

"We chose May because we felt that it would be long enough for guest to make time to come to the wedding. I can save up money between now and the week before and help pay for the wedding."

Joline says, "No, we'll help pay for it, Aliyah. You and Tim don't need to spend a dime on your own wedding."

Aliyah replies, "Tim's family is pitching in too. I know that if we need extra money Tim would be able to take care of it. But I feel like he takes care of too much. That's why I want to pitch in too."

Wendy says, "Aliyah let Tim be the provider he's working hard to be for you. There's nothing wrong with him taking care of things. I'm sure he doesn't mind as long as you're happy."

Aliyah says, "Helping out makes *me* feel happy too. I want to be a good partner for my future husband. Now come on we need to plan this wedding."

Amanda says, "Alright well who is going to be your maid of honor?"

Aliyah replies, "Well, I made a lot of friends in college and nursing school. But I didn't have anyone in mind. Amanda, Joline, I want you two to be my maids of honor."

Amanda and Joline become overjoyed, saying at once, "Really? Us?"

Amanda says, "You have to pick just one of us."

Joline adds, "Yes, it's tradition."

Aliyah smiles at the color schemes she has chosen as she says, "Well it doesn't have to be traditional does it? I just want to marry Tim. I consider you two my best friends. I want you to be my maids of honor."

Joline says, "You know what, Aliyah you're right. We would be honored to be your maids of honor."

Amanda adds, "It'll be easy for us to help you with it being two of us. We can divide jobs. I can do invitation and order decorations. Joline can help you pick out your dress as well as the bridesmaid dresses. I'm sure there's more to cover but the two of us can handle it."

Wendy joins, "If you two need help I'd be happy to aid. I was my best friend's maid of honor so I'm experienced with this sort of thing. It'll be fun."

They take a look at Aliyah's wedding planner as they begin discussing who will take which responsibilities. Tim walks into the kitchen casually. Aliyah gets up and walks to him as she holds the puppy.

She asks, "Honey do you want some lemonade?"

Tim looks at her saying, "Sure, but I'm going to get this furniture off of the truck first okay?"

She eagerly asks, "Ooh, can I help?"

He says, "I don't want you to hurt yourself. I can do it, sweetheart."

Aliyah walks the puppy to Wendy saying, "Could you hold her for a few minutes please? I'm going to help him get the stuff off of the truck."

Wendy happily takes the black puppy as Aliyah walks to Tim. She holds his hand and guides him outside. Tim looks around and smiles peacefully at the dreamlike scenery of their home. Aliyah leads him to the large rental truck.

"Okay sweetheart. Show me what you got us," she says.

Tim lifts the back door of the truck. Aliyah becomes wowed at the fancy yet obviously cozy furniture. She hops inside to admire the smooth, white and yellow sofas and resting chairs.

She says, "Tim these are perfect. You even got us desk and tables. You're freaking amazing."

He gets inside saying, "Haha it was your list of items dear. So you're the amazing one. I just follow instructions amazingly."

She kisses him and hugs him, saying, "We're both amazing handsome."

She kisses him passionately as she rubs on his arms. Tim holds her as she presses her body against him.

Tim says, "Are you alright?"

She answers, "I've just been really aroused lately. Waiting has been hard but now it's really hard. Tim I want you *now*. I want us to make love. It's been five years. Nothing bad can happen. We're getting married in two months and we love each other. We can have each other completely now. I want to be intimate with you on a physical level."

Tim holds her close as he feels on her soft and delicate body. He kisses her as he runs his fingers through her long brown hair. He gropes her gently as she lifts her leg slightly.

Tim says, "Just a little longer. We're almost there. If we do it now than it would be no different than doing it the first night we had the chance. Aliyah we have something deep and sacred. Let's make love the day we marry. We'll do it all night and every night after. We can do this."

Aliyah kisses him and says, "Okay baby. I guess I can wait another 60 days. But on that night you'd better be ready. It's been five years honey and I'm very tense if you know what I mean."

She teases him as she presses her breasts against his chest. He holds her and firmly grasps her rear. She lets out a surprised, but soft and pleased moan whimpering, "Agh."

Tim says, "Don't forget that it's been four years for me too, Miss Conrad. I'm very *firm*, if you know what I mean. It'll be a good night for us both, sweetheart."

Aliyah blushes and steps back, "Let's get this stuff off the truck before I rip your clothes off. I can only control myself for so long. You don't help much with those body heating words of yours."

Tim begins to move a table saying, "You're the one who put those mouth-watering breasts on me."

Aliyah laughs as she helps him take the table off of the truck. They begin moving furniture in and out of the house. Aliyah has trouble keeping up with Tim's strength but tries her best to help. Half of an hour passes and they make it halfway through the furniture. Aliyah stops to catch her breath as Tim prepares to move a large couch.

He looks to her with concern, saying, "Hey are you alright? Take a break sweetheart I can get this one."

She shakes her head no as she struggles to catch her breath, "No way. I'm helping you get all of this off of the truck. I just need a minute to get my energy back up."

She takes a seat on a resting chair in the truck. Tim walks to her and comforts her. He says, "Aliyah don't push yourself so hard. You've helped a lot. Let me take care of this."

She says, "No! You take care of everything."

Tim becomes confused saying, "I don't understand."

She explains, "You pay the bills, you buy the food, you picked out the house and you did everything for us through college. I don't want you to keep doing everything by yourself. I basically smooched off of you during college. I had no job and you paid for everything. You even helped with my student tuition."

She continues, "Well no more. After everything we've been through, it's finally my turn to help. I graduated, I have my degree and now I make money as a nurse. When we marry things will change, Tim. I promise. I will be an excellent wife and an even better mother. You won't have to do everything anymore I swear it."

Tim holds her and rubs her back, "Aliyah you're way too hard on yourself. I make money, writing books. When I was in high school, I never imagined selling my first novel so well. But thankfully it did and allowed me to publish more."

He continues, "Yes my writing career has supported most of the materialistic things we have in our life. But Aliyah you've been my source of inspiration this entire time. Your love and kind heart give me idea after idea. Without you, I doubt my books would have that spark that everyone seems to like. No one stays up reading over my manuscripts like you do. No one supports me every hour of the day like you do. No one gives me their love like you do.

"Aliyah none of this materialistic stuff matters to me. One day I might wake up and my career may be gone. But at the end of the day, I would give it all up just to hold you. Your love supports us Aliyah and you do help out. It's you who's carried the baton through this race. You're my anchor and I love you."

Aliyah's eyes gleam as she sheds a single tear. The moment gets interrupted as Joline says, "Aww! That was so sweet."

Aliyah and Tim look back to see her three cousins. Amanda holds her chest as she stares in awe. Wendy's face is red as she wipes her eye saying, "We needed to know what flavor you wanted your cake to be."

Aliyah smiles, softly saying, "Marble."

The three ladies walk back to the house as Tim and Aliyah hold each other.

Tim says, "Aliyah, I can see how important helping out is to you. I promise I'll start including you in on everything ok? But sweetheart, please don't push yourself too hard. We take care of each other."

She replies, "Tim I am fine. I'm tough ok? I can handle whatever comes my way. Let's get this furniture off of the truck."

T.Edward Redd

Tim gets up as she lifts one end of the couch. He lifts the other side saying, "You're so stubborn. Come on, let's hurry."

Their second round of moving furniture into the house begins. They spend another half hour moving furniture into the house. As they place the last couch into the living room they both let out a relieving sigh.

They lie down close beside each other on the soft and cozy carpet. Aliyah says, "How's that book coming along?"

He answers, "Editing. How's that nursing coming along?"

She replies, "That's good and you know, babies."

They laugh at eachother. Yet again, another one of their signature tickle wars begins as they lie beside each other. Aliyah tries to pin Tim down playfully. He flips her on her stomach gently and pins her down. She laughs hysterically as he lies on top of her. They slowly transition into passionate kissing.

"Oh my gosh. Don't you two have a bedroom?"

They become surprised to see Wendy standing before them smiling. Aliyah becomes embarrassed as she stands up and fixes her hair.

She says, "Sorry, auntie. We get like this pretty much every day. We aren't used to guests though."

Wendy replies, "It's your house, sweetheart. Your cousins and I have things pretty much figured out, so we're going to start making calls and arrangements. We're going to be staying with Alvin until everything is prepared. Joline and Amanda will probably call you a lot this month so be ready for whatever."

Aliyah says, "Okay. Thank you, Wendy."

Joline and Amanda walk in. They see Tim and Aliyah holding each other closely on the floor. Amanda says, "Wow I see you two don't waste anytime breaking in the carpet."

Aliyah laughs saying, "For your information we've never had sex with each other. We're waiting until marriage. Then it's going to be a love house for at least a few decades. Right, honey?"

He kisses her saying, "You got it, sweetheart."

Wendy says, "Aliyah how has your father been? He seemed pretty well at the wedding."

Aliyah replies, "He's been doing great. He helped Tim move a lot of our old things here. I work from 6a.m to 3p.m so it was hard for me to help. He's been sober for five years. I'm really proud of him. I'm still getting used to his girlfriend Sabrina though. But at least he's sticking to one woman this time. She seems good for him."

Wendy says, "It's good to hear he's doing well. It was nice seeing you two. We're going to head to your father's house. He's expecting us. Stay out of trouble you two."

She smiles as she begins to walk out of the house. Amanda and Joline follow.

Joline says to Aliyah, "Hey we'll call you when we need you. We'll need you for a few wedding arrangements. We'll be at Alvin's house until everything is planned. See you later. Don't get too crazy when we leave you two."

Tim and Aliyah watch as they leave. They lie beside each other as they relax. Aliyah looks at all of the furniture surrounding them. She smiles peacefully as she holds Tim, saying, "All of this is great honey."

Tim says, "So you like the house alright?"

She hugs him saying, "No, I'm loving it dear. I can't wait to start making a family and memories with you."

They cuddle on the carpet as they kiss each other gently. A small puppy-like whimper is heard as they kiss each other. They look back to see the puppy a few feet away. It nervously stands away as it watches them. It whimpers as it slightly moves forward and back.

Aliyah becomes sympathetic, "Aww, did they leave you by yourself?"

She slowly crawls to the puppy and holds out her hand. The puppy slowly moves to Aliyah. Tim watches besotted as she soothes the timid creature with her motherly nature. For a brief moment, he imagines her with a baby version of herself.

She smiles and says, "It's ok. Don't rush. I won't leave and I won't hurt you. You're safe here. You're home now."

The puppy looks at her as if it can understand her kind words. It licks her palm and slightly barks. Aliyah helps the dog into her hands. The dog's tail wags as it begins to rests in Aliyah's arms. Aliyah becomes attached as she smiles. She looks back at Tim. His day dreaming stops.

He says, "You're pretty good with that, Aliyah. I think she just decided who her owner is."

She pets the dog saying, "What will we name it?"

Tim says, "I'm not sure. Lyla sounds like a cool name."

Aliyah says, "No way. How about Fefe?"

Tim says, "I like that name babe. Why Fefe?"

Aliyah says, "It reminds me of a little girl I saw when I first started nursing school. She had brown hair and freckles. She was the coolest kid I'd ever seen. She was funny, smart and sensitive. I want to name the puppy, Fefe."

Tim smiles and says, "Alright Fefe it is."

Tim gets close to Aliyah saying, "I like that you can be motherly like that. You're going to be a really good mother, Aliyah."

She smiles saying, "That means a lot Tim. Thank you for always making me feel good. I'm looking forward to spending the rest of my life with you."

Tim holds her, saying, "I'm looking forward to spending my life with you as well, Aliyah." They hold each other.

Time passes as they spend time with one another. Aliyah continues making wedding arrangements with Joline and Amanda as the day of the wedding approaches.

April the 30th swiftly arrives as Aliyah and Tim prepare themselves for their wedding day. Aliyah stands in a mirror in a beautiful lime-green wedding dress, with elegant silk and green gloves reaching up her arms but below her elbows. Her gleaming brown hair flows down her backside as Amanda and Joline examine the dress for flaws.

Joline says, "Okay, it's a perfect fit, Aliyah. You look gorgeous."

Aliyah stares at herself in the mirror of a large bedroom in her and Tim's home. She begins to reflect on the days leading to the present moment. She smiles peacefully at the progress she has made, realizing she went from a weak and scared girl to a brave and strong woman.

"This is amazing, girls. Thank you for helping me," she says.

Amanda says, "No problem, Aliyah. This is one of the most important days for you and we want to make it as special as possible. You look so beautiful. I honestly didn't think green would look good. But you pull it off like a princess."

Aliyah examines herself in the mirror. She turns her back to the mirror saying, "Green is my favorite color. I didn't like anything else. Tim thinks the color fits the spring theme. I'm dying to see what he looks like. He dresses up pretty well. I bet he'll take my breath away."

She turns to the mirror and lets out a deep breath.

"Ok. Wow," she exhales.

Joline says, "You're nervous aren't you?"

She shakes her head, "Very much so, yes. Wow, I guess it's just starting to hit me that I'm about to marry the man of my dreams. He's been great to me these past few years. From day one he's always made me smile. Wow, this must be what he felt like when he proposed. Heh, I could faint."

Amanda comforts her, "It's alright Aliyah just breathe. It's normal that you're feeling this nervous. It's not like a date or anything. You're committing your life to someone you love dearly."

Aliyah bursts into tears, "I know and I'm just so happy. I love him so much and he's been so amazing. This moment is so special but I can't help but cry!"

Joline says, "Aww come here."

The girls hug her as she sobs happily in their arms. They cease their noises as they hear knocking at the door.

They hear Tim behind the door, "Hey? Aliyah, are you alright?"

She becomes surprised, "Timothy? Is that you, honey?"

She races to the door. Joline says, "Aliyah don't! It's bad luck to see the groom before the day of the wedding."

Aliyah stops herself from touching the knob. She places her hands on the door and gets close. She says, "Timothy, are you okay, sweetheart?"

Tim stands on the other side of the door dressed in a lime-green tuxedo suit with a tie.

He gets close to the door saying, "Yes, I just couldn't stand being away from you, you know? We have that whole Romeo and Juliet thing going on, at the moment."

Aliyah smiles smitten, "I know, honey. I want to see you too. Haha, but they won't let me come out because it's bad luck. It won't be long dear. Just think, tomorrow night you and I will finally, well you know."

Tim says, "Yeah, I know. Tell me I'm not the only one nervous here."

She says, "About making love or the wedding?"

Tim laughs saying, "Both."

She smiles in relief, "No sweetheart I'm as nervous as can be. I cried earlier because I was so happy. But everything will be fine and we're going to take each other's hand in marriage tomorrow and have our happy and magical ending ok baby?"

Tim smiles saying, "Ok, Miss Conrad."

Aliyah bites her lip saying, "Make that the last time you call me that. After tomorrow I'm Mrs. Derr, you got that?"

Tim says, "No problem, sweetheart. I'm going to go ok? I'll see you tomorrow."

Aliyah anxiously says, "Timothy."

He looks back and walks back to the door, "Yes?"

She says, "I love you. I'll miss you so much tonight. Don't you dare be late tomorrow? Be safe ok?"

He smiles saying, "I will, Aliyah. I love you too. I'll see you tomorrow princess."

He slowly backs away from the door as she says, "Until the dawn of tomorrow, my hero. Be safe."

He smiles as he walks away. Aliyah places her hand on her chest lovingly as she steps away from the door. She looks back as she realizes her two cousins have been watching the whole time.

She laughs, asking, "What?"

Joline says, "You two are like something out of a fairytale. It's really touching, Aliyah. Are you positive Tim doesn't have any brothers?"

Aliyah laughs saying, "Help me out of this dress."

The girls help Aliyah out of her wedding dress. Tim walks down a narrow hallway of the house. He meets his father and mother at the end of the hall.

Robert says, "You look great Tim. I'm proud of you son."

Tim smiles as his mother, Amber says, "You've turned out so well son. You and Aliyah are meant for each other I know it. You two help each other mature so much. It's beautiful and rare. Don't take it for granted."

Tim says, "Thanks you two and don't worry. I love Aliyah more than anything. It's hard to believe I marry tomorrow huh? Just yesterday I was a freshman in high school. Although we went to the same school for 4 years, I never noticed her until the fourth year. Life is strange. I love it.

Amber says, "So how are you and Aliyah spending your last night? Is she staying here or are you staying here?"

Tim says, "We agreed that neither one of us will stay here tonight. We'll sleep at our old homes and reunite here tomorrow night for our, err, um, well, after the wedding."

Robert says, "Ok son. Well it's 8p.m. I made dinner back at home and your sister is there too. Do you want to meet us there?"

Tim shakes his head yes as they begin walking towards the front of the house. He watches as his parents walk to their cars and drive away. One last time before getting into his car, he looks back at the house. He slowly begins to drive away as he begins thinking of past events leading into the present moment. He smiles peacefully as the night sky approaches, welcoming what's to come.

CHAPTER THIRTY-FOUR

Tim sleeps soundly in his childhood bed. The covers lie tangled around him as papers surround the bed. His hand rests on the nightstand close to his bed on a laptop.

"Ok Tim! We'll see you at the wedding in an hour. Good luck," a voice calls. Tim quickly opens his eyes.

He mutters, "An hour?" He looks around to see the room brightly lit by the morning sun. "Oh shoot! It's morning," he shouts.

He quickly sits up to check the time. He sees that it's 9:45 a.m. Quickly, he jumps out of bed but trips over the bed sheets entangling him. He sits up and unwraps himself.

"I guess it wasn't such a good idea to work on my writing the night before the wedding," he says.

He sits up to look at his laptop, "But I'm so close to finishing this project."

He saves his work to a flash drive and races into his bathroom and quickly gets into the shower. Swiftly he rushes to wash his body and brush his teeth at the same time in a furious hurry. Time seems to race against him as he frantically dries off and brushes his hair. He quickly gets into his tuxedo and puts on a tie.

He rushes out of the restroom and grabs his cell phone. Several text messages along with phone calls from many relatives, friends but most importantly his wife to be, Aliyah, fill his phone screen. He grabs a wedding band from his desk and shuts down his laptop.

427   *HERO'S ROMANCE*

After packing his laptop in a bag, he swiftly makes his way downstairs and out of the house. Checking the time, he sees it is 10:20a.m.

He drives a few miles as he checks his cell phone's message history. Several messages from Aliyah going from- *Good morning, honey.* to worried messages- *Babe where are you?? It's 10:20 and no one has seen you! The wedding is at 10:45 are you awake???*

Tim becomes more nervous as time begins to beat him. He becomes slightly less worried as he gets closer to the church on Brook School Road. He becomes shocked to see a huge traffic jam reaching from 116th street to Brook School Road.

He says in distress, "Oh no. You've got to be kidding me. It's a Tuesday. What could possibly be holding up traffic?"

He notices a limo in front of him with a banner saying, "Just married," and many cars in front of it. He realizes that they are guests heading to his wedding. Frustration fills his mind as traffic moves slower and slower. He stares at the church less than a block away.

"How can I be late to my own wedding? It's 10:40," he shouts.

His nerves begin to make him impatient. He stares at the church then the traffic. He looks behind him to see a long line of cars behind him.

"Aliyah you really do know how to draw a crowd don't you? There's no way all of these people are my guest," he says.

He sits impatiently as he stares nervously at the church. Aliyah keeps racing through his mind as his anxiety heightens. On impulse he shuts his car off, forgets to take out his keys and races out towards the church.

T.Edward Redd

Cars honk at him as people recognize their favorite author. He waves politely as he runs to the church.

In a dressing room in the church, Aliyah walks back and forth in her wedding dress nervously. Her bridesmaids stand before her in their light green dresses calmly. Wendy, Joline and Amanda stand near her as she paces back and forth.

"Where is he? He won't answer my calls and no one has seen or heard from him since last night. I know he wouldn't bail. Does he have cold feet," she says.

Amanda says, "Aliyah, relax. I'm sure he's on his way."

Aliyah says, "I can't relax! It's 10:50 a.m and my fiancé has disappeared from the face of the planet. Oh my gosh! What if he's been kidnapped? Someone probably caught him alone and took him hostage! We need money for the ransom. Go get our parents!"

Wendy holds her saying, "Aliyah, calm down. The likelihood of that man being kidnapped is as about as likely as this dress being pink. Give him a few minutes. I'm sure he's coming."

Aliyah says, "I'll have to go out soon. Where is he? Ugh! He's so in trouble when I get him alone. He had better hurry."

They hear wedding music play. The bridesmaids follow Wendy as she wishes Aliyah good luck. Aliyah becomes more and more worried as Joline and Amanda lead her out of the dressing room. She looks around anxiously for any signs of Tim.

They enter the sanctuary and begin to head towards an altar. Aliyah becomes disappointed not to see Tim waiting for her. Joline and Amanda try to calm her down as they get to the altar. The priest stands before them in white robes.

He says, "Are you ready to begin the wedding?"

Aliyah looks to the door of the sanctuary. She looks at Tim's parents who seem to be just as confused as she is. The priest begins the wedding ceremony.

"We are gathered here today, on this happy and beautiful occasion, to join this woman..." He looks to see a bride but no groom. He pauses his speech to whisper to Aliyah, "Where is the groom?"

She places her hand over her face in embarrassment and she says, "Just keep going. He will show. I know it. Continue the ceremony please."

The priest starts over, "We are gathered here today, on this happy and beautiful occasion, to join this woman and man in holy matrimony. Marriage is a solemn foundation held in by honor by all. It is the keystone of the family and community. It requires of those to embark on it a complete and absolute giving of one's self. It is not to be entered into lightly..."

As the priest continues, Aliyah looks around desperately for Tim. She leans to Amanda and Joline saying, "What if he doesn't show up? Where on earth could he be right now? He's never late. So why be late on the day of our wedding?"

The priest continues, "This pledge symbolizes the cherished sharing of two lives and still augmenting the individuality of the both of you."

The priest pauses to look at Aliyah, "Miss, this is the part where I ask your groom if he takes you to be his bride. Where is he? Am I marrying you to a ghost or what?"

Before she can speak they hear a loud bang. They look down the aisle to see Tim bursting through the sanctuary doors. The entire room looks back to see him standing at the door, hunching over on his knees. He breathes heavily as the doors shut behind him.

He struggles to catch his breath saying, "Sorry! A black cat crossed my path so I had to take the long way here."

Aliyah becomes relieved as she lets out a soft laugh at Tim's humor. He finally catches enough breath to walk as he heads towards the altar. He joins Aliyah slightly winded.

He says, "How late am I?"

The priest says, "Late enough to miss me greet the guest but just in time to speak your vows. Wait you look familiar. Are you a writer?"

Tim becomes embarrassed saying, "T.Edward Derr."

Before the priest can become excited Aliyah says, "Not now. Marry us first then you can talk to the famous author. Right now you have to marry us."

The priest says, "Yes, of course. Ahem, We are gathered here today on this happy and beautiful occasion…"

Tim looks to Aliyah saying, "You're beautiful sweetheart."

She leans to him and whispers, "You look pretty sharp yourself. What on earth took you so long? I thought someone had kidnapped you!"

He says, "Sorry, I overslept."

Aliyah laughs whispering, "On our wedding day dear? Why do you sound so out of breath? Are you nervous again?"

He whispers, "Traffic was backed up. I had to run a block, full sprint or I wouldn't have made it. I haven't run like that since junior year in high school. I'm out of shape."

431   *HERO'S ROMANCE*

Aliyah whispers, "Well I'm glad you got to warm up because you're going to need to be in shape for tonight. Catch my drift?"

The priest clears his throat to interrupt them as he finishes his speech. He whispers, "I know that you two are excited about intertwining your lives but keep in mind that we are in a church. Be respectful in the house of God."

Tim playfully jokes, "Well you know what the old man says, 'Be fruitful and multiply'."

Aliyah slightly elbows him as the priest gives him a serious look and becomes annoyed. The priest steps towards Tim saying, "Timothy Edward Derr, do you take this woman to be your wedded wife? Do you promise to love her, comfort her, honor and keep her in sickness and health, remaining faithful to her as long as you both shall live?"

Tim looks at Aliyah taking her hand, saying, "Aliyah, I've waited a long time for the moment that I would be standing before the love of my life. You've helped me grow so much these past five years and I'm honored to be the one to take your hand in marriage. I promise to always love, honor and protect you and your heart. I promise to stay by your side through everything that may come our way. I know that as one, you and I can survive the toughest storms."

Aliyah sheds a single tear, "Oh, Timothy."

Tim adds, "Oh and yes to everything he just said." He looks back to the priest saying, "I do."

The priest smirks at Tim as he walks to Aliyah.

"Aliyah Starla Conrad, do you take this talented and charming man to be you wedded husband? Do you promise to love him, comfort him, honor and keep him in sickness and health, remaining faithful to him as long as you both shall live?"

Aliyah smiles and looks to Tim saying, "Should I try and best you or do you want me to make it quick?"

Tim smirks and challenges her, "Show me what you've got, Mrs. Derr."

Aliyah blushes saying, "Ok. Timothy Edward Derr, we all know you have your way with words. You always know how to sweep me off of my feet, make me smile and even laugh. During my hardships it was you who made me smile when all I felt like doing was crying. Yes your words are a treasure, but your heart is out of this world."

Tim's eyes begin to water as she continues.

"You and I met either out of fate or a pure unorthodox circumstance. Either way, I am so happy that it was I, who on that fateful day received that birthday card. It would be a symbol that would bind our hearts together for a very long time. Timothy I love you for all that you are, good and bad. I am head over feet for you and till this day, you still give me butterflies.

"Yes, I promise to love this man, comfort him and honor him through all that is bad and all that is good. I'm his and he is mine so as long as we live, and even after death our hearts will live on."

The entire room becomes drawn to their love for one another as the two get close to each other.

"Timothy I love you," she says.

"Aliyah I love you too," he says.

They stare at each other deeply in the eyes holding back their passion as they wait for the priest's last words. The priest watches them not knowing that they are finished giving their vows. They look back at him. He becomes surprised saying, "Oh. You're ready. Then by the power invested in me, I now pronounce you husband and wife. You may now kiss the bride."

Tim and Aliyah begin to kiss passionately as they hold one another. Their audience applauds them as they kiss lovingly. Tim says, "Aliyah this is it. We're finally married. We can finally live as one and start our lives as…"

Aliyah kisses him fiercely and says, "Timothy I know honey. Haha, you don't have to say so much right now."

She says, "I'm pretty sure we both have the same thoughts. Let's head to the reception. We have to share ourselves with our families for a couple of hours before we sneak away with each other."

Tim says, "You got it princess."

He lifts her and carries her down the aisle in his arms. She laughs as she hugs him as the guests stand and applaud. He carries her to a dining hall within the church where the wedding reception takes place. They stare in amazement at the beautiful fairytale like surroundings.

Tables with white clothe are organized in rows circling around the center of the room. Flowers lie in the center of each table. Lime green drapery hang from the ceiling gracefully, welcoming the newly wedded couple.

They walk to a heavenly wedding cake. The cake is lime-green with darker green frosting on each of its five layers. Aliyah stares in amazement.

She says, "Oh my gosh Joline and Amanda went over the top didn't they?" She takes her finger and slightly digs into the cake and tastes the icing. She moans with satisfaction.

Tim laughs saying, "Honey, come on we have to wait until they cut it."

She takes another finger scoop saying, "No we don't baby. Come on this is our day. Rules are out the window, taste it sweetheart, here."

She places her finger close to his mouth and allows him to taste the icing. He smiles as the flavor tingles his taste buds.

Aliyah smiles, saying, "See, you like it don't you, sweetie?"

Tim smiles and gives her a peck on the cheek. The wedding guests begin to enter the room behind the couple's parents.

Aliyah says, "Here's the party. Let's have some fun ok? You can dance can't you? Because I want to dance with you tonight."

Tim smiles with her as the guests begin to take their sits. The couple greets them all and thanks them for coming. After their parents give their wedding toasts, everyone begins to have dinner after Tim and Aliyah get their meal. Following dinner the party begins to start dances.

Tim and Aliyah dance with each of their respective parents. The final dance is between Tim and Aliyah. The wedding guests allow them to dance in the center of the room by themselves.

Aliyah says, "Tell me something Tim, did you ever imagine that you would be married to me? The day that we first met, did you ever think you and I would be here?"

He holds her as they slow dance, "Honestly no hon. When we first met I misjudged you."

She smiles saying, "Oh really? What assumptions did you possess?"

He smiles at her as he twirls her, "Well, I'll be honest. I thought you were this spoiled rich girl who had hundreds of friends, a rich boyfriend and pretty much anything a teenager could dream of. I thought that you and I would never be able to understand each other."

Aliyah laughs teasingly, "Rich and spoiled? You nailed it Mr. Derr."

He holds her close, as he looks her deep in the eyes, "As we got closer and closer, you proved me wrong, repeatedly. Though you had everything a kid could dream of, you were still alone. My heart softened each time we spent time with each other. I wanted to wipe your tears and hold you. I wanted to be your hero."

She blushes as they continue to dance, "Well since we're being honest I'll go ahead and say that when we first met I really didn't think much of you. You were handsome but quiet and somewhat moody. But the more time we spent together the more I got to see this gentle and warm side of you, clouded by hurt and loneliness. I got drawn to you.

"It scared me that you were so amazing. You liked me for me and truly cared for me, wanting nothing in return but to see me smile and be safe. I didn't think I'd be good enough for someone like that. I was used to everyone treating me like I was nothing. But you never left me, you never hurt me and you were always there, even when I was cruel. I wanted you to be my hero. I wanted to be saved."

They hold each other as Tim says, "You're my princess, and I'm your hero. Now that we're one, we're going rule the world. No one can stop us, sweetheart."

She kisses him saying, "Let's give them a good show."

T.Edward Redd   **436**

They continue to dance as the guests begin to join them. The day speeds along as the reception goes by happily. Aliyah and Tim sit at a table eating wedding cake as they watch people dance. Aliyah sees a little girl with her mother having a good time.

Aliyah says, "Awe, baby isn't that sweet?"

Tim smiles, "Yeah it is. That'll be you someday honey."

Aliyah gets close to Tim saying, "Yes I know. You know today is the day we start practicing right?"

Tim chokes on his drink as she startles him. He spits up his pop. Aliyah holds him saying, "Are you ok?"

Tim says, "Yes I'm fine."

She gets close saying, "Sweetheart does it make you nervous? We've talked about this night for years. You can't chicken out. It's our night you know?"

Tim shakes his head yes saying, "I know, I know. It's been five years though and I've only had sex with one person. I'm somewhat nervous."

Aliyah kisses him on the cheek, "So am I. But we're going to help each other ok? Tonight will be passionate, deep and special for the both of us. Please don't be nervous. I know you're eager too."

She kisses him as she holds his hand. He slowly turns to her and places his hand on her hip as they kiss. He kisses her cheek then neck. She gently stops him, "Baby it's time. I can feel it."

Tim says, "Me too. I want you really bad right now."

He kisses her and holds her close. She gets up and leads him towards the back exit. They kiss each other fiercely as they walk to the marriage limo. They get inside.

Tim says, "Our house is just near Geist right after you get passed the gas station on 116th n Brook School road. Hurry."

The limo driver begins to drive as Tim and Aliyah begin to kiss each other more and more. They hold and feel on one another. Tim grabs her delicate thighs as she presses her breasts against his chest.

She says, "Tim I love you. I adore you and I just want to give myself to you."

She kisses him as he says, "I feel the same Aliyah. I feel so close to you and I've never been so synched with you. It feels right. It's our time."

He gropes her and hugs her close as she kisses his face and neck. The driver says, "Should I leave the car or were you two going to go inside?"

They look to see that they're at their home. Without any hesitation they rush out of the limo and towards the house. They get to the front door. Tim fiddles in his pockets for keys. Aliyah smiles eagerly and says, "Come on hurry, hurry!"

Tim says, "I can't find my keys! Shoot I must have left them in my car when I left it."

She grabs his hand and pulls him to the back of the house. They pass a beautiful pool as they go to a back door. Aliyah tries to open it but it is locked. She becomes anxious and opens a window near the door. She climbs through.

She looks out at Tim, "Come in baby!"

He smiles as he climbs through. Aliyah quickly attacks him with intense kisses as she pins him against the wall. She removes her shoes and gloves saying, "Ok, waiting is up. It's been almost five years. We're married now. My parts are tense as can be and you're going to relax them tonight. No excuses."

T.Edward Redd   **438**

She rips his suit off and rubs on his chest. He kisses her as he removes her dress smoothly. They unclothe each other down to their nightwear. They begin to caress one another's arousing body.

Aliyah stops Tim, "Wait."

He becomes eager, "What, what? You said no excuses."

She says, "Let's make love in our bed. I set everything up perfectly for tonight before I left yesterday. It's perfect come on."

They laugh playfully as they race to their bedroom. Tim trips over a power cord to his computer as they pass through the lounge. Aliyah laughs as she helps him up, "Are you ok Tim?"

He pinches her rear saying, "I will be. Come here!"

She giggles and screams as she runs away. He chases her to their bedroom. They stop at the door. Aliyah opens it. They both stare in amazement to see dimmed lighting above red and pink rose petals, leading to a king sized bed covered in red sheets. Soft white pillows and blankets cover the bed as Aliyah races to it and jumps in.

"Oh my gosh these sheets are amazing. I could die," she says. She adds the final touch to the romantic scene as she lights candles on nightstands lying next to the left and right side of the bed. She sits up and looks back at Tim, "Come here, Timothy. I'll be gentle. I promise."

Tim walks to the bed and sits beside her saying, "What if I don't want you to be gentle?"

He holds her head as he kisses her gently. She pulls him closer as she lies down saying, "Then I won't be."

They begin to kiss and cuddle each other lovingly. Tim brushes his fingers down her brown hair and teases her back dimples. She lets out a soft moan as she arches her back. She kisses him as he removes her bra. He begins to fondle her breast as they lie down. Aliyah let's out soft and pleasing moans as Tim begins to kiss and suck on her body.

He removes her green panties as he kisses her. She removes his underwear and lies back. She opens her legs and welcomes her beloved husband. Tim embraces her. She lets out another moan as they begin to finally act on their sexual urges.

Love fills the room as the two lovers make love. They please one another's every need without any reliance on words or signals. Their love is the only needed means of communication as their deep seeded bonds have begun to blossom beautifully for this long awaited moment. After an hour they transition into cuddling and playful fighting. They kiss each other in goofy manners as they laugh.

Aliyah hugs Tim saying, "I love you."

He hugs her back saying, "I love you too Aliyah."

Tim kisses Aliyah. She holds his face and blows into his mouth, filling his cheeks with air. She laughs as he coughs. Tim smiles and kisses her again. She tries to repeat her goofiness only to be countered with the same humor by Tim. They have mouth air battles as they laugh and hold each other.

They begin to pinch and tickle one another, yet again laughing until each of their stomachs ache. They hold each other romantically as they settle.

Aliyah says, "Tim I adore you so much. Tonight, no this whole day has been beautiful."

Tim says, "I know. Everything between us has been amazing. Even this moment. Even though we had sex, it's like the moment wasn't about sex. It's about our connection deepening. I love having you in my arms and cuddling against your soft body. We even have silly and lighthearted moments when we have sex. This is beautiful."

Aliyah says, "This is love baby."

They kiss each other as they begin another round of their embracing's of one another.

Tim and Aliyah start their lives as a married couple. They travel a few times during their summers. Eventually two years pass and they begin to start on raising a family.

Tim stands at a desk impatiently, as a lady talks to him. He says, "Miss, please, I need to see my wife."

The lady says, "My daughter would love it if I got you to autograph this book for her. You see she inspires to become a great writer someday. Of course she's only 15 but she's a very dedicated reader and writer. She's read 4 of your titles. There was *Hero's Wake, Blue Owl,* and *Tears.* Oh there was another. I forget which one it was."

Tim stands in a business button up shirt with a tie. He takes out a marker saying, "That's amazing. I didn't start writing until I was 17. If she stays focused she could publish before I did, granted she's as dedicated as I was at 18. I'm sure she'll do just fine. Writing isn't hard. Everyone has a story. Just write from the heart and add magic and fantasy. Ok where is the room?"

The lady takes the book saying, "She's right down the hall in room 30. Is she your wife?"

Tim says, "Yes, I should've been here hours ago but I got caught up in a meeting. Then some lady stopped me for an autograph that should've taken ten seconds. But she decided to make it ten minutes. Haha, tell your little girl good luck, dream big and write from the heart."

He races down the hall to room 30. He peeks inside.

"Aliyah, honey," he calls.

He sees her in a patient outfit surrounded by Alvin, his girlfriend, Wendy and Joline. She lies on the bed pregnant, breathing heavily as she sweats, saying, "Tim, baby you're finally here. Come close, sweetie."

He walks to her and hugs her gently, "Sweetheart, I'm so sorry I'm late. How are you?"

Aliyah says, "Tim, I'm scared. I was due last night but I'm still in labor. I hope the baby is ok."

Tim kisses her on the forehead saying, "Hey we've got to think positive ok? The baby will come when it's ready. Don't rush this. Just have faith. Maybe it was waiting for daddy to come," he laughs, "isn't that right?"

He gently rubs her stomach, as he gets close. Aliyah feels the baby move as Tim touches her stomach.

Aliyah gasps, "Baby, she moved!"

Tim says, "I know, I felt it. She always does that when I touch your stomach. Daddy's little girl."

Aliyah let's out a moan as she begins to have contractions. Tim gently holds her hand saying, "Breathe honey. In deep and out slowly. Everything will be ok. I'm right here."

Tim looks back to see Aliyah's father and relatives. He smiles and says, "Hey all. How's it going?"

T.Edward Redd   **442**

Wendy says, "Really well Tim, thank you. We're all pretty concerned about the baby though. She should've been here last night and Aliyah is barely having contractions."

Tim says, "You guys worry way too much. Trust me. My baby girl is going to be here before the night ends. I bet my life on it." He places his hand on Aliyah's stomach saying, "Isn't that right kiddo?"

Aliyah let's out another moan as she has another contraction. Her contractions get closer as Tim keeps his hand on Aliyah's stomach. Tim smiles confidently as he removes his hand.

He says, "Yeah, she'll be here alright. Give it two hours. So Alvin, how are things?"

Alvin smiles saying, "Great, son. Sabrina and I just got engaged a couple of months ago. We're set to marry in July. Isn't that great?"

Tim replies, "That's awesome."

Joline says, "Ugh, where is that doctor? This place is very unprofessional. This baby is going to need help."

Tim reassuringly says, "Come on you guys, relax. The baby is fine. She can probably here you talking negative like that. You have to encourage her."

He kneels to Aliyah's stomach saying, "It's ok. You take your time ok? We won't rush you. But we're ready to welcome you into this world as our own. We love you kid."

Aliyah moans as she has a contraction. She begins to breathe heavily.

Aliyah says, "Tim hold my hand sweetheart. She's trying to make her way through."

Tim holds her hand saying, "You got it Aliyah. I'm right here."

443   *HERO'S ROMANCE*

The doctor and a nurse walk in. The doctor says, "Sorry I was gone so long. I had to run to another patient on the far end of the building."

Wendy says, "What on earth is wrong with you people? She needs help with her baby. She was due last night and Aliyah is barely starting to have contractions."

Tim says, "Take it easy on him. He's got more than one patient. He can't help it. They may need him as much as we do. Besides our baby girl is fine."

As Tim rubs Aliyah's stomach she moans in pain as another contraction hits. She moans, "Ooooh. She's coming. I can feel it. She's coming. Agggh!"

Tim holds her hand, "Just breathe honey. I've got you."

The doctor walks to Aliyah saying, "She seems to be fine to me. Sometimes babies take longer than usual to come out."

Wendy says, "We've been here for hours and Aliyah is just now starting to have contractions. Something is wrong and you guys need to do your job and help her instead of slouching around."

Joline says, "Hey Tim, put your hand on her stomach again."

Tim looks at Joline as he places his hand gently on Aliyah's stomach. Not a moment after, Aliyah has another contraction. Tim pulls his hand away in fear.

He panics, "Oh no! Aliyah, did I hurt you?"

She fights the pain as she says, "No it's the baby. She's pretty fierce."

Joline gets eager saying, "Tim keep your hand on her stomach!"

Tim says, "Huh? Why?"

Joline rushes to Tim and places his hand on Aliyah's stomach. Aliyah let's out a scream as she has more contractions.

She says, "Don't you see? For some reason, when you put your hand on her stomach, the baby reacts to it."

Tim takes his hand off as he stares in confusion. Aliyah's contractions cease. He slowly places his hand back on her stomach and feels the baby move as Aliyah screams.

He says, "No way. That's incredible. Hey doctor check to see if she's dilating yet."

The doctor checks saying, "It looks to be about 7 centimeters. Still opening, strange."

Tim begins to soothingly rub Aliyah's stomach saying, "It's ok. Don't be shy. We love you and we're ready for you to come out and be with us."

Aliyah holds Tim's free hand as she breathes heavily, "Tim, my contractions get closer and closer the more you talk to her and rub her. I always thought it was strange how she only moved when you were around. Even when you talk I can feel her moving in there. She adores her daddy. Help her out, sweetheart."

Tim says, "I'm a writer so none of this should be weird to me. Ok, Lily it's ok to be shy. You see, I was shy too once. Way back when I was in high school, as a freshman I was really shy. I would have never dreamed of talking to your mom. But one day I realized that people aren't really that bad. It was your mother who taught me that."

The doctor says, "She's ready. Ok, Mrs. Derr, I need you to push when you're ready. She's ready to come out. I'll guide her out."

Aliyah says, "Tim."

Tim rubs Aliyah's stomach saying, "Don't be shy, Lily. It's your mother and I. We welcome you and we love you dearly."

Aliyah begins to push and moan as a contraction hits. She screams as the baby begins to come out of her. Tim watches in amazement as the doctor holds the newborn. Nurses come to his aid and help clean and drain the baby. It begins to cry as he gives it to Aliyah.

The nurses wrap Aliyah and the baby in clean towels. Tim watches as the baby stops crying while Aliyah soothes her.

She says, "Awe, she was a little shy. But daddy helped her out. Isn't that right, Lily?"

The family gets closer as they watch Tim and Aliyah comfort their baby girl. Joline says, "You two decided to name her Lily? That's a pretty name."

Aliyah says, "Yes, Lily Liel Derr is her full name. Lily comes from my name and her middle name is after Liel."

The baby opens its eyes and glances at Tim as she clings to Aliyah. Tim becomes surprised as the newborn stares at him. Aliyah notices as her daughter and husband share their first moment of connection.

Tim says, "She's staring right at me…"

Joline says, "Wow Tim, I think you're the first person she saw."

Aliyah smiles saying, "Aww, she's a daddy's girl already. I'm jealous. Tim you should hold her."

Tim says, "Huh? Me? Aliyah, are you sure? I mean she was just born. She should bond with you for a while."

Aliyah kindly says, "I've bonded with her for 9 months, sweetheart. Come and hold your daughter. I think she's been eager to meet you. You're the only person who she's ever kicked for."

Tim nervously steps to the bed saying, "Ok."

Aliyah guides his arms and shows him how to carry the baby. He holds his newborn daughter. He instantly becomes attached as the baby slightly smiles and tugs on his shirt. Tim can't help but smile as he sheds a tear.

He says, "Wow, this is different. Hey Lily. I've been dying to meet you too. I'm glad you finally came. Everyone including your mother was worried."

Aliyah laughs in a tired manner saying, "Hey I was only a little worried."

Tim winks at Aliyah as he speaks to Lily, "I knew you would come out sooner or later, Lily. You're just as I predicted. The best child I could have wished for. Welcome to the family."

Lily tugs on his shirt as she begins to fall asleep. Tim walks her to Aliyah saying, "She's a little tired. Here, sweetheart."

Aliyah says, "Tim she looks comfortable. Sit beside me and hold her a while longer. Don't worry about me. I'll be holding her quite a lot as I nurse her and bond with her. I want you to have your chance to connect with her. I held her for nine months and bonded with her. I want you to hold her for a while."

Tim sits beside Aliyah saying, "Ok. That makes sense. Wow, isn't she adorable, Aliyah? She has your complexion, nose, eyes and hair."

Aliyah looks at the baby smiling, "Aww, it looks like she got my mother's freckles too. Hey look at her ears and lips. Those are definitely from daddy. She's going to be gorgeous, Tim."

Tim smiles proudly as Lily rests in his arms. Tim and Aliyah spend a few hours in the hospital before Aliyah is released. They drive home. Tim guides Aliyah into the house as she holds Lily. Fefe races into the room wagging her tail happy to see her owners. She's grown to be a huge full-grown black Labrador retriever.

Tim pats the dog on her head saying, "Hey girl, look who we brought home. She's going to be your new friend pretty soon when she starts growing. Be very protective and nice towards her."

The dog barks loudly and happily as Tim pets her.

Aliyah says, "Tim don't get her excited. I don't want her scaring Lily. Sweetheart, could you help me to our room?"

Tim says, "Of course dear come on. Fefe stay."

Fefe sits as Tim begins walking Aliyah to their bedroom. He places several pillows towards the front of the bed so Aliyah can rest sitting up. She hands Tim the baby so she can get in a relaxed position in the bed. Tim places Lily in her arms.

Aliyah says, "She sleeps a lot huh?"

Tim sits beside her saying, "Yeah. She's not really loud. Not yet anyway. Aliyah, do you want or need anything?"

She replies, "Just you. Go grab your laptop and set up your workspace up here. I want you with me so we both can bond with Lily."

Tim smiles saying, "That sounds like a good plan, Aliyah."

Tim walks out of the room and walks down a staircase and grabs a laptop from a dining room table. He opens it up to see a project he has been working on since high school.

"I think you're finally ready to be published," he says.

He smirks proudly as he walks back to the bedroom where Aliyah and Lily rest. Tim sits beside Aliyah as he types.

She says, "What are you working on, sweetheart?"

Tim smiles saying, "Just an old project. Would you like to see?"

Aliyah looks to see the words *Hero's Romance* on a document on Tim's computer screen. She says, "The journal you made when you were in high school? I thought you gave up on it."

Tim shakes his head no, "It was just incomplete. I hadn't lived long enough to truly share my story with the world. But now that I've gotten this far, I think the book is finally ready to be published."

Aliyah stares with amazement seeing dates going back to 2009 to the current month, June 1st, 2018. She becomes intrigued realizing that he's been writing the story over the entire duration of their growing relationship.

She says, "Tim, what's in there?"

Tim replies, "Before I met you, this book focused mostly on the bad things in my life. But once you and I started growing with each other, I matured. I realized that the book was incomplete and that I needed to give it more time. In this book lies all of the memories you've helped me experience, along with my thoughts and feelings about the things that went on at the time."

Aliyah says, "Even your plan to propose?"

Tim replies, "Yes."

She adds, "What about our first date or the day we met? The baby's birth, buying Fefe, us reconciling with our parents and even our summer vacations?"

Tim replies, "All of it honey. I've been writing this diligently since the day you told me how dark you thought it was. When we went to see your father, my feelings had changed towards my mom. I wish I hadn't published the first version. But this newer version will sell big. I know it. When we started improving as one, I realized that our love could be a really good story to share. I just had to wait to see what happened and write. I'm naming it Hero's Romance."

Aliyah becomes amazed, as she looks at the document, she says, "Timothy this is amazing. I can't believe I didn't notice this. How did you manage publishing more books while working on this?"

Tim takes out a pocket sized notebook, "Copy and paste. All I had to do was record my thoughts and memories on some paper and type it when I had the chance.

Aliyah scrolls through the document while holding Lily.

She says, "Could I look at this? Lily is sleeping and I don't want to wake her. Can you scroll it for me?"

Tim says, "Of course, sweetheart. Tell me a day and I'll show you."

She says, "Hmmm, how about February 3rd, 2016."

Tim flips to the page. He reads out loud to her softly.

February 3rd, 2016

Today was one of the most nerve shaking days I have ever encountered. Though I prepared myself for this day, I was still extremely nervous. I love Aliyah so much and I knew that today was the day I stepped through another door, into another world as I left the other.

However it was like stepping into a door blindly. I didn't know what to expect. Though she said yes, the thought of her saying no was haunting. Stepping into a cold and dark world where the one I call sweetheart or love suddenly disappeared nearly brought me to tears.

I sat there watching her speak about her day gracefully. It was like our first date way back in 2011. I admire her happiness and that warm energy she gives off when she speaks. My heart pounded harder and harder as she spoke about her day. I fell deeper and deeper in love as she moved me by doing nothing more than being herself.

The moment of truth and courage came as she noticed I was troubled. It was funny yet embarrassing. As I stood to propose I bumped into a waiter who was carrying our food. We fell and food got all over my nice suit. But there she stood; ready to hold my hand as she always has been.

That's when it happened. Our hearts touched and the words just came out of my mouth. She cried as she listened. I cried as well as we held one another.

Apparently the entire eatery was watching because not a moment after she kissed me they started to applaud and cheer.

After that we celebrated with cake and wine, given to us for free by a waiter who wanted my autograph. The night took a comical twist as we went to a hotel for the night. I was too tired to drive and Aliyah was drunk and tired.

She was pretty naughty and fierce when she was in her drunken state. She kissed me, cuddled on me and wanted to make love. But I couldn't break our vow. Even though I wanted it too, I wanted to wait until we were married. It won't be too long, I know. She's lying on the bed right now as I type. She passed out an hour ago. She's a gift and I cherish her dearly.

Now that we're engaged we're going to look into houses and wedding arrangements this week. She'll be busy from mornings to the early afternoon now that she's become a nurse. So I'll have to do a lot, which I don't mind. I'm proud of her. I love her dearly.

End of entry

Aliyah looks at Tim as he smiles at her. They kiss one another. Tim asks, "What do you think?"

She replies, "Timothy I love it. I think your readers will too. Wow so you've been writing this since high school? And it's finished?"

Tim says, "Yes. I wrote my final entry after Lily was born. It was about an hour later when you fell asleep with her in your arms."

Aliyah asks, "Can you read it to me?"

Tim says, "You want to hear the final entry?"

Aliyah replies, "Well when you get it printed and published I would like to read all of it, honey. Do you think I should wait to read the final entry?"

Tim answers, " Well, there isn't really anything that you don't know besides the times before we met. We've experienced everything in this together. I don't see any reason why you should wait to read it, sweetheart. I'll read it.

Tim scrolls through many entries within the document. He gets to the last entry. Aliyah looks at him then the laptop as she waits in suspense.

June 1st, 2018

Today is without a doubt, one of my most treasured memories. Today I witnessed my three hour and a half old daughter, Lily, come into this world. I can't really put this into writing. It was just so, beautiful. When she was inside Aliyah, she would always kick when I touched Aliyah's stomach or move when she heard my voice.

As Aliyah held our daughter, Lily, for the first time, the little one glanced right at me. I was the first person she saw. It really shook me up. Not in a bad way, but a life changing way. I can't describe it. Aliyah insisted that I held her.

I didn't want to ruin the moment as Lily clanged to her mother, but she insisted.

As I held Lily she just stared into my eyes, as if she already knew who I was. It was breathtaking. Then I spoke to her and she smiled. I couldn't help but to cry and smile. She's everything I ever wished for. I always wanted a daughter and I always wanted a wife like Aliyah. Yes life is pretty amazing.

I remember how I was way back in 2011. I was withdrawn and detached. Then I met Aliyah. Since that day I've been changing and growing rapidly. She has grown and changed as well. All for the better. I'm thankful for her and the daughter that we've been blessed with.

It's strange how fast life can take such a drastic change. Back then I never imagined standing right here in this room, watching my wife sleep peacefully as our child rests in her arms. I could cry. I guess life really is too short for worry. All of this can be gone in a flash, that's why I try to treasure every second and thank God for every single breath I am able to breathe.

T.Edward Redd

I thank all of those who have taken the time to read my tale. If you have dreams, then capture them. Capture your dreams and cling to them tightly. If it seems too good to be true, than let it is just that. Don't try to fight it. Just accept the good things God blesses you with. If I hadn't accepted my feelings for Aliyah way back then, I wouldn't even be writing this last entry. Take care and never stop dreaming. Dream, but never sleep. Perhaps I'll write another tale in another five years. Take care and thanks again.